Moira had told Lily to stay away from her cousin, to let Moira know if there was anything strange going on, if Abby confided in her. She'd damn well learned her lesson—rely on no one else—and she prayed Lily was alive.

"We'll just look around the ruins for ten minutes," she said. "I'll know if the coven was here. Maybe we're not too late." She said it to give Jared hope; she didn't believe it.

Almost as soon as she'd stepped from the truck, Moira smelled evil. A subtle aroma on the edge of the ruins, growing with each step she took. Incense. Poisoned incense. Strong herbs and odors to control spirits. But it was the sulphuric stench of Hell itself that raised the skin on her arms and made the scar on her neck burn. As Moira neared the midpoint of the spirit trap, she slowed her pace, her feet heavy as lead. Slower. Slower. She wanted to run back to the small, safe island off Sicily and lock herself inside St. Michael's fortress. She didn't need this, didn't want it, but she could not shirk her responsibility.

All that is necessary for evil to triumph is for good men—and women—to do nothing.

As Moira approached the wide circle painted in white on the ground, it became clear that the ritual had been interrupted. There were signs of violence—overturned candles, disturbed earth, a feeling of unrest, of commotion. While no candles burned, the scent of extinguished flames hung in the low-lying fog.

There, in the middle of the circle, was a dead body.

ORIGINAL SIN

THE 7 SEVEN DEADLY SINS

ALLISON BRENNAN

BALLANTINE BOOKS • NEW YORK

A Ballantine Books Mass Market Original

Copyright © 2010 by Allison Brennan
Excerpt from *Carnal Sin* copyright © 2010 by Allison Brennan

Published in the United States by Ballantine Books, an imprint of The Random House Publishing Group, a division of Random House, Inc., New York.

BALLANTINE and colophon are trademarks of Random House, Inc.

This book contains an excerpt from the forthcoming book *Carnal Sin* by Allison Brennan. This excerpt has been set for this edition only and may not reflect the final content of the forthcoming edition.

ISBN 978-0-345-51167-6

Cover art: Tony Mauro
Cover design: Scott Biel

Printed in the United States of America

www.ballantinebooks.com

9 8 7 6 5 4 3 2 1

For my two oldest children
Katie and Kelly

I will forever remember our girls' nights munching popcorn and nachos watching *Supernatural* and *Veronica Mars* and *Buffy* and all the scary movies we screamed at and laughed over. I will remember you both growing from sweet, inquisitive children into mostly sweet and curious teenagers, and I know you'll be charming, smart, and spirited adults.

Katie: I am in awe of your strong, innate sense of justice, of right and wrong, of defending the underdog and standing up for your beliefs. Your self-confidence will take you far, your common sense will keep you safe, and you can do anything you set your mind to.

Kelly: Your creative talent is far beyond your years, and I marvel at your artistry. Your imagination is boundless, and your perceptions surprisingly mature. Don't doubt yourself, and you'll be able to do anything.

I am so very proud of you both.

ACKNOWLEDGMENTS

In addition to the usual suspects—my agent Kim Whalen, my incredible editors Charlotte Herscher and Dana Isaacson, and the entire Ballantine team—there are a few people I want to acknowledge for their help with this book.

First, my daughter Kelly Brennan who came up with the cover concept for *Original Sin* and created the original illustration in this book. We had a lot of fun and energetic conversations about the Book of Genesis and the seven deadly sins in the world today. And the designer, Scott Biel, who took our vision and created an amazing cover.

My writing buddies, especially the talented Toni McGee Causey, who read a very early, very rough version of this book and helped talk through my worldbuilding, playing both devil's advocate and biggest fan. She was also there to listen to me whine, complain, cry, and celebrate. I owe you big time. (And thank goodness for free long distance calling!)

My amazing blog partners at murdershewrites.com and murderati.com who may not keep me sane, but are crazy enough that I appear surprisingly ordinary.

My kids for understanding that the writer's life is not normal and putting up with my late nights and caffeine fueled mornings; my husband for bringing me Starbucks even when I don't ask; and my mom for being a surrogate chauffeur and terrific grandmother.

And finally, especially, thank you to my readers, for indulging me this deviation into the supernatural world. This story has been in my head for more than six years, and I'm thrilled and grateful that I'm able to share it.

We always long for the forbidden things,
and desire what is denied us.

—François Rabelais (1494–1553)

PROLOGUE

Ten Weeks Ago

No one could hear Moira's piercing screams; they were in her head, as trapped as she was by the ancient demon who was luring the man she loved to his death.

Peter, her lover, her life, the reason she wanted to survive, held out the cross and chanted an ancient exorcism.

Her palms went up, facing him. The demonic energy building within pulsated outward and grabbed her lover by his throat. Squeezed. It was as if her own hands were tightening around Peter's neck with inhuman strength. But Moira was many feet away from him, the demon using her body to channel his satanic energy. Peter was dying, struggling for breath as he collapsed to the floor, scratching at invisible hands around his neck, drawing his own blood.

Moira witnessed the shock on Peter's face. The pain. The disbelief. With a flick of her wrist, the malevolent demon hurled him across the room with enough force to crack the stone wall. Peter dropped twelve feet to the ground, dead . . .

Moira O'Donnell jolted awake, her breath coming in gasps, the cheap, scratchy motel sheets damp from perspiration, her skin slick and hot to the touch. As always, after this nightmare came a vision, hitting so hard and fast and fading so rapidly that every time she tried to focus on a detail, it would disappear like a wisp of smoke. But fear still clung tenaciously to every cell in her body, squeezing her tight until she was nearly blind with panic.

She'd been having nightmares every night. And just as the nightmares were the real past, the visions that invariably followed were the real present. They were far from useful: even as Moira witnessed events happening *right now,* she was powerless to stop the endless cycle of destruction. How could she balance the scales if evil kept winning?

It didn't help that her visions were difficult to decipher, snippets of startling images and intense feelings, strangers' faces and places she'd never been. She suffered with people she didn't know, feeling their pain, sharing their terror, and was unable to do a damn thing to stop it. Father Philip explained to her there was a deeper meaning, to be patient, but Moira was tired of waiting for answers that never came. She was exhausted from watching the underworld win yet another battle, and seeing countless more innocent people suffer.

Moira was tired of living when she had nothing to live for.

She sat up, head in her hands, doing what Father Philip told her to do after a vision. Try to remember. Search for clues.

You are seeing these things for a reason. Ask questions, listen for answers. They will be there when you need them, but you must be alert.

Sure, rip open my soul to be tortured again and again,

always searching for answers when I don't even know the damn questions!

She heard the crashing of waves against cliffs far beneath her.

Moira could practically smell the salt air. Salt air tinged with smoke, ash, sulphur. She focused on remembering the images she didn't want to see.

A demon. The stench of burning sulphur, so thick her tongue was coated with it, mixed with the sick, sweet, metallic taste of blood. A burning house. Screams of agony. Not only from those trapped inside, but all around her. All around, and down below . . .

Moira jumped out of bed, unsteady. It was a portal. A gateway to Hell, a place where the supernatural barrier between this world and the underworld was so thin and weak that it took little effort to bring forth evil, or send souls into the fiery pit.

Joyous laughter cackled loudly as evil watched death win a victory for its master. The house collapsed into itself, down, down into the molten pit far, far below . . . the gate was opening . . .

Fiona.

Fiona was responsible. Moira knew it as certainly as she knew that she was just as responsible as her mother for Peter's death.

Once again, Moira was too late to stop Fiona—a witch, a magician, an evil bitch, any of the names worked—from unleashing darkness into the world. Her laugh, her *scent* of lavender and musk, filled the air but disappeared as soon as Moira concentrated on the details of the vision, something, anything that might tell Moira where Fiona was *right now*. As soon as she focused, the sights and sounds faded away.

Would she ever figure this vision thing out? Would it ever *help* her find her mother, or would it only continue to taunt her, tease her, haunt her?

Moira sat back on the bed and stared at the long, unblinking cat's eye where the depressing yellow streetlight cast shadows through the slit where the curtains didn't quite meet. It was late November and the bitter cold would most certainly bring snow to this small, depressed town in upstate New York. The blustery weather reminded Moira of her childhood in Ireland, but here there was no green, not even a hint of spring, no salty air or the sweet warmth of burning peat.

A glance at the puke-green digital numbers on the old alarm clock had her swearing under her breath. Three fucking a.m. Ninety minutes of sleep. No way was she getting any more downtime tonight. She got up, switched on the desk lamp, pulled off her damp T-shirt, and walked over to the sink in an alcove. Even the shower wasn't private, simply a cheap plastic curtain hiding stained green tiles. Only the toilet was behind a door in a closet barely wide enough to turn around in. She splashed water on her face and under her arms and efficiently brushed her thick, black hair into a long, wavy ponytail.

The scar on the left side of her neck caught her attention. She tilted her head to view the odd-shaped discoloration that could be mistaken for a strawberry birthmark if anyone else actually saw it. Though barely noticeable after seven years, the scar was forever imprinted in her mind. If only having the memories—and nightmares—removed could be as easy as removing the demon's mark her mother had branded on her.

She leaned over, holding the stained porcelain with

white-knuckled fingers, drinking water from the faucet, the St. Michael's medallion she never removed clattering against the sink. Her face flushed with fear and the urge to run; she splashed icy water over her skin. Panic would get her and others killed. Too many people counted on her to find Fiona.

How do you kill your own mother?

She looked at the scar again. It burned beneath her skin as it had thirteen years ago, when Fiona had marked her on her sixteenth birthday. A memory of the pain . . .

It was no memory. *The scar was burning.*

Moira checked the salt seals on the windows and door. There was little that could stop demons, but she could slow them down, weaken them. It had saved her more than once, giving her time to disappear.

The time for hiding is over.

She picked up her cell phone. It was noon in Italy. Father Philip would be meditating in prayer. He was not to be disturbed during this hour, except in an emergency like this.

"St. Michael's," a calm male voice answered.

"Father Philip, please," she said, the Irish lilt all too obvious in her voice.

"He's not available right now."

"This is Moira O'Donnell. It's extremely important."

The monk didn't comment or hang up. She heard the receiver being placed on the wood table.

The only phone at St. Michael's Monastery was in the library. She pictured the tall, narrow windows with stained glass in the arches; the stone floor covered with a huge, impossibly old, faded Persian rug. The worn leather sofas, the reading lamps, the peace. This was a sanctuary for study and rest. The intensive, hands-on training—the physical training—was done far away in America, maybe to separate the violence from the research, but most likely to protect the Order from being annihilated in one attack.

Moira had spent countless hours in the library with Peter, studying the old texts. Many of the others were skeptical of her, but Father Philip had allowed her to stay. He'd saved her life and cared about her when she thought there was no hope left. He'd brought her to the sanctuary, taught her, encouraged Peter to help her. That the priest felt responsible for the tragedy that followed deeply pained her. It wasn't his fault she'd disobeyed his command to steer clear of magic. She'd wanted to undo the damage her mother and the coven had done, and the only way she knew how to battle magic was with magic. But she and Peter had gone too far. She hadn't realized the price would be so great, but learned the hard way that even with good intentions, sorcery begot only evil.

Father Philip broke her contemplation when he picked up the receiver, saying in his soft measured accent, "Moira. It's been six months."

She didn't want to explain to Father why she hadn't contacted him, or anyone, affiliated with St. Michael's all these months. Her doubts? Fears? Or was it the loneliness of her solitary mission she wanted to keep hidden from the few people who cared enough about her to notice her pain.

But this vision was different and Father was the only one who might have answers. "I had another vision. I don't remember much of it, but a gateway to Hell is opening."

"Where?"

"I don't know!" She bit her tongue. She wasn't angry with the old priest, but frustrated with herself. Frustrated and alone. She desperately missed Peter, but every time she allowed herself to think of him, she remembered only his death.

"Where are you?"

"Upstate New York. I was looking into a ritualistic murder that occurred on Halloween. It was just a stupid serial killer, his sixth murder in two years. It had nothing to do with Fiona." She was disgusted with herself for being drawn here just because the woman was killed at a graveyard. Fiona wasn't that uncouth.

Moira's mother killed with style.

She added, "My scar hurts. I've never felt it like this before."

Father Philip didn't answer. Her heart raced; what was he thinking? That she was going to be possessed again? That she was making it up? That she had truly lost her mind and was now seeing signs of demonic activity everywhere?

She fumbled around in her backpack for her aspirin bottle and shook four out, dry swallowing them. The bitter, chalky taste coated her tongue. She cupped water from the tap into her hands and drank, her shoulder holding the phone against her ear.

"Father?"

He cleared his throat. "It's a sign."

"I can't go through that again." Every time she had a vision, it ended poorly. She almost laughed at her thought—what an understatement!

"I didn't say it was a bad sign. I need to research."

What about "portal to Hell" wasn't bad? But Moira

swallowed her sarcasm and said, "Tell me the truth, Father, please."

"I don't know for certain; it's a hunch. Let me—"

"Tell me," she interrupted. "Father. I must know."

He sighed, and she could picture him taking off his small, silver-framed glasses and polishing them absently with his handkerchief. Philip was not only "Father" as in priest, but also the only father figure—the only *sane* father figure—she'd ever had. But Moira had been unable to remain at St. Michael's when the majority of its residents accused her with their silence. She couldn't take fearful refuge in the monastery while Fiona was free, gaining power, forging alliances with the darkest souls on and beneath the earth.

So she'd left for Olivet, an abbey in Montana named after the Mount of Olives in Jerusalem. Olivet was the go-to place for intensive physical training to be a demon hunter and, Moira supposed, the place where those in the thick of it went afterward to lick their wounds and regroup. It was the only place she could learn to use skills other than witchcraft to find and stop her mother's insane plans.

St. Michael's Monastery was the academic branch of the Order. They studied, prayed, raised up the young warriors, and fully educated them—until their gifts were discerned and they were assigned elsewhere, or sent to Olivet for training.

It had been whispered that St. Michael's hunted human evil, and Olivet hunted supernatural evil. Few acknowledged that they all were both predators and prey, hunting evil while trying to protect their Order from external—and internal—enemies.

The sole reason Moira was trained as a demon hunter

was to battle demons Fiona put in her path. Rico, the head of Olivet and her trainer, had made it clear that she wasn't truly one of them: a chosen warrior raised at St. Michael's. Moira's only purpose was to find, and stop, Fiona. Because dark covens used demons to defend them, learning to battle demons was essential to stopping witches.

Loneliness had been added to her guilt.

"A gateway to Hell is open?" Father Philip asked.

"*Opening.*"

"Why do you say it like that?"

She wasn't sure. "When I had the vision, that's what I thought. Something is beginning. I can't explain it; it's just what I felt." Moira hated unclear visions, interpretations, vague ideas of what it all supposedly meant. She wanted—*needed*—a path to follow. Explicit instructions, a solid plan. Once again, God showed his dark cosmic humor in her life.

"Then there's time," Father Philip pronounced from across the ocean.

"What about the scar?"

"You've been having the visions since Peter died."

Her heart twisted at the mere mention of his name. "Yes."

"These visions involve the barrier between us and the underworld."

"More or less." She shifted uncomfortably. "I've only had a few." A dozen, more or less. "It's not like I'm ready for the rubber room."

"No, no you're not." It had been a joke, but he'd answered as if she'd been serious. "It's a sign. You have a spiritual link to the underworld."

"No, no, *no!* Absolutely *not!*" She was shaking. St.

Michael's newest demon hunter shaking in fear. What a world!

"Moira, I believe you do. And you're going to have to learn to use your powers to our advantage. We must fight back. Too long we've been reactionaries, not acting until they brought forth evil spirits. The one right thing you and Peter did was to be proactive."

"Father—please." She could not talk about Peter.

"Peter made many mistakes."

"*I* made the mistakes, Father."

"But Peter knew better."

"Don't say that."

"Daughter—" He sighed. Moira's heart swelled. She loved to hear Father Philip call her *daughter*. It was an endearment that kept her grounded in love and hope. An assurance that even with everything she'd done, all the mistakes she—and Peter—had made, there was someone who cared about what happened to her. She was not alone, no matter how alone she felt.

Father said, "We absolutely cannot afford to be reactive. The signs have been many, and after the tragedy at the mission—"

"What mission? What happened?"

"At Santa Louisa de Los Padres. There was a demonic ritual there that led to the murders of twelve priests."

Her stomach rose to her throat. "Father—"

"I knew many of them."

"I'm so sorry."

"We were too late. Perhaps that was your vision. It happened three days ago."

Though she couldn't remember her vision image by image, only the overall feeling, she still recalled snapshots. "It happened tonight. A great fire, complete destruction."

"Moira, you must open yourself to the visions. Learn to read them."

"What if they're from Hell? What if I'm being misled?"

"Every vision you've had has been of an event that *is* happening, not a deception."

"That can change. They can use me to hurt people." *To hurt you.*

"I will continue to research. Consult Rico, others. We can be proactive. With you, we have foreknowledge."

"Foreknowledge? If it's happening *now,* how can that help us?"

"You said that the portal was *opening*—which means we can stop it or close it. This is our advantage, and the only way to stop them."

Rico had taught her everything he could during her time at Olivet, including his creed: gather intelligence, create a plan, execute the plan. It worked, and she liked the structure and preparation that went with being a demon hunter. But being given inside information? That scared her. What if Father Philip was wrong? What if Fiona and the demons were trying to deceive her? Trap her? What if Moira misinterpreted the visions? What if her mistakes cost more innocent souls their lives?

She just wanted to stop Fiona. She didn't want— couldn't bear—the fate of mankind on her shoulders.

Reluctantly, she asked, "What do I need to do?"

"Find where the gateway is opening. Go there."

"How?"

"Meditate. Pray."

Never. But Moira didn't tell him that. She'd use more contemporary methods, starting with the Internet.

"And how do I close it?"

"I don't know."

"Terrific. I'll just throw my body into the pit and battle it out to the death."

"Do not be flippant." Father sounded irritated. "I will find out how to close it. Let me know as soon as you locate it. I will need the specifics of how it was created and why. That might be harder to discover than its location."

Moira closed her eyes. Everything was spiraling out of control. She didn't want this responsibility. When she'd first accepted this mission, it was to locate Fiona, not a gateway to Hell.

But she had no choice. Fiona was somehow involved, and Fiona was her responsibility. "Fine, I'll do it. But Father, I feel out of balance."

"You need assistance."

"No." She wasn't about to work with a partner. She wasn't going to kill anyone again. *Except* Fiona, of course.

"My sweet child, your heart is broken, but your soul is intact. Give your pain over to God; you will heal."

She snapped, "I don't trust Him." She didn't buy into the whole benevolent God angle. Yeah, He was around, but it was hands off, fend for yourselves, children.

"Moira, go to Olivet and work with Rico on—"

"I'll call when I find something." Before hanging up, she added softly, "Good-bye, Father. I miss you."

Moira picked up her pack, gathered her few things, and left the squalid motel room. She had no intention of returning to Olivet, not without answers. She scanned the parking lot. Slim pickings. Only five parked cars. She settled on the lone truck because she remembered the owner—he'd been drinking heavily in the greasy road-side restaurant when she'd stopped in earlier to order a BLT. She hoped he'd sleep through the sound of his truck starting up. She didn't need the vehicle for long, just to get to a bigger town where she could use a li-brary, find a coffee shop, and figure out where the damn door to Hell had cracked. She'd ditch it with a full tank of gas and twenty dollars in the glove box, the best she could do on her meager funds.

As she crossed the uneven concrete parking lot, the first snowflake of the season landed on her cheek. She brushed it aside like a cold tear. She wouldn't be around long enough to enjoy any white winter.

ONE

Present Day

It was the darkest hour of the night.

Fiona stood within the protective double circle that framed the perfect hexagram within a perfect triangle. Bowls of incense burned within triangles, six of which were perfectly and evenly cast between the inner and outer circles at the apex of each point of the hexagram, smoke slowly rising. Only when the fumes breached the invisible shield did the wind carry them off, swirling violently into the black night. The laws of physics did not apply to Hell's gateway.

As it is below, so it is above.

The seventh bowl sat in the center, at the base of the altar. The trap was complete.

Her filmy, translucent white gown was unique in its meticulous and detailed silver embroidery. Woven through Fiona's fiery hair was a knotted scarlet rope. Flames from the black candles at each point of the hexagram were virtually still, a testament to her careful preparation and growing power.

Seven of her coven stood sentry beside the seven triangles. They, too, wore white gowns with nothing beneath. Her obedient daughter Serena was at her left hand. Three men guarded the altar. And the key to the gateway to Hell lay naked upon the altar, covered with only a sacred red sheet. Abby was a beautiful sacrifice, her long, golden hair fanned out beneath her. She had no fear. She'd been taught well.

Fiona listened to Serena speak the ancient words from the *Conoscenza*, murmuring as if speaking to a lover. She'd searched her entire life for this book of knowledge, the book so many believed to have been destroyed. Fiona had never lost hope, never given up. And now it was hers.

Nine days of fasting, nine days of purification, nine days of denial culminating in tonight and the fulfillment of her promise. With power comes responsibility, and Fiona kept her word. With the knowledge contained in the *Conoscenza*, her gain would be far greater control and power over the elements, the spirits, the universe. One step closer to immortality. She saw it, tasted it, reveled in the electricity of the forces within her and around her.

As Serena spoke, her servants chanted their response. As she incanted, their voices swelled, fueling Fiona's power. The energy grew, pulled into their sacred circle. She commanded the wind, she would command all!

This was only the beginning, and there was to be no end.

"Anoint our vessel," Fiona commanded the three men.

Serena handed Garrett a gold chalice with a mixture of herbs, resins, and human blood. As he dipped his left thumb into the cup, Serena began to turn the supernatural key by reciting from the book. Garrett marked the vessel, ensuring that the Seven would soon be under Fiona's command.

"As it is below, so it is above," Fiona intoned. "For every good there is an evil, for every virtue there is a vice."

Garrett put his thumb on the vessel's forehead and drew a triangle. One of the women entered the inner circle and lit one of the seven candles, reciting a prayer of obedience.

Fiona continued the ritual, moving from triangle to triangle, with Garrett anointing and Serena reading from the book. He looked at Fiona over the cup, his eyes on fire. His lust, his fever, inspired her and she summoned each woman in turn, each a chosen guardian of one of the Seven.

Serena stepped away from the altar in the middle of the ritual and Fiona whirled around. "No one breaks the circle!"

"She's here."

Fiona looked upon her coven, smiling victoriously. She'd told them the *arca* would come.

—And the blood of the virtuous will seal the seven, and thee who seals the arca will rule—

Lily Ellis stood outside the double circle. Her long, pale red hair whipped about her face, her fair skin nearly translucent. She was rail thin, a wisp of a girl, but with the power of virtue and a soul dedicated to this moment. Fiona knew the girl's inner strength would be strong enough, as she had been prepared as the vessel had been. If not, she'd die tonight, and Fiona would find another *arca*. There were others who had been dedicated; others who could serve her purpose. But the signs weren't wrong: Lily Ellis was the one.

Fiona whispered to Serena, "Are you ready?"

"Yes."

"Bring her forth."

Serena walked to the edge of the circle. She'd been cleansed and could not break the circle without harm, but Fiona was certain Lily Ellis did not know this, nor that once Lily entered the circle she would not be allowed to leave until the ritual was complete. And when the Seven were trapped, Fiona would have the power of legions of demons on her side, and elevate herself to a mortal god. Closer to victory over death, victory over age, victory over humanity.

"We will not harm you."

Lily said, her voice shaking, "Pul-please let her go."

"You would take her place?" Serena asked.

Serena understood the power of words. *Would* take her place was not an offering or an exchange, it was a question. Because no one could save Abby. She was the sacrifice through which the Seven would come forth; Abby was the key that unsealed the prison. She had been recruited because she was the *arca*'s closest friend and blood relative, a cousin. Both only daughters of witches who were only daughters of witches. Not necessary for the ritual, but Fiona preferred balance and rhythm in her rituals, and Lily and Abby provided a nice, even canvas.

The girl's lips trembled. She had not dressed for the chill, her arms pulling her thin sweater tight around her. The fog rose from the ocean, rolling over the edge of the cliffs toward their circle. "Please—"

"Would you?" Serena asked.

Tears glistened in the candlelight. "Y-Yes."

Serena put out her hand, palm up.

Lily hesitated. Fiona closed her eyes and pictured the surroundings. She sent out her Third Eye, her psychic self, looking for anyone lurking in the cypress. Beyond that was open space, cliffs, and the highway more than a mile to the west. Open space protected them. There was no one to stop her. She'd know long before anyone could get close. Victory was in her grasp. Power swelled in her breast.

Lily had to cross the circle of her own free will.

She had to agree to taste the forbidden fruit.

Lily looked around at the cloaked men and women. Nervous, scared, uncertain. Fiona nodded to Garrett. He pushed back his hood and turned to face Lily.

The *arca* gasped. "Pastor Garrett—"

"Come, child." He opened his arms to her, palms up like Serena. Welcoming. Benign. His strikingly handsome face seduced women of all ages to do exactly what he wanted.

Lily swallowed, then stepped into the circle. She stopped, her face twisted in fearful confusion as the stillness of the air within the circle surprised her.

Serena removed the extra gown from her shoulders and said, "Wear this."

Lily looked around, her eyes darting nervously from Garrett to the other men.

Serena laughed lightly. "Would you like them to close their eyes?"

She nodded, shaking. Fiona put up her hand and nodded to the men. "The *arca* commands privacy."

Ian and Richard closed their eyes. Garrett smiled at Fiona as he put his hood back on, then closed his as well. She allowed him to gloat. Fiona had been skeptical of a seventeen-year-old virgin, but Garrett was never wrong about these things.

The girl took off her clothes, not meeting the eyes of

the women who watched. Abby, a willing participant only because she didn't know that her death was required, said, "Lily, there's nothing to be scared about."

"Abby—" Lily glanced around, her big, brown eyes wide, the reflection of the candles making them seem bottomless. "Please, let's go."

"No," Abby said, irritated. "I thought you wanted to share this with me."

Lily opened her mouth to speak, but Fiona could not allow her to cast doubt within Abby. Fiona said, "Relax, Abby, you need to be perfectly calm in order to achieve your elevated state."

"Yes, *medea*."

"The anointing," Fiona said.

Serena had a small gold triangle-shaped box in her hand. The box contained a resin, made in part with blood of a newborn goat, olive oil, scammony, myrrh, and civet. The recipe came from the *Conoscenza* to aid the Seven in finding the *arca* once they were released. Serena marked Lily with the seven signs, on her forehead, each hand, her heart, her stomach, her pubis, and her left hip. There was an opening in the gown at each point so the mark wouldn't be concealed. At each step, Serena whispered the commands in Latin, so the girl wouldn't be afraid.

Garrett handed Serena a closed ball of simmering henbane. Serena opened it, allowing the hallucinogenic fumes to flow into Lily's senses. *One. Two. Three.*

She closed the ball, handed it back to Garrett, and took Lily's hand. The henbane would keep her compliant, for Fiona couldn't have her fight back now. The wine she would soon drink—willingly or not—would attract the Seven to her, like a bitch in heat attracts a male dog. If the Seven escaped the *arca* it would be impossible to recapture all of them. At this momentous time, there was no room for error.

Serena brought Lily to the altar and laid her on her back, the top of her head touching Abby's head. One was a vessel through which the demons would enter the world, the other was a container where they would be trapped.

It was perfect.

"Abby," Lily whispered.

"Silence," Fiona ordered. "It has begun."

She continued the ritual she'd begun before the *arca* arrived, the growing tension and excitement filling her with physical and spiritual power.

Fiona would succeed where other, weaker magicians had failed. For centuries, individual witches and covens had attempted to locate the *Conoscenza* and failed. Attempted to find the Tree of Life and failed. Many had died in their failures.

Fiona would not fail. She would not die.

She would live forever.

TWO

Courage is not the absence of fear,
but rather the judgment that something else
is more important than fear.
—AMBROSE REDMOON

Moira jolted upright, her breath coming in gasps, her heart racing. The nightmare rapidly faded, but the terror that clutched her held on tight.

It wasn't a nightmare, it was a vision, just like the terrible one she'd had ten weeks before. But this was far more vivid than any she'd ever experienced.

For a long moment, she forgot where she was. She willed her heart to slow, trying to gain mastery over her fear. This morning's motel room was the same as so many before it. The stale smells, the strange thumps, the yellow lights and thin sheets. Days had rolled into weeks with Moira barely acknowledging the passage of time, blending together Ft. Lauderdale and Ocean City, Astoria and Santa Louisa, and in between dozens of towns, big and small. At last Moira was in the right place.

"Santa Louisa," she whispered in the dark. The town wasn't far from the mission massacre Father Philip had told her about. She realized now that she should have headed here directly after that phone conversation. If only she'd known the mountains in eastern Santa Louisa were a mere thirty miles from the Pacific Ocean!

She'd arrived in the picturesque central California

town nearly a week ago, remaining after sensing this was the right place. Her research and her finely tuned instincts told her the gateway to Hell was here in Santa Louisa.

On the Internet message board she frequented that discussed supernatural phenomena, she'd encountered a teenager who described cliffs in the area that seemed strikingly similar to those in her vision. He'd been concerned because a mysterious fire had destroyed a local house and there'd been other odd occurances. His name was Jared Santos and everything he told her confirmed that these were the cliffs of her vision. She'd immediately headed to Santa Louisa.

The cliffs—the ruins of the destroyed house—terrified Moira even in daylight. Frightening images and thoughts flooded her mind whenever she went near the place.

She'd stood where evil radiated from the ground like heat from a furnace set on high.

Evil surrounded her. Evil didn't float in the air, it was the air. The earth didn't smell like earth, it reeked of the dead, of terror, of lost souls clawing through moldy dirt, desperate to escape their fate. She'd passed dead birds, rodents, a mutilated dog as she neared the center of the ruins on the cliffs. Her heart strained, told her to leave, but she looked down, and for a second that seemed to last forever, Moira saw a river of fire beneath the surface. She felt the heat rising. The soles of her feet burning, she ran.

That first night, in the dark, she'd hid among the cypress, waiting, the fear gnawing at her. She'd forced herself to stay, hoping—and fearing—her mother would appear.

Fiona hadn't come. No one had. The following day,

Moira had contacted Father Philip and told him what she'd learned. About the fire and the two deaths inside the house. That the house had been completely destroyed was frightening enough. Worse, Moira knew that portals like this could be opened only through human sacrifice.

Father asked her to stay on site and watch, to be diligent, and she had been. Or so she'd thought.

Fiona spoke, surrounded by energy so evil Moira began to shake. She could see nothing else, nothing but her mother's flaming red hair, everything obscured by a smoky curtain that Moira couldn't penetrate. Dark shapes took form within the curtain, whether human or demon she didn't know. The gates of hell were open and Moira was too late.

Dammit, no! She couldn't be too late. Father was certain Fiona wouldn't act until the first of February, when the worlds were naturally closer. Moira had agreed, but they were wrong. It was happening *now*. How could she face her mother and whatever evil she had summoned and defeat it? *Alone?*

Yet how could she not?

She sensed beyond a shadow of a doubt that right now—at this very moment—Fiona was on those cliffs finishing what she'd started more than two months before. Two months? Fiona had been seeking immortality her entire forty-eight years, continuing the journey that started with the first covens assembled in ancient times. But Fiona was the first witch to come this close.

"Shit," Moira muttered, "that's going to go straight to her head." She couldn't let her succeed.

She slid from between the worn sheets, clothed in a blue T-shirt and black panties. She switched on the desk lamp, pulled on her jeans, then tossed her sweat-soaked T-shirt into a plastic bag.

How the *fuck* was she going to stop her mother? She had no backup, few tools, and too little information to go head to head against Fiona. Father Philip hadn't figured out what the gateway would bring forth, and without that knowledge Moira might as well be sprinkling holy water on Satan himself. A mere sizzle within an apocalyptic inferno.

She couldn't let Fiona go through with the ritual. It would end in murder. It always did.

The mark on her neck burned.

Moira snapped on a bra and pulled a black turtleneck over her head, then slid into the custom-made leather jacket Rico had given her. With special pockets for special things.

"I'm not a hunter," she'd told him, holding the jacket as if it were on fire.

"No, you're a huntress," her trainer said. Rico pushed her chin up. *"Despero caveat, mei amica. Despair lets them in. Despair means no hope, and there's always hope."*

Anger fueled her fear, both volatile emotions that could be used against her. She didn't know how to control them. That lack of control had screwed her big-time in the past, often enough to force her to pause now and breathe deeply. She remembered that there was more at stake tonight than her life.

If she failed, the covens would grow even stronger, more powerful, aided by demons at their side. St. Michael's Order would be in great peril. One by one, Peter's brothers-in-arms would die. Horribly. Violently. Painfully.

Move it, Moira. Stop feeling so damn sorry for your-self.

She grabbed her bag and opened the door.

Outside something—some*one*—moved.

She quickly stepped back into the shadows of her room as she sensed before she saw a person approaching through the dense fog. Her knife was in her hand before she knew it, sweat on her brow. Though she'd yet to do it alone, she knew how to stop a demon. It was extremely difficult outside of a controlled environment—like the monastery—to banish the demon and not kill the human being it possessed. And even then, survival of the victim or the exorcist was not assured. She wanted no more deaths on her conscience.

There was only so much that intensive training could do, even with Rico—the best instructor the Order had—in her corner. Experience trumped the classroom every time. But she had no choice at this point. Fiona was here because Moira had made a deadly mistake. A mistake she couldn't make again.

She recognized the visitor. Jared Santos, eighteen, her sole friend in this country.

Shocked, Jared's dark eyes went to her knife and she quickly pocketed it. "I didn't know who you were."

"So you pull a knife? This is Santa Louisa, not Detroit."

She ignored his comment. He still didn't understand what they were up against, but she'd needed someone who knew the locals and the area. Jared had been her lifeline for the last week, providing her with information and transportation. He didn't completely believe what she told him, but he'd seen and heard enough that he hadn't turned her in to the police. And considering his father was a deputy sheriff, that was a *real* good thing.

"What are you doing here?" she asked. "You're supposed to be watching Lily."

"She's gone."

Moira's nagging fear deepened. She knew where the girl had gone, but she didn't know why. She had come to Santa Louisa because Jared had told her on the message board about several odd incidents he and his girlfriend Lily had uncovered about her cousin Abby's new group of friends. The fire on the cliffs—occurring the same night as her vision more than two months before— sealed the deal. Everything Moira heard was stamped with the M.O. of an actively recruiting coven. That Abby had been overweight until recently and had few friends, outside of Lily, was another big flashing neon sign warning Moira.

"We have to find her. When did she leave? Why did you let her go?"

Jared began, "I didn't—"

"I told you what was at stake!"

He ran his hands through his short buzzcut, a pained expression on his face. "I don't know what happened."

"You fell asleep." *Geez.* She shouldn't have trusted him.

"I don't know. I—I didn't mean to. My head's foggy; I guess I haven't been sleeping so good lately."

Fiona or one of her minions must have cast a spell over Jared. Or drugged him. Something had enabled Lily to slip away. The girl was crazy, that's all there was to it. Moira had told her what Abby and the others were up to, but Lily didn't believe her. "*I know it's not safe, but—*"

"There are no 'buts,' Lily! They are not playing games. They are deadly serious, and outsiders are not invited into their coven for a cup of tea. They are invited to be sacrificed."

She'd gone too far revealing that detail. No one believed in human sacrifices because the evidence disappeared. Just because there were no publicly recorded cases of human sacrifices in America, that sure didn't mean they didn't happen. Moira knew for a fact they did.

"She promised she would tell me before she went to the meeting," Jared insisted. "I don't understand why—"

"We haven't time." Moira cut him off and pushed him out the door, rolling her eyes, having no patience for the kid's excuses. *Meeting.* Nice way to sugarcoat deadly occult rituals.

She spotted Jared's black truck parked at the end of the front row. She started to run. "Let's go. The cliffs."

"Is Lily really in danger?"

"Yes."

"But—"

She abruptly turned around and he stumbled to avoid running into her. "You told me about the fire," she said with frightening vehemence. "About the dead animals near the cliffs, Lily's cousin Abby and all the weird things you saw. Everything matches what I know about these rituals. It's the timing I don't understand, but I do know we have to go right *now.*"

Moira didn't give him time to answer or argue. She ran around to the passenger side and hopped into the truck. He quickly followed and headed for the cliffs.

During the ten-mile drive, she called Father Philip. When he came to the phone, he sounded extremely worried. She hated that she'd caused him to fear for her safety.

"Moira, where are you? You haven't called in three days. I was worried."

"I'm still in Santa Louisa."

"I'm checking out one more thing; then I hope to know more." She hoped to still be alive. She very much wanted to be wrong about tonight.

"Have you seen Anthony?"

Her hand tightened on the phone at the mention of the name. Father Philip had told her the demonologist was in town, but because they both thought there was time, they hadn't contacted him. Not that Moira would. Anthony despised her because of what had happened to Peter. He blamed her, even more than she blamed herself.

"No. I told you—"

"I should have called him when you arrived," Father Philip said.

"So he could get himself killed?"

"He's much stronger than he was seven years ago."

"He's not a hunter," she protested.

"He's gifted in other ways."

"He hates my guts."

"He hates no one."

Father didn't know what he was saying. "I can't risk him, too." Her voice cracked. Damn, she didn't even *like* Anthony—the man Peter had called brother—and she had to worry about him now.

"Anthony is a grown man. He's faced his own battles, and survived."

Father Philip believed in forgiveness; Anthony did not. But Moira couldn't tell Father that. He wouldn't believe it, or if he did, it would hurt him. And he was the last person on the planet Moira wanted to hurt.

"You are certain about the gateway," he said quietly.

"Yes."

"Don't go back."

"I have to. There's a coven in town; all the signs are here. If this is Fiona—I have to stop her."

Father Philip said, "I'll call Anthony."

"No!"

"Moira, child, you can't do this alone."

"He's not going to help me."

"Yes, he will. You need to have faith and trust, Moira."

"And a little bit of pixie dust?"

"Excuse me?"

"A joke." If she didn't laugh, she was going to fall apart.

"I'll call Anthony and be mediator. You need to explain your visions. Don't go to the site again until you have backup."

"Too late, Father. I'm on my way. Something's happening right now."

"Moira—"

"I'll be careful." She hung up.

"Maybe," Jared said as he drove too damn slowly, too damn cautiously, through the thickening fog, "I should call my father—"

"Sure. Call him. Tell him you're working with Moira O'Donnell, P.I., as in *Paranormal Investigations*. That you contacted me to check out supernatural phenomena in the area and oh, by the way, there's a coven of witches on the cliffs about to open a big-ass gateway to Hell and release Lord knows what demonic forces into the world."

"You don't have to be sarcastic."

"I'm *not*. If you want to call him, fine, but you're already risking your life to help your girlfriend. I don't know what we're facing, and if you want to get out now, fine by me." She didn't want him to leave her alone, even though he didn't know what he was doing. But she didn't want to risk his life, either.

"I love her," he said. He didn't make a move, either to leave her by the side of the road or to make a call. *Love* Moira understood. It made you do stupid things and it hurt worse than a knife to the gut.

She wished she had someone to back her up other than a testosterone-fueled teenager playing Romeo to Lily's Juliet. At least she had a getaway driver. And Father Philip would call Anthony. She knew that as certainly as she knew the sun would rise in a few hours. Whether she lived to see the next day was another story.

"Step on it, Jared. We might already be too late." None of Moira's visions had been about a future event, but Fiona was still around. Rituals took time, especially with Fiona, who liked all the bells and whistles, especially with complex rituals. Moira knew this was a big one. If she cut off the head of the coven, the rest would scatter, and hopefully whatever evil they'd summoned would turn on them.

A confrontation with her mother would likely kill Moira, but she also knew that if she didn't stop her, Fiona would destroy innocent people in far more painful ways. It was now or never.

On the horizon, in the direction they were headed, lightning slashed the fog. It was too close to the ground.

Rivers of bright lava crossed the road in front of them. Above them, a fluttering of bats . . . but they weren't bats. *They* were an "it," one large dark cloud with mass, with volume, evil to its core.

She screamed and Jared jumped.

The fires were gone, but she'd seen them. She'd *seen* them. Hadn't she? Was she losing her mind?

"What the fuck? You scared the he—"

"Didn't you see it? The fire? The . . . *dark cloud*?"

He frowned. "I—it was just birds. It's the middle of the night; they got startled or something."

"Denial will get you killed."

"What do you think that was?"

She swallowed. She didn't know, but whatever it was, it wasn't supposed to be *here*. "Hell on earth," she whispered. Then, more urgently, she said, "Go faster, Jared."

THREE

●

Lonely is the night when you find yourself alone
Your demons come to light and your mind is not your own
—BILLY SQUIRE, "Lonely Is the Night"

"Dear God, why are you doing this to me?"

Biting back a curse, Rafe Cooper stumbled along the rocky cliffs that, to him, marked the edge of the world. It was a long, long way from his youthful island home in the blissful isolation of Sicily's St. Michael's.

Earlier tonight, he'd been in a hospital bed. He'd opened his eyes with the overwhelming, undeniable compulsion to leave. How he got from there to here he didn't know, only snippets of his two-hour journey remaining.

When he tried to think—to *remember*—knifelike pain sliced through his head, lights and shadows exploding, and he had to stop until the intensity subsided.

He knew who he was—Raphael Cooper—and he knew why he'd been in the hospital—the attack at the mission. He'd been the sole survivor. Uninjured while the others had been butchered. Comatose, according to the doctors, but that couldn't be right. He'd been unable to see or speak, but he heard everything. He heard far too much, so why couldn't he remember now?

Again, pain sliced through his skull as he tried to recall what had happened during the months he'd been in the hospital.

A grove of cypress trees provided a canopy and a place of rest. He sat on a lightning-split trunk and let out a long breath. Every limb shook, his feet were numb, and his mind raced faster than he could think. He didn't know why he'd come here, why he was compelled as if he had no control over his actions.

A car was parked on the north side of the cypress grove, but no one was inside. The *tick-tick* of the engine told him that someone had stopped here recently, and he looked around, confused and curious. He seemed to be in the middle of nowhere, but he wasn't alone.

South of the grove he saw light within the thickening fog. Flickering light, from candles, a mere football-field length from him. Shadows of people—a dozen or more blurry figures—moved within the fog, among the flames. Fear clawed at the base of his skull; his blood alternated between hot and icy cold. Something evil was at hand.

How do you know that?

He considered, and shards of pain stabbed his head again, blinding him, bringing him to his knees in supplication, until his mind again went blank. He screamed, but no sound came from his lungs.

He refocused on the scene, the still, low fog casting an ethereal glow in the vicinity.

Be quiet, be very quiet, don't think, don't think a word . . .

Salt air rising from the inky depths of the ocean mingled with the pungent fragrance of myrrh and musk and other scents he couldn't identify. The candle-holding figures wore white, their gowns shimmering in the quickly disappearing moonlight.

A coven.

Don't think, just act, don't think, do, quiet quiet quiet, they won't see me, don't let them see me . . .

Rafe didn't know how he knew what the coven was doing, but as he neared the assembled group he understood everything as if he'd known it all along. Yet when he tried to concentrate on individual thoughts they disappeared, like a partial recognition of an old friend, or a suspected enemy. You know you *know* them, but you don't remember where or why or when.

He didn't need to know why or how he knew, he just needed to accept the truth: this coven was summoning demons and sacrificing the girls on the altar to do it.

Neither girl would survive when it was over. That he knew with certainty.

Rafe told himself this was foolish, one weak man against a dozen witches. How long had he been asleep? How long had he been in the hospital, knowing time passed but not knowing why?

Painful memories cut into his thoughts. He pushed aside the blood-soaked helplessness of his past . . . He had been unable to stop the witches before, when he was physically and spiritually strong; how could he stop them tonight, when he was weak and doubting? He would die in such a confrontation.

He deserved to die. Maybe this battle was meant to be. His death to save someone he didn't know. Dying would give him peace, silence the constant pain and pressure and agonizing memories of his murdered friends. He was supposed to protect the priests who sought forgiveness and healing at Santa Louisa de los Padres Mission; instead, he'd allowed their slaughter through his own blindness.

How do you know what they're doing, Raphael?

Rafe pushed the question aside, the overwhelming urge to hurry forcing him to walk faster until he was running, and before long he stood on the edge of their circle. Even though the demon trap was in the center of a clearing, the witches were so engrossed in their ritual that at first they didn't notice him through the fog and smoke.

The High Priestess, with dark red hair that shimmered in the light, held a bowl over a naked girl, and said:

"Ashes to ashes and dust to dust, as God in Heaven created the angels from nothing, so I command the Seven to rise through the gate which I have opened. In the name of Barbiel, Azza, and Mammon; in the name of Moloch, Olivier, and Sammael; in the name of Beelzebub and all the Fallen: come through the keyhole and submit to my command."

The body of the naked girl began to convulse, and a hooded woman next to the High Priestess held a dagger above her, as if to ward off an attack. The hooded woman was familiar . . . but Rafe couldn't focus on her as the earth rumbled, a growl that shot primal fear directly to his heart, putting every one of his senses on high alert.

The girl was lifted from the ground by unseen forces as she writhed. The gowned girl next to her was still, and at first Rafe thought she was dead. But then her eyes moved, her face twisting in panic. She was an unwilling sacrifice.

Save the arca . . .

A deafening roar filled the circle and the naked girl screamed and convulsed as around her black smoke rose from the ground, then swirled like a hurricane above the coven. Lightning flashed as unformed demons crashed and collided. As the six witches within the double circle, and the one in the center, chanted urgently, the demons were drawn against their will into the double ring, swirling, straining, screaming, until they were wrenched apart, separated, into seven distinct columns that rose from ceremonial bowls into the sky. The column in the middle grew bigger, wider, darker.

Pride.

Rafe was too late to stop the opening of the gates of Hell. The demons were here, and he didn't know how to send them back.

Save the arca . . .

The *arca?* He laid eyes on the terrified, frozen girl on the altar. The naked girl was dead; Rafe knew it as certainly as he knew he was alive. But with the knowledge that he could—that he *had* to—save the other girl, the *arca,* he broke the circle.

All eyes shot to him. Shock registered on the High Priestess's face as he spoke.

The words were foreign to his tongue; he'd never heard them before. But as soon as he spoke, his voice took on a deep, resonant command and the earth shook beneath him.

"Stop! You don't know what you're doing!" the High Priestess screamed. "Raphael Cooper! Stop!"

She countered him with a curse that he could almost see bounce off him. Sharp pain in his chest told him she'd hit close. He didn't know who or what was protecting him, but he didn't have time to figure that out, just like he couldn't reflect on how the redheaded witch knew his name.

Rafe walked to the altar and pulled the girl, the *arca,* to her unsteady feet.

The High Priestess began another chant, aided by the familiar witch in a different language. A language he *almost* knew. She was finishing the invocation that would make this girl her weapon. His head ached as he looked into the girl's wide pupils. She was drugged, her eyes darting and unfocused, her face flushed. The incense burned low to the ground where the girls had lain, making her drunk with the poisonous, hallucinatory fumes. They would soon affect Rafe. If this girl didn't escape, he would have to kill her to stop the ritual—a ritual that would have far more deadly results than the loss of one innocent life.

He didn't want to kill her. But if the ritual was complete, not only would she die anyway, but the coven would be impossible to stop.

"Run," he commanded the girl. "Run or you'll die."

A low rumble and an overwhelming feeling of unbalance ripped Anthony Zaccardi out of a restless sleep at two that morning. He sat up, the sheet, damp from his perspiration, falling off his chest. It took a moment for him to recognize the cluttered room he'd been sleeping in for the past ten weeks, the lacey femininity of Skye McPherson's bedroom so different than the no-nonsense cop she was outside of her home.

He swung his legs off the side of the bed, squeezed his temples, and prayed for answers to questions he didn't know.

"What's wrong?" Skye asked, putting a cool hand on his bare back.

"Sorry," he murmured. "I didn't want to wake you."

"Your thousand-degree body woke me. I swear, I'll save a fortune on heating bills with you in my bed."

He stared at Skye in her gray cotton tank top, her long, blond hair tangled and damp from sleep. It took a moment for his head to clear, then he touched her beautiful face. "I am sorry, *mia amore*."

He'd heard something but couldn't remember what had awakened him. A deep sense of foreboding filled him. It was the same fear that had built in him more than ten weeks ago when he'd first arrived in Santa Louisa from St. Michael's in Italy. The closer he'd gotten to the mission, the more apprehensive he'd become. For good reason. He'd been able to save only one man from the horrors at Santa Louisa de los Padres: Rafe. The others, all twelve priests, had died.

Could he have saved them if he'd arrived earlier? He studied demons, he didn't hunt them; he could exorcize weak demons from inanimate objects like buildings and artifacts, but he was ill prepared to battle demons who had a plan.

Skye frowned, her brows knit with worry, her cop eyes sharp and focused in the dark. "It was a joke, Anthony. What's going on?"

"You'll think I'm being foolish."

"Never." She sat up next to him, her bare thigh pressing against his shorts.

He touched her again, needing to ground himself. Despite being together a short time her love gave him great strength. He soaked in her presence and said, "I want to go to the house again."

They both knew he meant the empty lot on the cliffs where once a house had been, before it burned and tumbled into the pits of Hell, just three days after the slaughter at the mission. Skye thought he was obsessed with the ruins, but he still went out there several times a week. He'd tried every trick in the book to figure out what bothered him about the place, other than the fact that both he and Skye almost died that fiery night on the cliffs in November. He'd even performed an exorcism a couple of weeks ago and felt absolutely ridiculous, because of course there was nothing there to be possessed. He'd tested for sulphur, for blood, for anything that would signal to the demonologist that an evil spirit was in the soil itself. All negative.

"First thing in the morning," Skye said, putting a hand on his arm. "You haven't been sleeping well for weeks, you're exhausted. Between rebuilding the mission and sitting with Rafe at the hospital, you haven't had time to yourself."

"Or for you." He kissed her. She was his lifeline in these troubled times. She had faith in him, and even when he did things she didn't understand, she stood by him. "I love you."

She smiled and put her hand on the back of his neck. "Lie down," she whispered and kissed him lightly. "I know how to get rid of that headache."

He took her hand into his and kissed it. "I want to go to the house now."

She silently stared at him, trying to hide her concern, but he saw the worry in her green eyes, in the way she tried to shield them when he frowned.

She relented. "All right, we'll go."

"I can do it alone."

"No."

"Skye—"

"You're not going alone. If something is going on, I need to be there."

"It may not be a crime in your jurisdiction, Sheriff."

He tried to keep his voice light, but the seriousness of the matter overshadowed his attempt.

"You're not going alone," she repeated. "We're in this together."

As they dressed, Skye asked, "Why tonight?"

"I heard something."

"The ruins are miles away."

He didn't respond. "The earth shook. It woke me."

She cocked her head. "Earthquakes are common in California."

"I told you you'd think I was foolish."

She crossed the room and grabbed his shoulders. "And I said I'll never think you're foolish." She was angry with him. "I don't understand everything you do; I don't have your faith or your experience. But I love *you,* and I have faith in *you.* That's all I need. If you heard something, if you felt something, then we'll go to the ruins and make sure no one is messing around. I don't want that—that *thing* back in my town."

He touched her face. *"Mia amore."*

"Let's do this fast so I can bring you back to bed." She smiled and nipped his ear playfully.

He returned her kiss, but when she turned to check her gun and holster it, his smile disappeared. He'd like nothing more than to make love to Skye and fall back to sleep until dawn, but he wasn't wrong about the ruins. There would be no more rest tonight.

FOUR

Fiona's temper flared as Raphael Cooper—who shouldn't even be here, let alone awake!—repelled her energy right back at her.

She diverted the cosmic electricity into the ground, making the earth shiver. The trapped demons growled as they began to take form. She had to complete the ritual before they regained their strength.

She'd wanted Cooper dead from the beginning because he represented the only true threat to her plans. However, others in her coven believed he'd gleaned important information from the priests at the mission—knowledge that would be valuable to them in their quest. In addition, Cooper was of St. Michael's Order and therefore knew many of their secrets. That had been the turning point for Fiona. She wanted to crush the Order for what they'd done to her and her ancestors. So she agreed to allow him to live on the condition that he was kept under the coven's control in order to extract what he'd learned.

But they hadn't pulled out a fraction of the information in his head, and now—somehow—he'd awakened from the coma they'd put him in.

"You have no idea what you are doing, you fool!" she screamed at Cooper. Lily broke through the circle, causing a psychic fissure. The trapped demons growled, sensing the deterioration of the invisible chains that kept them imprisoned. Fiona couldn't send any of her coven after Lily without further weakening the traps and risking their lives. She used all her power to fortify the double circle that kept the demons under her control. Over the increasing rumble above and below the earth, Serena began the final spell from the *Conoscenza* that would bind the Seven to the *arca*.

But it was too late. The *arca* was running away.

"Sancte Michaël Archangele, defende nos in prælio et colluctatione," Cooper began.

"Stop him!" Fiona realized he was attempting to send the Seven back through the gateway! It would not work. He spoke in Latin, an exorcism rite, but there were no demonic possessions here. Not yet. And the *arca* was getting away.

The rage she felt was immeasurable. For decades, she'd sought the *Conoscenza*. She'd believed in it when others—some who perceived they were wiser and more powerful than she—insisted it had been destroyed. She'd proven them wrong! She'd embarrassed St. Michael's Order because they'd emphatically stated that the book had been destroyed. Now, Fiona commanded respect from covens across the world. And this *man*, this *diolain*, was not only jeopardizing decades of *her* work, but centuries of preparation by her ancestors.

She raised her hand. "In the name of Belial, I command thee to thy knees!"

The layers between Hell and earth were thin here, and the simple demand shook the ground. Cooper paused, pain crossing his gaunt face, before he continued his verbal assault.

She turned to Garrett. "Take him down."

Garrett rushed the intruder, but Cooper held out his hand and spoke in a language even more ancient than Latin. Garrett bounced off an invisible shield and dropped to the ground.

"Fiona," Serena exclaimed, eyes wide, "that's the language of the *Conoscenza*!"

Fiona couldn't think now of how Cooper knew the book, as the demons roared from their traps, shaking the foundation of her control. They could not be contained in the bowls forever, and with Cooper trying to reverse the ritual, she was losing them.

He continued to speak in the most ancient of languages and Serena murmured spells to counter him.

"Turn the bowls," Fiona commanded her coven. "Release the Seven."

Her followers stared at her, surprised. They were *not* allowed to question her.

"Do it! Or my wrath will be greater than any demon on earth! Turn the bowls and protect yourselves!"

The women turned the bowls that contained the demons and, while chanting protective spells, stepped into the inner circle. The demons roared, now free from the chains of Hell. They swirled within the trap, frenzied by their freedom. If the *arca* were here, the ritual would be near complete. The next step was for the *arca* to draw them inside herself.

If not for Raphael Cooper! He had sent her off, and now the demons had nowhere to go. Nowhere but freedom to roam the earth.

"You are to blame!" she pointed her finger at him. "You take responsibility for the deaths and souls the Seven will claim!"

She turned her face to the heavens and chanted, "Belial, Hecate, Sammael, and all the named and nameless fallen ones, I command thee to shield thy servants, protect the sanctified, and mark the one who thwarted my will!"

The demons broke through their traps, swirling within the double circle, faster and faster, a tornado of smoke and fire, as the Seven lost their growing physical forms and melded within each other, in and out, gaining strength and speed and volume as they rose like a column and surrounded the coven.

Cooper was brought to his knees by a screeching tumult of such intensity that it vibrated within the circle. All dropped to the ground, unable to stand, holding their ears. The candles were snuffed out all at once, and blackness fell. It was chaos as the light vanished—no moon, no stars, no flame. The gut-wrenching sound of demonic screams filled the void.

With an invisible explosion, the Seven burst through the double circle, up and out, into the world.

"Get him," Fiona told Garrett as she rose from the ground. "Now I will learn his secrets." She would take deep pleasure in torturing Raphael Cooper. He would tell all he knew before she was through. He would renounce all he believed in and swear allegiance to Fiona!

She would make Cooper suffer. Suffer for as long as it took her to hunt down each and every one of the Seven, even to the ends of the earth. He would pay dearly for his interference.

"He's gone," Garrett said.

"He's not gone. Serena! Light!" Cooper could not have fled so quickly.

Serena fumbled in the dark and came up with a flashlight. She cast its beam around the circle.

The coven members were rising from the ground, the stench of fear rising from their skin. Pitiful.

Cooper was nowhere to be seen.

"How did he breach the circle?" Fiona demanded.

"How did he know the language?" Serena countered.

"Garrett, you and Ian stay and destroy the circle and bring the vessel." She waved irritably toward Abby's dead body. "Then find him. I want Raphael Cooper in front of me before sunrise."

She looked at the others. "Disperse! Quickly! Speak to no one of this. Punishments you could never even imagine await anyone who betrays me."

"Dammit!"

Moira slammed her fist on Jared's dashboard as he stopped his pickup truck at the end of the short road that led to ruins along the cliffs.

"They're gone," she lamented. And for a split second, she was relieved. She wasn't ready for this confrontation; she wasn't ready to die. Guilt washed over her— she needed to prepare herself for the inevitable. She'd been trained for this moment, and now she wanted to run? She could never live with herself if she did.

"Maybe you're wrong," Jared said. "Maybe this isn't what you thought."

For a split second Moira hoped she *had* been wrong. It had been a mistake to come here, and she'd misread the vision. The feeling she had ten days ago when she walked across the scarred foundation and saw a burning river of tortured souls beneath the earth's surface. No, she knew she was right about Santa Louisa, but that didn't mean she knew what she was doing. What made her think she could beat her mother at her own evil game?

Fiona had a lifetime of experience and a passionate—
obsessive—desire to control the underworld. The power
of Hell was on her side. Moira had fear, revenge, and a
couple of years' training with the top demon hunter in
the world. That made her little better than a novice. An
amateur. And amateurs died while masters prospered.
Fiona, most certainly, was a master.

But if she didn't do *something* to stop Fiona, Peter's
death wouldn't be avenged. If she didn't stand against
evil, she stood for it. If she didn't die fighting evil, she allowed it to flourish.

Rico always quoted some guy who'd said *all that is
necessary for the triumph of evil is that good* men *do
nothing*. Being cocky, and scared, finally Moira had
countered with, "You're a man, I'm a woman. So you
do it." Rico just stared. He had *no* sense of humor. And
when you faced life and death on a regular basis, Moira
didn't understand how anyone survived without enjoying a little humor in life.

She took a flashlight from her pocket and opened the
passenger door. "I'm checking it out." The interior light
came on, and she quickly reached up and flicked it off.

Jared became incensed. "We have to find Lily! She's
not here, no one's here! Where's her car?"

She understood the kid's frustration. What if . . . She
shot a glance at Jared. Her instincts told her he wasn't
possessed or under a spell, and both Father Philip and
Rico told her to trust her instincts, but she still doubted
herself. With minimal movement, she reached into a
hidden pocket and pulled out a small bottle that looked
like Visine. She squirted it toward Jared and the holy
water hit him on the cheek.

"Hey!" He wiped his face, scowling. No mark, no

steam, no rage, no rolling eyes. Even the strongest of demons couldn't hide their first pained reaction after being hit with holy water, even if it was no more annoying than a bee sting.

"Sorry." She pretended to put a drop in her eyes and pocketed her emergency "test" kit. She didn't know why she had it. When she'd faced someone possessed, she *knew* it as certainly as she knew her name. But Rico insisted, and she was good at following orders. Most of the time. Sort of.

"I should have gone to Abby's house first," Jared mumbled. "Lily is probably there."

"You did the right thing."

"I've called her cell phone ten times . . . maybe she's mad at me."

"Stop second-guessing yourself." Moira should have sat on the girl, or pushed her harder. Lily had seemed too fragile to handle all the information about the dangerous game Abby was playing with magic, and Moira had avoided the harder truths. Some people weren't ready for *any* truth, let alone the tough facts. Friends who played with the dark arts were already too far gone, but Lily wouldn't have been able to accept that truth about her cousin and confidante, Abby Weatherby. Once committed, there was no turning back. Once a person tasted dark power, giving it up was impossible.

So Moira had told Lily to stay away from her cousin, to let Moira know if there was anything strange going on, if Abby confided in her. She'd damn well learned her lesson—rely on no one else—and she prayed Lily was alive.

"We'll just look around the ruins for ten minutes," she said. "I'll know if the coven was here. Maybe we're not too late." She said it to give Jared hope; she didn't believe it.

A reluctant Jared followed her into the night. Almost as soon as she'd stepped from the truck, Moira smelled evil. A subtle aroma on the edge of the ruins, growing with each step she took. Incense. Poisoned incense. Strong herbs and odors to control spirits. But it was the sulphuric stench of Hell itself that raised the hair on her arms and made the scar on her neck burn. As Moira neared the midpoint of the spirit trap, she slowed her pace, her feet heavy as lead. Slower. Slower. She wanted to run back to the small, safe island off Sicily and lock herself inside St. Michael's fortress. She didn't need this, didn't want it, but she could not shirk her responsibility.

All that is necessary for evil to triumph is for good men—and women—to do nothing.

As Moira approached the wide circle painted in white on the ground, it became clear that the ritual had been interrupted. There were signs of violence—overturned candles, disturbed earth, a feeling of unrest, of commotion. While no candles burned, the scent of extinguished flames hung in the low-lying fog.

There, in the middle of the circle, was a dead body.

Jared saw it right after she did.

"Lily!" he cried.

"Don't—" Moira tried to stop him, but he pushed her aside and ran into the center of the ruins.

Moira hated being this exposed. There was nowhere to hide, but at least she'd be able to see anyone approach as easily as that person could see her. A small consolation.

Jared knelt next to the body. When Moira looked over

his shoulder, she saw it was not Lily, but her cousin Abby.

She lay naked and dead on a red silk sheet. Her eyes were open, her mouth gaping, but there were no wounds on her body. No knife marks, no claw marks, no burns or any external sign of how she died.

Could she have been poisoned? There were impressions in the sheet and ground where bowls of incense had burned, and in the daylight Moira could probably identify what herbs and resins had been used, by scouring the ground for spillage and faint smells. But Fiona and her coven were smarter than that; they wanted to intoxicate their victims, not poison them. They didn't make those kinds of mistakes.

If Abby Weatherby was dead, they wanted her to be dead.

Jared put his fingers to Abby's neck, presumably to check for a pulse, but Moira snapped, "Don't touch her!"

"We have to get her to a hospital," he said.

"She's dead."

"How do you know? You don't know that. She could be—"

Moira said, "Look at her eyes, Jared. Open, glassy, and her mouth—dammit, she's dead and you must not touch her."

She didn't know why that was important, or even if it was. Maybe it was more important for the cops, none of whom would believe that something supernatural had killed the teenager. Without a doubt this was Fiona's handiwork. The drama, the location, the oversized circle, the elaborate symbols.

Moira cast her light around the site. She hated being inside this spirit trap, even though it had been violently broken. A pile of incense was scattered across the linen. Dried candle wax mixed with dirt and rocks. Any vegetation or plants, here at the lot where the house had burned, were all dead. Nothing living could survive above a gateway to Hell.

What had happened? The ritual circle was a mess. It was a big no-no in the occult world to leave behind signs of any rituals. Witches were hunted as fiercely as they themselves hunted. If demon hunters—like her, Moira acknowledged—could trace a coven's symbols, they could better track and stop them.

Leaving *anything* here, at the ruins on the cliffs, told her that Fiona and her minions had been stopped.

Before or after they summoned the demons? Moira didn't know for certain. But based on the earlier lightning and darkness flying over them, Moira suspected there was at least one more demon on earth tonight.

Jared paced. "Where's Lily? What happened to Abby? Why is she naked? What's going on, Moira? You didn't tell me anyone was going to die!"

Moira countered his hysteria with a calm voice. "I don't know where Lily is. She and Abby were playing with dangerous things. Where there's danger, there can damn well be death."

Moira turned away from the dead teenager, deeply sad and angry at the loss of life. She said, "I don't know what happened here, but there was a fight—and they left fast. Picked up most of their supplies, but there are two candles over there." She gestured toward two black pillars on the edge of the circle. "And they didn't completely eradicate the symbols. Very sloppy, and Fiona is not sloppy."

Leaving Abby here . . . that was plain stupid. They always disposed of their victims. They had to, or news of the crime would get out to the public and they would have to be even more cautious. Murder was a crime; occult worship was not.

Ignoring her own advice to Jared, Moira squatted next to Abby and touched her body with two fingers. Her skin was cool and slick with moisture from the ocean fog. Moira was no cop, but she didn't think the girl had been dead long. And the recent dead were ripe for the picking of demons. If Fiona had brought forth something, it would be around. Or coming back. Demons always returned to their origins—one of many truths Rico had pounded into Moira's head during their lessons.

She pulled out a container of salt from her pack and poured it in a circle around Abby's body. She didn't know whether it would do any good—if the demon was powerful enough, it could just lift her body out of the circle. But it would slow him enough to buy her time. Salt was a purifier and a preservative, a mineral that naturally repelled demons. But like virulent bacteria, the strongest demons built up resistance to any defenses, including ancient defenses like salt.

"What are you *doing*?" Jared asked her, looking at Moira as if she were a nut job. She was used to it. She'd never been normal, and it seemed that now, at the ripe age of twenty-nine, normal wasn't in her future, either.

"The salt will stop a demon from snatching Abby's body. She hasn't been dead for long. After an hour or two"—Moira honestly didn't know how long, Rico had only told her to guard the recent dead because they could be summoned—"it won't matter, because the demons won't be able to inhabit her. Sort of like animals who only eat fresh kills." She guessed.

Jared shivered.

"What about Lily? Where is she?"

Moira looked around the area. The ocean waves, less than a hundred yards west and a hundred yards down, crashed unseen against the rocks. In different circumstances they would have soothed her, reminded her of the west coast of Ireland, the only place she'd had peace.

"I'm going to call someone to pick up Abby's body," she said. Damn, she dreaded making this call. The minute Father Philip had told her Anthony was in Santa Louisa, she knew she'd have to make contact eventually. She'd be lucky if he didn't kill her. If he weren't such a damn high-and-mighty ethical demonologist, he wouldn't hesitate to slit her throat and blame it on her demonic soul.

"My dad will have to come out," Jared said, staring at Abby's body. "I can't believe she's dead."

"Your dad doesn't understand what's happened here."

"What does he need to understand? We found Abby dead! He's a cop. He'll call the crime scene people, find out who did this. Find Lily."

"*Who* did *what*? Come on, Jared! I told you how these people operate."

He was torn, Moira saw the conflict and confusion in his pained expression, but she wasn't about to sugarcoat the truth.

"Yes, we need to find Lily," she said. "I don't know if they have her, but if they do we have to try and save her. If they don't, we have to find and protect her. I'm with you on that, Jared. But this"—she gestured toward the partially obliterated occult symbols—"needs someone who specializes in . . . this," she ended lamely.

Moira no longer wanted Jared here because she feared Fiona's minions *would* return. He could hardly be expected to defend himself against magic he didn't understand, and she couldn't protect both him and herself. Not against Fiona's coven. If there was more than one magician, Moira would have her own battle to wage. And she could *not* let them take possession of Abby's body. The girl deserved a proper burial—*after* she was cremated into three pounds of ash.

But Moira also couldn't let Jared search for Lily on his own . . . what if Fiona's coven was watching? They didn't have to be too close, there were other ways . . . She shivered. "Trust me."

Jared scowled. Trust her. *Right.* She barely knew him. He'd frequented an online message board about supernatural phenomena, but he was in no way prepared for this.

Jared bent down and picked up two articles of female clothing. Jeans and a pale pink sweater. He looked ill. "Lily was wearing this sweater today."

A distant scream pierced the night. Moira jumped. It came from the woods, far on the other side of the road. Then there was silence, which sounded even worse.

"Lily!" Jared exclaimed. "I have to find her. I'm sorry, Moira, I—she must be terrified." He ran to his truck, ignoring her protests that he shouldn't go off alone.

His truck was driving away when she whispered, "Don't leave me."

The wind whipped up from the ocean, salt air stinging her cheeks. She felt as though she was being watched, but there was no place nearby to hide . . . No one was watching, no one was here. But telling herself that did little to alleviate her rising panic.

She shook her head, thinking herself foolish, and looked again at poor Abby. She wished she had Rico or Father Philip here to tell her what to do.

Anthony. She had to bring him in. She pulled out her cell phone and dialed Father Philip.

She was surprised when he answered the phone himself after the first ring.

"Father, it's Moira."

"Are you all right?"

"Yes. But it's bad, Father. I think—I don't know what to think. Something happened at the cliffs. There are signs of violence, a spirit trap, obscure symbols I've never seen before. And no one is here, except"—she glanced at Abby's naked corpse—"a dead teenager."

"Holy Mother of God."

She smiled; otherwise she would cry at Father's version of cussing.

"I'm worried about Anthony," Father continued. "He's not answering his phone."

Bright lights shot out at her from the road and approached quickly. As soon as the spotlight hit her body, the red and blue rotating spheres clicked on.

Fuck.

"Father, I need to go."

"Moira, wait—what's wrong?"

"Keep trying Anthony, and hope that he has a get-out-of-jail-free card in his pocket. I think I'm going to need it."

She hung up and pocketed her cell phone.

A voice said over a speaker: "This is the Santa Louisa County Sheriff's Department. Stay where you are with your hands visible."

Moira kept her hands in front of her, plainly in sight, and fought the urge to bolt.

FIVE

Moira had to come up with a plausible story as to why she was here in the middle of the night with a dead girl. Maybe . . . she'd been walking in the area and . . . *right*. Like anyone would believe she'd *walked* the ten miles from her motel to the cliffs. At two in the *morning*. And she was in the middle of friggin' *nowhere* with three abandoned, boarded-up houses on an unpaved road next to a cursed lot. She got lost? *Sure*. She'd wandered aimlessly near the edge of dangerous cliffs in the fog, just happening to stumble across a corpse.

But she certainly couldn't say anything about what had happened—what she *thought* had happened. Moira had to carefully maneuver a tightrope. She wasn't an American citizen. She could be deported, her student visa revoked. Father Philip had arranged with Rico to "enroll" her in Olivet, and no one in the States had yet questioned that Olivet was an all-male theology seminary. *Yet*. And she didn't want to shine a light on them, because they weren't *really* a seminary. Olivet was the western hemisphere university for demon hunters and not officially recognized by the Vatican or any quasi-legitimate authority, as opposed to St. Michael's, which had some protection from the powers that be. If people sniffed around, they might discover that no priests actually graduated from Olivet.

Fortunately, she'd wisely left her gun back at the motel, but the dagger wouldn't go over too well with the sheriff. And who would believe her that there had been an occult ritual here? *Exactly*—no one.

An officer shined a light in her face. Moira couldn't see beyond the brightness, could barely make out the two shadowy figures when she squinted. Suddenly the idea that Fiona's coven was bigger than her mother traditionally maintained—Fiona plus twelve in the inner court, and a few strays used for muscle and eyes and grunt work—terrified her. What if someone in the police department was part of it? What if Fiona controlled the town? This had happened before in small towns, and Santa Louisa had only thirty thousand residents. Moira should have put her own pride aside and contacted Anthony when she'd first discovered he was in town. At least she'd then have someone on her side who understood what they were up against, and maybe he'd know whom to trust.

"*Always have backup,*" Rico had said during their training. "*Never go blind into a situation, even if you think there's nothing going on.*"

"*I don't have a partner,*" she'd said. "*And I don't want one.*"

"What are you doing out here?" a female voice asked, jolting Moira from her memory.

"Are you the sheriff?"

"Sheriff Skye McPherson. And you are?"

"Moira O'Donnell. I was with Jared Santos, but he ran off after—"

A man in plainclothes stepped forward from behind the sheriff. Moira shielded her eyes from the light and squinted. She could see no details, but the way he moved was familiar, like a big, caged cat.

The sheriff reached out to grab him. "Wait, Anthony—"

Anthony brushed off her hand and quickly approached Moira, stopping only a foot from her. Disbelief and anger rolled off him in palpable waves.

Anthony Zaccardi. Though she knew he was in town, she was still stunned to see him again after all this time. The towering demonologist's middle name could have been *Intimidation*.

"Moira O'Donnell." He spoke the name as if it were a curse. "I should have known where there is trouble from the underworld, you would be nearby, *puttana*."

"Prick."

She held her ground, though Anthony's hostility put her on edge. He hadn't liked her even before she'd killed Peter. If Father Philip hadn't been there, Moira was absolutely certain Anthony would have killed her that same night.

"What did you do?" Anthony glanced briefly at Abby's body, then his gaze focused on her.

Sheriff McPherson walked over to the body and, careful not to disturb anything or turn her back to Moira, bent down to feel for a pulse. "Shit," she mumbled. "You said you were here with Jared Santos? Where is he? I want the God's honest truth. What happened here? Were you drinking? Getting high?"

"Summoning demons?" Anthony whispered.

Moira said, "We thought Jared's girlfriend, Lily Ellis, was coming here. We found Abby instead of Lily."

"You know Abby Weatherby?" Skye asked as she approached, standing beside Anthony.

"Not personally."

"Anthony?" Skye asked. "Do you know this woman? Can you vouch for her?"

"Vouch? I can vouch that she's a killer."

"Fuck off," Moira snapped. "Look around, Zaccardi. I didn't do this, and you damn well know it. And Sheriff, this has nothing to do with kids getting high or drunk; Abby died because she was *sacrificed*. Lily Ellis is missing. We think she came here to try and talk Abby out of the coven, but—"

"Coven?" Anthony shook his head. "That sounds familiar—something you know really well. What was your part in it? Or are you going to pretend you were possessed again?"

"*Pretend*? You bastard!" She swung her arm out to slap him. He grabbed her wrist and squeezed so tightly she thought her bone would snap. She kicked him in the shin and he let go, wincing. She turned and walked several feet away. She had to control her temper around Anthony. It would get her in trouble.

"That's enough!" Skye said. "Anthony, let me ask the questions, okay?"

Anthony backed off.

Skye radioed for the coroner, crime scene unit, and backup. She glanced at Moira, then added into her mic, "Call Deputy Santos. He's off-duty. Patch him through to me when you reach him. Over."

Skye shot Anthony a glare, then asked Moira, "Do you have some identification?"

Moira pulled out her wallet from the inside pocket of her leather jacket and held it out. Skye retrieved it, opened the flap, and saw her passport. "You're from Ireland."

"Yes."

"You've traveled a lot."

She shrugged.

"Student visa. Olivet in Pinesdale? Where's that?"

"Montana," Moira said.

Anthony grabbed the passport and took a close look at her entry date. "You've been here for six months!"

"I've been in Santa Louisa for a week, but yeah, in America for six months." *This time.*

Skye retrieved the passport from Anthony. There was an ease and familiarity between the two. Why was he with Skye in the middle of the night? Interesting.

She raised an eyebrow and gave Anthony a cocky half-smile. "So Santa Louisa has a demonologist on the payroll?"

"No one has to answer to you," Anthony snapped.

"Excuse me." Skye motioned for Anthony to follow her. Moira couldn't help but grin. She had to like anyone who stood up to the arrogant demonologist. Peter had done it, often. Her smile faltered. Maybe if Peter had listened to Anthony's warnings, he'd still be alive.

A car pulled onto the road and they all turned to look at it. It wasn't Jared's truck, it was another cop.

As Skye walked over to the new arrival, Anthony approached Moira. "Don't even think of running. I will hunt you down like a dog."

"I'd like to see you try."

She glared at him and he turned away, flashlight in hand, and began to walk the perimeter. She took an uneasy breath. If she gave any hint of how much he was upsetting her, he'd continue poking with a sharp stick until she was a basket case.

The fog was thin and low, obscuring the symbols and

signs on the ground, but Moira recognized the remnants of witchcraft. Black candles, the foul stench of herbs used for protection and control and warding off evil spirits. Moira could laugh at the thought—they were summoning demons, but used herbs and spells to keep themselves from being possessed.

If they only knew . . .

Of course, Fiona *did* know. Her mother knew exactly what she was doing, and she didn't need the candles or herbs or red silk sheets laid on a makeshift altar. All she needed were the right incantations, the proper demon trap, the *will* to call forth evil, and the strength to control it. When you were a magician for as long as Fiona had been, when you trained and practiced day in and day out and didn't care who you hurt or what you did, power became both addictive and easy.

For years, Moira had studied witchcraft with no idea why, other than to please her mother. From the beginning, it terrified her, but she did it because she knew no other way to gain Fiona's favor. She'd continued until she was sixteen and unwittingly participated in a human sacrifice—a sacrifice that dedicated *her* to the underworld, as the "Mediator." It was during that ceremony that she was branded, the scar still on her neck. It was then that she learned Fiona's plans not only for youth and beauty and finding the Book of Knowledge, but for Moira's future.

To be sacrificed on her twenty-first birthday to serve as Mediator between Hell and the Magicians.

It was the highest honor, Fiona had told her. "You have no idea what goes into creating a Mediator, to properly conceive, train, and place one. We haven't had a good Mediator in generations; they've all managed to self-destruct or be killed by an order." An "order," in Fiona-speak, was a group of people, generally worshipping God and affiliated with a church, fanatics who were devoted to the repression of the transformative knowledge and cathartic oneness gained from magic and working with the underworld.

"We are *the trees of knowledge*," Fiona often said. "The reason God forbade His people from practicing sorcery is because He wanted to deny us. He wanted to keep us from knowing the truth, the true power, of the universe. But with magic, we gain. We become more powerful, more beautiful, live longer, gain wisdom that was wrongfully reserved only for the angels above and below."

And Moira was a believer for years. She had done everything Fiona wanted. Learned everything she taught, and more. Moira desperately wanted to please her.

Then, on her sixteenth birthday, she went to her dedication ritual. They'd traveled for two days, but Moira wasn't sure where they were—someplace in Europe. It marked the beginning of the five-year journey where she would learn spells and protections that few witches knew. At first she was as excited as she was nervous.

The excitement quickly ended.

"Today, you begin your final journey here on earth," Fiona said, beaming at Moira, proud of her. But Moira didn't like what her mother was saying.

"I don't understand."

"You will be able to walk between the worlds at will. You will be able to control spirits with a command, initiate requests from every coven on earth."

"I still—"

"You will understand!" Fiona was losing her temper and Moira shut up. She couldn't face Fiona's wrath, not on this day.

She was treated like a princess, and even Serena, her eleven-year-old half-sister, was excited for her. "You're going to be a goddess. Forever."

But Moira was skeptical. Mediator? Goddess? Walking between the worlds? It sounded like she was to be a spirit herself, a ghost, trapped into slavery, doing the bidding of whatever witch summoned her . . .

Then that night . . .

Moira would never forget the screams of the two men who were stabbed in the chest with a glowing dagger.

Her mother's fury when she didn't drink their blood.

The chaos when her refusal caused the demons they'd trapped to break their restraints and torture those whose protective shields were weak. Fiona had then used all her power to send them back to Hell. Moira helped out of fear more than rage.

"You will comply!" Fiona said, coming at her with a dagger dripping with human blood. "You are here because I made you. You will serve me or you will burn!"

Moira ran, tossing spells out almost without thought, stopping those who tried to capture her . . . she didn't even know where she was until she ran out, saw signs in French, and wondered how she'd been ignorant for so long. She hadn't even remembered the journey! Had she been drugged? Under a spell?

She ran, hid, ran again, covered herself with protective spells and shields and anything she could think of. Anything and everything except calling forth a demon to do her bidding.

This was so wrong, people dying—how could Fiona have killed those men? For her? *So she could be a* slave?

That was the first night she'd ever been alone. But Fiona soon found and punished her. Afterward, Moira played the good daughter as long as she could. She learned as much as she could to fight her mother, to stop her, studying Fiona's enemies, particularly St. Michael's Order, a much hated group.

And then at last, she escaped. And this time, she knew enough to keep her whereabouts hidden from her mother.

She had heard about Father Philip of St. Michael's, and that he might be able to help her, but had no information about where he lived or what he could do for her. She tried to find him by leaving coded messages at every Catholic church she entered, not knowing whom to trust. After more than a year, she started finding messages from Father Philip when she went to the churches, in the middle of the night, to steal holy water. Slowly, he told her of many atrocities her mother had committed over the years, awful things in which Moira had unknowingly participated. Horrified, she worked to undo the damage they'd caused, righting wrongs, hiding from Fiona while seeking more information from the elusive Father Philip.

She didn't realize until later that St. Michael's Order had been trying to find her. Or that until she escaped her mother, they would have killed her to stop Fiona. To stop her from becoming the Mediator. And she still didn't fully understand what being the Mediator meant!

After two years of running and despair, the holy man arranged to meet her at dawn, in a small church in rural Italy.

She knew him the moment she laid eyes on him.

"Father Philip?"

He nodded, then crossed the stone floor, the rising sun streaming through ancient stained-glass windows. Father Philip was older than she'd thought, with trimmed silver hair and wire-rimmed glasses, but he was spry, stood straight, but was still several inches shorter than she. "Child, at last. We've been looking for you."

She frowned. The notes they'd left for her over the years had been pretty clear: they did not want to have anything to do with her personally, but they would feed her information.

"But the messages you left for me—"

"That was Pietro. You will meet him. He insisted that we test you, to make sure you weren't setting a trap. This is the first time I've stepped outside our sanctuary in many years. There are some who—" He stopped, put his hands on her shoulders. "Some people who want to hurt me. Like your mother."

She became suddenly scared and confused, and started trembling, sitting down heavily.

"Moira, what is it?"

What if this was a trap . . . for her?

When she didn't answer, he said, "I will show you something that may give you a modicum of peace."

He removed his clerical collar, then pulled back the neck of his shirt far enough to show her his upper right breast.

On his tan skin was the tattooed symbol of St. Michael's Order that she'd seen in one of the ancient books she'd found during her search. The sword of St. Michael the Archangel slaying the serpent, an elaborate triangle behind it to represent the Holy Trinity.

"You are strong, child," Father Philip told her, replacing his collar, "with a well-formed conscience. Your heart is pure; your quest has come with a price and a reward."

"I don't understand—"

"Join us. Let me teach you the ways of St. Michael's. The decision is yours." He sat on the pew. "Or continue running from Fiona."

She shook her head. "I—I'm so lost. I didn't know what she was doing."

"The road you have chosen is not easy. But it is your path. I can't walk it for you. Believe me when I tell you that every man at St. Michael's would walk in your shoes if they could. But you are unique, Moira. And in time, you will understand that. Until then, I'm here to help you. I can teach you to avoid or confront obstacles on your path. I can give you the tools to survive. Though in the end, I cannot take your place." He gently touched her face, his eyes watering. "I would if I could, my dear."

Her lip quivered. "I'm so tired."

"You are not alone, Moira."

"She has to be stopped, but I am so scared."

"God tells us, 'Do not be afraid.' But there are many things that are fearsome. There are good reasons to be afraid, and while we can be confident in our eternal life, we may be terrified on earth. We have a sacred duty to save as many souls as we can. Fiona and her kind have turned so many souls black. Hardened their hearts, devoted them to serving her and covens like hers, seeking answers where there are only dark lies. Come with me, and we can help."

"I'm cursed." She pulled down her turtleneck, reveal-

ing the mark of the demon on the side of her neck. "I'm
theirs." *Her voice choked.*

"No, you are not."

"You can help me?"

"I will help you, and you will stop her. You are
stronger than you know. But first, from this moment
forward, you must promise me no more magic. It's your
magic that is leaving a trail for Fiona to follow. It's why
she's close."

"But it'll leave me unprotected! I can't, it's—"

"Even magic used for good leads to evil. Never forget
that."

She'd tried to live according to Father Philip's rules.
He taught her everything about St. Michael's Order.
And her knowledge of Fiona and covens would help
them stop the evildoers. Father Philip and his order had
been floundering ever since Fiona began to unite the in-
dependent covens. Moira's unique position gave them
intelligence they'd never had before.

She wanted to help, and did. But it felt . . . passive. It
became increasingly difficult to follow Father Philip's
rules. She wanted to be out of the walls of St. Michael's,
out tracking Fiona herself! But Father said she was un-
safe outside the monastery's walls. She'd traded fear and
hunger for security in a beautiful sanctuary that too
often felt like prison. And then there was Peter . . .

Together, they'd begun to use magic to undo the
damage that Fiona had done. As a team, they were so
powerful, and they were doing good! They had great
successes, though even those they kept secret. Rico and
the others believed that it was their own handiwork,

while Peter and Moira were aiding them from afar. They were . . .

. . . *leading Fiona right to them*. It was the magic that revealed Moira's location, the magic that led Fiona to St. Michael's, and no amount of protection could shield Moira from her own arrogance.

Fiona found her, sent a demon to possess her, and with her own hands Moira had killed the one man she loved.

SIX

Oh mama, I'm in fear for my life from the long arm of the law
Lawman has put an end to my running
and I'm so far from my home.
—STYX, "Renegade"

Moira had to steer well clear of any self-pity, especially now when Anthony had the opportunity to chip away at her carefully constructed shields. Glancing over her shoulder, she saw Skye McPherson approaching Anthony, who was standing near the edge of the cliffs. Skye and Anthony talked, and Moira knew damn well what Anthony would say about her.

Moira turned on her flashlight and shined it on the ground, looking for more clues.

It was obvious—at least to her—that there had been a full, protective circle here. Anthony knew how to read the signs and symbols, how to trace their magical supplies. As a demonologist, he might even know which demons had been summoned. But most of the symbols were obscured. Some attempt had been made at collecting the supplies—she saw only two candles, yet the wax in the dirt indicated many more. Something violent had wreaked havoc here. Maybe she could piece it all together and somehow discover Fiona's weak spot.

If only it weren't just about her, Moira wouldn't hesitate to use magic to find and destroy her mother, even knowing that she herself would likely die and her soul would be lost. What did Moira have to live for but regret?

But she couldn't risk innocents. Lily, or Jared, or even that bastard Anthony Zaccardi. She'd told Father Philip she couldn't bring Anthony in because she didn't want to risk his life, and while on the surface it sounded altruistic, it was purely selfish. She didn't care if Anthony was dead or alive, as long as he was dead through natural means. Then his eternal fate was between him and the Big Guy. But witches? Possession? *Hell?* She couldn't suffer through that again.

You're pathetic. Get over it already.

Good going, Mo. Practice that tough love on yourself; maybe you'll believe it one of these days.

Moira walked along the perimeter of what had been the outer circle and suddenly spotted something. She stopped, squatted, and inspected the earth.

There had been a double circle, and the remnants of a hexagram. But this hexagram had crossed the inner circle and touched the outer circle. Generally, the hexagram was constrained by the inner circle. She hadn't seen one of these before, but she knew the triangles at the tips of the hexagram within the double circle were for specific, ancient rituals. They were not well known, not practiced by most covens because most covens were novices working basic spells that did nothing but add to the fissure between the underworld and humans.

For Moira's entire life, her mother had been obsessed with finding the *Conoscenza.* Everything that she and Peter had uncovered years ago told them that the *Conoscenza,* the Book of Knowledge, the key to finding the Tree of Life, was gone forever. What if they'd been wrong? What if Fiona had found it? How in the world had her mother even read and understood it? It wasn't written in a known language; it was so foreign, so old, that it was rumored to have first been written in the generation after the fall of man, by fallen angels and the humans they seduced into rebellion.

The two types of demons—fallen angels and lost souls—had one thing in common: they wanted out of Hell. Lost souls were dangerous, but they needed a body to possess. They were weaker than fallen angels, more susceptible to traditional exorcism rites, vulnerable to certain weapons such as iron.

Fallen angels, they were spirits. They were a whole other breed of demon—deadly, dangerous, and wholly evil. They didn't need a human host, though they could take one easily if they wanted. God put them in Hell for a reason, and dammit, they should stay in Hell!

The *Conoscenza* gave these dangerous incorporeal creatures an opportunity to escape. Humans, playing with matches and lighting the eternal fire. Manipulating demons with magic took extreme power and fine control, which few witches possessed. It would be far too easy for the demons to break free of restraint and gain the freedom they desperately wanted.

Fiona had been so certain the evil book still existed. She had lusted for it, obsessed over it.

If it existed, great, untold evils would be unleashed on unsuspecting humans. There would literally be Hell on earth until the End Times.

Heat rose from the ground, dark fog swirled around and around and Moira nearly screamed. But Skye and Anthony were still talking off to the side, and they didn't see anything, didn't feel the heat that saturated Moira. Sweat rolled down the back of her neck, her skin burned, and in the dark she saw the eye of evil itself, staring at her, marking her. Beneath her feet the river of fire returned, its flames reaching out for her. Her mouth opened in a silent scream . . .

. . . then it disappeared. She fell to her knees, caught her breath, and knew beyond a shadow of a doubt that she stood over Hell itself.

"Moira?"

She jumped up and whirled around, fists on the rise until she realized that it was McPherson, who had approached so quietly that Moira questioned her own instincts, her training, her will to live.

"Sorry." Skye assessed Moira and frowned. "Are you all right? Are you sick?"

She must look like crap for the sheriff to sound so concerned. "Fine." Her voice was rough. She cleared her throat. "I'm fine. So what are you doing now? Did you call Jared Santos, verify that everything I told you is the truth?"

Skye didn't answer her question directly. "The crime scene team is on its way; I need to ask you to leave. I shouldn't have let you stay here in the first place. I've just been used to letting Anthony help . . ." Her voice trailed off as she glanced over at Anthony, who was inspecting something on the ground.

"I understand," Moira said even though she didn't. Anthony aiding the police?

But Moira could learn nothing more here. She needed to make sure Lily was safe, find out if Jared had found her. She pulled out her cell phone and texted Jared:

When you find Lily take her to my motel room. Tell no one. Do not let her out of your sight. Call me!

She sent it, then deleted all her messages with three quick strokes, just in case the cop wanted to look.

Skye looked at her suspiciously. "You and Anthony have a history."

The cop's face was blank, but Moira could read her eyes. The sheriff believed everything Anthony told her, and she now had complete disdain for Moira. It angered and embarrassed her. She reacted with sarcasm.

"Yeah, we go *way* back," she replied, adding with a wink, "but he meant nothing to me."

Skye was not amused. For a moment, Moira saw a hint of jealousy, which the cop quickly covered up. Anthony and a cop. That was one for the record books.

"Tell me what happened. Start at the beginning. Why are you in Santa Louisa?"

"You wouldn't believe me if I told you."

"You might be surprised."

Anthony stood only feet away. He was listening, pretending to examine one of the symbols painted onto the ground. *Jerk*. He could have made this so much easier if he'd just vouched for her.

If Skye McPherson was involved with Anthony, she wasn't ignorant of what was *really* going on in, above, below, and through the world.

Moira couldn't exactly tell the complete truth. Anthony knew enough to be dangerous to her, but he didn't know everything. "I investigate supernatural phenomena. I believe that the fire here a couple of months ago opened a gateway from Hell. A back door of sorts. And a particularly dangerous coven has been preparing for tonight, sacrificing one of their own to bring forth something evil." She glanced at Abby's corpse.

Wow, four sentences and not a lie in them! She was good.

"What specifically were they trying to summon?"

"Demons, of course."

"When you say 'coven,' do you mean witches?"

She shrugged. "Or magicians. You say tomato, I say tomahto."

"Excuse me?"

"Witches and magicians are essentially the same thing, sort of like . . ." She thought about it. "All magicians are witches, but not all witches are magicians."

"Which means what exactly?"

Moira was getting irritated. She really didn't have time to educate the sheriff—why hadn't Anthony done it? "Whatever the hell you want it to mean."

"Don't screw with me, Ms. O'Donnell. I have one dead teenager, one missing teenager, and when I get back to the station I'll have the D.A., reporters, parents, and cops to answer to. I don't have time to play twenty questions."

"And I don't have *time* to explain the nuances of the black arts! Go ask your pet demonologist and leave me the hell alone!"

Moira knew she was overstepping, but she *really* hated being here. She was worried about Jared and Lily, not to mention that the ground she stood on was a portal to Hell.

Anthony stepped forward to defend Skye. "Watch yourself, Witch."

"Asshole."

"Enough!" Skye said. "Why would they *want* to bring up a demon?"

, At least she wasn't calling her crazy, Moira thought. That was a first. She noticed that Skye and Anthony exchanged significant glances.

Moira ignored Anthony and continued. "It's always about power and knowledge. This group is already potent. They've been summoning evil spirits for generations. The leader—"

"You know who did this?"

Moira bit her lower lip. "I suspect."

"Who?"

"You can't confront her. She'll have you running in circles until you drop dead."

Skye tilted her head. "Look, Ms. O'Donnell, I'm trying to understand your position, but don't play me for the fool. Abby Weatherby is dead. I need to talk to everyone who might be responsible. It's my job."

Moira said, "Abby was in the coven. You don't think they haven't protected themselves? I would have gotten the hell out of Dodge as soon as I smelled the sulphur if I hadn't found her body. They want this body; they aren't usually this messy."

"You lost me. What do you mean that they want her body? You mean to destroy evidence? To bury her, cover up the crime?"

Of course she thought like a cop. "There're two main reasons black-art covens don't leave bodies lying around. One is because of people like you. You see a dead person, you start investigating. So yeah—evidence, I guess you could call it. Which is why magicians are so good at . . . disappearing the dead. Really, do you think all the missing people in the world are still alive?"

The sheriff wanted to ask her more questions about it

but changed gears and said, "You said you know who's the leader of this coven."

"I haven't any proof."

Skye said, "But I can interview them. Ask questions."

"No."

"You're obstructing an investigation."

"I didn't see anything. I don't have firsthand knowledge of who was here. When I arrived, the only thing I saw was this body and the disturbance you saw on the ground."

"When did you arrive?"

"Maybe ten minutes after the ritual was over. We—Jared Santos and I—saw a—" How could she explain what she'd seen in the distance? And make it sound sane? "We were still a couple of miles away and there was a fluttering, like thousands of bats all rose into the air at once. But it wasn't bats. It was something dark and thick and alive, but nothing I've seen before."

That wasn't the entire truth. She'd seen it before. She'd dreamed it, had nightmares about the dark overtaking the light, throwing humanity into a self-made prison, where people maimed and tortured and raped and killed without thought or remorse, where magic was the norm and evil ruled. Where pleasure was pain and pain pleasure, where there was no justice, no light, no hope . . .

She said, "When we got here, there was chaos all around—see?" She gestured to the candles and the linen under Abby's body. "They didn't even gather up all their supplies. They didn't erase the circle. And there was sulphur in the air, incense and poison." Moira was unconsciously rubbing her scar. She stuffed her hands in her pockets.

"Are you saying Abby was poisoned?"

"No. Maybe. She *might* have been, but that's not how she died."

"How did she die?"

Moira took a deep breath and looked at Anthony. "Anthony knows."

Skye sounded irritated. "Can the *woo-woo*. Just tell me the truth or I'll arrest you."

Moira bristled. "Abby was a sacrifice, necessary to bring forth the demon."

"Not just one demon," Anthony interrupted.

Moira and Skye turned to him.

"How do you know?" Skye asked.

He said, "The symbols. There are seven."

"I only saw three," Moira said.

"They were deliberately obscured."

"Seven?" she asked, incredulous. "At one time?"

He addressed Moira with a subtle nod. "The ritual could easily have been Abby's cause of death."

"Anthony, please—" the sheriff said wearily.

"Skye," he said softly, and for the first time Moira saw a tenderness she'd never before seen in the demonologist. "We have an extremely serious situation here. The Seven may have been released."

Moira blanched. Anthony was about to confirm her greatest fear.

Anthony gestured with his flashlight to the triangles and symbols outside the circle. "I don't know how they did it, how they found the spell. The book was supposed to have been destroyed hundreds of years ago, but this is the same as I've seen in two different sets of ruins, one in Ireland that is five hundred years old, and one in Italy that is nearly a thousand years old. There were more at-

tempts, but we don't know where or when. Every one
has failed."

A chill ran down Moira's arms. "They probably failed
too," she said. "Look around, it's chaos."

"I don't know," Anthony said.

"The Seven?" Skye asked.

"The Seven Deadly Sins. If they've been freed, we have
a supernatural war on our hands. And we are not prepared."

It was the *Conoscenza*. Only the Book of Knowledge
had the proper spell to release the Seven Deadly Sins
from Hell. Fiona had found it.

Anthony stared at Moira. "Arrest her."

"What?" Moira and Skye said together.

"Moira O'Donnell is a witch. She has the power to do
this."

"Bullshit! You damn well know I had nothing to do
with any of this!"

"She's here illegally," he continued, facing Skye and
ignoring Moira. "Olivet is a reclusive, all-male theolog-
ical college similar to St. Michael's, where I'm from. She
couldn't have legitimately gotten a student visa. I sent a
friend of mine a message." He glanced at Moira, tri-
umphant, and Moira knew exactly what he was going to
say. "They've been expecting her for months. She never
showed."

Skye said, "That's an Immigration issue, Anthony. I
don't have grounds to arrest her unless she committed a
crime."

What Anthony said was true, she was supposed to return to Olivet after learning the deaths she'd investi-
gated in upstate New York three months ago weren't
related to supernatural forces. But both Father Philip

and Rico knew she was following her mother's trail. They kept her involvement under wraps for a whole host of reasons, not least among them was the division she'd caused among the Order after Peter's death.

But she wasn't going to prison over their secret. "Call Rico Cortese," she told Anthony. "If he didn't tell anyone about my trip to Santa Louisa, I'm sure he had good reason. Need to know and all that—oh, I get it, you're just pissed off that you weren't in the loop."

Anthony stepped forward and grabbed Moira's wrists before she'd seen him move. Okay, maybe it wasn't such a good idea to bait him. "Rico picked the wrong witch to train," he said under his breath, then added to Skye, "Left inside pocket. She has a knife."

Skye's face darkened. She reached where Anthony told her and extracted the knife. It was a dagger with a double-edged blade, in iron. The handle was gold, inlaid with the relics of saints. It had been Peter's. She always carried it with her. She had little else from Peter.

"Any other weapons?" the sheriff asked angrily.

"Nothing that can hurt a human being," Moria snapped. She glared at Anthony. He was trying to keep his face impassive, but he recognized the knife as well. The fury simmered inside him; she felt it rippling through his body. Moira almost didn't blame him. She was angry with herself, too.

But she had never hated him more than she did right now. She couldn't go to jail. If Fiona had failed, she'd try again. If she had Lily, she most certainly would restage the ritual as soon as physically possible—possibly as soon as tomorrow night. If she'd been successful, Moira had to undo the damage. How, she had no idea. But first, she needed to confirm exactly what happened here.

If the Seven Deadly Sins were on earth, she had to figure out how to send them back to Hell and stop Fiona.

Skye searched Moira and pulled out salt, several vials of holy water, and a long, thin iron chain.

"A garrote?" Skye asked.

"A devil's cuff."

"Excuse me?"

Anthony explained. "A means of restraining a possessed human. It prevents the demon from escaping, and makes it easier to interrogate the beast without harm to the human." He then added, "It doesn't always work."

Moira glared at him; Anthony stared her down. She bit back a sarcastic remark.

Skye looked torn. She asked Moira, "Why are you here?"

"I told you. I found the gateway and I had to stop her."

"Who?"

Moira squirmed.

Anthony answered for her. "Fiona O'Donnell. Her mother."

Two cars pulled up behind the sheriff's truck. "That's the crime scene team and coroner," Skye said. She pocketed Moira's passport. "I think it would be best if you came down to the station so we can talk, until I find Jared and Lily to corroborate your story."

For a brief moment, Moira considered magic. She could find Fiona and hurt Anthony. Her urge to cause him pain for everything he'd said tonight and in the past scared her so deeply that her skin crawled and she felt physically ill.

Magic was evil, even if her purposes were noble. That Anthony had been able to even get her to consider it, just for that moment, pained her. She was worse than a drunk, worse than a drug addict. Magic was the greatest power, the greatest high on earth, and resulted in the steepest fall.

Anthony saw her internal battle and smiled cruelly.

"I knew you'd never change. I warned Peter, but he trusted you. Now he's dead."

She decked him.

SEVEN

Fiona strode through the secluded mansion on the outskirts of Santa Louisa, her footfalls echoing through the cavernous halls, a virtual electric storm in her wake. Serena had rarely seen her mother so furious. Though she'd been equally upset—and shocked—when Rafe Cooper walked into the middle of their ritual, she couldn't help but feel a little gleeful that her mother's lack of foresight had bit her in the ass.

"Why didn't you know?" Fiona turned on Dr. Richard Bertrand when they reached the towering library in the back of the house. The property was owned by Good Shepherd Church, and Serena was usually amused knowing that the contributions to Pastor Garrett Pennington's ostensibly Christian church were used to allow her and her mother to live in luxury.

"Richard!" Fiona shouted when he didn't immediately answer her. She sent a pulse of energy toward the double doors, forcing them to slam shut, to emphasize her anger. Richard winced as if physically assaulted.

The doctor groveled. Typical, Serena thought. Few people had the backbone to stand up to Fiona. But Rafe had been his resposibility. Richard had ensured everyone that Rafe Cooper would never awaken. Richard would be lucky if he was alive at dawn.

"He shouldn't have woken up," Richard whined.

"*Shouldn't have?* Richard, since when have you re-duced yourself to ridiculous understatements?" Fiona turned to Serena. "And *you* were supposed to kill him months ago!"

Serena straightened her spine and kept her chin up. She wasn't going to let her mother reinvent the past. "When Rafe Cooper went into the coma, *you* said he was more use to us alive than dead," she retorted.

"He should have been dead that night!"

Fiona flung open the doors of her library with a flick of her wrist—a neat trick, but a parlor trick nonetheless. Serena had lived with her mother long enough to discern the difference between games and power. No doubt about it—Fiona controlled more otherworldly forces than any magician Serena had ever known, but she also enjoyed the bells and whistles that went along with power. There had been no need for half the games she'd played at the ruins. Had she forsaken the frills for expe-diency, they would have been done trapping the demons in the *arca* long before Rafe Cooper broke their circle.

Fiona whirled around and glared at her as if Serena had verbalized her criticisms. Her mother couldn't read minds, but she had a sixth sense that had kept Serena in line. "When I find Raphael Cooper I will make him suf-fer," Fiona said, leaving no doubt in anyone's mind that she would torture and kill him with great pleasure.

"Serena, go! Check on the others. Make sure they un-derstand the consequences of disobedience."

"Mother, I think—"

Fiona stared at her daughter and raised her brow. "I didn't ask you to think." Serena knew better than to countermand Fiona's orders, especially when others were present. When it was just the two of them, they often battled verbally, and sometimes with magic. Fiona always declared herself the victor.

But someday, Fiona would learn who had the real power in the family.

As she left the library, Serena whispered, "Your wish is my command."

Fiona watched her daughter walk out, considering whether her sarcasm should be punished. But when Richard opened his mouth, Serena's slight was forgotten.

"I don't understand how Cooper could have walked out of the hospital," Richard said, "not without help."

"Of course he had help," Fiona snapped. "I want to know if it was human or other."

She paced the length of her expansive library, picking up the *Conoscenza* where Serena had placed it on the desk. She flipped pages rapidly, searching for answers. None came because she couldn't read the damn book, only Serena could. Why was that? Why did her foolish daughter have the gift, and not she?

And how had Raphael Cooper known the language? Impossibly enough, he had saved the *arca* and cost Fiona her prize.

It was doubtful that Cooper even knew what he had done. She'd find him, put him in her own, special reverse devil's trap, summoning spirits one by one to torture him. He would beg to die. He would kill himself and be dragged under, a special offering that would gain her much favor and more power.

After tonight, she needed it.

She almost threw the *Conoscenza* across the room,

but as if the book itself lived, as if sensing her intent, the ancient text became hot. Fiona dropped it on the table.

She picked up another thick tome, *Twilight,* and threw it instead. Its spine cracked when it hit the wall and dropped to the floor. She grabbed another, and this time threw it at Richard. He ducked, but the book hit him in the head, and she smiled.

"How did Cooper awaken? Tonight of all nights?"

"I swear, Fiona, *medea,* I do not know! I did everything I could to keep him in sleep. When I left he was the same as always."

"Zaccardi?"

"Nowhere. He came by the hospital this morning, like every morning, but didn't stay longer than usual. Cooper was in the same condition. No one even called me to report he'd awakened. I swear—"

"Go. Get back there right now. Find out what happened, if anyone helped him. If your magic is so weak that you can't give me the answers I need, I will send Serena."

"I will, but—"

"Richard, I just gave you simple orders. Find out how Raphael Cooper woke up and left the hospital." Her voice was suddenly eerily calm, which might have been even more frightening.

He left briskly. When she was alone, Fiona turned back to the *Conoscenza.*

"Why am I not given the gift?" She slammed her hand down on the book, challenging it. A puff of smoke escaped, her palm burned, and she jerked it away.

"It's not fair," Fiona whispered.

She was the daughter of a witch, the granddaughter of a witch, and the great-granddaughter of one of the

greatest magicians in Ireland. In the world. Her lineage
went back to the beginning of magic itself, she'd learned
after years of meditation and study. While anyone could
practice witchcraft, Fiona had a natural talent, a skill
and finesse and inner strength that put her head and
shoulders above even the strongest magicians in the
world. Few could compete with her. When some tried,
she always won.

Fiona fought fiercely when challenged, so most of her
competitors were dead. Those who were not dead became her subordinates, but she watched them closely.
She quelled potential mutinies long before they became
cancerous.

With all her strength, her heritage, her talent, she
hadn't been given the ability to read the old language. If
she had the knowledge, she could have stopped Cooper.
Serena had never been one to think on her feet; she was
too rigid, too restrained. Fiona could have twisted the
spells to battle Cooper. It was her destiny to unite the
covens of the world, to stir the cauldron of human apathy and discontent into a frenzy. With her at the helm,
they would quash St. Michael's Order and the last remnants of the great witch hunt would die away.

They would no longer need to practice in the dark of
night, in the alleys and fields and hidden niches of the
world. Fiona already had several high-placed witches in
positions of power, elected officials and businessmen,
the rich and the powerful, the leaders and the teachers.
By controlling the Seven released at the cliffs, she would
gather more support from the covens. Once she had
them contained, once the covens united under her
command, she would at long last be able to breach St.
Michael's sanctuary.

The fools there did not know what they had. If they did, they would have destroyed it long ago.

The library doors swung open and Fiona whirled around, furious that the intruder hadn't knocked.

It was Garrett, with Serena behind him.

"We have a problem," he said. "I had to leave her, there was—"

"A problem? Where's the vessel?" Fiona demanded. "You didn't clean up?"

"I began to, but the police came."

Fiona clenched her fists. Sparks of electricity snapped around her.

"And Cooper?" she asked, her voice a mere whisper.

"We searched at a distance after the police arrived, but we couldn't pick up his path in the rocky soil. The police—"

She put her hand up, not wanting another excuse from him. The electricity charges snapped on the ends of her fingers. She wanted to hurt him, but she was disciplined and caught herself. Instead, she flung her energy away from him and Serena, across the room, into the fish tank against the far wall. The water bubbled and boiled, steam rising as the fish floated to the top.

"Fiona, we have a bigger problem," Garrett said.

Fiona's eyes flashed. "There can be no bigger problem than the Seven out of my control!"

"Moira."

"That name is forbidden."

"I saw her," Garrett said. "She showed up minutes after you and the others left. She didn't see me, I stayed hidden among the cypress, and when the boy she was with left I was going to grab her, but then the police arrived."

"No!" Fiona was emphatic. "I would know if that traitor was near!"

"She must have protection," Serena mused.

Fiona paced, furious. Even Serena didn't know the extent of Moira's betrayal. The suffering and sacrifice that Fiona had to endure to regain her lost power, all because of her ungrateful firstborn!

She wanted Andra Moira to suffer for eternity. Fiona would bring this about with her own mind and hands, with her magic, her power, her demons. The traitor would be torn apart, put back together, torn apart . . . Moira would watch those she loved, those she cared about, clawed and eaten by the vilest of demons that feasted on human flesh; she would be subjected to a thousand lashings, over and over, until she bled from every inch of her flesh, bleeding but still alive; and Fiona would joyfully sic the leeches on her, to painfully suck her dry like dozens of small vampires.

The last time Fiona sought to punish Moira, the girl had fought back and turned the effort against her. If her bratty spawn had been practicing all these years since, Fiona didn't know if she could defeat her one-on-one.

Fiona could turn the Seven on her traitorous daughter and, once and for all, pay back a debt long overdue. That is, once she trapped the demons again. Once she found the *arca*.

"Serena! Get my map. I will find her."

"No need," Garrett said. "I know where she is. Zaccardi had his bitch arrest her."

Fiona laughed. Oh, maybe the universe had sided with her tonight.

"The traitor is in jail?"

"Yes. I saw her in cuffs."

"Beautiful. Serena, continue researching our problem with the Seven." Fiona walked across the library, her bright gown flowing behind her, her red hair bouncing luxuriously off her back. Regal and knowing exactly how she looked to those around her. Beautiful. She put on her cape and added, "I'm going to make you an only child tonight."

Serena nodded. She picked up the *Conoscenza* and hugged the book. "I'll find the answers."

Fiona stopped next to her fish tank and frowned, suddenly sad. "Serena, fetch Margo. My poor fish. I can't bear to see them dead."

Skye wasn't happy about arresting Moira O'Donnell. She didn't understand Anthony's vicious reaction to the woman who obviously was in his same strange business, but when Moira slugged Anthony—catching him by surprise—Skye had reacted. The woman had committed assault, and no law officer could let that slide. She'd been armed with a dagger, but also with paraphernalia that Skye herself had around the house ever since Anthony had walked into her life and into her heart. When she put Moira in the back of Deputy Young's car, she couldn't help but think that maybe she was overreacting. Jared Santos was a good kid. If he could vouch that they were together when they found the body, Skye would release her—decking Anthony notwithstanding.

Deep down, she realized she was jealous. She'd known Anthony for fewer than three months. They lived together, they loved each other, but Anthony had lived a long and strange life before he arrived in Santa Louisa. He'd brought the bizarre into her life.

She'd seen things she couldn't explain. She'd been drugged, attacked, kidnapped, restrained, and nearly died at the hands of her best friend and head detective, Juan Martinez, while he'd been possessed. She'd actually seen the demon when it had been exorcized from Juan's body. Anthony had cut his leg with a special dagger—not unlike the one she had confiscated from Moira O'Donnell—to save Juan.

So she believed Anthony when he said that the Seven Deadly Sins were more than a fable or religious fairy tale. If Anthony told her they were demons, then dammit, they were demons, and she had to find a way to save her town, the small piece of the world that Skye had sworn to protect and serve.

But if anyone other than Anthony had told her that the Seven Deadly Sins were real, she would have laughed or committed him for seventy-two hours in the psych ward.

Dr. Rod Fielding approached Skye with a nod as Young drove off with Moira O'Donnell. The head crime scene investigator was now the acting coroner, after Rich Willem surprised her by retiring at the end of the year. Skye had tried to convince Rod to take the appointment, but he declined, telling her it was just temporary while she searched for Willem's replacement.

Rod headed for the corpse, then stopped and looked around. "What happened here?" he asked. He saw Anthony standing on the far edge of the lot, talking on his cell. "This isn't—" He saw the symbols, even though they had been partly concealed. He noticed the red silk linens, the naked body, the spilled candles.

"Dear Lord."

"It's Abby Weatherby," Skye said.

"I know Abby's parents." The pain in his voice was real.

He rubbed his eyes, then pulled on gloves as he said, "What happened?"

"Hope you can tell *me*."

They crossed over to the body and Rod frowned. "She's naked. Any sign of sexual assault?"

"Not that I could see externally—there's no blood on her body, no visible bruising. There are no external wounds, I can't see any obvious cause of death."

"Did anyone touch or move the body?"

Skye hesitated. "Possibly. Jared Santos and a friend of his found her. I don't think they disturbed her, but I can't say for certain."

"Where is he? Can you ask him? Or his friend?"

"I haven't spoken to Jared yet. And I took Moira O'Donnell into custody. She—" Skye hesitated. Rod was one of the few people who knew what *really* happened last November, but Skye felt strange talking about supernatural events as if she were discussing common crime. "O'Donnell is from Anthony's . . . group." That sounded lame, but how else could she explain it?

"Why'd you arrest her?"

"She assaulted Anthony."

Rod grinned. "She hit him? Really."

"Don't look so happy about it." Skye changed the subject. "Anthony thinks there were other people here—a, um, coven." She mumbled the last word.

"He thinks *what*? Did you say *coven*? As in *witches*?" Rod looked around, taking in what she and Anthony had catalogued earlier. "It's certainly freaky, but we've been having trouble keeping trespassers off this site ever since the fire. These kids are dumb-asses, you know that as well as I do. I'll do a full tox screen of Abby, but I know you're thinking exactly what I am. We've talked about it before."

"Kids partying, getting high, OD."

"Exactly. I'm not rushing to a conclusion, but honestly, this isn't new. We've seen it time and time again, and you and I both know Abby was running wild this past year. Senior, about to leave home, breaking away from strict parents. We've seen it here and in every other town big and small in America. I'm just disheartened to see so much potential gone to shit."

Maybe Anthony was wrong, or the demonic symbols were a game, not truly meant to summon demons or anything else. Just kids messing around. Maybe there *had* been a supernatural ritual here, but before Abby arrived. Or she interrupted something . . .

"I'll track down her boyfriend if she has one, talk to her friends. Someone will crack."

Rod squatted next to Abby's body and did a visual inspection, then pulled on gloves and touched the body in several areas. "When was she discovered?"

"Approximately two a.m."

He glanced at his watch, made a note in his book. "About ninety minutes ago—take or leave. She hasn't been dead much longer than that. She's in the very early stages of rigor, which is likely with the low temperature—I'd put her death no more than two hours."

He looked in her mouth, eyes, nose, throat. He spread her legs to check for obvious sexual assault, found none, and rolled her to check for injuries on her back.

"Nothing physical. Honestly, this looks like her and

her boyfriend came out here to screw and get high. She OD'd and he fled."

"He took off with her clothes?" Skye doubted it but didn't say anything. Rod was a veteran, nearing retirement age but sharp as a tack. He was also the one who'd come up with the key to solving the murders of the priests at the mission last November. She trusted his judgment, but wondered if his knee-jerk response now was because he didn't want to contemplate something . . . *otherworldly.*

As Rod eased the victim's body back into its original position, she saw something. "What's that on the back of her neck? Move her hair." Skye pulled on one latex glove and gently pushed the girl onto her side. "There."

She pointed to an elaborate and colorful tattoo on the back of her neck—right where the neck touched the shoulders.

"Looks like a professional tattoo," Rod said after inspecting it. "I'll take photos at the morgue."

She glanced at Anthony and saw that he was talking on the phone. She bit her lip and hated that she wanted to eavesdrop.

"I'm going to collect her with this linen," Rod said, "to preserve trace evidence. But I've done all I can do here. I'll tag and bag her and transport her to the morgue."

"What time can you do the autopsy?"

"Right away. I'll prep her, then begin at eight a.m. You coming?"

"Absolutely." She looked over at Anthony, who was still deep in conversation and worried. He caught her eye, then turned his back to her. Something was up, Skye thought as she went to help catalogue the rest of the crime scene.

Anthony listened intently to Father Philip, disliking the direction of the conversation.

"You need to help her," Father said after telling Anthony that he'd known all along that Moira O'Donnell was in the States—even before Anthony had left the island for Santa Louisa last November.

"You knew that witch was here?"

"Now is not the time for this argument."

"She is a Jezebel, she has deceived you." Anthony's stomach turned. He and the Father had had this argument many times, and neither could convince the other of the rightness of his position. There was nothing Father Philip, or Rico, or any of the others who held Moira blameless could say to convince Anthony that she was not a threat to St. Michael's Order, and nothing *he* said nor the facts he presented about her culpability in Peter's death swayed them either. She had brought the demon into St. Michael's. She was responsible for its crimes.

Father Philip ignored his comment and said, "She called me tonight when she found out about the ritual on the cliffs. I told her to call you, but as there has been considerable animosity between you two, I'm not surprised she didn't. But you knew—"

He didn't want to discuss his strange connection to the ruins, so he interrupted. "I check the cliffs every night because of the darkness that surrounds the place." It was like a black hole, with mass and depth, as if the laws of physics didn't apply. Not now, not tonight—whatever the coven did here changed the place. "There have been some signs of occult activity over the last two months, but nothing like what I found tonight."

"What happened? I've been trying to reach Moira, but she's not answering her phone."

"According to the signs, the Seven have been released. A teenager died in the process—possibly a sacrifice. Moira O'Donnell was in the middle of it. She claims she found the body, but I don't buy it. Why can't you see that she's the problem? She's been part of the under-world uprising from the beginning—she started with her mother, and while she may not be working with Fiona anymore, she had her own brand of magic, and it got Peter killed. I called Olivet tonight and learned that she was supposed to arrive there months ago but never showed. She's a loose cannon—and I honestly don't care what her motives are. You—"

"Anthony," Father snapped, interrupting him. "You're wrong about Moira, and while she was supposed to re-turn to Olivet, Rico knew her plans. But we haven't time for this discussion now. Are you certain about the Seven?"

Anthony hesitated, feeling like an admonished child. "Yes," he replied. "I'm certain that's who they were summoning, but I can't say whether it worked, or why they need the Seven, or who specifically is behind it. This is bigger than anything I've dealt with. I need my books, I need to research." He felt far more confident poring over ancient texts than battling demons face-to-face. He'd done it once to save Skye—he didn't want to go through that horrible experience again.

"Good, I'll send you anything you need. But please, let Moira do her job."

"Job? What job?"

"I can't tell you over the phone."

Anthony froze. Father Philip was his mentor, had been

since he was a small boy. They shared the same last name, because that was the way it was at the monastery with the orphans—one of the priests or monks "adopted" the child and was his primary caregiver. Father Philip had taken him . . . and Peter. Which was why Anthony didn't understand Father's acceptance of that witch, Moira O'Donnell.

"Has this *job* been going on while she was supposed to be at Olivet?"

"Longer. Anthony—I will explain when we are face-to-face. Or you can ask Moira herself."

"Neither will happen soon."

"It may be time for a council at Olivet."

Anthony couldn't control the hurt he felt deep inside that Father had kept something as important as this from him for so long. But he said, "I understand."

"Anthony, I need to talk to Moira, where is she?"

"Jail."

"You need to get her out as soon as possible! Anthony, she needs your protection."

"Protection?" He rubbed his jaw. "Hardly."

"Fiona will find her in jail! The police wouldn't allow her to have any of her protective gear. You know that!"

For a moment, Anthony felt a twinge of guilt.

Father said quietly, "You and Peter were close. I understand. I loved Peter deeply. What happened was a grave mistake; it was hard on all of us. But you must forgive Moira. Both she and Peter were culpable, but in the end, it was Fiona and her demon who killed Peter, not Moira, and not Peter himself." Father Philip's voice deepened. "Anthony, you are very special. Exceptional and gifted by God. You are vital to our calling. But your weakness will be your destruction. If the Seven have been released, your anger will be used against you. You must pray for the strength to forgive."

Anthony felt the reprimand from thousands of miles away, even though Father hadn't raised his voice. "Now, tell me, how long has she been unprotected?"

Anthony swallowed a retort and said, "An hour."

"Don't let Fiona find Moira. I will leave for Olivet tomorrow."

"You're coming to America?"

"I must. Promise me you will get Moira out of jail."

Anthony struggled, not wanting to obey. "Yes, Father, I will."

EIGHT

Philip Zaccardi packed light—he didn't need much.

The priest despised travel. He rarely left St. Michael's. His fellow monks, the young men he trained, thought it was because he was fearful of flying. They were right about one thing: he was afraid. But it had nothing to do with airplanes.

If Anthony knew the private revelation Philip had been entrusted with years ago, the young demonologist would insist he never leave the island. But Philip had told no one; it was a revelation meant only for him.

The time had come. If he was right—and he believed he was—people would die. If his interpretation was wrong? He'd set into motion a chain of events where far more would suffer and die, including those he deeply cared for. But inaction, doing nothing in the face of evil, was a sin, and to many—including himself—inaction was an even greater sin than being wrong. No one could sit on the fence in the battle of good versus evil. The line had been drawn eons ago, when the serpent first lied to Eve. Sides were still being chosen. Only God knew the outcome, and He wasn't sharing.

Philip sought out Bishop Pietro Aretino, the elderly vicar who handled the day-to-day spiritual needs of the priests and monks. It was time for confession.

One might think the sins of a devout priest were few,

but Philip's mind was a maze of conflict and doubt. Doubt showed lack of faith, which increased fear, endangering him and others both physically and spiritually.

Philip's entire life had been filled with doubt and questions. And yet, he persevered. Still, he stood against evil.

After he received dispensation, the bishop took him on a walk through the garden. The garden that he'd at one time cherished was going the way of weeds. Such was the reality of the twenty-first century: fewer young priests with strong backs, more elderly priests with weak bones. At one time, decades in the past, when Philip had been new to St. Michael's, it was common to have three, four, or even five infants left on the island each year. These young ones were to be raised and trained in the battle against evil. Now? *Four* in the last twenty years. Did that mean the final battle was near? Would ten-year-old James Parisi be the last warrior in an order that had been founded hundreds of years before?

"You're leaving," Pietro said.

Philip had said nothing of his journey during confession, but the bishop was astute, even in his advanced age. "Yes."

They walked in silence. It was midday, the clouds obscuring the descending sun. Philip paused to pull weeds that surrounded the tree they'd planted after Peter's death. So many trees in this row . . . too many trees. Peter. Lorenzo. Elijah. And more.

"Take Gideon with you."

Philip hesitated, then slowly rose and faced Pietro. "I thought we'd decided Gideon would stay another year."

"We haven't the luxury of time."

Philip didn't want to disobey orders, but he wanted to keep Gideon safe. His mentor had died last year, and Gideon's training here was complete. His calling was still obscure, but his gifts were many. Dangerous gifts, and easy for misinterpretation by the young man.

Pietro resumed walking down the broken stone path with deliberate steps, his age forcing him to walk slowly and carefully. "You have affection for the boy."

Philip followed. "No more so than the others." Was that a lie? Not a deliberate lie. To clarify, he added, "He reminds me of Peter."

Pietro nodded.

"Peter failed."

"Did he?"

"He believed he was stronger than he was; he believed he could turn dark power into light. He kept secrets."

"You fear for young Gideon's soul. Your greatest failing, Philip, is your greatest strength."

When the older priest didn't elaborate, Philip said. "I'm going to Olivet. I'll need your blessing and authority."

Pietro nodded. "You have it."

"Anthony is asking questions."

"As he always has. Let him ask. He'll find answers when he asks the right questions."

"If he's right about the Seven—"

"He is."

Philip stopped walking. "You know something of this?"

"I know the *Conoscenza* was not destroyed at Santa Louisa."

"In Santa Louisa! The *Conoscenza* was destroyed hundreds of years ago. Here, in Italy—"

"A book that had been called the *Conoscenza* was destroyed, a brilliant forgery. But the real *Conoscenza,* the one written in ink tainted with demon blood, the one written by demonic hands, the original, which is older than Moses and unintelligible to most humans, is still on earth. Our ancestors in the Order were misguided, led by their own pride and erroneous sense of invulnerability. They were deceived. One of their own betrayed them, a Judas, who forged the book and hid the original so well that no one knew it existed."

"Why was this kept secret? We needed this information. How can—"

"Philip, we weren't certain until today."

"Because of Anthony's report about the Seven."

Pietro nodded. "It confirms out deepest fears. We had no proof, but Anthony is not generally wrong about these things."

"He's not, but—"

Pietro held up his hand. "I know this is hard to believe, and I didn't want to believe myself."

The old man sat on a bench under a plane tree, one that had been planted more than four decades before, its gnarled trunk rising into countless branches. It was Father Lucca Zaccardi's tree, planted after his death during a violent exorcism when Philip was still training under him. Philip often sat in this spot when he meditated, or when he doubted. Father Lucca had been a pillar of strength, much like Anthony. Philip felt weak between the two men, and was usually comforted here. Not today.

Pietro continued. "Father Salazar contacted me from the Santa Louisa Mission four months before the murders there. Poor Herve expressed a rather . . . paranoid, for lack of a better word . . . belief that the book was alive."

"Alive?"

"His word, but fitting considering the origins of the book. The inner council didn't want to accept it, but I believed him. So did the Cardinal."

There were many cardinals in the Church, but only one cardinal publicly associated with the Order: Francis Cardinal DeLucca. He was their main benefactor, the one who ensured that St. Michael's Order survived from his position high in the Vatican. Other high-ranking supporters did so with much discretion.

"The Cardinal sent Raphael to the mission at Santa Louisa to find the *Conoscenza*."

Philip had to sit down at this revelation. He hadn't known. How could he have not known? He looked up at the gray sky, through the leafless branches of the plane tree, and knew with certainty that he wouldn't see spring blossom on the island.

Pietro continued. "It wasn't until after the murders that the idea that the *Conoscenza* was at the mission took hold. The witch's belief that her mother was searching for it meant we needed to—"

"The witch? You call Moira O'Donnell a witch?"

Pietro stopped for a moment, sat next to Philip, and said, "I'm sorry. I know you have affection for the girl." He went on. "The Cardinal sent Raphael into the mission to assess the situation. You understand that we still don't know his calling."

By the age of twenty-one, the "calling" of all St. Michael's children was clear. Whether they were to be priests, exorcists, empaths, demon hunters, demonologists, scholars, linguists, or one of many other specialties was discerned no later than twenty-one. Some, like Anthony, had been discerned at an early age. Others, like Raphael, were more elusive. He was in his thirties and still unsettled.

Pietro continued. "After Father Salazar's cryptic messages, we sent Raphael to Santa Lousia, but we also began to discreetly investigate all the men at the mission. You know why they were there."

"Because they'd been spiritually and emotionally damaged by evil."

"And we have sympathy for our people. But—"

"You knew about the priest Jeremiah Hatch."

Pietro paused long enough that Philip wondered if he was working on a fabrication, or if he simply didn't want to comment. "We began to suspect Hatch was a practicing magician," Pietro said. "It was in retracing his steps in Guatemala that we discovered some inconsistencies with his story, and in those inconsistencies accepted that he may have uncovered the *Conoscenza*."

"By design."

"We don't know how the book came to be in Central America, or how Hatch learned it was there. But he was missing for three years, and everyone who was lost with him is still missing. They are likely dead. Hatch returned to America, and is the only priest who *asked* to be sent to Santa Louisa."

"If you knew, why didn't you stop him before the murders?"

"We *didn't* know! We didn't have all the information until after the massacre. If Anthony is right about the Seven, the only known spell to draw them from Hell is in the *Conoscenza*. You sent the wi—Moira—to track Fiona's coven, and she lands in Santa Louisa. The same place that we were looking for proof that the *Conoscenza* survived all these years. Now that the Seven may well be on earth, we face an ancient evil we are ill prepared for." He sighed wearily as the sky grew darker, as the sun slid farther down and the clouds grew heavy. The light breeze that had flitted through the courtyard all day strengthened, pushing at the men.

"There are times, Philip, when I want to close my eyes and leave it all for the End Times. There will be an end, and I am so tired."

Philip refused to live his life in the belief that nothing he said or did mattered. Forgiveness was commanded by the Lord, even for those who had done unspeakable acts. And if Philip died because he obeyed, then he was ready to die.

"If we do not fight against evil, we are as those who celebrate it."

Pietro didn't comment, and Philip felt very alone. He was considered an idealist, known for his passion and compassion. But Pietro was a realist, and realists often looked only at the facts—that Judgment Day was inevitable, regardless of what they did or didn't do. Arrogant, Philip believed. This arrogance—*pride*—was the fall of many in the Order. That they were pure and thus could turn their back on the masses of God's children.

Philip had always been drawn to the parable of the lost sheep. That the Lord would sacrifice the pious to save the one who wandered. That *the one* mattered. Raphael . . . Anthony . . . Philip . . . Moira . . . even Peter, who had made wrong choices for the right reasons. That the Lord would forgive, would search for His lost sheep night and day, endlessly, and have mercy on them.

Lord, please be with your lost sheep today and forever.

"You, Philip," Pietro said quietly, "are a rare soul."

"I am who I am, nothing more than a servant for the Lord." They sat in silence for many minutes, until the clouds opened and a solitary drop of rain fell on the ground.

Philip accepted his fate and rose, his bones cracking audibly. Despite the infirmities of old age, he no longer regretted his lost youth. "I should finish my preparations. It is a long journey."

Pietro remained sitting and caught Philip's eye. "As you know, the *Conoscenza* can only be destroyed by a very specific person."

Philip's stomach rose. "A witch."

"Moira."

"But you still call her Witch."

"She will always be a witch."

Philip shook his head, wiping raindrops from his brow. "You can't believe that. We all can be forgiven."

"'Tis true, but she is what she is. Forgiven or not, she is our one best hope. Only a mortal witch can destroy the book written in the blood of a union between demons and humans. She is a descendant of the fall of man."

"We all are."

"But you know what I speak of."

Of course Philip understood what Pietro meant. After humans were banished from the Garden of Eden, after the first taste of knowledge from the forbidden fruit, a few in the following generations turned to magic, and demons roamed the earth with them. It was that first

coven, the first magicians on earth, from which Fiona
had come. And, thus, Moira.

"Are you certain?" Philip asked as the rain fell more
steadily and they began the walk back to the building.

"I am," Pietro said.

A chill ran down Philip's spine. As if sensing his fear
and hesitation, the wind whipped up around them, coming down into the fortress as if blown in from the heavens. Pietro pulled his handmade sweater tighter around
him.

"I know you are upset with me, Philip, and I am sincerely sorry that I had to keep information from you.
Rico needed Moira to believe that she was to be one of
us, but it was simply to divert her questions. He never
lied to her." He hesitated. "Since you're reluctant to
bring Gideon, instead John will escort you to Santa
Louisa."

"I'm going to Olivet." Even as he said it, Philip realized that he'd been unconsciously planning to go directly to Santa Louisa. Anthony, Moira, Raphael—they
were in danger, and they needed the truth if they were to
have a chance.

Philip wiped drops of rain from his cheek. "They deserve the truth."

"Perhaps. Philip, up until now, Moira's visions have
been of the present; if she begins to see the future we
have to stop it."

Philip shook his head. "There are gifts—"

"Her gifts are not from God. Philip, you are blind
when it comes to Moira. I need you to be safe. John will
escort you to Santa Louisa. He can protect you."

What Pietro was implying . . . "Moira would never
hurt me, or any of us. It took her years to accept the as-

signment to"—Philip hesitated, unable to say the word *kill,* in violation of all he believed—"*stop* her mother and the coven."

As he passed Peter's tree again, he glanced over, his heart heavy. Pietro had said all he had to say.

They stepped inside the stone halls, water sliding off their clothes onto the ancient floor. Philip said, "I will leave tomorrow. Gideon will stay here, yes?"

Pietro nodded solemnly. "Agreed. Gideon will join you later. I will prepare John to escort you. You'll both leave at dawn." He took Philip by the arm. "We cannot lose you, Philip. I've been . . . uneasy lately. Without you, we lose our center."

"I am merely a man."

"You are a rock, Philip. I remember when you arrived at the gates. I was ten, not privy to much, but I heard Father Lucca say, 'This one, he is of the foundation. We must protect him as long as possible.' And he took you under his wing. It was a first for him; he'd never raised one of us."

Philip had never heard that story before, and it moved him. "Are you keeping anything else from me?" he whispered.

"You now know everything I know, but—" He stopped.

"But? Pietro, please. I must know."

"The Cardinal knows more."

NINE

All hope abandon, ye who enter here!
—DANTE ALIGHIERI

Moira realized after hitting Anthony that she'd let her temper get the better of her, but connecting her hand with his arrogant face had been so damn satisfying that she gloated for the first five minutes she was locked behind bars. True, she probably couldn't take Zaccardi out in a fair fight, but she didn't care if she played fair, and she'd surprised him. *Wham!* Down on his knees. She wished she'd broken his nose, but no such luck. She rubbed her hand. Rico had taught her how to pull punches to minimize damage to herself, but damn, her palm was still sore.

There were only four cells in the Santa Louisa County jail, plus a larger "drunk tank." There were two men in the drunk tank—sleeping. Only one other cell was occupied, and that man was sleeping as well. Though the place was clean, she occasionally caught a whiff of stale urine or vomit underneath the antiseptic cleanser.

Her cell, surrounded by three smooth, gray cinderblock walls, was on the opposite side of the wide walkway. Narrow steel bars and the three sleeping prisoners were her only view.

Six minutes of incarceration and the walls began to

shrink. Her heart raced as the floor seemed to rise. She knew she was panicking, but knowing it didn't stop the pressure in her chest, or the sweat from breaking out on her neck, between her breasts, and on her palms.

She'd been in prison before, only nothing as lavish as the Santa Louisa Sheriff's Department.

The first time Moira had run away she was sixteen. And because she'd been stupid and unskilled in survival, Fiona had found her. Punished her. Sent her underground, in a dungeon of an abandoned castle in Ireland. Dark. Cold. Damp. With the foul stench of mold and decay, of dead, rotting rodents. She heard the rats scurrying all around her, above her on the beams, in the corners, in and out of the bars of her cell. It could have been the seventeenth century as easily as the twenty-first.

Fiona had left Moira for a week. Alone. With only enough food and water to ensure survival. Into her dreams, Fiona had sent monsters so real Moira didn't know whether they were nightmares or reality. She hallucinated and had nearly been broken. *Nearly.* Except for the hard rock of hatred in the core of her heart, hatred of Fiona. It kept her alive, it kept her breathing, and when she was free she played Fiona's game for months. When she ran again, Fiona didn't find her for nearly five years.

Moira's breath caught and she stared at three barred, horizontal windows on the far wall. Tilting her head up, she stared greedily at the dark sky, a nearly full moon blurred by high clouds. She had to get hold of herself. She wasn't underground, this wasn't a dungeon, and Fiona didn't know she was here. She focused on the red planet through a small opening in the clouds. Mars was so bright tonight! She watched it appear and disappear as the clouds and earth moved. Imagined being outside, beneath a vast array of stars, in an open field, physically free and emotionally calm. Without trouble, without the pain of regret, without the torture of memories that burned.

It felt like hours, but it had only been ten minutes since she'd begun to panic. The terror subsided, but she felt . . . prickly, as if she were being watched. Tense, knowing that the panic of confinement was just beneath the surface, just waiting for something to draw it out.

The deputy who had brought Moira in had left, but he had to be nearby, didn't he? They wouldn't leave her in a locked cell without being able to see or hear her. She called out, "Hey! Come on, let me out! Please! Find the sheriff—" What was her name? "Skye! Are you there?"

"The courts open at nine a.m.," the man alone in his cell said from across the corridor. "Shut up or you'll wake the boys. They'll puke up their rotgut dinner and we'll be smelling that shit for hours."

Moira wasn't getting into a conversation with anyone. Instead she focused on paying Anthony back. She'd deck him again—out of sight of his girlfriend the cop.

"You're too fresh-faced and pretty to be a hooker," the prisoner said. "And you don't look drunk. Drugs?"

She didn't respond.

"Come on, sweet thing, talk to me. I don't bite, unless you want me to." He laughed at his stupid joke.

She glared at him and turned her back.

"Bitch," he mumbled. "Hope you go to State; the dykes would love to wipe the floor with your attitude."

Anthony wouldn't let it go that far, would he? Send her to prison for years? No, he couldn't. Father Philip would get her out. First call she made would be to Rico.

He'd get here fast in his private plane. No way he'd let her stay in prison. And he'd beat the living daylights out of Anthony for putting her here. She hoped she could watch. No one fought better—meaner or dirtier—than Rico.

The door opened at the guard station. Finally.

Moira was about to rip Sheriff Skye McPherson a new one, but she bit her tongue.

It wasn't the sheriff coming through the door. Even before she saw the woman, she knew who it was.

Fiona.

An exotic, seductive scent—lavender and orchids and dark ocean breezes floating on a rich, musky base. Unique, enchanting, deadly.

Moira quietly backed against the wall closest to the door, where Fiona wouldn't first see her—not that it mattered. Fiona knew she was here; otherwise she wouldn't have come, wouldn't have risked exposing herself. But Moira needed a minute, a few *seconds,* to adjust to seeing her mother again for the first time in seven years, when she'd blindly caught up with Fiona after Peter's death. Rico had risked his life to save her. She hadn't deserved to be saved.

Three primary emotions battled: pain, rage, and fear. Fiona had channeled dark powers for years, had become far more powerful than even when she'd summoned the demon that possessed Moira seven years ago. Fiona could easily kill her without a man-made weapon. And Moira couldn't fight back. Even if she had kept her abilities sharp and honed, she couldn't fight Fiona with magic without breaking her promise to Father Philip. She'd rather die than do that. Even magic with good intentions killed, because it all came from the same source of pure evil.

It had killed Peter. It had almost killed her. Now, trapped in this prison—the physical jail cell and her own morality—she'd be dead before dawn.

"Well, well, well, hell-*lo*, hot stuff." The sober prisoner sat up on his cot and gave Fiona an appraising look.

Both Fiona and Moira ignored him. Moira had no idea how Fiona had found her, how her mother knew she was in town and specifically in prison, but she damn well knew *why* she'd come. Seven years ago when Rico and Father Philip saved her, Fiona had said:

"You are cursed, firstborn daughter. I will find you. I will hunt you down, I will destroy you inside and out. I will wring your soul dry until it's begging for mercy, of which I have none to spare you."

Anthony wouldn't have let it out that she was in jail. If he'd known where Fiona was, he'd have gone after her himself. And he still believed Moira was working either with her mother or another coven. But Sheriff Skye McPherson—was she part of the coven? Covens loved to recruit people in positions of power. Cops, teachers, ministers. Anyone with authority and trust.

And then there was Jared, who'd disappeared to find his girlfriend right before the police came. Could he have alerted Fiona? Perhaps his original intent in bringing her to the cliffs was to lure Moira into a trap, but something went wrong and the coven had dispersed.

"Cead inion." First daughter. Some might think it was a term of endearment, but Moira knew better. To Fiona, it meant she was property.

"Cailleach."

Fiona smiled at the insult—Moira didn't know what offended her more, the "old" part or the "hag" part. Her red, glossy lips wide, teeth so white they seemed false. Some might have called her grin inviting. But Moira knew better. She was a shark, circling her prey.

Fiona's brilliant, dark blue eyes matched Moira's; her hair, a shiny, golden red, was thick and curly and impossibly long. Moira had the same curls, but she kept her black hair up or braided and out of the way. Fiona's skin was smooth and flawless, her cheekbones high and aristocratic. Her mother had always been a dramatically beautiful woman. She hadn't changed. She hadn't changed physically *at all* from when Moira had last seen her. Fiona was forty-eight. She looked . . . younger. Stunning. Twenty-eight, maybe, but not forty-eight.

"Andra Moira." Her full name rolled off Fiona's tongue with the Irish lilt and the proper accent. *An-drah Mor-rah*. Moira hated it. She preferred the wrong way everyone else in the world pronounced her name, with three syllables instead of two. And she refused to use her first name, Andra, knowing whom she was named for and why. An ancient goddess who relished blood and human sacrifice . . .

Moira stared at her, tense and watchful. Wishing the damn sheriff would get her ass in here. How had Fiona gotten in? Had she killed someone . . .

"You're weak." Fiona walked to the center of the jail and stared at Moira with both shock and contempt. "You haven't been practicing! Pathetic."

She sounded disappointed, as if she'd wanted some sort of supernatural battle between them. But Moira had learned the hard way that all supernatural power came from the wrong side of the tracks, and payment for borrowing it was steep.

"I know what you did on the cliffs," said Moira. "I know what you're up to."

"You can't possibly imagine in your small mind what I am doing." Her eyes glowed with excitement—from Moira's entrapment or her own plans, Moira didn't know. Probably both. "You are fortunate that I am forgiving."

"As forgiving as the devil himself," Moira snapped. "Oh, wait, he's one of your friends."

Fiona's throat tensed, revealing delicate bones under flawless skin. "You should be more respectful of your father."

"Bullshit." A chill started in the center of her bones, hardening her gut, bringing the panic on, but she stood perfectly still. Moira had never known her father. For all she knew, her mother had slit his throat after mating. Moira's bravado was a farce, and she damn well knew that if Fiona smelled fear, she would pounce. She crossed herself more to goad her mother than to proclaim faith.

Fiona murmured a spell aimed at Moira, but at the last minute tossed it toward the drunk cell with a flip of her wrist. Moira could almost see the gray smoke, even though she knew it wasn't physically there, but merely an illusion.

The drunks both groaned in their stupor, the nightmare Fiona had thrown into their minds taking hold.

Fiona paced the length of the walk. The velvety blue gown swirling around her gave the illusion that she was floating. Wisely, the man in the far cell said nothing.

"What did you do to the guards?" Moira asked.

"They're sleeping."

Fiona stopped dead center in front of Moira's cell. "Andra Moira, I am granting you a choice." She raised her left hand with flair, her jewels sparkling in the artificial light. "On the one hand, I will let you out. You come with me and fulfill your role as it was decided before your conception. You, the first daughter of a virgin womb, sacrificed to be the goddess of the underworld. Such a high status for doing nothing but being born. You are of the chosen, for I am of the chosen. I gave my body to the gods so you could exist.

"On the other hand," she waved her right hand as if swatting away a fly, "you will die now, and I will rip your soul from your body and send it into the pit to be tortured forever. She who gives life can also take it away."

Fiona held her palms up, as if in a peace offering. Moira stared, feeling an unspoken spell building. On Fiona's open palms, two worlds balanced: one of fire, the other identical but with Moira in the middle, her face melting to bone, the bones turning to ash.

Another illusion. Moira willed her mind to see only what was in front of her, to repel the telepathy that her mother was using to send images into her mind.

She blinked and it worked. She saw only her mother. Rico had trained her well.

"Free will conquers magic. Use your mind, your thoughts, your free will in battle. Turn not to external forces, but to the strength that God gave you."

An irritated scowl crossed Fiona's face and she dropped her hands.

"You released the Seven Deadly Sins from Hell," Moira said, emboldened by her small victory. "There's no reason—"

"I didn't free them! They were to be mine. It was that—" She stopped, straightened, and glared at Moira. "Your decision. Now! Come with me or die."

They were to be mine. Fiona did nothing without a reason, but Moira couldn't come up with even one idea as to why Fiona wanted to claim, or keep, the Seven.

Moira's words were clear. "I am not yours. I refuse to be sacrificed to any of your demons. Go ahead and try to send me to Hell; if you succeed, I know ways to come back and thwart every one of your plans."

Fiona laughed.

"You fool," she said between bouts of laughter. "You know nothing. Those pathetic men on that ridiculous island have no idea of the power to be had. The wall separating the worlds is so thin, it is close to crumbling. Between the here and now, the underworld and time; I am the weakest link, where the membrane between humans and the supernatural universe is thinnest. You will never defeat me."

In ancient Latin she spoke a spell that Moira had never heard before. The words seemed to be aimed at her through a fast-moving tunnel. Moira's vision faded. She put her hands out and screamed, but felt no vibration in her throat. She was falling, falling, deeper and deeper into her mind.

It's not real, it's not real, it's not real.

She lay naked on a bed of feathers, the sunlight streaming through the high windows of the retreat on the far side of the island off Sicily. This was her cottage, where the priests had hidden her while she, Peter, and the others tried to find a way to save her and defeat Fiona.

Peter came to her, glorious with his olive complexion,

broad chest, long sun-streaked brown hair. They were in love, had fought their feelings for months, knowing that giving in to the desire building inside of them would be violating everything that Peter held dear.

"Loving you isn't wrong," Peter told her as he slid into bed with her. "Loving you is heaven on earth."

She felt his hands, his lips, his breath on her neck. So tender but determined; confident but timid. The conflict was in both of them. Guilt battled need, pleasure battled duty. He skimmed her breasts, her stomach; his hands were between her legs, then he was sliding inside her, filling her, loving her . . .

"Loving me is deadly." Her hands went up around his neck and squeezed him. "Your fall from grace was of your own accord. You will burn in Hell!"

No, no, this never happened! But Moira couldn't push the vision from her mind. She tried to fight it, and as she fought she heard distant laughter. Her mother.

See him now, see him now, see him now.

Suddenly, she was free-falling and floating, as if having an out-of-body experience. She saw Peter.

Peter! My love, I miss you, I love you, I'm so sorry . . .

He was in the middle of an Irish meadow, the grassy knoll outside her grandmother's cottage. She wanted to run to him, fly to him, but she was trapped, held back by invisible hands. The meadow turned to fire. Peter stood on an island in the middle of lava, whips of flame slicing his back, leaving red welts. Over and over and over . . .

"You *bitch!*"

Moira pulled herself from the spell . . .

. . . use your mind, look inside . . .

. . . Rico was talking. *Focus, focus, focus.* She built the

wall around her mind, like a caterpillar built a cocoon, fighting back as best she could.

Your will is powerful. Focus.

The laughter rang louder. "Poor girl," Fiona said, mocking.

Moira was pushed by an unseen force against the back wall. The wind was violently knocked out of her and she couldn't draw in another breath. She was suffocating. She would die in this cell, not a mark on her, and Fiona would win. She'd take the Seven Deadly Sins and complete whatever fearsome plan she had.

Fiona released her and Moira fell to the cement floor, gasping for air. She had nothing to protect her. The sheriff had confiscated her knives, her cross, her holy water, her medallion, the medal that Rico had told her never to remove.

"You were chosen, and you rejected the greatest gift in the universe!" Fiona said. "You damaged me. But I fought for what was mine and I'm stronger now. More powerful than you or any of your kind."

Moira's head ached and she mentally pushed back, fighting whatever images Fiona tried to plant inside her. Her head felt as if it would explode.

She felt something wet and sticky on the ground; she touched her face and came away with blood. Her nose was bleeding like a waterfall. She would bleed to death. Here. It would be called natural causes. A fluke. And no one would believe the prisoner in the far cell, that a beautiful woman had killed Moira without touching her. Who would?

"I wish I had time to toy with you, *fealltóir*. But I have work to do."

Moira looked up from where she bled on the floor.

Fiona sounded irritated, and her brow was wrinkled, showing frustration.

"If I want it done right," Fiona murmured, then turned her attention back to Moira. She stepped as close to the bars as she could without touching and smiled.

Fiona's lips moved, but Moira couldn't hear what she said, or read her lips. Her lungs grew heavy, as if filling with water, and Moira felt as though she were drowning. She couldn't breathe. She grabbed her throat, the sensation of choking so real—suddenly, she coughed up water, a half cup, then more.

Fiona watched. "It would be such fun practicing on you, but I don't have time. I'm going to share something with you before you die, though. Something to take with you."

Moira screamed as if a knife had pierced her brain. The pain was so excruciating that Moira prayed to God to just kill her now. The invisible knife twisted, twisted, her skull pounding in agony. Her eyes rolled back in her head and she curled up in a fetal position, wanting to pound her head into the cement because anything would feel better than this.

She tried but failed to use her will to hold back the pain, to stop the inevitable. Fiona was too strong, too powerful. Rico had been wrong. Moira's will was far too weak to fight. She'd told him before that she couldn't battle Fiona without magic, and now she was proven right. Her will . . . useless.

Suddenly a flood of images cascaded through her mind. Women. Naked, virgins, all sacrificed brutally, bloodily. Dead because Moira had escaped her fate, had run away from being goddess of the underworld, liaison to the magicians, the Mediator.

She whimpered, unable to speak. Fiona said, "Do you know how many had to die in your place? Eleven. One for each month I couldn't find you during the year you hid from me. By the time you reached your twenty-second year, it was too late. The window was gone. You did that. To all of them. The priest was icing on the cake."

She laughed, but there was no humor, just cold pleasure. Moira tried to crawl into the corner, as far from Fiona as she could get, but the pain stayed. She was dying. She could move no more than a few excruciating inches, her nose still dripping blood. She swallowed and tasted her blood, her mouth coated with the sweetly metallic flavor.

The priest was icing on the cake. Peter. Dear God, how could you let this happen? How could you allow Fiona to hurt so many?

Fiona said, "I wish I could have shared those sacrifices with you a long time ago, but the one thing you are good at is running and hiding. You should have stayed hidden, Andra Moira, because you are incapable and weak. You will never defeat me."

Moira's body rose from the floor and hovered in midair before Fiona's telekinetic magic threw her across the cell, against the far wall, where an unseen force had her pinned. Moira began to speak Hebrew through the blood in her mouth, the blood flowing from her nose. Weak, weaker, weakest . . . she was weakest. She began to fade, her mind mush, black then white then dark again.

Moira knew little Hebrew, but she remembered this one protective prayer Peter had taught her to hide her soul from Fiona. All her concentration went to remembering the words, and repeating them over and over. She was going to die, but she couldn't lose her soul. Fiona would torture her for eternity, torture those she cared about.

"Your pathetic attempt at fighting me will fail," Fiona said, and the pain inside Moira's head exploded so she couldn't remember her name, let alone an ancient Jewish prayer.

Suddenly the pain stopped, and Moira lay in a pool of blood. She thought she was dead, until the pain returned—throbbing, aching, bruising pain, but not the unbearable agony of before. Tolerable.

Fiona was on her cell phone. "I need a few more minutes." She scowled and stared at Moira.

"It seems, *a chailín mo chroí,* that you have a temporary reprieve," she said sarcastically. "But I will not forget. To quote a little book you may know—'Stay awake! You do not know the day or the hour.'"

"I will kill you," Moira whispered, trying, failing, to stand. "I will undo the damage you have done!"

Fiona whispered to Moira, barely loud enough for her to hear, "Remember the damage *you've* done."

On a curse, Fiona left the jail the same way she came in: without incident.

TEN

Skye pulled into her parking place at the sheriff's department. She turned off the cruiser's engine and turned to face Anthony. Anthony put his hand on the door—worried that Father Philip was right and Fiona O'Donnell would go after Moira—but Skye stopped him.

She said, "I let my anger convince me to arrest her, and now you want her out." She tenderly touched his jaw. It was a bit swollen and sore, but nothing was broken. Anthony was more irritated than hurt. "There's obviously a dicey history between you two."

"She killed a friend of mine. Seduced and murdered him."

"Why isn't she in prison? Is she a fugitive? Do I need to contact ICE?"

Anthony shook his head. "Peter was a monk at the monastery where I lived. She seduced him into breaking his vows. Put him in the middle of something extremely dangerous." He didn't know everything that had happened during the years before Peter died. He'd been in the middle of his own training that included extensive travel studying ancient architecture and artifacts. Peter was younger, sometimes annoying in his eagerness to please, and while Anthony had always considered him his little brother, he also considered him a neophyte, one of the Order who was part of the whole but not singularly necessary.

His arrogance had known no bounds then, and Anthony sincerely regretted it.

"Father Philip found Moira in Italy. She'd been running from her mother, hiding to avoid being detected by Fiona O'Donnell's coven." Anthony feared Father was right and Moira was in trouble, and while on one hand he didn't care what happened to the witch, he *did* care what Father Philip thought of him and his decisions. "Basically, her mother wanted to sacrifice her to the underworld in a ritual that would have given Fiona's coven more power than any other coven on earth."

"How many of these covens—witches, whatever—are we talking about?"

She was talking the way she had before—before she'd seen evil with her own eyes. Her dismissal disturbed him, but he tried to explain. "Hundreds of covens, thousands—probably tens of thousands—of witches, some practicing alone, some in covens. Most have little or no power. The larger, more powerful groups usually splinter off but remain affiliated with their founder. Fiona controls more covens than any other magician on earth."

"Please try to understand my position on this. It's new to me. You're going to have to give me a bit more before I launch a modern-day Salem witch hunt."

Anthony waved his hand. "The fools in colonial times didn't understand dark magic. They killed more innocent women than true witches."

She didn't say anything, and Anthony realized that not only was Skye skeptical, but he must sound foolish to her. The average person did not believe witches—like

Fiona O'Donnell and her kind—existed, or that they had power over dark forces.

His word, his experience, wouldn't be enough to convince Skye. Like the last time, she had to see it. That put the woman he loved in danger, because the dark arts were alive and well, thriving in these times, and now here in Santa Louïsa.

"She needs to be deported," he finally said. It was the only way to get Moira out of Santa Louisa. Father Philip trusted her, but she wasn't to be trusted. Guilt niggled in the back of his head. He felt as if he were somehow deceiving Father. Anthony couldn't let her roam free. Even if she wasn't working with Fiona, Moira O'Donnell was still a witch.

"First you want me to arrest her. Then you want me to let her out. Now you want me to deport her. I suppose I could call Immigration, send them her credentials, see if *they* have a reason to deport her, but it's not within my power to do so."

"We have a crisis on our hands, and Moira O'Donnell in the mix makes it more complex and dangerous."

She looked as confused and frustrated as he felt. "I want to believe you, but I don't understand. I need to understand. You said the Seven Deadly Sins were released. What does that mean?"

"The roots of the Seven go much deeper than two thousand years of Christianity. The sins have been written about, with different names, different ideas, from the beginning of humanity. Ancient people told stories of the sins in pictographs on the walls of caves and pyramids and in Roman architecture. Even further back in Mesopotamic time. Most people believe sins are internal, personal battles we all must face. In one sense, that is true. Since the fall of man, all humans are capable of great evil. We want, we envy, we lust—we battle every day to keep these feelings, these primal urges, in check.

"But the Seven aren't internal sins. They are supernatural. They are mutations. They are among the Fallen Ones."

"You're getting woo-woo on me, Anthony. Just lay it out for me. Logically. I trust you; I need you to be straight with me."

Would she believe the truth? "Some of my people think that the Seven are fallen angels."

"Fallen angels," she said flatly. "Like Lucifer."

"Yes."

He read in her eyes confusion, uncertainty. She bit her lip in an effort not to tell him she didn't believe him, or questioned him. It upset Anthony, but he couldn't entirely blame her.

"What do *you* think?" she asked quietly.

He touched her face. So beautiful, so strong, so full of justice that it ate her up inside and out. Her heart led her to truth, to righting wrongs, and he loved that about her. "I believe that they are here. I believe they are dangerous, that they are not like demons I know and understand, but far deadlier. I don't know how to stop them, I don't know how to send them back, but I will find out. I promise you, I'm not resting until I figure out how to send them back to Hell before more people die."

She reached out for him. "I trust you, Anthony. You do everything you can to find out what happened on the cliffs last night, and I'll do everything I can to find the people involved. Whether or not something—demonic— is on the loose, you and I both know that a flesh-and-blood human being is ultimately responsible for Abby's death. I want that person in jail."

"On what charge?"

"Murder, of course! A teenager is dead."

It would be almost impossible to pin the girl's death on a coven of witches without hard, physical evidence. And if Skye became troublesome to the group, to protect themselves they'd use their dark powers to hurt her, turn her, destroy her.

A chill ran through Anthony. He had to find some way to protect Skye from their trickery. "I need to go to the mission." He'd been rebuilding the library there, having books sent to him from his cottage in Italy. "But first—how do we deport O'Donnell?"

"I'll talk to the D.A. Are you still dropping charges?"

"Yes—but I don't want her to run. I need to know where she is at all times."

"I can keep her passport. She is a material witness. If you want to take my truck to the mission, I'll be here awhile. Abby's autopsy is in a few hours . . . I can grab a car from the pool if I need it."

He kissed her. He would do everything to protect Skye, whether she believed what he said or not. "I love you, Skye."

Her face softened and he touched her chin, her cheek, her soft blond hair. *Love* was not an adequate word for his feelings. "Be careful, *mia amore*."

"You too." She kissed him lightly, then slid out the driver's door and he moved into the driver's seat.

"I'll return this afternoon," he said.

Skye watched Anthony pull out of the parking lot, driving too fast. She cringed. She probably shouldn't have let him drive her official vehicle, but Santa Louisa had always been more laid-back than most counties in California. With fewer than twenty-nine thousand residents, it landed near the bottom of the population list, so small by West Coast standards that most California residents couldn't pinpoint it on a map.

She walked in through the main doors and heard the phone ringing. It was barely daybreak and the phone was ringing? She smelled something odd—but couldn't identify it.

The desk sergeant was asleep, the phone ringing next to him having no effect.

Asleep or . . .

She drew her firearm and looked cautiously as she approached Deputy Jorgenson to see if he was injured. The phone stopped ringing; the silence made her heart race. She felt his pulse. Strong.

"Deputy Jorgenson!" Skye shook him by the shoulders. "Are you sick? Bruce!"

Jorgenson wasn't yet fully alert, but he struggled to speak and stand. She caught a whiff of something that smelled like rosemary and . . . something like baking. Food poisoning?

"I—don't know."

A fine, off-white powder covered his dark hair and shoulders, some falling on his desk.

"Have you been drinking?" She touched the powder, sniffed it. Definitely a hint of rosemary, and lavender, and other herbs.

"No!" He coughed.

"Sit tight, be alert."

She didn't know if he'd been drugged or not, but she didn't want him covering her back if he wasn't one hundred percent alert. She spoke into her lapel mic, "All available units, 10-34. I repeat, officer needs assistance at headquarters."

Another phone rang, but there were no voices. They had a minimum of four officers at headquarters during graveyard shift, more if the four jail cells were full. Where was everyone?

The phone stopped ringing and Skye heard the faint sound of the television in the break room. The twenty-four-hour sports channel. Then steady banging, coming from the jail.

She had no intention of walking into the jail cell without backup, but when she saw two more deputies sleeping at their desks, one right outside the holding pen, she feared for the lives of her men.

Damn, damn, damn! She glanced at the log, noted that there were four prisoners, two drunk and disorderly, one grand-theft auto, and Moira O'Donnell.

Just as she was about to enter the holding pen, Young walked in. "What happened, Sheriff?"

"I don't know. Jorgenson, the others appear to have been drugged. Did you see anything when you brought O'Donnell in?"

"No, I booked her, then went on break across the street at the coffee shop."

"We're going in. Ready?"

He took out his sidearm and nodded.

"On three." She held up her fingers. *One, two, three.*"

She opened the door with her key, slowly and quietly. She smelled blood and her heart skipped a beat, her mind transported back to the slaughter at the mission ten weeks ago. The murders had been human, but the cause was supernatural.

She glanced around and noted the banging was Mr.

Grand Theft Auto pounding the heel of his sneaker on the bars.

"It's about fucking time!" he yelled when he saw her.

Skye saw Moira O'Donnell, sprawled on the cement floor, blood pooled around her and smears on the wall. Her first thought was murder. Skye had Young cover the door while she quickly searched—there were no hiding spaces in the jail.

She opened the cell and checked Moira's pulse. Strong. Her eyes opened, then closed again.

"Moira!" Skye exclaimed. "What happened?"

The auto thief said, "She's bleeding to death, what do you think?"

"Shut up," Skye ordered.

He continued. "This crazy dame walked in, some kind of psychic or something, and the babe just flopped against the wall like some big beefy guy was holding her up, and then her nose started bleeding like a fucking waterfall."

Moira groaned and tried to get up. "Relax," Skye told her. Protocols would demand that Skye wait for additional backup, secure the prisoner, and arrange for transport to the hospital. But Anthony had dropped the charges, Moira wasn't a threat to her. Could a demon have done this?

She said, "Anthony dropped the charges against you, Ms. O'Donnell. You're free to go. I'll call a medic, get you to the hospital."

Moira rolled over onto her back, wiping the blood from her face with her stained shirt. She began to laugh, borderline hysterical, and Skye tensed. "She found me. Seven years and she never found me until now."

"Who?"

She continued to laugh. "You—you think you can arrest Fiona O'Donnell? For what?" She sat up. Skye offered her hand, but Moira ignored it, crawling over to the bars and pulling herself up onto unsteady legs. Skye was stunned at the huge amount of blood left behind on the floor. It had presumably come from her nose, but Moira also had scrapes on her face and arms, and a nasty bruise on the side of her head, partly obscured by her hair.

"Let's get you to the hospital—" Skye said.

"No. No. I just need a bathroom for a few minutes."

"You lost a lot of blood."

"I just need a few minutes," Moira repeated. "And orange juice. If you have any. Or water."

Skye was inclined to take the woman back into custody and force her to go to the hospital, but what would she tell the ER doc? That no one touched her? She stared into Moira's eyes, so incredibly blue—both dark and bright—that Skye felt entranced.

"All right," she reluctantly agreed. "Then I'll drive you back to your motel."

She planned to argue, Skye could tell from her posture. Then she relented. "Thank you."

ELEVEN

During the fifteen-minute drive from the jail to the motel on the edge of town, Moira didn't speak unless the sheriff asked her a direct question. She was numb from both physical and emotional pain. All she wanted was to return to the Italian sanctuary of St. Michael's and lick her wounds.

But of course she couldn't run away, and not just because the sheriff had kept her passport. The time for running was over. Her mother was here in Santa Louisa, and she had to be stopped. Fiona had done awful things in her life—kidnapping, torture, murder, a seemingly endless spree all done for power. Power begets power—the more control Fiona exercised over dark forces, the more power she craved.

But it wasn't simply the lust for power that drove Fiona and other magicians. It was the thirst for knowledge that could never be satisfied. One taste of the infinite possibilities and the need for more grew, all-consuming, never ending until death. And for Fiona, death was merely an obstacle that could be avoided, within reach was the golden trophy: becoming a demigod.

Moira had to stand in Fiona's way. She accepted that she would die—she deserved to—but Fiona would as well. Pure justice.

Yet if Moira was caught again by surprise, trapped, there was no way she'd survive long enough to stop her mother. She could protect herself if she were free, but locked up—she was a sitting duck. She'd make sure that never happened again)

Skye pulled into the motel parking lot. "Thanks for the lift," Moira said as she reached for the door handle.

"You didn't listen to anything I said."

"I have a headache, it's been a shitty day. I promise, I'm not going anywhere. Besides, you have my passport."

"What did she do to you?" Skye asked.

"You wouldn't believe it. Best thing you can do is stay out of my way."

Skye turned off the ignition and bristled. "I don't like threats."

"I'm trying to save your ass. Fiona won't go after you unless you try to stop her from getting what she wants. She doesn't know what tricks Anthony has up his sleeve, but you can bet she knows you're screwing him and she'll use that against you if she can."

Skye blanched. "I'm not—I mean, it's—"

"Save it."

"I'm not going to let anyone hurt Anthony, or get away with murder."

"You don't understand."

"Shit, I hate it when Anthony says that and I *really* hate it when you say it."

Moira asked, "How'd you and Anthony hook up?"

"You know about what happened at the mission?"

"Santa Louisa de los Padres? Of course. A demon-driven murder-suicide."

"More like drug-induced murder-suicide. The priests

were poisoned. There was one survivor, Anthony's friend Rafe Cooper. Know him?"

Rafe Cooper. Raphael Cooper?

She shrugged, disguising her interest. "Not personally." Of course she'd heard of him. He was from St. Michael's. Moira glanced toward her motel room. No light.

She'd left a light on.

She discreetly looked around the parking lot. Jared. His truck was parked on the far side. Had he found Lily? Moira hoped so . . . and that he'd actually listened to her and brought his girlfriend here.

Moira itched to get inside, but she also didn't know if she could trust the sheriff completely. Yet based on the phone conversation Fiona had while torturing Moira, someone had tipped her off that the sheriff was coming in. Who? A cop?

"So, where's Anthony now?" she asked Skye.

"Researching."

Moira couldn't help but smile. Some things never changed. "I hope he finds something useful. I don't know how much time we have, but Fiona will be working all hours of the day and night to finish what she started."

"And exactly just what *did* she start?"

"You heard Anthony. He told you about the Seven. And—" She hesitated.

"And what?"

"Fiona said something that had me thinking her ritual went wrong. I don't think she has the Seven Deadly Sins under her control. Not yet."

"Then where are they? Still in Hell?"

Moira glanced at Skye, impressed that the cop was thinking like a paranormal investigator. "Possibly. Either there, or out and about, and wreaking havoc in the world."

"Why do you think that?"

"Because she was frustrated about it. Also, if she had them under her control, she wouldn't have time to spend trying to kill me. It's not like she can put them in a cage and walk away. She would need to maintain a demon trap, which is difficult in the short term and nearly impossible in the long term. Either way, she'd need to focus all her psychic magic on the trap, not walking away and playing games with her traitorous daughter."

"And why aren't they still in Hell?"

"They could be, but . . ." But what? "It's just a feeling. And what I saw out there." Moira didn't want to explain her vision standing at the ruins, which would inevitably open the door to more questions that she didn't have the time for. She itched to get inside and talk to Jared.

Skye had more questions, but Moira cut her off with, "I'm really tired. Can I go in?"

"Are you sure you don't want to go to the hospital?"

"I'm fine." She held up the quart of orange juice Skye had bought her at the mini-mart near the jail. "This helped, and with a few hours' sleep I'll be good." She didn't plan on sleeping.

"Don't do anything stupid."

"I'll try to be smart." She put her hand on the door, then asked, "What's going to happen with Abby's body?"

"Why?"

"You absolutely must convince the family to cremate her body."

"It's not my place."

"You don't underst—"

"Stop!" Skye ran a hand through her hastily pinned-back hair. "You and Anthony—I swear, I understand a hell of a lot more than either of you give me credit for. Why, dammit, is her body so important?"

She wanted honesty? "The human remains from a sacrifice are divided up for use in a variety of divinations. Her heart. Her liver. Her ovaries. Her eyes. Her organs have value. They'll cut her up and use her for years. It's sick, but it's very effective. And it traps her soul. She'll wander, restless, divided. Evil spirits are truly dangerous, because they usually can't be destroyed until all their remains are destroyed. As soon as her remains are divided, she'll be nearly unstoppable."

Skye looked ill. "I'm going to get some sleep," Moira said. "Do what you can." She wasn't holding her breath. Moira herself would have to find the body and destroy it. There was no other option. Unless she could convince Anthony to do it. He would understand the dangers.

She started to get out of the truck, but Skye grabbed her arm. "If you're right, they've done this before. So why isn't the world overrun with evil spirits?"

Moira stared at her, a half-smile on her face. "Who says it isn't?"

Skye downed her third cup of foul-tasting sweetened black coffee and still felt fuzzy after two hours' sleep and eight hours of investigation.

She watched the medical examiner, her longtime colleague Dr. Rod Fielding, cut into the body of seventeen-year-old Abigail Weatherby.

She had to admit that she was unnerved by the conversation she'd had with Moira O'Donnell on the way from the jail to the motel. She caught herself biting her thumbnail, and pulled out a pair of latex gloves from the box on Rod's workbench to stop the nervous habit.

Anthony didn't like Moira because he thought she was a witch responsible for the death of one of his "brothers"—the boys he'd grown up with at the orphanage. She supposed it wasn't *technically* an orphanage— Anthony had never referred to St. Michael's as such—but Skye didn't know how else to think about it. None of the boys there had parents, and they'd all taken the last name of one of the priests or monks in residence.

Odd, but Skye had never contemplated Anthony's unusual upbringing largely because he didn't hide anything. Still, she couldn't stop thinking about how many kids were abandoned by their mothers at a monastery to be raised as warriors for God. The entire *idea* sounded suspect to her analytical cop mind.

Yet her mother had left when she was fourteen, walked out with a man who made lots of promises, then killed her. Abandonment wasn't foreign to Skye, either.

And she loved Anthony. She accepted what he said as truth, even though it was unusual.

Then Moira O'Donnell showed up, and Skye saw a side of Anthony she'd only glimpsed briefly during the few months she'd known him. Anger and hostility. Had he and Moira been involved? She tried to brush it off as cop instincts, not feminine insecurities, but it wasn't working.

Rod was unusually quiet as he performed the autopsy, but he was generally more reticent when working on young people. Focused, deliberate, with none of the banter Skye was used to. It made the autopsy that much more uncomfortable. If it was a drunk or a sixty-year-old heart attack victim or even a gang shooting, Rod would joke to relieve the tension. But Abby was seventeen; she'd had her whole future ahead. Everything . . .

Skye had come to the autopsy after telling Abby's parents of her death. They had been sitting at the kitchen table drinking coffee, both of them believing that Abby was still sleeping in her bed. It was the hardest damn thing she'd ever done. She knew Hiram Weatherby, and she also knew that Hiram would be on her ass day and night until she solved the crime.

He was, after all, the mayor, and the council member who'd led the charge to appoint her sheriff.

She said to Rod, "You're killing me here. It's been thirty minutes." All he'd spoken were clipped orders to his young assistant.

"I have nothing," he snapped. "Nothing."

"Nothing . . . what the hell does that mean?"

"Heart—perfect. Lungs—strong. No sign of cancer, heart attack, internal bleeding, physical signs of OD—I sent the labs over as a rush, and Monica just walked over tissue samples from every major organ, as well as skin and hair samples. I have a second set being worked up to send to the state lab for additional testing, beyond our capabilities. But sudden, violent overdoses would normally show *something* somewhere. Needle pricks in her arm? No. Bloody nose? Nope. No signs of sores or burns in her mouth. Hell, she probably has never even smoked a cigarette; her lungs are in great condition. Her stomach contents are next to nothing, some liquid—probably tea—no solids. Sent that over too."

"There was an odd smell at the scene when we

arrived—maybe she was poisoned through the air, breathed it in."

"No sign of violence to her nasal cavities or throat or lungs. It's like her heart just . . . stopped for no damn reason."

Skye wanted something scientific to hold on to, but Rod wasn't giving her anything.

He continued. "I saw the destruction on the cliffs, Skye. There had to have been more than one person on scene before or during her death. We didn't find her clothing or her car, and she couldn't have walked there without shoes—her feet are dirty, but no cuts or bruising. Someone had to have brought her out; someone had to have taken her clothing. Why? She should be alive. She's perfect in every way."

"This morning her father said she'd recently lost a lot of weight, that she'd been exercising."

"How recent? Sudden weight loss, or over time?"

"He said she started losing at the beginning of the school year. Lost twenty pounds or so, according to her mother."

"Twenty pounds in five months? Not common, but certainly possible." He inspected her body. "Yeah, I see the loose skin here . . . here. But if she was popping pills, I'll know when I get the bloodwork back. I'm running everything I can think of."

"Sexual abuse?"

"No sign of recent or habitual abuse. No signs of forced entry or violence or bruising in the vaginal area."

He handed her a Polaroid photograph. "Here's a copy of her tattoo."

Skye stared at the photo. The colorful tattoo was eerily beautiful, a circle with crisscrossing curvy lines that narrowed in the center. It was the same image upside down. "What is it?" she asked.

"I don't know, but it's a bit unusual. I thought you might need it, show it to the parents. Maybe one of her friends knows something about it."

She stuffed it into her notebook. "Lots of girls these days get tattoos."

"I've seen. Usually when they're dead. And one more thing."

Rod turned Abby on her side and touched the small of her back. "I didn't notice this at the site, but she has a faint birthmark here."

The pale strawberry stain looked like a sun, with a filled, near-perfect circle in the middle of faint lines reminiscent of varicose veins, except they were red. Almost as if smeared, the birthmark spread around her to her side, ending in a crescent.

"A lot of people have birthmarks. What's unusual about it?"

"It seems too perfect for a natural mark. I'm wondering if it's scarring left over from a previous tattoo. But she's underage, she'd need parental permission to both get and remove a tattoo."

Skye shook her head. "In California, but it's pretty easy to go to Nevada and get a tat, and there are plenty of people here who'll do it for the right price. Did it contribute to her death?"

"Doubtful, but since I don't know what killed her, I'm not going to discount anything. I took a skin graft and should have some answers."

"Are you thinking maybe an infection from a bad needle?"

"Again, doubtful—her white blood cell count is normal. She's a little on the anemic side, but not danger-ously low. But hell, Skye, I'm willing to look at every cell in her body if it'll tell me what happened to her."

Her phone vibrated. Normally she wouldn't answer it during an autopsy, but it was the hospital calling. "Sheriff McPherson."

"Sheriff, this is Doctor Bertrand at Santa Louisa Gen-eral. I need to report a missing person."

"Doctor, I'm in the middle of—"

"You're the contact. It's my coma patient, in the hos-pice wing. Raphael Cooper."

Skye straightened. Rafe Cooper was missing? "What happened? When?"

"I don't exactly know—he apparently walked out just after midnight."

"Walked out?"

"I've already ordered a copy of the security tapes for you, but I saw it myself. He walked out of the hospital. Extremely odd."

Odd? That wasn't the word Skye would use.

Especially since he'd apparently gone missing two hours before Abby Weatherby died. He'd also been the prime suspect in the slaughter of twelve priests, until Anthony Zaccardi convinced her that a demon was re-sponsible.

Maybe Raphael Cooper wasn't as innocent as An-thony made him out to be.

"I'm on my way."

TWELVE

Moira listened to Lily's account of what happened on the cliffs. According to her, Fiona's coven had killed Abby, though she didn't know exactly how. *Something* had come out of the ground around Abby's body, but she couldn't say what.

At least a dozen people had been involved, many from Santa Louisa. Lily hadn't seen the faces of everyone in the circle, but she recognized some.

Moira realized the absolute worst had happened. Not only had the Seven been freed, but no one had control over them. Neither Fiona nor anyone else. They were on the loose, and anything could happen.

"My pastor was there," Lily said. "Pastor Garrett. Why?"

"Why did you go to the cliffs in the first place?" Moira demanded to know. "What were you thinking?" She breathed deeply, and her chest ached from the earlier attack.

"I—" Lily glanced at Jared.

"Don't look at him," Moira snapped. She was too tired and sore to coddle the teenager. She swallowed three aspirin and chased them with lukewarm water. "You went to the cliffs when I told you to stay the hell away from Abby. I told you she was up to something.

You were supposed to tell me when the coven was meeting!"

Lily blinked back tears and Jared jumped to her defense. "Don't yell at her! She just saw her best friend die—her cousin she's known her entire life—and saw things no one's seen before."

Moira held back an outpouring of *truths* these kids needed to hear before it was too late; she wasn't in the right frame of mind. Instead, she bit her tongue.

Lily said quietly, "I thought I could help Abby. I thought that's what she wanted, but didn't know how to ask. But when I got there—she—she—" Lily stuttered, not knowing how to describe it.

"Abby wanted to be there," Moira said evenly.

"Yes."

"You said they called you the *arca*. Is that right?"

She nodded, accepting with a smile the water Jared offered her. "I don't know what it meant, but they painted these symbols on me—"

"Symbols? Show me."

"I showered. I felt so disgusting, dirty—I can't."

Moira wanted to throttle her, but asked calmly, "Can you draw them for me?"

"Maybe." She bit her lip, obviously not knowing what was written on her.

"I remember one or two of them," Jared said.

Moira tossed him a notepad and pencil.

"Did you voluntarily cross into the circle?" she asked Lily.

"I don't understand."

"Did they drag you kicking and screaming to their altar, or did you walk into the circle of your own free will?"

"I—walked in, but I was worried—"

"What does that matter?" Jared interrupted.

Moira didn't want to go into the nuances of human sacrifices and dark magic. She recited the CliffsNotes version. "Human beings have free will. We make our own decisions. Many rituals—especially the ancient rites—require a conscious choice."

"I just wanted to help Abby. I didn't know—"

"I told you!" Moira pressed her thumb in the center of her forehead. She'd warned her, she'd warned Jared— and she didn't pull any punches. Maybe they hadn't truly believed her because she was *too* blunt.

Moira needed a good twelve hours of sleep but doubted she'd get ten minutes before dark. She pulled the makeshift compress from her lower back, squeezed out the water from the melted ice, and added fresh ice. Her entire body ached; she needed an icy bath to numb the pain and stop the swelling. She put the compress on the back of her head now that her back was so cold she could barely feel the bruising.

"Something went wrong with the ritual and you ran away," Moira prompted, wanting to get to the end of Lily's story and figure out what to do with her while she called around to friends and "frenemies" to find out what *arca* meant. It was a container of some sort, but what could Lily have that was valuable to Fiona? "You're certain you saw demons? What did they look like?"

"Dark. Smoke, but thicker, and they had shapes— faces, tails, not like us. They changed, looked more like animals—monsters—than people. But they looked human, too." She choked back a sob and Jared sat next to her on the edge of the bed. He took her hand.

"It's okay," he murmured.

"I didn't want to look, I closed my eyes, but then the stranger told me to run or I would die."

Moira's head snapped up. "Stranger? What stranger? Someone from the coven?"

"No—he came right after Abby died. Just walked up and started saying these things—I didn't understand him. It was a foreign language, really weird, and then he looked at me, told me to run or I would die. I ran. Then there were the most inhuman screams I've ever heard and I glanced back and the sky was like on fire, with lightning, thunder, screams, all there around the circle, and then they were gone like the fluttering of thousands, hundreds of thousands, of birds. I thought he was behind me, and I was scared of him, but he'd saved my life. I thought he might be an angel, but he wasn't. He was running, but then he wasn't behind me and I was alone."

"Describe the stranger," Moira said, then added, "please."

"He was wearing green hospital scrubs—you know, like what surgeons wear, or orderlies. He looked sick— pale. Dark hair. Black or dark brown. His eyes—I don't know, they were . . . honest. Very—I can't explain it, but when he told me to run, I ran. I trusted him. He stopped them, stopped them from killing me. But he was too late for Abby." She was crying now, and Jared pulled her to his chest, rocking her.

Moira pulled out her iPhone and brought up the Santa Louisa newspaper. Her conversation with Father Philip had been running through her head, and then what Fiona had said in the jail—she knew something that they didn't know, and Moira thought she'd figured out exactly what it was.

She retrieved articles about Santa Louisa de los Padres Mission. Skimmed them. Anthony Zaccardi, historical architect rebuilding . . . the fire . . . the murders . . .

Jared said, "What are you doing?"

"I have an idea about who that man was, I'm trying to find a picture."

Moira touched article after article on the small screen until she found what she was looking for.

Raphael Cooper, psychologist and seminarian from St. John's in Menlo Park, was assigned by the Vatican to Santa Louisa de los Padres Mission four months prior to the murders. A spokesman for the Vatican, Samuel Cardinal Benvenuti, declined to comment, releasing a written statement that briefly said, "The prayers of the Holy See are with the victims of this unconscionable attack, and with Mr. Cooper for a full recovery." A spokesman from St. John's Seminary said only that Cooper was abandoned by his parents as a young child and raised in an orphanage. He became a naturalized American citizen when he arrived in California twelve years ago.

An orphan? Friends with Anthony? He was one of them, Moira was certain—like Peter and Anthony and Rico and others, left on the doorstep of St. Michael's.

A photo—tagged as from St. John's Seminary five years earlier—showed Raphael Cooper in his late twenties. His dark hair was short and conservative; his eyes at first glance looked black, but Moira realized they were dark blue. He was handsome, broad-shouldered, with a strong, square jaw. On his neck was an inch-long scar. Pure Irish oozed from every pore. How had an Irish baby ended up at St. Michael's? Moira knew not all of the infants left were Italian, but most of them were.

She skimmed the article. Cooper was thirty-two. Peter would have been thirty-two had he lived. Cooper hadn't been at St. Michael's during the time Moira lived there, but Peter must have known him.

"Is this the man?" She showed Lily the picture.

Lily nodded. "Yes—but his hair is longer and he's lost weight. He has that scar, right there, on his neck."

"And he just told you to run and he stayed behind?"

"I thought he followed me, but then there was an earthquake, and the screams—nothing I've heard before."

"Fuck!"

Lily jumped at Moira's language and Moira bit back the stream of profanity she wanted to spew. She'd bet her life that the screams were the demons' call. When two or more demons were together, fighting being controlled by the witches who summoned them, they screamed a cackle unheard by most people.

"Did it sound like laughter?"

"No—well, maybe. Sick laughter. Like they were crazy."

"They're demons."

Lily was shaking and Jared held her close, glaring at Moira. "I thought you could help. All you're doing is hurting her."

"No," Lily said quietly. "She *is* helping."

Lily stared at Moira with wide eyes. "They called me the *arca,* Abby the *key.* She never wanted to die. She wanted to live forever. She wanted—"

"Live forever?" Moira asked. "Damn, damn, damn!"

"What—" Jared began.

Moira cut him off. "Stay here. Do not call anyone. Do not leave this room. I have a stash of food and water. When I leave, seal the door with salt." She tossed a bag of special salts at Jared; he caught it. "I don't care who it is, do not let anyone in no matter what they say."

She stuffed equipment in her backpack. Salt. Her backup knife—the sheriff hadn't returned hers because it was a weapon—her cross, and holy water, and she pulled on her leather jacket.

"Where are you going?"

"Not to sleep," she mumbled. "I have to find Rafe Cooper."

"Not alone," Jared said.

"Of course alone," she snapped. "Lily has to be protected, and you'd damn well better do a better job of it this time. Lily, you said your minister was there. One of them."

"Yes."

"What's his name?"

"Garrett Pennington. From Good Shepherd Church."

"Catholic?" Moira wouldn't be surprised. The best— and the worst—in this battle were in the Church.

She shook her head. "Just, you know, regular Christian."

"When did Pennington open his church?"

"He took over for Pastor Matthew at the end of the summer. His mother got very sick and he wanted to be with her. I miss him—I really liked him, though my mom didn't. She adores Pastor Garrett, and I liked him too, until . . . "

"He's no man of God." Moira didn't know if there were any left, but she didn't say that. "What about your parents?"

"It's just my mom. She thinks Pas—um, Mr. Pennington walks on water. Sunday services went from less than fifty of us to over three hundred. He's a great speaker."

If Ms. Ellis had been sucked in by the witch, then Moira couldn't let Lily go home. She could very well be turned over to them, and Ms. Ellis wouldn't even realize what she was doing to her daughter.

"Jared, I don't know why they wanted Lily, but she's important to them, which means she's in danger. You can't let her out of your sight. I have my phone. Call me, text me, do anything—but if she's in trouble? Get me the message."

She reached behind the dresser and pulled out the little .22-caliber Beretta she'd hidden earlier. Some things protected you against demons, but when facing human evil, nothing worked as well as a bullet through the head.

"We should come with you," Lily said.

"No. Can I borrow your truck?"

Jared tossed her his keys.

"Thanks. Use the salt. Don't open the door."

She looked from Jared to the teenage girl holding his hand as they sat on the edge of the bed. They both looked so innocent . . . young . . . trusting.

They trusted her. They believed she knew what she was doing, that she could protect them.

Doubt and fear battled her need to be proactive. She couldn't be trusted because she didn't know what the hell she was doing; and as far as protecting them? She couldn't even protect herself.

She gave them a half-smile. "If anything happens out of the ordinary—and for some reason you can't reach me—call Anthony Zaccardi."

Jared looked at her quizzically. "The guy rebuilding the mission? Why?"

"He's your best shot at staying alive."

There was a knock on the door and Moira, right on the other side, jumped and put her hand to her mouth, the other hand on her gun. She motioned for Jared and Lily to stay quiet. She was about to look through the peephole when there was another loud rap.

"Jared, it's your father. I know you're in there; open the door."

Moira shook her head and mouthed *no*.

Jared looked stricken.

"Jared, dammit! Open the door or I'll break it open and arrest you for leaving the scene of a crime after the fact, statutory rape, and anything else I can think of."

This was Jared's father? Moira was inclined to let him break down the door. She felt like shit after the beating Fiona gave her, but she knew some tricks—tricks that had nothing to do with magic—and she didn't like Hank Santos. She wouldn't mind practicing on him.

Except he was a cop, and the last thing she wanted was to be trapped in a jail cell again. Next time, Fiona wouldn't let her survive.

Jared was torn, but Moira saw in his expression that Deputy Santos would break down the door if she didn't open it.

Fuck fuck fuck.

She stared at the ceiling for a brief moment. She rarely prayed, but she muttered under her breath, "God, this is *so* not funny."

She hid her Beretta and opened the door.

Deputy Hank Santos was several inches shorter than his tall, lanky son, darker in skin tone, with broad shoulders and a stance that radiated authority. His dark eyes assessed both her and the room quickly, then focused on Jared—who stood behind her—then on Lily, sitting on the bed. Finally, they turned back to Moira where she saw extreme dislike—some might call it hatred—in his expression.

Fine with her; she didn't like Hank Santos either, not one little bit.

"Jared, Lily, come with me."

"Dad," Jared began.

Hank interrupted. "You've greatly embarrassed me. I had a call from another deputy that your truck was here, at this sleazy motel. The manager said you've been here a lot lately." He stared at Moira, looking her up and down in such a vile way that she knew exactly what he was thinking.

"Don't make any assumptions," she said, pissed off.

He diverted his eyes in disgust. "I know women like you."

"You're out of line, Dad." Jared stepped forward. Moira glanced over at the young man. She saw strength of character she hadn't seen in him before, protectiveness and chivalry. She didn't know why she was surprised, but then realized she hadn't really considered Jared—or Lily—as *people* as much as *problems*.

"You have a lot of explaining to do, Jared. I'm disappointed in you. Screwing around with women is one thing, you're eighteen—but dragging your girlfriend into it, sleeping around, lying, sneaking out of the house—I don't know what's gotten into you, but your mother is turning over in her grave."

The anger and intense pain in Jared's face had Moira reeling. He had far more depth than she'd given him credit for.

"Don't drag Mom into this."

"You wouldn't be behaving like an asshole if she were alive."

"Mr. Santos," Lily began, but the man ignored her.

Jared reddened and didn't back down. "This is about *you*. You bully your way in here, insulting me, my girlfriend, my friend, jumping to conclusions because you have this warped idea that I've gone wild since Mom died. This is more about *you* than it is about *me*. You feel guilty because you're dating again—"

"Do not change the subject and drag Nicole into this," Santos said. "This is between you and me."

"You've dragged *my* girlfriend into it!"

Santos looked pointedly around the motel room. Moira resisted the urge to wince. It was the type of flea-bag motel that looked the other way when hookers rented a room.

"And look where I found you."

"Don't change the subject. Mom died of *cancer*. She was dying for *years* and I hated every minute because I didn't want to lose her, but I've accepted it. I hated it, but accepted it. And I am the man I am today because she told me to stand strong. I'm not wild, I'm not lying. The least you could do is listen to me!"

"Listen? You snuck out of the house—"

"I'm eighteen."

"You're still living under my roof and I demand you respect my authority."

"You wouldn't understand—"

"I didn't know where you were last night! It turns out you were at the scene of a crime, left your friend dead! What if you could have saved her?"

Lily was on the verge of tears as Jared said, "Abby was already dead when Moira and I arrived, and Lily was in trouble."

"And you didn't call the police? Or take Lily to the hospital? The police station?" He stepped over the threshold and Moira twitched. Something had her instincts humming. A demon? Yet he'd crossed the salt line without hesitating or reacting even a bit. He didn't even notice it. She took a step back, staying farther than arm's length away from the cop. This situation felt . . . odd. Over the top. Maybe it was because he seemed so incredibly stubborn, but Moira was used to stubborn. It was more than his attitude. She watched him carefully, trying to keep her hands from shaking.

She'd never exorcised a demon by herself before. She'd never protected anyone from a demon. And exorcisms were safest under controlled circumstances, with a spirit trap to protect the exorcist and the victim. Here, without a safety net, she'd have to stab the victim with her knife—a very specific, very special knife—and hope she didn't hit a major artery, hope she didn't kill the innocent along with vanquishing the demon.

And even then, there were other concerns . . . such as whether the demon was strong enough after the ritual to possess someone *else*. Or strong enough to take its own shape and form.

"Dad," Jared said, "Lily just needed a little time before all the 'rents started in on her. I was going to bring her home and then talk to Sheriff McPherson. I promise, just give me an hour."

"You missed classes this morning, contributed to Lily's delinquency. I'm taking Lily home—her mother is frantic—and then you and I will sit down with Sheriff McPherson."

Moira couldn't allow Lily to be alone. Fiona wanted her for a reason. "They can stay here," Moira offered. "I don't mind."

Deputy Santos looked at her as if she were trash. Moira straightened her spine, but she couldn't help but feel inferior and defensive under his intense disapproval. "Ms. O'Donnell, you've caused enough trouble."

"I haven't done anything!"

"You have Jared lying to me. You got him involved in God knows what—sex games? Drugs? I don't know, but Abigail Weatherby is dead and both you and my son were there."

Lily spoke, her big brown eyes wide. "Mr. Santos, I was there when Abby died. Jared came later, trying to find me. He had nothing to do with it. It was an awful accident, and—"

"Lily—" Moira interrupted.

"Stay out of it or I'll take you down to the station," Santos said.

"I'll take Lily home," Moira said, grasping at straws. Someone had to keep an eye out for her.

"Dad—"

"Enough!" Santos's face was getting red. "Jared, Lily, come now or I'll put you both under arrest."

"You can't—"

Santos stepped toward Moira. "Don't talk. Not a

word. I heard that something bizarre happened at the station this morning, and it involved *you*. You have unduly influenced these kids; you are trouble. I don't know what your game is, but it's over as far as my son is concerned. One word and you'll be back in jail in fifteen minutes."

"It's okay, Moira," Jared said. "I'll take care of Lily." He took his girlfriend's hand.

It wasn't okay, but Moira didn't know what else to do. She couldn't go back to jail, and if she tried to stop the cop, she had no doubt that he'd arrest her. Either way, Lily would still be home, alone and unprotected. Worse, Santos would find her gun and her knives, and take them. She'd be defenseless again. She couldn't face Fiona empty-handed—no weapons, no open space, no magic.

Moira had no choice but to let them go.

"Now," Hank said. He stepped through the door and looked up into the gray, overcast sky. The day looked as dreary as Moira's mood.

Jared picked Lily up off the bed.

"I'm sure she can walk," Hank said.

"Her feet are cut from running," Jared said quietly. Moira glanced over; Lily wasn't wearing any shoes, but had on a pair of Moira's socks pulled up high. Blood had seeped through the bottom.

"Be careful," Moira whispered as Jared passed by her. "Call me if anything happens."

Jared whispered, "Take my truck." He nodded toward the keys still in her hand.

Hank glanced over his shoulder, but Moira had already pocketed the keys. "Jared!" Hank barked.

Moira stared at the back of Hank's neck. His hair was

cut short, a little longer than a buzzcut, and it looked like there was dried blood right above his collar. She almost said something, then he shifted as she realized it wasn't blood but a birthmark, a port wine stain that was centered at the base of his skull and went beneath his collar.

She was tired. Exhausted, more like it, seeing things. But she had no time to rest now. Finding Raphael Cooper was number one on her list, then destroying Abby Weatherby's corpse before Fiona got her hands on it or summoned Abby's vengeful spirit. She'd have to call Anthony, urge him to find a way to keep an eye on Lily. Surely he could do *something*, considering he was sleeping with the top cop in town.

Moira waited until Hank had driven off with Jared and Lily. Then she slipped out and drove Jared's truck in the opposite direction, toward the cliffs, hoping she could retrace Cooper's steps and find him before Fiona did.

Rafe didn't know how long he'd been asleep, or unconscious. As his eyes slowly opened, he saw shades of light in the dark shadows of the abandoned cabin.

He was huddled in the corner of the filthy, foul-smelling room, shaking, cold and hungry, unable to move. He tried to stretch his quivering limbs, told himself he had to do it, but his body did not respond, paralyzed. He'd never felt so completely drained that he had no will to do anything. He would certainly die here, for even the thought that he *would* die if he didn't leave gave him no strength to stand, or even crawl.

He'd expended every ounce of his energy in saving the girl and escaping the witches and demons.

The wind howled around the cabin, the boarded-up windows providing a break from the damp salt air.

Rafe had no idea how he'd found this cabin when he fled the chaos he'd caused.

Intellectually, he'd known that it wasn't his fault that the demons had been released. He hadn't started the deadly ritual; he would never have even flirted with the dark arts or any form of magic. It was antithetical to everything St. Michael's Order stood for. He was one of the chosen few who was charged with stopping the spread of witchcraft, of sealing breaches between this world and the underworld. Even within St. Michael's, he'd had talent—special gifts in their fight against evil.

Yet he'd had no part in any of the battles of late. He'd been most recently at St. John's, hoping to become a priest but unable to say his vows. His mentor told him he should look deeper, try to better discern his calling. He'd thought helping the tortured priests at Santa Louisa de los Padres Mission was the answer.

He was wrong.

In his heart, he feared that somehow, he was just as culpable as the coven for what happened last night. When he stopped the demons from possessing the girl's body, the *arca*, he'd known exactly what he was doing. Now? He tried to remember, tried to find the words, or at least understand their meaning, and nothing. Nothing but pain, in his head, in his heart, in every muscle of his body.

And now the demons were on earth, free. He had to find them, stop them. Demons could only be sent back to Hell; they couldn't be killed.

Yes they can.

He frowned, trying to chase the words in his mind, to

find the solution to the problem. If demons could be killed, how?

A sharp pain shot through his ear and his hands grabbed his head. *Make the ringing stop!* His stomach retched, but there was nothing inside, nothing to throw up, and he dry heaved until his gut ached.

He closed his eyes.

God, help me.

He slipped into sleep, or unconsciousness, or death . . . but the dead didn't dream or remember, did they?

THIRTEEN

Skye watched the security tape twice without comment.

Rafe Cooper had been recorded four different times on three different cameras. The first was outside the elevator bank closest to his room—he'd shuffled by, wearing a hospital gown and appearing disoriented, confused, and in pain. A few minutes later he was seen entering the staff lounge at the opposite end of the floor. He seemed steadier, as if walking had given him strength, but he was still slow.

When he emerged—a good fifteen minutes later and in hospital scrubs he'd stolen from an employee locker—he still looked pale but walked with purpose, slow and steady. He was neither looking at the camera nor trying to avoid detection.

The last camera that caught him was mounted just outside the emergency room doors. He walked right out of the hospital.

"How does someone usually wake up from a coma?" Skye asked Cooper's doctor, Richard Bertrand.

"There's no typical way. I've seen a coma patient wake up after eight days with no side effects, ready to walk out the door. Mr. Cooper has received daily physical therapy and quality care, but his muscles would still have atrophied some after ten weeks, and he'd be too

weak to walk. It normally takes weeks to fully recuper-
ate. But Mr. Cooper's unconsciousness—while technically a coma—was uncommon in itself. As I explained
to you when he first came to me in November, he had no
head trauma. No tumor, no aneurysm, no brain damage.
His brain waves showed signs of REM sleep, but little
activity during his so-called waking periods. It's an atyp-
ical case, and while not the only such documented case,
certainly rare."

Skye was ticked off and worried. Where did this put
her investigation? She had to talk to Cooper; he was still
technically a material witness to the murders at the mission. She couldn't very well put in her police report that
a demon had been involved.

District Attorney Martin Truxel was going to be the
biggest problem. The D.A. had made it clear that
Cooper was *his* suspect, and when she reminded him
that he was a prosecutor, not a cop, he told her flat out
that she'd fucked up the entire case and it would cost her
the election.

The D.A. had made it no secret that he was support-
ing Assistant Sheriff Thomas Williams, who'd recently
filed to run against Skye for Sheriff. The election was
five months away, and right now it was between Skye
and Williams. With Cooper waking up—and walking
out of the hospital—the murders at the mission would
once again take front and center in the local media. The
Santa Louisa Courier covered a small territory, but the
four-person staff was dogged. Everyone in town read the
paper daily, commented on the popular *Courier* website,
and believed what was printed. If *The Courier* wrote it,
it had to be true.

And on top of all that, she had daily messages on her desk from a Los Angeles crime reporter who was writing a damn *book* about the mission and the murders. It was enough to make Skye throw her hands up and take a full-page ad out in the *Courier* telling everyone *exactly* what happened—demonic possession and all.

Then Williams would win the election; her best friend, Detective Juan Martinez, would be either in prison or a mental hospital; and she'd probably be sued for wrongful death by the family of the deputy who had died on the cliffs, not to mention prosecuted for gross negligence. Because no one would believe that a demon—let alone witchcraft!—had been involved in the murders at the mission or the fire on the cliffs two nights later.

"No one saw him?" she asked Dr. Bertrand, incredulous that a formerly comatose patient could walk out of the hospital without *anyone* trying to stop him.

"A nurse checked his vitals at eleven p.m. before the shift change. At one a.m. the new shift was in, and the nurse who did rounds assumed he'd been taken for tests or moved, because his chart was missing. We've moved him a couple of times. And while tests aren't common at night, because of tight budgets I run some of the scans then, when there is less demand on the equipment. I had been running REM tests on Mr. Cooper, trying to figure out what was causing the coma. The only answer is psychosomatic. He'd experienced a major trauma. His brain just shut down."

Skye spoke to the nurse who'd found Cooper's bed empty, the nurse who last checked his vitals, and everyone still in the building who'd been on duty between 12:07 and 12:29 a.m. while he'd been moving around the hospital before walking out of the building. No one remembered seeing him.

She finally said, "If he shows up back here at the hospital, call me." She wrote her cell phone number on the back of her card and handed it to Dr. Bertand. "I'll put an APB on Cooper, and anyone who finds him will be instructed to bring him back here for medical evaluation, under guard, until I know what's going on. You good with that?"

"Of course," Dr. Bertrand said.

She glanced at her watch. "Damn, I'm late."

She'd spoken on the phone to the high school principal earlier this morning about the death of Abby Weatherby, and had asked to address the entire school in an assembly before lunch. Someone there knew something, and dammit, she wanted to find out what had *really* happened out on the cliffs—supernatural or not.

Anthony didn't scare easily but when he'd learned more about the ritual that brought the Seven Deadly Sins forth, he was terrified for humanity.

At his desk in one of the two rooms left standing at the mission, poring over ancient texts and other research materials, he paused and contemplated the worst that could happen. It was a situation as dire as it could be.

Dr. Franz Lieber, a wheelchair-bound ninety-year-old theologian from Switzerland whom Anthony had met many years ago, had sent St. Michael's a copy of all his notes. As far as Anthony knew, he had the only copy in his possession, the original still with Lieber, who was more reclusive than anyone Anthony had ever met.

Lieber doubted whether the *Conoscenza* still existed,

but he had written at the beginning of his notes on the book:

There is very little information or rumor about the Conoscenza. The book itself is unnamed, given "Conoscenza" circa 1520 by Bishop Paulo Giovanni of St. Michael's Order. Prior to then, it had been called both "The Book of Knowledge" and "The Book of Death," depending on whether the speaker was a magician or one of the righteous.

The Conoscenza was most likely destroyed in a deadly ritual in 1698 in France, where there was a powerful coven led by High Priestess Tara Rafferty and her common-law husband, Detrich Ehrenbach. Neither Rafferty, Ehrenbach, their coven membership, nor the six priests and demon hunters from St. Michael's Order survived. Everything in the immediate area was destroyed—obliterated. To this day, some believe that those grounds are either haunted or cursed. No one lives on the desecrated site, all attempts to do so end in violence.

Though Lieber didn't believe that the Conoscenza still existed, he knew a lot about what was within its evil covers. It was a grimoire—a book of spells. These dark spells were specifically aimed at conjuring spirits, summoning demons, and controlling both.

The origin of the book was in dispute. Some scholars felt it had been compiled over time with contributions from multiple generations of magicians, the spells evolving and gaining strength. Others believed that it had been written many thousands of years ago during the time of Moses in an ancient language that could not be understood without demonic guidance. And still others, including Father Philip, believed that the book had been written in demon blood only a few generations after the fall of man, in the language of the fallen angels, unreadable to all except the few who had been chosen by Satan himself.

But it was certain, at least during Anthony's five hours of intensive research, that the *Conoscenza* contained the ritual to unleash the Seven Deadly Sins into the world.

And he'd yet to find any theorizing on how to send them back. Lieber opined:

> The one certainty we know, should the Seven be freed, is that, according to the legends, they will disperse, spread themselves far apart. Logic dictates that they would be stronger together, but in truth they gain their strength from psychic unions with humans. They cannot compete for the same person, for the victim would die without fueling the demon. This seems to be the antithesis of all we know and understand of the adage of strength in numbers, but for the Seven they are equals and cannot share the same space without devastating results for them and humans. They seek the weak and are lured by sin. Sin makes them stronger. Lust finds lust; greed finds greed. The longer they are free, the more powerful they become.
>
> The Seven are not demons who can be exorcised using traditional ritual exorcisms, because they do not need to possess a body to survive. They are spirits. They laugh in the face of the Faithful and do not obey orders of those who summon them. They are the Tricksters of Hell, Fallen Angels, among the highest

order of angels who plummeted during the Great Battle. Woe to the world who sees the Seven on earth.

Anthony learned two important things.

The first was why Fiona's ritual had taken place at the ruins on the cliffs. In a handwritten diary of an Olivet graduate nearly three hundred years ago, shortly after the book was thought destroyed, he read:

> *Any place where the blood of the righteous is spilled in the battle of good and evil, heaven and hell, and where also a human being is sacrificed, weakens the protective barrier between earth and the netherworld. At such a place, with the proper ritual, training, desire, and power, a fearless magician can open a gate for demons to pass through. Some magicians believe that they can move freely between the demonic world and our own, a deadly proposition. Many things must align for all the elements to be in place for such a gate, and there are only a few known gateways over the last millennium, all of which have been sealed and consecrated. But there will be more. Magicians will continue to create these openings when possible, and the greater in number, the weaker the entire threshold. Some believe that a great battle on earth will ensue, spilling the blood of the righteous and leading to murder and desecration. The battle will weaken the barrier between earth and Hell until the End Times, allowing free movement of demons through the membrane. Chaos will reign. This will, some believe, be the signal of the Second Coming.*
>
> *Some will wait and watch and not impede the successes of magicians.*

Some, including this scholar, believe such a strategy sets up many for eternal death through inaction.

Though none of the scholars Anthony read had specific knowledge of how the ritual worked, they all were in agreement that to summon the Seven at one time there was the need for not only a powerful magician, but two sacrifices: a vessel and an *arca*.

The vessel, also called a "key" by Lieber, was a magician who used her powers combined with the others in the coven to draw out the Seven from Hell. Her death was a sacrifice necessary to bring them forth, as no one could survive such a violent spiritual assault. Her soul in exchange, according to Lieber, would have strength in the afterlife, which could be used by the coven as tenuous control over the Seven—in theory.

Was Abby Weatherby the key? The means to draw out the Seven? It would appear so, but Anthony didn't know enough about what powers she may have had. Everything he knew and understood about the afterlife put souls in two places: purgatory en route to Heaven. or firmly in Hell. There were hierarchies of angels and hierarchies of demons, but human souls with power in Hell? He had never heard such a thing, and it greatly disturbed him.

If Abby was the *key*, that meant there had to be an *arca*.

The girl Moira spoke of, Lily. The teenager who went to the cliffs to save her cousin, Abby.

Anthony was poring over everything he could find about what the *arca* was—if in fact it was a person and not a thing—and how it was used. There were far fewer specifics about the *arca* than the *key*, but based on subtext he determined that the *arca* was a human 'container' that trapped the Seven.

> The arca must have been consecrated for the purpose. Arcas, like other warriors for the underworld, are conceived during rituals. Some believe such individuals, whether they know of their purpose or not, must be sacrificed by the just or the end result will be devastating for many, many innocent souls. Others believe such individuals can be saved. But as I live and breathe today, it remains the truth that none have been saved; once told of their position and potential for power, they grow in darkness. The allure of evil is great, and the lies of demons many.

Moira O'Donnell.
Anthony slowly shut the heavy book.
None have been saved.
Father Philip must have known the truth about Moira before Peter died. Moira had sought him out; they all knew she was a witch.
Such individuals . . . must be sacrificed by the just . . .
Anthony couldn't kill Moira without cause. He wasn't a cold-blooded murderer, and one opinion in an old book didn't provide adequate justification. There had to be another answer. He would find it. Not to save Moira, but to save them all.

He frowned, staring at the stacks of faded books and papers spread across his desk at the mission. He knew enough of Moira's past, how her mother had conceived her to serve as a liaison between the covens and the underworld, but what of the *arca* last night on the cliffs? If Lily Ellis was the *arca*, she was one of the unsaved.

He refused to believe it. God didn't work that way. Everyone could be saved.

None have been saved.

That didn't mean they *couldn't* be. He opened an old, thin tome about demon traps. The Seven were not traditional demons, and Anthony needed to better understand all types of spirit traps.

His phone vibrated and he grabbed it, startled. It was Skye.

"Working?" she asked.

"Yes."

"You have answers?"

"I'm getting there. It'll take a little more time."

She didn't say anything.

"Skye? Are you there?"

"Rafe Cooper left the hospital last night. Walked out, just after midnight. No one has seen him since."

Anthony rose from his chair. "You're certain he left on his own? After ten weeks in a coma?"

"I saw him leave on the security tape. He's gone. I put an APB out on him, and need to get him back in the hospital for tests, and I have to talk to him about the mission murders. He's our only living witness."

Anthony didn't have to read between the lines. "And your only suspect."

"I believe you," she said to the question he did not ask.

"It does not sound that way."

"Dammit, Anthony, I know that not everything in this world can be explained with scientific logic. But I'm also the sheriff and I need to follow through on the investigation. Rafe's disappearing act isn't going to help his cause."

"I will look for him," Anthony told Skye.

"I still need to talk to him," Skye said warily.

"Of course."

"Be careful."

"You as well, *mia amore*."

"I'm going over to the high school to talk to Abby's fellow students. I'm hoping that one of them will feel so damn guilty that she's dead that they'll spill the beans as to what really happened on the cliffs last night."

"We know what happened," Anthony said.

"We *think* we know what happened, but someone—someone human—was also responsible for Abby's death. I want that person—those *people*—in jail. Someone must be punished, Anthony. Someone here on earth. God can have them after I'm done."

FOURTEEN

Even before the Santa Louisa sheriff spoke to the general assembly at the beginning of their lunch break, there wasn't a person at Santa Louisa High School who didn't know that Abby Weatherby had died at the ruins on the cliffs. Everyone had a theory. Some rumors were true—that Abby was naked, for example. Others were false—like one that she'd killed herself. But as Chris Kidd sat in the last row of chairs in the auditorium and rubbed his sore neck, he knew some of what had really happened.

His girlfriend, Ari Blair, had told him.

He had mixed feelings about what she'd said, and he couldn't help but think that Ari didn't *really* remember what happened. She'd hedged, making him think she was lying when she caught up with him earlier at his locker between first and second period. She said she wasn't drinking at the time of the incident, but *might* have been drugged. She also said that something "otherworldly" happened, which made him think that she'd been royally fucked up. He didn't want Ari getting in trouble—she was a straight-A student, the student body president, and had offers from three top colleges around the country. But he told her she had to talk to the police, it was the right thing to do. She'd kissed him and run off to class, leaving Chris feeling oddly disconnected and worried.

The principal walked onstage and called for everyone to quiet down. Still concerned about his girlfriend, Chris listened to Mr. Lawrence, hoping the Sheriff's Department had answers that didn't involve Ari.

"I'm sure all of you know that Abigail Weatherby died last night on the cliffs near Cypress Point. There is a lot of misinformation going around, and Sheriff McPherson wanted to speak to the student body to put the rumors to rest.

"There will be counselors on site during lunch, after school, and all day tomorrow if anyone here would like to speak with someone about this tragedy. Abby will be missed by many."

The blond sheriff walked briskly onstage, thanked the principal, and stood at the podium. Chris had forgotten the sheriff was a girl. She looked too young and too hot to be a cop.

"Thank you," she said, breathless and distracted. "I'm Sheriff Skye McPherson. I graduated from Santa Louisa High thirteen years ago, so I know you're thinking what the heck is going on? So I'm going to tell you what I know, and ask for your help.

"The circumstances of Abby Weatherby's death are unclear. The Santa Louisa Medical Examiner and my office are right now processing evidence that will hopefully lead to the truth. The community deserves it, Abby's parents deserve it." She looked out into the audience, her expression stern.

"Abby's body was found last night on the cliffs outside of town. There was evidence at the scene that more than one person was on the cliffs at some point prior to, or up until, her death. We know that the cliffs are a popular gathering place for young people. How do we know this? Because most of the deputies in my office grew up here, too, and I've been told it's a well-known make-out spot."

There were some giggles and nervous laughter, but the sheriff didn't crack a smile.

"At this point, we cannot definitely say whether Abby's death was an accident or homicide." She let that sink in, and there were additional murmurings.

McPherson continued, "Perhaps Abby died accidentally—such as by a drug overdose or falling—or through a natural cause like an aneurysm. I can imagine how difficult it would be to witness an accidental death and not know what to do. Sometimes we might make a decision that is wrong, and then we don't know how to make it right afterward."

She looked out over the audience carefully, from one side to the other.

Any nervousness was gone, her voice forceful and commanding. "I want to know what happened to Abby Weatherby last night. I want to know the truth. And I *know* that at least one person in this room was with Abby last night."

Again, she paused, but cut off the murmurs with a firm announcement: "Every teacher has a set of my business cards. They will be left all over the school. Call me day or night and I will meet with you, I'll talk to you, I'll keep it confidential as much as I can. If you're a witness to something other than an accident, I can and will protect you.

"I need the truth. It's what Abby and her family deserve."

The sheriff walked offstage and Chris looked around for Ari. She was on the far side of the gym.

He and Ari had been exclusively dating for nearly two years. He didn't know if he loved her, but he couldn't stand the thought of any other guy dating her. And they all wanted to. She was gorgeous. Blond hair, blue eyes, big tits, and hot in her cheerleading uniform. He loved watching her when he was on the bench, or getting that short little skirt off her in the bed of his truck.

Other guys wanted to do the same. Like his best bud, Travis. Was that Travis talking to her now? Chris started over to the corner, but the crush of students delayed him. By the time he got over there, she was gone.

His head pounded and he squeezed his eyes shut. The image of Travis screwing Ari hit him, and he had a hard time getting rid of it. Travis wouldn't do that to him. Ari wouldn't. What was he thinking?

Chris left the auditorium, the damp fog and steady drizzle feeling surprisingly good on his hot skin. He felt ill; he knew better than to work out and not eat. But when he'd heard the news about Abby, he couldn't think about food. Now he was paying for it.

He looked around. A few other students were talking outside, but most were in the cafeteria, where it was warm and dry.

Where was Ari?

Chris walked slowly around campus looking for her. When he walked out into the parking lot, he saw the sheriff getting into a cruiser. He hesitated, not wanting to get Ari in trouble, but she'd been shaking this morning. She couldn't fake being that scared.

He walked over to Sheriff McPherson. "Sheriff? Do you have a minute?"

The cop nodded. "Why don't you get in and stay dry?" She motioned to the passenger side.

Chris did, and began. "I'm worried about my girl-friend."

Skye McPherson took notes as Chris told her every-thing Ari had said.

Anthony locked his books and papers in his small office—one of the two rooms still standing at the mission—and drove as fast as he dared in the thickening drizzle. It was as if the air had expanded; every breath he took was cold and wet, filling him. The twenty-minute drive down the winding mountain road became thirty minutes, as the slick pavement prevented him from reaching the posted limit.

He absolutely had to find Rafe before the police did. To prepare him for the inevitable questions, the accusa-tions. Skye was only doing her job, and she would be fair, but Anthony had no idea what condition Rafe was in.

His cell phone rang with an unfamiliar number show-ing. "Hello," he answered curtly, keeping his eyes on the slick road.

"It's Moira. I'm heading out to the cliffs right now to find Raphael Cooper."

"What?" He slowed down, his attention now divided. "What do you know about Rafe?"

"When I got back to my motel room, Lily filled me in. Everything we suspected about her adventures on the cliffs was true, except for one surprising fact. A guy in hospital scrubs walked up and created chaos during the ritual. Told Lily to get the hell out of Dodge, then disappeared. Lily identified him as Cooper when I showed her his picture."

Anthony said, "Rafe walked out of the hospital at midnight last night. No one has seen him, yet he was way out at the ruins last night?"

"No doubt it was him. I don't know how he got there, but he saved Lily's life. I'm going to try to retrace his steps."

"Maybe the coven kidnapped him," Anthony said. *Or killed him.* He pressed the gas pedal harder.

"I don't think so."

"You can't possibly know!"

"Something Fiona said this morning made me think he got away. Did your girlfriend tell you about how Fiona tried to kill me?"

He sighed. "What did Fiona say?"

"It was more the subtext of what she said. She implied that someone had stopped her from completing the ritual. Lily confirmed that demons were released, and that Rafe was trying to stop them."

"I'll meet you at the cliffs."

"I'm practically there."

"Wait for me."

"No, I can't stay here. There're . . . *things* still going on. The electric charge is high; I smell Hell. It's right here. No way I'm staying. I'll call you when I find him."

"But—"

"I wanted to tell you what Lily told me, and because she said something else and I don't know what it means. Fiona called her the *arca*. What the hell does that mean?"

"Is Lily still at the motel? I need to send Lily away, to protect her. She's in grave danger."

"She's not there. Jared's father, a cop, tracked them to my room and took them away. He said he was taking Lily home."

"And you let him?"

"I wasn't going to jail again, not that it matters to you."

Anthony asked, "Where does Lily live?"

"Foxglove—1300. What does *arca* mean?"

"She's a spirit trap."

"What the fuck? Humans can't trap demons."

"Can you speak without swearing every other sentence?"

"Fuck, no," she snapped.

Anthony supposed he'd walked into that one, and said, "She was dedicated for the purpose at her conception. You know something about that, don't you?" He didn't mean to be cruel, and almost took it back. But didn't.

"Her mother . . . Anthony, Jared's father took her home more than an hour ago. Her mother must be part of it."

"I'll get her," Anthony said. "You find Rafe." His stomach churned. He didn't want to leave Rafe in Moira's hands, but he didn't see what choice he had. If the coven got hold of Lily, they might be able to re-create the ritual to reunite the Seven.

"I need a place for Rafe and me to stay. My motel room is no longer safe. What about your girlfriend's place? Is there a friendly church around here?"

Anthony considered it but knew neither idea would

work. "There's a hotel on the coast, the Santa Louisa Coastal Inn. The owner is a friend of mine. I'll call him and register a room. I'll put the room under your name, and I'll let him know you'll be coming."

"Why can't—"

He knew what she was going to ask. "I want to talk to Rafe before the police."

After hanging up with Moira, Anthony put Lily's address into Skye's GPS system, then called Father Philip, not caring how late it was in Italy. He was surprised that the Father had already left.

"When did Father leave for Olivet?" he asked.

"One moment," the monk said. Moments later, Bishop Pietro Aretino came on the phone.

"Anthony," Bishop Aretino said, "Philip isn't going to Olivet. He's on his way to Santa Louisa."

"Why? He told me—"

The bishop interrupted. "He has his reasons. But he left before dawn, without his assigned escort."

"What?" Dread filled Anthony. That Father Philip was leaving the sanctuary for Olivet was dangerous in itself, but that he would come here without a bodyguard was foolhardy. Both he and Father Philip knew that his life was in grave danger. He was on the inner council, was privy to information that few had. Information that the covens would love to have, and would be pleased to torture out of the old priest.

"We don't know exactly when he left, and John is leaving now. We hope he can catch up with Philip before . . ."

"That's not soon enough! We have a crisis here," Anthony said. "The Seven Deadly Sins have been released."

"You think Santa Louisa is the only major problem

we're facing?" Pietro admonished him. "Our ranks are thinner than ever. I'd send Rico, but he has to protect his people or we have no hope. You have more people in Santa Louisa to help than any of our other hot spots. Be careful, Anthony. God bless you."

He needed all the blessings he could get. But the motto of St. Michael's was *God helps those who help themselves*.

He had his work cut out for him. Finally off the treacherous mountain, Anthony sped up, and hoped that he wasn't too late to save Lily Ellis, the *arca*.

FIFTEEN

within my envy, within my envy, within my envy grows
—CALM, "Envy"

Chris couldn't find Ari after school, and several of her friends said she hadn't come back after lunch. He tried her cell phone, but there was no answer. He wanted to explain that he'd talked to the sheriff because he was worried about Ari, not because he wanted to get her into any trouble.

"Hey, Kidd, you're late," his friend Travis said when Chris walked into the locker room.

He jerked his chin up. "Sec," he said. He left another message for Ari, then grabbed his gym bag from his locker and jogged to where Travis was waiting by the door. They were the last two players to leave for the bus.

Travis Ehrlich was one of the few black guys at the central coast high school and they'd been friends since day one, when Travis moved to Santa Louisa in the seventh grade. Travis made varsity his freshman year, almost unheard of. He had NBA scouts watching him and a full ride to UCLA—a PAC-10 school—where he'd probably be a starter his freshman year.

Today all Chris could think about was how Travis had everything Chris wanted—and at the assembly, hadn't

Travis had been sniffing around Ari? Was that why Ari had left early?

He shook his head as the headache he'd had all day worsened.

"What's up?" Travis asked. "You got your game on?"

"It's on."

"You look sick."

Chris hit him good-naturedly in the arm. "Freak."

Chris had a scholarship, just like Travis. Why was he beating himself up because Travis was going into PAC-10? Chris was happy with his deal.

Travis had a better deal. *Prick.*

"Chris?" Travis prompted.

He grinned. "Fooled ya."

"Coach is pissed. Look at his face—it's beet red."

"Hot tamale, get a move on." Chris slapped Travis on the back, and they ran toward the bus that would take them to the away game.

"Watch out!" Travis grabbed Chris by the shirt and pulled him out of the path of a classic bright-red Mustang speeding through the parking lot. It came within inches of running over his toes.

"What the fuck?" Chris said. "That's Mr. Ayers's car."

"That wasn't Mr. Ayers driving. It looked like Ms. Peterson."

"Ms. Peterson? The *librarian?*" Chris stared after the Mustang as it took a corner too fast and too sharp, clipping a stop sign it didn't even slow down for. "Shit."

Travis shook his head as they boarded the bus. "I swear, *everyone* has been acting weird today."

The Ellis house was at a crossroads—three roads coming together—signifying a place where deals were made.

If that were the only sign, Anthony might not have given it a second thought. But there were more. Subtle, understood only by those familiar with magic.

Moira would know.

He pushed the vixen from his mind. He'd regretted his decision not to join Moira O'Donnell on the cliffs to search for Rafe. By his actions, he'd given her implicit sanction to take Rafe under her protective wing, and he feared her "protection" would get his brother killed.

Or worse.

Anthony walked up the Ellises' front path of limestone edged with moss. The garden was full of herbs, plants, and flowers used in witchcraft, but more than that, they were arranged in specific ways to protect the house and its occupants from evil spirits. Some relatively innocent witches—those dabbling in witchcraft without evil intent—might protect their homes against accidents. But a supposed churchgoing Christian didn't go to such elaborate lengths, preferring the traditional and effective crucifix.

Anthony had no choice but to continue up the walk, his apprehension growing. More than Lily Ellis's life was in danger. If the coven possessed the *arca*, they could re-create the ritual, bringing the demons under their control to use at will.

He hesitated. If he had the *arca* he could trap the Seven, giving him more time to find the prayer that would send them back to Hell.

It might kill Lily.

It would kill her.

Yet it might be his only recourse. He pushed the thought aside. Father Philip had instilled in him the supremacy of the individual, that human sacrifice even for a good reason was still murder.

"It's one thing to nobly give up your life to save your brothers," Father had said, *"but quite another to sacrifice an innocent even if it appears to be for the greater good. Appearances are deceiving."*

Anthony had to keep Lily out of the coven's hands; then he could research further, find an answer that didn't involve using Lily Ellis to trap the demons.

Anthony stuffed his hands in the deep pockets of his trenchcoat, the handle of his blessed dagger-cross comforting in his grip. He was already damp from the fog as he walked up the wooden steps to the wide porch of the restored Victorian. The roof sheltered him from the rain, but the hair on his skin rose. He knocked on the door, stepped back, and glanced around. Something gave him an itchy feeling.

Anthony looked up. The wood was slightly different, a fraction lighter, directly above him. He glanced at the large doormat beneath his feet, stepped back, and lifted up the corner.

A demon trap had been etched into the wood. Most assuredly beneath the new wood above him was a similar trap. They were used to protect a house against evil spirits. Traps—barriers—had been placed near each entrance. He dropped the mat and straightened. Anthony wasn't as well versed in witchcraft, but there were other reasons for the traps as well. He almost called Moira to ask her, but he heard someone approaching the door.

The door opened. Through the thick screen, Anthony couldn't see much of anything, only the outline of a woman much shorter than he. Older than a teenager, she had blond hair tied up on her head and wore a long dress.

She said, "You're not with the Sheriff's Department."

Anthony glanced behind him, almost forgetting that he'd been driving Skye's truck all day.

"Ma'am, my name is Anthony Zaccardi and I—"

"I know who you are. You're not welcome here."

"Excuse me, I'm just—"

"Don't play dumb. There's just one reason you'd come here, and that's to take my daughter."

Anthony stepped forward, grim and determined. In a low voice, he told the witch, "You don't know what you're messing with."

Laughter, light and airy, rang out. "It's *you* who don't know what you're up against. Leave now, or you'll regret it."

She slammed the door in his face.

Anger simmering, Anthony walked off the porch, through the paths of myrrh and lavender and henbane, back to the truck. Elizabeth Ellis was part of Fiona's coven, and extremely dangerous. She had a solid standing in the town. No one would believe she'd be party to having her daughter sacrificed.

SIXTEEN

The only sound was the fierce wind as it whipped around Moira, slapping her face with moisture as the soggy fog turned to drizzle and the drizzle to a cold, stinging rain. If she listened carefully enough, though, she could hear the Pacific Ocean crashing on the rocks beneath the cliffs. However, if she listened *that* carefully, she also heard the screams. She didn't know if the panicked pleas were real or in her imagination, on the surface of the earth or beneath it.

She stood several feet from the ritual circle and stared. Though broken, there was still some residual magic. Residual evil. A rotten, cloying scent of sulphur mixed with mold and dirt. It wasn't mist that skimmed the ground; it was steam. Heat rose from the earth.

As she stared, a river of bloodred fire bubbled beneath the surface.

She turned away from the image, heart racing, the electricity in the air unnatural and almost unreal, unsure whether what she saw was real or her imagination, a vision or insanity.

She ran back to Jared's truck, slapping her hands on the still-warm hood, taking deep breaths and gathering her wits.

Fear could be a healthy response, but uncontrolled fear was deadly.

She tilted her head up and faced the gray afternoon, knowing the sky was there but unable to see anything but bleakness, light without depth, shadowless, surreal.

Thin rain stung her face as she shouted, "I don't want to be a martyr!" Her long hair whipped around her face, pulled from the loose braid she'd fastened in haste earlier. "I don't want to watch people die!"

She squeezed back her tears, fists clenched, wanting to hit someone, take out her pain and anger on *something*. Rico had taught her to use the gym or to run, but she didn't want to battle a sandbag or run ten miles, twenty miles, more, until her legs ached and her lungs burned and she threw up. She was always running. Anthony Zaccardi was right about that. She ran and ran and ran, never facing the truth.

She was cursed. She was going to die.

"I don't want to die," she whispered.

Moira turned to face the ruins, this time from a distance. The house had stood about a hundred yards from the edge of the cliffs. That was where the demons had been released, the back door into Hell created by the fire two months ago. Moira knew a bit about creating gateways. It was difficult and extremely dangerous, but of course Fiona and her people regularly attempted—and often succeeded in—establishing the thin membranes between earth and Hell.

Moira frowned. Why hadn't Anthony done something to close the gateway? He'd been in Santa Louisa for months, knew what had happened at the ruins—he was a demonologist and couldn't be ignorant about what was so obviously here. Or maybe she was sickly aware of evil because she'd lived with it for so long. Maybe she had a black heart, hard and tainted and cursed.

The edge of the continent looked eerie and surreal through the fog. She knew how these rituals went, and could picture Fiona and her people casting the circle, protecting themselves, excited and arrogant and fearful.

Lily's observations of the ritual were tainted by her ignorance. She didn't know anything about coven practices or how demons operated. But Lily was clear in what she *had* seen even if she didn't understand it. Such as demons leaving Abby's body as it levitated inches above the altar. Abby was part of the puzzle, a necessary piece to draw out the demons from the gateway.

Lily had been adamant about the black clouds being outside the circle. But there were *two* circles, a double circle, and Lily may not have made note of that. What about the witches standing in that double circle? How had they been protected? And how did Raphael Cooper affect the ritual?

Moira shook her head, frustrated. So many questions, too few answers.

She was alone and scared. Maybe she should have asked Anthony to meet her. Loneliness wasn't new—Moira had been lonely most of her life. But she hadn't felt so much despair since the night Peter died. She didn't know whom she could trust, and those she did trust in this battle—those like Anthony Zaccardi—wanted nothing to do with her. Hated her. Blamed her for things that weren't her fault. And for some things that were.

Hell churned here, in Santa Louisa. They had a war on their hands. She'd participated in some of the battles that came before, but she'd only heard about others; most which were fought before she was even born—and few came close to what they now faced.

If Moira succeeded in stopping Fiona, another magician would take her place. There were always more waiting in the wings, studying, practicing, looking for an opening to seize power and wrestle control away from the demons. It was as euphoric as it was deadly, as addictive as it was dangerous.

It was Fiona who'd united the covens and magicians in pursuit of her goal, Fiona who'd convinced them that together, they had influence. She'd been right. And the more control she wielded, the more covens would join her, a never-ending cycle that had to be stopped.

Moira felt like a pawn, expendable, used first by her mother from the moment of her conception, then by St. Michael's Order. They didn't care what happened to her. Deep down, she knew it. They wanted one thing from her: a weapon against the rising dominance of Fiona O'Donnell and the legions of covens she directed.

Sometimes Moira wished she'd let her mother sacrifice her.

Sometimes she wished she could just disappear forever.

Most of the time she wished she'd never been born.

Her eyes burned with unshed tears.

Self-pity is for the weak; regret is for the hopeless.

"Shut up, Rico," she whispered.

God may have forsaken her, but evil couldn't triumph. If she lost to Fiona, every sacrifice Peter had made would be for nothing. His death would be for nothing. The cycle would repeat like a violent *No Exit*. Sartre would be amused, perhaps, at the endless game where the end was certain, but irrelevant.

Peter.

She fell to her knees in the wet, sandy soil, her body vibrating with restrained sorrow. Tears, mingling with the rain, fell to the rocky earth.

"It's not fair!" She pounded the ground with her fists. She missed him so much! Her voice cracked and she absently pushed the hair back from her face.

She stared at the ground. There was a symbol here, vague and disappearing in the rain. She crawled several feet to where it was clear, touched it.

It had been disturbed during the ritual and she couldn't make it out completely, but seeing it stopped her numbing inaction. She knew exactly what was happening to her.

Slowly, she rose to her feet and looked around. The rain was slow but steady and she was drenched, but that didn't bother her, nor did the cold that seeped into her bones. This place was evil. She'd told Anthony just that. She had been standing here doing *nothing* but feeling sorry for herself and thinking through her problems over and over and over . . . inaction.

Sloth.

One of the seven deadly sins.

She looked at her watch. *Hours* had passed. It was five o'clock, the light had changed, and she realized then the terrible risk Santa Louisa—and the world—faced with the Seven on the loose.

As soon as she realized what had been happening to her, her mind cleared. She admonished herself, drenched to the skin, but resolved. She had come out here to find Raphael Cooper, and she'd allow nothing to stop her.

After stealing the Mustang from Frank, high school librarian Bea Peterson pulled over and took the top down. She didn't care that it was raining, or that she would ruin the beautifully restored seats, or stain the red carpet. She wanted to drive with the top down.

Nor did she care that she wasn't dressed for the weather, wearing the thin wool sweater she kept at the library to stave off the chill. Her graying hair first frizzed in the moisture and wind, then the wavy strands hung heavy with the weight of the rainwater. Her thick makeup ran down her face, turning her from a moderately attractive, overweight middle-aged librarian into a sad clown—or to some she might appear deranged, her wild eyes giving light to something far more sinister and feral than anyone at the school expected from sweet Bea Peterson.

Bea drove, without thought, without regret. Carefree and single-minded, she laughed out loud as she sped around the bends of the cliff-side highway too fast. When she skidded, or spun the wheels in the narrow sandy shoulder, she whooped and hollered, as if she were on an amusement-park roller coaster. In the rain, this road was used only by necessity. The few drivers Bea passed honked at her reckless driving, but she laughed. They didn't know what freedom felt like. They didn't know how much pleasure there was to be had driving a classic car like this. It was hers!

Just before she crossed the Santa Louisa County line into San Luis Obispo, Bea stopped the Mustang in the middle of her lane. She stared toward the ocean, except the fog was so thick and wet she couldn't see the water. Her heart raced. She didn't want to give *her car* back to Frank, but she'd have to if she went back to the school. And he'd be angry with her for getting the interior wet and for the scratch on the door when she went around a corner too fast.

She'd seen his face in the rearview mirror when she drove away, running after his car. It pleased her that he was shocked and angry and sad that he'd lost it. She frowned. Why? Why was she so happy that Frank was miserable?

Her breaths came sharp and quick as she replayed the last hour, from seeing Frank drive into the parking lot to her grabbing his keys and driving away in his car. *Her car.* From sideswiping a car taking the turn out of town to taking the top down to hitting nearly one hundred on her drive. Reckless. Foolish.

She didn't understand why she'd done it. Except that she wanted *this* car. This Mustang. It had to be hers. The urge had been so powerful, so overwhelming, that she couldn't see anything but the need to have it.

She needed to go back. To apologize. Maybe he'd understand. Maybe Frank would forgive her.

No.

She cried. The car reminded her of what could have been, of the choices and decisions she'd made—right and wrong.

It's your car now.

Go back.

Go forward.

The bend in the road up ahead was so sharp that directly forward led into the ocean. Straight down to the rocky coastline below.

They won't let you keep the car. They'll give it back to Frank and you'll be arrested. Lose your job. Maybe go to jail.

They're not going to let you keep the car.

They're going to take your car.

Bea put the car in drive and pressed the accelerator, turned the wheel sharply to the left, and she was flying . . . flying off the cliff. She held on to the steering wheel as her body pulled from the seat—the old Mustang didn't have seat belts. Then she was flying. Flying, falling, hearing but not seeing the crashing waves, the salty mist reaching up to catch her.

She hit a protruding rock, her body bouncing off and into the water, where it was tossed onto more rocks.

By then she was dead.

SEVENTEEN

Lonely, lonely, lonely—your spirits sinkin' down
You find you're not the only stranger in this town
—BILLY SQUIRE, "Lonely Is the Night"

Moira slowed Jared's truck to a crawl as she neared the end of the narrow road, the windshield wipers moving intermittently back and forth, visibility so poor she was unsure she was even going in the right direction anymore.

Then she saw the broken sign, so weathered from age it was colorless.

LCOME TO P AC   GE RESO
O ETS

Her heart raced as she realized this was an abandoned motel or lodge of some sort, with separate cabins all boarded up. She released the brake just enough that the truck moved forward, the road turning to gravel overgrown with small shrubs. A sign posted on the first cabin read:

Property of the State of California
Trespassers will be prosecuted

Each abandoned cabin appeared to be a large, single room facing the ocean, far off the main road and obscured by trees. In the dark, Lily could have easily passed by and not known they were here. A perfect hiding place.

She stopped the truck, turned off the ignition, and walked cautiously through the weed-strewn central courtyard. The cabins were about twenty, perhaps thirty feet apart. Cypress and eucalyptus trees shielded the area from view. Only a few hundred yards away was the main access road into the mountains—the access road Lily had found—but unless you knew these cabins were here, you wouldn't find them.

Moira stumbled over tree roots and caught herself on the leaves of a prickly shrub.

"Damn." She pulled two thin, sharp thorns from her right palm as she righted herself. She shivered uncontrollably, her wet clothes plastered to her skin, her hair heavy with the weight of rainwater down her back. She wanted nothing more than to get back into the warm truck and return to her miserable motel and sleep.

She didn't believe in luck, but a spike of adrenaline hit her bloodstream as she thought of her *luck* in finding this place. If, in fact, Rafe Cooper was here. Could it be logic? Maybe. But still . . . the whole thing felt oddly fortuitous to her. She didn't like being manipulated, by either humans or supernatural beings.

"There are always signs, there is always a helping hand. It's understanding the signs, accepting the help, which is difficult for everyone—and you. That's where your bias, your fear, your arrogance, and your ignorance will get you killed if you can't see the truth."

"Shut up, Rico," she muttered again. She wished she'd never trained with him, because she couldn't get his damn lectures out of her head. She pushed aside her concerns—the idea that this place was a *sign* she'd somehow unknowingly followed—and walked among the cabins.

Each cabin was locked tight, windows boarded up, locks on the doors, all in disrepair, abandoned for many years. But there was something different about the third cabin from the end. She stared, tilted her head, and squinted through the still fog.

She approached the house cautiously, walked the perimeter slowly.

Then she saw what had caught her eye.

The front door was splintered just a bit, the freshly split wood bright against the weathered door frame.

The lock was still on the knob, but the doorjamb had been broken. Moira hesitated. Human or possessed? She didn't know what was going on with Raphael Cooper, but she couldn't take chances. She pulled out a large crucifix on a chain from a deep pocket inside her jacket and put it around her neck, then pulled the Beretta out of her concealed pocket holster.

No movement, no sign of anyone watching. She opened all her senses, listened, *felt* the atmosphere around her. No electrical charge in the air. No smell of sulphur or rotting meat. No extreme heat from one of Hell's gateways, nor the ice-cold sensation of ghosts. Nothing. Still, that didn't mean that her truck hadn't drawn attention, or that there wasn't a way for Cooper to see out a crack in the barricaded windows—if it was Cooper inside. She didn't think he was dangerous—he'd saved Lily and stopped Fiona—but Moira couldn't afford to be wrong.

She pushed on the door firmly and it opened, a thick sliver of wood falling to the ground.

In the darkness, Moira caught sight of a gutted kitchenette to the right and a door in the rear. As her eyes adjusted to the near black, the only light coming from the diminishing gray day behind her, she saw a man in hospital scrubs huddled in the far corner of the empty room.

She approached cautiously and said, "Cooper? Raphael Cooper?"

He didn't move. She squatted, the crucifix swinging on her chain between them, and checked his pulse. It was strong. She let out a long breath.

"What happened to you last night?" she whispered.

She pulled out a flashlight, turned it on, and popped out the bottom to rest on the wood floor. The glow lit the entire room like a lantern. The scrubs Cooper wore were torn. His skin was cold, and he was huddled tightly for warmth, though sweat and a day's growth of beard covered his face. His hair was longer than in his picture, damp and curling at the ends from the moisture. As she watched, his body began to shake and he shouted out a command of sorts.

It was in Spanish, a language Moira recognized but didn't understand beyond the basics. He continued, his voice fearful and commanding at the same time. She touched his sweating forehead, smoothed back his hair, and murmured, "Shh, you're having a bad dream."

Suddenly, he sat bolt upright, eyes frightened and lost. He pulled himself into the corner, shaking.

"Raphael, my name is Moira O'Donnell. I'm a friend of Father Philip."

He stared at her and she wasn't sure he'd understood her.

"Do you remember what happened last night? On the cliffs? The coven?" She paused. "The Seven Deadly Sins?"

Slowly, he shook his head. His voice was rough and low when he said, "She's dead." He coughed to clear his voice.

"No, she's not. You saved her. You saved Lily." Moira took his hands, squeezed them. "Lily wore the white dress. You told her to run and not look back." She pulled a water bottle from her jacket and handed it to him.

He looked at the water, then at her, then took the bottle.

"It's okay," she said, reassuring both him and herself.

"She's dead," he repeated. He sipped the water, then coughed.

"Yes, Abby died," Moira said. "Abby was also there. But you saved Lily. The girl in the white gown. She's alive and well and safe." At least she hoped Anthony had been able to find and protect her.

As Rafe remembered the night before, relief crossed his face. "Lily?" he asked. He sipped more water, then drank fully.

"I need to get you out of here," she said.

"No. No. Give me a minute."

"Excuse me, but you look like death warmed over. Anthony has a place for you—"

"Anthony. He's here." A statement, not a question.

"Has been the whole time. Raphael, I'm—"

"Rafe. My friends call me Rafe."

"I'm Moira."

"Moi-rah," he whispered, smiling. He pronounced her name right, and she liked the way he said it.

He took a deep breath and straightened his legs, leaning against the wall. "Thank you." He finished the water. "I'm not usually this out of sorts."

She couldn't help but smile. "I think I can forgive you, considering."

"Considering." He gave her a half-smile. "I'm getting my strength back."

"A miracle," she said, not realizing until the words were out that she sounded sarcastic.

"You don't believe in miracles."

"Sure I do. I just haven't seen any lately."

He looked beyond her, at what she didn't want to think about. He was a seminarian; of course he had stronger faith than she did. So had Peter, and look where it got him.

He shook his head. "I didn't stop them. They're out there. They're everywhere . . ."

Moira wasn't certain whether he was talking about the demons or Fiona's coven.

"We'll get them back."

"Oo'la te-ellan l'niss-yoona: il-la paç-çan min beesha."

Moira wasn't sure what language he was speaking, but it sounded familiar. "What did you say?"

He stared at her. "Aramaic." That didn't answer her question, but he continued, frowning. "The *Conoscenza* was stolen. My fault."

Moira sat next to him in the dark, dank cabin, her back against the wall, facing the door. Though he'd lost too much weight since he'd had his picture taken for the paper, he was a tall man, with broad shoulders. She felt small sitting next to him, even though she wasn't short.

He touched her shoulder, her damp hair, and said, "You seem . . . familiar."

He was changing the subject. For now, she could play along, but Rafe would need to answer the hard questions. "I lived at St. Michael's seven years ago," she told him.

He shook his head. "I left twelve years ago and never returned."

"Never?"

He finished the water and put the bottle next to him, his index finger fingering the top. "I've had some things to work out. It took longer than I thought."

She shifted uncomfortably. The way Rafe spoke, the way he looked off but didn't see anything in front of him—it made her think he was listening to something else, seeing something that wasn't there.

The rain pounded on the roof; the wind rattled the sides of the cabin. The weather was getting worse. "We have to leave," she said. "There's a lot to do."

"Do?"

"To stop Fiona." Rafe closed his eyes. Damn, she needed a little help getting him to the truck. "Rafe—please, the high priestess of the coven is furious with you."

"She's mortal. There are seven demons out there. Immortal, powerful demons."

"What do you know about the Seven?"

She didn't want to go back into the foul weather, but she didn't want to stay here, either, and listen to someone who sounded far too much like Peter. It made her extremely uncomfortable.

Rafe said, "The fallen angels were banished to the underworld for disobedience and pride. They envied God; they envied humans. They hated us because we were chosen, yet we were corporeal. Not spirits. They wanted everything, to be favored, to be chosen.

"As there is a hierarchy of angels, there is a hierarchy of demons. The Seven have been around since the first angels. They know everything there is to know about Heaven and Hell. They know everything there is to know about human beings, intimate knowledge of our weaknesses. Our foolishness. Our desires and our fears. They have control over their spirit. They don't need to possess a human body, though they can when it suits them. Instead, they roam free, feeding on sin. They strip out our God-given conscience and feed on our darkest desires. Lust becomes uncontrollable, and in our need they feed. Greed turns insatiable, and they feed. They will never be satisfied, they seek *more* . . . more sex, more money, more food, more time. They become stronger, more destructive, deadlier, as they spread their virus. They're like legendary vampires, but instead of sucking blood they crave our greatest weaknesses, drawing them to the surface, pushing us to act on sins that hurt not only us, but others. And the more we give in, the more we want. The more we *need*."

Moira listened, captivated, amazed that Rafe Cooper, who seemed so fragile a moment ago, was speaking so clearly, so firmly. It scared her. His understanding of these demons was uncommon; even Anthony hadn't figured it all out yet. How had Rafe picked up on the demons' nature so quickly?

She swallowed and inched away from him just a fraction. Saw his water bottle. An idea came to her. She was being foolish . . . but as Rico always told her:

First, stay alive.

"They are out there," Rafe continued, almost in a trance. "Spreading iniquity. Drawing out our sins. They'll go where they are coveted. We are up against not only evil itself, but the evil within us. How can we run from ourselves?"

Moira handed Rafe a half-filled water bottle. Her hand was shaking. She willed it to stop, but it didn't.

He looked at her. "You're different," he said, and she didn't know whether that was good or bad. He took the water bottle and drank.

Swallowed.

"Okay, I'm ready," he said. "I might need a little help."

She let out a slow sigh of relief. The holy water she'd poured into the plastic bottle went into Rafe smoothly. He wasn't possessed. He wasn't being controlled by a demon. He was human, fully human, and she almost cried with relief.

She was losing it. Lack of sleep, the attack by her mother, seeing Anthony, remembering Peter.

"Moira."

Rafe touched her chin and she looked at him in the dim light.

"Why are you crying?"

"I'm not."

He brushed his thumb against her cheek. "Yes, you are."

She cleared her throat. "It's from the rain."

He looked at her, didn't believe her; she didn't expect him to.

"You're shaking." He ran his hand up her sleeve.

"And wet. You came through the storm to find me. How?"

"Lucky guess."

"I don't believe in luck," he said. "Divine intervention."

"Don't start down that path, Rafe," she whispered.

He rubbed her arms, put his arm around her shoulders, and pulled her close to him. Her heart was racing. Why was she nervous around him? He wasn't possessed, he wasn't a spirit; he was unusual, and strange, but he was a person. A man.

"Let's go," she said.

"I'm in your hands."

Something shifted painfully inside her. Moira had always been a loner, especially after Peter died. But just lately, people were depending on her. Jared. Lily. And now Rafe Cooper.

She didn't want the responsibility. All Moira wanted was to stop her mother.

She pulled away from Rafe and stood, holding out her hand. He looked at it for a moment, then grasped it with a strength that surprised her given his ill appearance. She pulled him up; her workouts with Rico and her daily exercises kept her fit. But suddenly Rafe towered over her and she took a step back, startled.

Then he staggered, dizzy, and she caught him.

"Let's go slowly," she said.

She eased Rafe out of the cabin, into the dark, misty rain, and down the unpaved road to the truck. By the time she got him into the passenger seat, Rafe was weakening, and once again in pain. She didn't want to take him to the hospital, but if he was in serious distress she didn't think she'd have a choice.

She hopped into the driver's seat and said, "Are you sure you don't need a doctor?"

"I'm not sure about anything, but I can't go back to the hospital. I wasn't in a coma, but I wasn't awake either. I don't know what they were doing to me, but something . . . I just . . ." He stopped, looked at her, and Moira felt the anguish and confusion rolling off him.

"It's okay." She reached for him, held his hand and squeezed. "I have a safe place."

He stared at her, his dark eyes troubled, fathomless. "There's no place safe enough for either of us. But if we go back to the hospital, they'll kill me."

They won the game, no thanks to Chris.

"Don't sweat it, you had a bad day. It happens to all of us." Travis slapped Chris on the back as they boarded the bus back to school. "You'll be on your game next week."

Chris shrugged off his friend's comments. Bad days didn't happen to Travis Ehrlich. He was perfect, he had everything, he had the scholarship to UCLA and was MVP and scored twenty-fucking-eight points—including six three-pointers—in the game.

"Let's hang at my place," Travis said. "My mom's working late; we'll have the place to ourselves. 'Kay?"

"Whatever." Chris didn't want to look at Travis, let alone spend any time with him. He took a seat in the back of the bus and sulked while Travis took kudos from the coach and the rest of the team.

After the bus started down the dark highway, Coach sat across from Chris. "Listen, Kidd, you screwed up but I know you're better than this. Get your head to-

gether and we'll work one-on-one tomorrow after practice." He slapped him on the shoulder, then went back
to the front of the bus.

It was obvious to Chris that Coach was simply placat-
ing him. Coach could care less about Chris and his future. It was all Travis all the time. The Santa Louisa Star
Player, the Local Boy Done Good. Asshole. Prick.

Why did Travis have all the talent? Because he was
black, that's why. God gave black guys all the moves. It
had nothing to do with working harder, practicing, it
was because they were born black and sports just came
easier to them. Chris had to work his ass off for every
point, every ounce of sweat. That should matter, dammit,
it should *mean* something, but it fucking meant *nothing,*
and Travis just walked into being the MVP and scholar-
ships because of randomness.

Forty minutes later, the bus pulled into the school
parking lot and everyone got out, unusually quiet after a
win. As they were gathering their gear from the under-
carriage storage, Chris overheard Coach tell Travis,
"You're Kidd's buddy, see what you can do with him."

Can *do* with him? Right.

Travis came over to Chris, his duffel tossed over his
shoulder. He handed Chris his bag. "My place?"

Chris stared at the bag. What the fuck was wrong
with him? Travis was his best friend; they'd been buddies since Travis moved up from L.A. six years ago after
his dad died. His dad had been a beat cop, killed by
gangbangers as part of a ritual stunt. Travis wanted to
be a cop; his basketball scholarship was his ticket to college because his mom couldn't afford to send him.

And Chris wanted to kill him. His hands itched to

punch Travis's face, to beat him to death. His anger and jealously surged, and Chris shook his head, trying to rid his mind of the violent image.

No!

Excruciating, blinding pain hit Chris all at once. It was as if a knife were slowing carving his scalp from his skull, and he fell to his knees, his hands holding his head.

"Chris? Coach! *Coach! Chris is bleeding!*"

Chris didn't hear anything but the drumbeat in his brain. His hands were sticky and he was choking on something. But the foul, metallic taste was nothing compared to the numbing pain.

He mumbled something, over and over, but didn't know if his brain translated it to his mouth.

Sorry, Travis, I'm sorry, I'm sorry . . .

Coach ran over, knelt beside him. "What happened?"

"I don't know! He just fell over. Why are his ears bleeding? What's happening?"

"Chris, can you hear me?" Coach shouted.

Make the pain stop. I'm sorry, Travis, I'm so sorry, I would never hurt you, buddy, oh God, oh God, the pain, make it stop!

Travis knelt beside him, took his hand. "Hold on, Chris."

"Sorry sorry sorry."

"Call 911," Coach said as he took off his jacket and stuffed it under Chris's head. He pulled off his T-shirt and wrapped it around Chris's ears and skull, tightening it, and applied pressure as Travis dialed 911.

The last thing Chris heard before he lost consciousness was Travis on the phone. "I need an ambulance at

Santa Louisa High School. My buddy is bleeding a lot. Coach—"

Coach took the phone, but Chris didn't hear what he said.

He died in the ambulance.

EIGHTEEN

And it's never pretty when somebody's dream dies
But those are the rules in a mean little town
—HOWLING DIABLOS, "Mean Little Town"

At 1830 hours, a 911 call of shots fired came in from Rittenhouse Furniture Emporium. Now, thirty-three minutes later, Skye commanded the crime scene from a makeshift staging area, the beams from several squad cars lighting up the parking lot. Inside the store, an employee held several hostages at gunpoint.

Skye listened in as Deputy David Collins talked on his phone to a victim, the manager Grace Chin, who was hiding in a bathroom stall and had had the wherewithal to call out using her cell phone.

The situation was grim. Grace was trapped in the bathroom with no way out except the door that led to the shooter, whom she identified as Ned Nichols, a long-time salesman for Rittenhouse. He'd shot three people and was holding hostage a customer, Ashley Beecher McCracken.

Skye knew Nichols. Though he was two years older, she remembered him from school. In a town like Santa Louisa, you knew pretty much everyone who grew up here. She'd already sent another cop in search of everything they could get on Nichols, starting with his cell phone number, because he wasn't answering the Ritten-house telephone line.

A deputy came up and handed Skye the blueprints of the building. "The owner, Rittenhouse, just arrived with these. He wants to know what's happening."

Skye put her hand over her phone. "I'll talk to him when I can."

"What do you want me to say? His sister-in-law was shot."

His sister-in-law was Betsy Rittenhouse, who'd been shot in the leg as she fled the building. She was on her way to the hospital.

"Tell him there's one confirmed gunman inside, with hostages. That's it."

"Got it," he said, and left.

She spread out the blueprints, and she and David stud-ied them under a bright portable light. There were three offices on the east side of the building, the break room in the rear, what looked like a large janitor's closet that had access to the electrical room, and a large L-shaped showroom that took up more than 80 percent of the square footage. She tapped her finger on the women's bathroom next to the break room.

"You're in the women's room?" David clarified over the phone.

"Y-Yes," Grace said.

"Where do you think Nichols is now?"

"I don't know. I don't know!"

"Can you hear anything?"

She didn't say anything for a long moment.

"He's talking," she said. "Ranting about something; I can't hear the words. Ashley's crying. I think they're just outside the offices."

Nichols had shut down the overhead lighting, but dim lights from the back of the building, near the offices, illuminated the interior well enough.

As David continued to extract information from the victim, Skye finally received the information she needed: Nichols's cell phone number.

She showed David and put a finger to her lips. David told Grace that he was still there, but they had to be silent for a minute.

"You ready?" David asked her.

"Yeah." No, but she had no choice. She called Nichols.

Four rings later, his voicemail picked up. His recorded voice sounded normal and calm, not the voice of a killer.

She said, "Hi, Ned, this is Skye McPherson. Remember me from high school? I'm now Sheriff McPherson, and we need to talk." She left her number and hung up. Then she called again. Again it went to voicemail. She hung up without leaving a message. Waited a moment. Called a third time.

It took sixteen calls before Nichols picked up.

"No!" he shouted into the phone. "I'm not talking to you, stop calling me!"

"Ned, it's Skye McPherson."

"I don't care, I'm through with everyone. It's not fair!"

"What's not fair, Ned?"

"Everything. Deric doesn't deserve the sales; he did nothing that I couldn't have done! It's random, all random, all a game; it's not fair, I'm good enough."

"Of course you're good enough, Ned. Let's talk about this. If you come out now, you and I can talk. Just the two of us. You can tell me everything."

David was nodding at her, making the hand motion to keep talking.

"Ned, I know you don't want to hurt anyone. Let's talk this out, and—"

Nichols cut her off. "You know why she got the promotion? Do you know why?"

She? He wasn't talking about Deric anymore. Skye needed to keep him talking, so asked, "Why?"

"Because she fucked him. I should have gotten the promotion, but she's a little whore; it's the only way she could have gotten the *job that was mine!*"

Skye motioned toward the owner, who was sitting in a squad car on the perimeter. David nodded and ran over there to ask what Nichols was talking about.

Skye said, "That's not fair. Why don't you come out so we can talk about this face-to-face?"

"Did you fuck your way to the top, too?" His voice was taking on a more fevered pitch, and she heard a female crying in the background. Skye didn't know if he was talking to the hostage or to her.

"If we—"

He cut her off. "I did everything right. Everything. I came to work. I was friendly. I talked to everyone. I sold. I sold well, but the fucking *luck of the draw* and Deric gets the cash cow. He did nothing for it, nothing! I've been here for seven years; he's been here six months. It should be mine!"

By the changes in his tone, and that she no longer heard crying, Skye realized Nicholas was moving through the building. A door opened. Closed.

Skye didn't like how Nichols was switching back and forth between outrages. If he were a bank robber, she could handle him. They wanted to get away, were willing to negotiate to buy time until they realized it was hopeless. If he were a drunk husband, she'd have a chance to talk him down while David's team got into position. But Ned Nichols sounded totally crazy. To say it was hard to deal with the criminally insane was a huge understatement.

"What do want, Ned? What can I do for you so that you'll let those people go?"

"I want everything to be fair. I want to be manager— I'm better than any of them. I want to be top salesman. I only want what's right!"

David ran back to the command center and scrawled:

Grace Chin was promoted to manager nine months ago. Deric Costigan was hired six months ago, he's a cousin to the Rittenhouse family and was training to take over the business.

"I think we can talk about all of that," Skye said. "You're right, everything should be fair. How about coming outside, and we'll talk about how we can make everything fair?" She stared at David and shook her head.

"No." Nichols hung up.

"We have to go in now," David said. "He's ready to pop."

"I agree. Take the first good shot."

He nodded solemnly and handed her the phone.

Skye put David's phone to her ear. "Grace? This is Sheriff McPherson. Stay put. We're on our way in—"

A door slammed open.

Grace screamed.

Gunshots blasted over the receiver, then the phone went dead.

"Where have you been?" Anthony answered Moira's call on the first ring.

"Long story," she said, not wanting to explain about losing so much time on the cliffs. "I found him. He's okay. Tired, but okay." Whether he was truly *okay* was a matter of internal debate for Moira. She was incredibly worried about Rafe.

"Where are you now?" Anthony asked.

"I just pulled into the hotel. Did you get us a room?"

"It's under your name. Can you get checked in first? Rafe shouldn't be in public. People are looking for him."

"If Fiona finds him we're in trouble."

"The police have questions and he's going to have to answer them eventually, but not yet. Not until we know exactly what's going on."

Moira glanced at Rafe, who appeared to be sleeping in the passenger seat, though she didn't think he was actually asleep. "He thinks someone at the hospital wants to kill him."

"Tell him," Rafe murmured without opening his eyes, "to check into the doctors."

"Rafe wants you to check out the doctors at the hospital."

"Let me talk to him."

Moira said to Rafe, "Anthony wants to talk to you."

Rafe sighed, took the phone.

Moira could hear Anthony's voice clearly. "Rafe?"

"It's me."

"Thank God. I'll be there in thirty minutes. Don't talk to anyone."

"I won't."

"Don't trust Moira. Once a witch, always a witch. You know that."

Moira's eyes stung. Dammit, she would *not* shed a tear. Why did it bother her so much that Anthony was tainting her reputation with Rafe? Rafe was one of them, one of St. Michael's Order; most of them hated her anyway. Why shouldn't Rafe hate her too? It wasn't as though what Anthony said *wasn't* true. She had been a practicing witch, and like an alcoholic she would always be a witch. She could fall off the wagon anytime, anywhere.

Still holding the phone to his ear, Rafe took Moira's hand. She whipped her head around, eyes wide, unable to keep the shock from her face. He was staring at her, his eyes so dark blue they looked black. A minute ago he was weak and could barely speak; now he seemed almost radiant with strength, as if it were glowing within and under his pale skin.

"Anthony, where's the *arca*?" Rafe asked.

"I can't get to her right now. We have a problem. Her mother is a witch. There were many signs at their house, which is at a crossroads. I don't know where she's keeping Lily, but I can't get inside. She knew who I was."

"I can," Rafe said.

"No."

"I'll explain when you get here." He snapped the phone closed before Anthony said anything more. "Anthony is single-minded. Don't let him hurt you."

"He hasn't."

Rafe squeezed her hand so hard it hurt. He glared at

her. "Don't lie to me, Moira. Ever. I have to know that I can trust you *always*."

She didn't know what to say. "Are you empathic?" she whispered.

He shook his head, his eyes wet with tears of pain.

"I need to get you inside," she said.

He nodded, his jaw clenched.

"You need to let go of my hand." He did, reluctantly. "Stay here, I'll be right back," she told him.

Rafe watched Moira run across the parking lot and into the hotel. Only when she was inside did he breathe easier.

Once a witch, always a witch.

Anthony believed in black and white, and Rafe loved him for it. They needed the moral compass that Anthony provided, the depth of knowledge and experience. His concrete faith. But something had happened to Rafe while he was in the hospital; that was the only explanation for what he was feeling, thinking, *knowing*. Never had he felt so lost or confused.

He feared he knew more than he should. When he stopped the Seven Deadly Sins from inhabiting the *arca*, he felt something . . . a power he couldn't explain. He *knew* things he shouldn't know, that he never remembered learning. He feared he was being used by someone . . . or something. What if it was witchcraft? What if he was a pawn between warring covens? He'd been out of his mind for more than two months, what if someone else had gotten in?

The things he remembered from the hospital . . .

Pain sliced through his head and all thought disappeared. He lay on the seat of the truck cab, praying to God to take the pain away.

The door opened. "You're here." Moira sounded both irritated and worried, but mostly relieved.

He instantly felt the pain subside enough that he could think. She was a lifeline. He held up his hand.

"I thought you'd done a stupid move and left," she said, helping him from the truck.

"I need rest."

"Glad you're finally admitting it." She put his arm around her shoulder, wrapped her right arm around his waist, supported him. She was seven or eight inches shorter than he was, skinny, but solid muscle. "We have a room. I wanted the first floor, but they were all booked. I don't like it, but we're on the second floor."

"It's okay for now."

Why did he know that? He didn't *want* to know the future. Seeking that knowledge was akin to buying a ticket to Hell. He didn't want the future; he wanted to go back to before the murders, to before he'd fallen prey to seduction, to when he was safe at St. John's.

Safe and hiding.

Hiding from his dreams. His nightmares. The nightmares that had come long before he arrived at Santa Louisa Mission.

Hiding from his fate.

NINETEEN

Calamities are of two kinds:
Misfortune to ourselves, and good fortune to others.
—AMBROSE BIERCE

Patience had never been her mother's strong suit.

Serena tried to ignore Fiona's pacing in the library, but it had begun to irritate her when Fiona asked, exasperated, "Is it ready?"

Serena frowned as she added the final ingredient to the glass bowl. She was at a delicate point in the spell; her mind needed to focus, as spells were as much willed as they were created. Fiona had incredible control over external forces, but it was the quiet concentration of spell casting that held true superiority.

Though some witches preferred wood or stone, Serena liked the conductive force of a perfectly formed, clear, pure glass bowl. Her *peculiarities,* as Fiona called them, had gained her the respect and awe of many. It was *her* magic that Fiona used to keep the other covens under her thumb. No one in their world doubted Serena's ability. She had full command of the tools of her trade. Serena had taken magic to the next level, and beyond—a feat even her mother, on occasion, admired.

Not that Fiona would admit to anyone that Serena was as powerful as she was . . . or *more* powerful.

If you only knew what I could do, Mother.

"Serena!" Fiona snapped. "Answer me!"

Ever since Fiona's Third Eye had been unable to locate Raphael Cooper, she'd grown increasingly irritable. Serena suspected it was more because Fiona needed to ask her for help, and Fiona did not like giving up control to any of them, even her own daughter.

Fiona had put herself in a trance and sent out her psychic "Third Eye"—an ability that worked most of the time. She tracked Rafe from the cliffs to a nearby abandoned cabin, but when she sent two of her men out to capture him, he wasn't there. She'd been so certain, but she hadn't allowed Serena to verify the information before impulsively acting on it.

Another rash act. Fiona's going to the jail early this morning in her attempt to kill Moira had been particularly unwise. Now Moira knew for certain that Fiona was nearby, and probably Anthony Zaccardi did as well. The coven had been protected here in Santa Louisa partly out of ignorance—St. Michael's Order didn't know where they were. But now it was only a matter of time before hordes of witch hunters descended on the town and their efforts were hampered. She didn't want to leave and stake out new territory—Santa Louisa was perfect for their purposes for many reasons.

After the failure to apprehend Rafe at the abandoned cabin, Fiona sent out her Third Eye again, but Rafe seemed to have learned how to shield his aura from exposure—a difficult and almost impossible task against Fiona's psychic eye. Whether she was conscious of it or not, Serena didn't know, but the more Fiona tried to find him—and failed—the more irritable she became. Now she was on the verge of exploding.

"The ingredients need to sit." Serena put a clear crystal into the bowl and recited the spell that summoned Prziel, the demon of lost enemies, and trapped him in the crystal. Once the crystal glowed red, Prziel could be used to find nearly anyone, though he was primarily used against enemies.

Fiona paced. "When I get my hands on Raphael Cooper, he will understand true pain. If he thinks he can walk away with what I need . . ."

"He doesn't know what he has locked in his mind," Serena interrupted.

Fiona whipped around and angrily shot an electric charge at Serena. Used to her mother's mood swings, Serena held up her hand and sent the charge into the fish tank. The water sizzled and steamed, and in seconds more fish were floating on the surface. Dammit, Margo had just put in the new fish three hours ago.

Fiona barely noticed. She whirled around and peered into the mirror, inspecting her perfect skin with a critical eye.

"We have the *arca* back," Serena reminded Fiona.

"But we don't have the Seven and they're becoming stronger. I need them under my control before they gather so much strength even *I* can't control them. We don't have the time to screw around. I'll pull the information from Raphael Cooper's mind if it kills him."

It likely would, and if it didn't, Fiona would find other ways to torture him and make him beg for death.

Serena didn't want Rafe to suffer, but he'd made his decision when he fought them ten weeks ago at the mission. There was nothing Serena could do to end Fiona's wrath. If only the process had been completed then, they would have had the Seven under their control the night of the fire on the cliffs when they first opened the gates.

But Rafe had led Anthony Zaccardi to Santa Louisa. The demonologist's presence had forced them to be cautious, lest he discover them. They'd been smart, and while he was suspicious and had walked the ruins nearly every day, he hadn't figured out *why* he was suspicious, and that enabled them to continue their work.

But Moira had somehow tracked them to Santa Louisa. Fiona thought Moira was weak, foolish, annoying—a pest, a gnat to swat dead. Fiona wanted to torment her for fun and revenge, but didn't consider her a real threat.

Serena suspected that Fiona underestimated Moira.

Serena had once dreamed that she and Moira would band together and defeat their psycho mother. Together, they would be more powerful than anyone could imagine. But Moira didn't want to run the coven and had turned her back on their gifts.

Serena desperately missed her sister, loving and hating her at the same time. Did Moira ever think about her? Did she remember that there was a time when they were best friends? Did she know that it was Serena who put a magical shield around her so Fiona didn't know she'd slipped out? Did Moira know that Serena had saved her life?

Serena stared at the glass bowl. The clear liquid began to bubble, though it was nowhere near a source of heat.

"I need his blood," she said.

Fiona walked over to the locked mini-fridge behind her desk and typed in the secret code. She didn't trust anyone, even Serena, with that information, though Serena had broken the code many times. Fiona always underestimated her, just as she underestimated Moira. It pleased Serena to have so many secrets from the sorceress, the one who believed no one could lie to her.

Fiona handed over the small test tube of Rafe's blood that Richard had obtained for them. They had only a few left—in a rage, Fiona had once fried the fridge, destroying everything inside. They were still rebuilding their supplies.

Serena held up the tube of Rafe's blood, opened the stopper, and chanted the words she knew by heart, a spell she had perfected. Few witches today did anything but what the old books told them; Serena could write her own *grimoire* with powerful, original spells. She understood more than even the most seasoned of witches, more than Fiona herself, though Serena wouldn't say that out loud.

She dripped two drops of Rafe's blood into the potion. "As it is above," she said, adding two more drops, "it is below." Two final drops were added and she sealed the tube. Fiona took it from her but didn't return it to the fridge. She, too, was entranced by the metaphysical reaction in the bowl.

The clear liquid turned blood red, bubbling and churning. A whirlpool began to move faster and faster, and the table the bowl rested on began to shake violently. Serena held the sides of the bowl so it wouldn't crash to the floor, the liquid warm but not burning.

She chanted the name Prziel over and over and suddenly the shaking stopped; the potion settled and returned to its clear color. At the bottom of the bowl, the crystal, now red, glowed.

Serena removed the crystal with iron tongs to prevent the demon from escaping into her. She carried it over to

a map of Santa Louisa County and put it down, spin-
ning it gently with the tip of the tong.

"Find him, find this blood," she commanded the
demon.

The crystal moved across the map. It started lazily,
then began to spin faster like a child's top, all over the
map. Faster, faster, faster, until it spun itself off the table
and across the room, hitting the wall with enough force
to embed it inside the wood.

Fiona ignored the trapped demon and looked at the
map. "There!" she announced excitedly.

One blood-red drop told them that Raphael Cooper
was at the Santa Louisa Coastal Inn.

Rafe pretended to be asleep when Anthony arrived in
the two-room suite. Moira was arguing with Anthony.

"Don't wake him. Give him an hour, at least, okay?"

Movement at the partially open door. Rafe felt it was
Anthony, making sure he was both alive and present.

"Did you seal both rooms?" he whispered.

"Of course," Moira snapped. "I'm not a complete
novice."

"No, you're not."

It wasn't a friendly comment.

Rafe breathed a sigh of relief when Anthony didn't
try to wake him. It's not that he didn't want to talk to
Anthony—he wanted to see his old friend. But he felt
safe here, at least for the time being. Safe enough to try
to organize his thoughts before Anthony bombarded
him with questions. Moira already had many; Rafe had
seen them in her brilliant blue eyes.

Moira had insisted he lie down while she sealed the

rooms against demons and witchcraft, but he watched her. She was meticulous, pouring salt, reciting prayers as if they were spells, not leaving any edge unprotected. But while demons couldn't come in, and spells couldn't attack them, both he and Moira knew that the protections were mere stopgaps in the battle. A temporary fort that could be breached with time and strength.

He prayed silently in the dark, blocking out the loud whispers of Anthony and Moira in the room next door. A verse from the Book of Sirach came to him, and he shuddered:

* *there is anger and envy and trouble and unrest,*
 and fear of death, and fury and strife.
 And when one rests upon his bed,
 his sleep at night confuses his mind.

Sleep . . . how could he sleep? He'd been in a state of sleep for ten weeks. Ten weeks of a coma? A drug-induced sleep? A spell-induced sleep? He didn't know, but his thoughts were filled with confusion and sorrow.

I failed and they died.

He'd not only been tempted, but he'd given in to his temptation. He'd lusted, and his weakness had brought death into the mission.

He closed his eyes and pictured *her,* the woman who had lied to him, had seduced him, had brought evil into the mission. Seduced him—he was a willing partner. He'd seen her as the sign he'd been waiting for that God wasn't calling him, that He'd never called him into the priesthood. He'd been dangerously wrong.

He wanted to sleep, here, safe, knowing Anthony and Moira would be sentries against the evil that wanted him. But he couldn't sleep. His mind was a mess; he could hardly keep his thoughts straight.

When he'd first seen Moira O'Donnell, he was certain they'd met before—talked before. He remembered her hair, her voice with her subtle Irish lilt, her long, elegant fingers . . . But they'd never met. He *knew* they'd never met.

It was as if she were meant to find him. But that scared him as well, because he was a pawn in a larger game.

And last night on the cliffs—the words he knew, the phrases, the commands. He didn't question, just spoke—ordered—*commanded*—and the *arca*, Lily Ellis, was saved. As hard as he tried now, he couldn't remember what he'd said.

He hadn't been possessed, but nor was he quite himself. It was as if his brain had many rooms, and someone had unlocked a door he'd never known was there, then slammed it shut—and locked it—after he had a glimpse inside. Try as he might, he couldn't open the door again. This wasn't the first time, and he feared it wouldn't be the last.

He closed his eyes, hoping to sleep undisturbed by the nightmares—real and imagined—that had haunted him during the three months he was in a coma. He had to tell Anthony about the dreams, but would Anthony believe what Rafe had seen? The dreams felt so *real* that Rafe was certain they were memories, but that was ridiculous. It was more likely the work of one of the local witches—and there were many, as he knew from his time at the mission. They had blinded him to their evil intent, and when he finally learned the truth, it had been too late. They'd planted dreams and nightmares in his mind during his coma to torment him.

He moaned out loud, his chest tight with emotional pain, as images of the vivid, blood-soaked chapel snapped into his head. He'd been blinded, true, but not just because of the witches. What if he couldn't stop the evil that threatened them? What if he'd unknowingly unleashed the *arca* when he saved Lily Ellis? He'd saved one, but many more were in jeopardy.

He slipped into an uneasy sleep . . . And the dreams returned. And try as he did to wake himself, he couldn't. Just like he couldn't awaken for the last ten weeks, though he'd desperately tried.

The priest prepared the homily as he always did, after prayer and fasting.

The African villagers Isa served had nothing. Some went days without food. Water was scarce. Children were starving.

What could he say to them tomorrow? They stared at him with blank expressions, sitting in the tent church, converting to Christianity because they received a small wafer of bread. The bread of life . . .

"Give me faith, Lord."

He had great faith, which was why he'd been sent to Kenya. Missionaries died here. They were tortured and murdered for giving hope to a hopeless people. Death didn't scare him. He believed in Paradise.

"Abba! Abba!" The boy, ten, ran into the small hut Father Isa Tucci lived in behind the tent church. He grinned, carrying a long animal in his bony black arms. "I hunt him."

At first, Isa panicked. He had a great fear of snakes. But this snake was dead, a nonpoisonous boa.

Isa smiled at the boy. "Let's prepare a fire."

How could he feed two hundred people with one snake? He would make a stew. And he prayed for a miracle akin to the loaves and fishes. These children of God needed a miracle.

They needed food.

The potatoes he grew were small, but they would make a good starch. He used the last of the beans, only three handfuls now, feeling a bit like the foolish boy who bought magic beans hoping to grow a beanstalk to the heavens. Everyone in the village contributed something. There was laughter and talk.

Father Isa looked on in approval, humbled. "Thank you, Lord."

Hours later, they went to sleep with full stomachs and hope. There were leftovers—enough for a small bowl tomorrow for every man, woman, and child.

In the middle of the night Isa woke to the familiar sound of many Jeeps. Fear clutched his heart. Evil lived in darkness.

He emerged from his hut and saw that the tribal chief had also stepped out. "We must hide," Isa told him.

He shook his head. "It's too late."

"No—"

"Save the children." Children were being brought from their huts as gunfire rang out nearby.

There were thirty-six children under age thirteen in the tribe, but he could find only fifteen of them. They silently followed Isa to their hiding spot in the ground. They hid for hours. Through gunfire. Screams. Cries for mercy that did not come. Isa prayed. The gunmen were above them but did not see their camouflaged entry.

When the silence outside matched the silence of the children inside the cramped shelter, Isa stepped out.

The stench of blood filled his senses.

Winged predators—vultures—were already feasting on the remains. There would be more predators soon. He walked slowly through the village.

The women had been butchered, the men tortured and killed. The children that had been left behind were no longer there. They'd been taken for slaves.

He turned, saw one boy who'd been left. The boy who had hunted the snake. His hands were cut off. His feet. His tongue. Isa realized then that the child had stolen, not hunted, the snake.

As he watched, baby snakes poured out of the boy's body, from every limb that had been severed. Isa screamed and closed his eyes. When he opened them, the snakes were gone. But the boy was still butchered.

The slaughter was for revenge. One theft and nearly two hundred innocent people were dead.

Isa fell to his knees and cursed God.

Rafe sat upright in bed, the scent of blood wafting through the motel room, the air so hot his tongue was dusty and dry. For a split second he saw snakes, hundreds of them, slithering around the room, and he stifled a cry while praying for deliverance.

Then the snakes were gone, and the reality of his nightmare hit him.

Father Isa Tucci was one of the priests who'd been murdered at the mission. For months Rafe had encouraged Father Tucci to talk about the demon he'd confronted in Africa, but he'd refused. What he'd suffered then, the choice he'd had to make, had tormented him for more than a decade. Rafe understood now, understood as he never had while Father Tucci was alive.

"You had no choice, Father," Rafe whispered. "God forgives you; you must forgive yourself."

The room grew cold and the door between the rooms slowly shut without sound.

A flutter of wings sounded, but Rafe saw nothing.

Cold . . . a ghost? Father Tucci?

Rafe rose from the bed. He heard Anthony and Moira talking in hushed but firm voices. He shouldn't have feigned sleep earlier; the relaxation had led to real sleep and the nightmare about Father Tucci. He checked the seals at the doors, the windows, the corners, the vents. Moira had been meticulous, ingenious even in sealing the hotel vents with salt and sticking a crucifix above the opening. She was exceptional in her complexity, and anyone who went head to head against Anthony had courage. Anthony was the golden child of St. Michael's, an empath of sorts and a demonologist of the highest order, but he was also vulnerable in that he wasn't a trained hunter.

Rafe had been at Olivet for a year after walking away from his ordination the first time. Rico had wanted him to study hunting, to discern whether they'd missed his calling on the island.

But after completing the training, he still wasn't a hunter. He couldn't make the commitment and walked away. As with music, some could play the notes perfectly but couldn't make music. And some musicians made errors, but their songs were infinitely sweet. Rafe could hunt demons, but he didn't have the core instinct that made him a demon hunter.

He'd failed at St. John's, failed at Olivet, and failed at Santa Louisa. And now he was jeopardizing his friends, new friends and old, and risking the lives of innocent people.

He frowned. How could he know that? How could he know what had happened to Father Tucci? There was no one here—no ghost—yet why was it so cold?

He breathed deeply, realized that the chill was gone, and wondered whether the sensation had been his imagination. Or residual nightmares that clouded his physical perceptions.

He had to face Moira and Anthony. He had to take responsibility.

TWENTY

you envy and you fear, so have no envy, no fear
—JOSHUA RADIN

Moira squeezed her eyes shut. She and Anthony had been going round and round about their next step and Moira was fed up with inaction.

"Lily will die if we wait around here much longer," Moira said to Anthony, glancing anxiously around the hotel room. "Her mother is a witch, and if she was out on the cliffs last night she knows exactly what will happen to Lily. If you're not going to help me rescue her, I'll do it myself."

"What about Rafe?" Anthony asked, his voice low and harsh as he glanced toward the adjoining door. "If he wasn't in a coma, but under a spell—" He frowned. "I protected his room from demons."

"Protection isn't foolproof," Moira said, feeling a smidgen of sympathy for the demonologist. He cared about his friend, and the idea that Rafe had suffered for weeks in a magic-induced limbo disturbed both of them. "And spells are like bacteria. They adapt, become stronger, defeat the standard protection the way bacteria can sometimes survive even with antibiotics. I don't know what they did, but they could have moved him from his room, removed any amulet you had on his body. We don't know, but we have to assume that they did something to him. But why?"

Anthony stared at the door. "I wish I knew. He's not possessed, but he's not himself."

"He's not under a spell," she said quietly.

Anthony turned his attention from Rafe's door to her. She felt uneasy under his silent scrutiny, his face hard and disapproving. She knew exactly what he was thinking, and her heart twisted.

"I'll get Lily," she said quietly. "If she's not at her house, I'll track her down."

"How?"

"Her boyfriend. Jared knows more than he realizes. But I'll need a safe house to take her to."

"Bring her to Skye's place."

"The sheriff? Aren't you putting her in a difficult position? I'm talking about *kidnapping* a minor. Lily is seventeen. Her mother is a witch, but she'll use the law when it suits her. Even if Lily wants to come with me, you're risking your girlfriend's career."

"Some things are more important."

"What about Rafe? I can't take him there, too, and we need to stick together. If we spread out too thin, we weaken the team." She glanced around the hotel room. Much nicer than what she was used to. "Maybe I can bring Lily here, but I don't know how safe this place is."

"You diligently protected—"

"It doesn't matter how well I protected these rooms against witchcraft or demons; there are ways to get to him—and you—and me. And Lily. We're *all* in danger; it's just a matter of time. Fiona made that perfectly clear this morning. We can't leave Rafe alone, so are you suggesting we bring him to Skye's house as well? She'll have to bring him in for questioning; he's probably under suspicion for murder—"

"*What?*"

"Give it up, Anthony. I *know* Rafe didn't hurt Abby, but people aren't going to listen to our arguments without tossing us into a padded cell or prison, which is exactly where Fiona wants us. Where she can get to us."

"Do not treat me like a novice, Moira. You have no idea what I've faced here since the murders at the mission. Antagonism. Hatred. Adoration and idol worship. Some people think I'm a religious nutcase, others think I'm a prophet, others are starting a cult. People have bowed at my feet and spit in my face. Skye has been under close scrutiny by the city council, and the fact that the daughter of the mayor is dead and there are occult overtones is going to make it much worse for Rafe. I know exactly how the town will respond when the truth comes out about Rafe, which is why I want to send him back to St. Michael's. Except—"

He stopped mid-sentence. Moira was surprised at how much Anthony confided in her about what he'd gone through these last weeks. He had no intention of befriending her, but she understood him and what he'd been through more than anyone else could.

"Except we need Rafe here, in the middle of the battle," she finished quietly. "Okay, truce. Please, Anthony, until we figure out exactly *what* has happened and how to track those seven demons, we need to be on the same side. We should wake Rafe; he needs to be part of the planning. In fact, I'd suggest you stay here with him and I'll get Lily tonight. Can we take her to the mission? Is it safe?"

"Yes, but you can't drive that road now. It's extremely

dangerous in the rain, and if someone—or some*thing*—
is tracking you it would be far too easy to push you off
the edge. I'll check out the cliffs on my way home; you
stay here with Rafe. I—"

"I won't let anything happen to him," she said. She
looked at the door that separated her from Rafe. He was
listening—the door was ajar, and she sensed him standing right on the other side.

Anthony stared at her and nodded. "I'll return at
dawn to talk to Rafe while you find Lily and take her to
the mission."

"That's six hours," she said.

"Like you said, we don't have much time."

Moira hesitated. She had no intention of waiting until
dawn to grab Lily. But she'd have to take Rafe with her,
and she didn't want to jeopardize him.

Anthony said, "I still don't trust you."

"I know. And believe me, I hate that I *do* trust you."

Rafe heard Moira approach the partially closed door.

"He's gone," Moira said. Rafe smiled. She'd known
he was standing there, listening.

He opened the door and stepped through.

She looked him up and down. "Glad the clothes fit."

Anthony had brought him jeans and a black cotton
T-shirt. "They're loose."

"You lost weight while you were at the hospital 're-
sort.' I have some power bars here, water, not much else.
Though we can raid the mini-fridge. It's on Anthony's
tab." She grinned.

Moira was a beautiful woman, he realized, classical
Irish beauty. No makeup; smooth, creamy skin with a
smattering of faint freckles on her nose; thick wavy

black hair that shined under the light. Tall, lithe, and athletic, all movement and muscle. She wasn't a woman to sit still, he noted. Even when she was standing, her hands were in her pockets, or running through her hair, or tapping, full of energy.

Beautiful for certain, but with sad eyes. Brilliant blue eyes, the color of the eastern sky just before dawn broke, so alluring he wanted to lose himself under her gaze.

He sat on the sofa and diverted his gaze. He shouldn't be looking at Moira as he was, yearning for something he couldn't have. He'd lost so much already because he'd lusted; he'd allowed himself to be seduced by a witch. He wouldn't do it again.

He felt as if he knew things about Moira, things he couldn't know, but every time he tried to concentrate, the memory—if that's what it was—flitted away. He wanted to believe it was nothing, just a comfort he'd felt when he was with Moira from the moment she found him.

He knew it was more than that.

She was looking at him quizzically, but he didn't have the answer he knew she wanted. Not yet. So he said, "I agree we need to find Lily. But I'm not staying here while you put yourself in harm's way."

She sat on the small table across from him. "You're not a hundred percent." She smiled, tried to make a joke. "Being in a coma can be tiring."

He didn't smile. He touched the side of her face where a bruise had formed, from her neck up to her cheek. "What happened? This is recent."

"Fiona. My mother." Moira glanced away, uncomfortable with his touch. He dropped his hand.

"The head of the coven."

"Look, Rafe." She rose, fidgeting, picked up her water bottle from the desk, and drank heavily. "Fiona is planning another ritual using Lily as bait for the Seven. So let's get her, bring her back here, and take turns sleeping, okay? Two hours and I'll be good."

She tossed him a power bar and water bottle. "Eat up." She opened her own and took a bite. "You need your strength," she said with her mouth full.

He took a bite of the tasteless food. Chewed. Swallowed.

Moira was openly watching him, her enquiring expression curious and honest. Her strength moved him. Not just the physical strength he'd witnessed when she found him at the cabin and practically carried him back to the truck, or when she brought him to the hotel room, but her inner strength. Her character was so solid, so steadfast and resolute, that he trusted her. The odd sensation that they'd met before came and went again. He let it go, knowing that if he chased the memory, his headache would return.

Quietly, he confided in her. "I remember . . . things."

She leaned against the desk, studying him with her sharp eyes. "Like what?"

"I've been thinking about this all day, all night. I heard what you said to Anthony, that his protections might have protected my hospital room, but not me. I was taken somewhere, Moira. Almost every night. It was in the hospital—I think I can find the room if I go back. There might be information there that can help me figure out what they did to me."

Moira believed Rafe, believed everything he said and things he didn't say. Rafe was both solid and ethereal, tough but yet vulnerable. He wasn't intentionally being deceptive, yet in her heart she felt he was holding back—that while he wasn't lying to her, he wasn't telling her everything. She didn't expect him to open up completely about what had happened to him at the mission and in the hospital, but she *did* expect him to lay out the important facts. The things that could get her and others killed. Or worse.

There were worse things than dying.

"Tell me what you're hiding," she said.

He tilted his head, bemused and surprised. It was an endearing gesture, and it took all her willpower not to simply look away to avoid it. She couldn't be soft around him. Not because *he* would hurt her, but because if she relaxed with him, her senses might not be in tune with everything that was going on around them. If she let her guard down, evil would have a way in.

"How do you know I'm hiding anything, Moira?"

"I read people very well. It's kept me alive for a long time." Now she did look away, making the excuse that she needed more water. She picked up her bottle again, realized it was empty, and put it down. What she wouldn't give for a pint of Guinness! Not the bottled crap they sold in America, but the perfectly drawn pint from an oak cask in her quiet hometown of Kilrush, Ireland.

But there was no going home, no drinking on the job, and her job was now 24/7.

"I don't want to talk about it," he said.

"You're going to have to. Dammit, Rafe! My life is a damn open book; crack your spine a bit and cough it up. What is going on with you? Other than the fact that you were out of it for two months, what do you know?"

"That's just it—I know things I shouldn't! Things I

don't remember learning. I don't know if they did something to me at the hospital, I don't know if—" he stopped himself.

"If what?" she prompted.

"If I'm dangerous! I need answers. That's why I need to go to the hospital. Answers are there. Please, believe me."

As he stood, a wave of pain crossed his face, but he pushed forward, pacing slowly. She watched, leaning against the desk, resisting the urge to help or console him. Rafe had the same physical presence as most of the men from St. Michael's. Calm on the outside but with energy rippling beneath the surface. The quiet intensity, the vibrancy of being *alive* and fighting, and part of a world most people didn't know existed, let alone have any true understanding of what they faced daily.

He said, "When I stopped the ritual on the cliffs, I spoke in a language I do not know. I *knew* what they were doing even though I've never had more than a cursory study of demonology and witchcraft. I failed as a hunter, I failed as a seminarian, and I failed the men at the mission. What good am I if I can't see evil when it's right in front of me? I thought I found my calling here in Santa Louisa, but then my brothers were murdered. Mentally tortured and slaughtered like animals. Poisoned under my watch. Poisoned, because I was blinded—"

He cut himself off and put his hands on the wall, his back to her. A chill ran down her spine, but her voice was surprisingly calm when she asked, "Are you using magic?"

"No!" he shouted, turning to face her. His pale face was twisted in distress. "No," he repeated. "Not on purpose. But I don't know what I did, how I stopped them—maybe whatever Dr. Bertrand was doing to me turned me into one of them. What if I'm risking everyone? What if I'm the one who set the demons free?"

Now, Moira did cross the room. She put her hands on his shoulders and shook him. Though he had at least fifty pounds on her, he moved back and forth as if he were a leaf.

"Fiona and her coven are to blame. Not you. You can't do that to yourself. Do you think that any of us are perfect? We *all* make mistakes. We *all* screw up big-time. If they did something to you, we'll find out what and we'll reverse it."

"What if they're using me? Using me for something I don't even understand! I can't fight against the unknown!"

"Well, I can tell you that you're not possessed and you're not under a spell. If you were cursed, we'd know it here, in this room." She gestured toward the doors, windows, and vents she'd sealed. "So rule that out. I'm a witch, Rafe. I don't use magic, but there're some things I know because I was born this way. Conceived to be this way." She spat out the last sentence, her anger getting the better of her. She took a deep breath. It was true that she could sense when someone was possessed or when witchcraft was in the air, but she wasn't entirely convinced it was because she was born that way. Father Philip thought that after her possession seven years ago she was connected, somehow, to that other world. To her, it made her cursed. Father thought it might lead to victory. She hoped he was right.

"We'll figure it out," she repeated. "First, Lily. She's in danger. Then, after Lily is safe, I'll go to the hospital."

"Not alone."

"I've been alone most of my life, Rafe, and frankly, I like it that way. No one else gets hurt."

Rafe watched her turn abruptly from him, mumbling an excuse as she stepped into the bathroom, shutting the door behind her.

The pain in her voice was tangible, and Rafe wanted to take it away.

Moira was wrestling with something deep inside, as insidious as a snake, twisting her as it did him. A powerful urge to protect her washed through him, followed by a desire he knew he could never act on.

Only a moment later she stepped from the bathroom and said, "Ready?"

"Let me get my shoes."

He stepped into the adjoining room and heard a card slide into the lock. He stopped.

Moira was right behind him. "What?"

Someone swore outside the door and moved away.

"Who was that?" he asked.

"I don't know." She was concerned, her voice tight. She walked over to the door, listened. "They're gone." She frowned. "No—someone is there. Voices." She closed her eyes. Rafe slipped on the shoes Anthony had brought with the clothing.

"Moira—"

"Shh."

She was listening so intently, Rafe wondered if she could hear his heart beating.

Suddenly she said, "They know we're here. We need to get out of here." She ran back to the main room and grabbed her bag.

He followed her. "But they can't get in. It's safer if we stay."

She shook her head. "Sure, we're just fine for a while, but those guys were human. They can walk right in and do whatever they damn well please. And I don't want to kill anyone, okay?" She frowned. "We can't go out the door; I don't know how many there are and they might be waiting for us to leave. The key didn't work because they'd cast a spell on it, and at least my protections worked long enough to keep them out. The balcony— hey!"

Before she could finish her sentence, the lights went out. The emergency lights flickered on, blue and low to the ground.

"We're so fucked," Moira said.

TWENTY-ONE

Years of living in motel rooms and cheap apartments had trained Moira to travel light and stay packed. She had everything she needed in her bag and slung it on her back.

"Stay out of sight," she said.

Moira crossed to the balcony and, while squatting, slowly opened the door but not the drapes. So far so good. She heard people in the hallway, guests complaining or worried about the power outage. Also good. She said to Rafe, "Stay here, by the door, don't go out. I have an idea."

"What?"

"Chaos. That's a strategy that usually works."

She ran to the door and listened again, but there were at least a half dozen people chatting in the hallway and she couldn't distinguish the voices of the men she'd heard outside Rafe's door. She closed her eyes, picturing the hall as she'd seen it when they first came in. They were three rooms from the end. To the left was the main hallway, and at the far end, the elevators. To the right was the staircase. The bad guys would assume they'd go to the staircase since it was closer. She hoped.

But next to the staircase was the fire alarm.

Outside her door she heard the shrill voice of a

woman. "I was drying my hair! My hair is going to frizz if I can't dry it! Kenny, can't you do something?"

Moira took that moment to open her door and step out. The woman jumped. "Watch where you're going!"

By the time she finished her sentence, Moira had opened the small door of the alarm and set it off.

The clanging of the emergency bells and a piercing siren trilled through the hallway.

"What are you doing?" the woman demanded as Moira stepped back into her room, shut the door, and slid both the bolt and the chain.

A swirling red light in the corner of the room had gone on with the alarm, along with a mechanical voice informing them of a possible fire and to leave the building.

"Let's go," she said to Rafe. "Stay low."

"Why'd you do that?"

"Ask questions later. We're going to jump. It's only about twelve feet."

In case someone was watching the balcony, she didn't want to be obvious. The power outage helped some, though the emergency lights didn't.

"On three," she said.

They counted together, then she pushed open the sliding glass door and without hesitating, they both ran to the far corner of the wide balcony. They jumped together, rolling to soften the fall, and then were up and running low toward the trees on the north side of the lot where she had parked Jared's truck.

Moira kept pace with Rafe, who didn't have all his strength back but was moving fast enough. She spotted Jared's truck under a street light and turned in that direction, Rafe right behind her. The fire alarm faded in the distance, but she couldn't hear any sirens. She glanced behind her and saw no one in pursuit, but she didn't dare slow down.

She hadn't told Rafe what she'd overheard in the hall, but he needed to know as soon as they were clear that he was in danger. The thugs hadn't said a word about Moira but had mentioned Rafe by name.

Moira sprinted the last fifty feet so she could get the car open and started by the time Rafe got inside. Keys in hand, she clicked the unlock button and reached for the door at the same time that someone leaped out from between two cars in the next aisle. It happened so fast, while she was focused on who might be behind them, that the tall guy had an extra few seconds to grab her, and he slammed her head against the glass.

Shit! She tried to shake her head to rid it of the stars in her eyes. She was furious with herself; her instincts weren't as sharp as they needed to be.

"Well, surprise surprise! It's little Andra Moira," the asshole cooed.

"Don't say that name," she hissed, jerking against him. He whipped out a knife and spun her around, holding the blade against her throat.

He laughed. "Your mother will be so pleased to see you again, *Andra*."

Rafe watched as Moira was grabbed by the beefy thug and ran forward as if to tackle the attacker, halting ten feet from the truck when the man put a knife at her throat. Blood seeped through a cut on Moira's forehead. Rafe's chest burned, but everything around him stilled, his eyesight sharpened, and he focused on the immediate danger to Moira.

"Cooper," the attacker said, pressing the knife into

Moira's flesh. "Come with me and I won't kill her."
Blood dotted her pale skin.

"He's lying." Moira's eyes were dark with fear, but her
voice was steady. "Run."

He wouldn't be alone, Rafe knew. There had been at
least two people outside his room, and someone had
turned off the power to the hotel. They would be
nearby. He didn't have time to escape, nor would he
leave Moira. Moira had dropped the keys when she was
grabbed. Rafe had no weapon.

He said, "Let her go and I'll come."

"Get out of here, Rafe!" Moira ordered.

"I'm not leaving you."

"Dammit!" She was angry and fought against her attacker's arm.

Rafe pointedly glanced to Moira's left and saw that
she understood his signal, even though they'd never
trained together.

It was going to be risky, because he had to wait. Wait
until the attacker's backup was in sight in order to create a distraction.

"You work for Fiona," Moira said to the attacker.
"You won't let me live."

"For a while."

"Téigh trasna ort féin," Moira said. Rafe had no idea
what it meant, but it sounded insulting and the thug
tightened his hold. The knife dug deeper into her skin.
Rafe was slow to anger, but seeing Moira in pain, blood
dripping down her neck, had him raging inside. He
swallowed the emotion, knowing it would hinder him.
Only complete calm and focus could save her.

Rafe saw two men jogging toward them from behind
the hotel. He turned his head to get Moira's attacker's

attention. When he looked in that direction, the knife wavered just a fraction.

Simultaneously, Moira reached up between the attacker's hand and her body, grabbed the man's wrist, twisted it, and slammed it against the cab of the truck so hard Rafe heard a bone snap. She kicked the creep in the groin as Rafe reached down for the keys on the ground. He came up and grabbed the man's other arm, pulling him away from the truck and pushing him hard into the ground as Moira grabbed the knife he'd dropped when she broke his wrist. Rafe slipped Moira the keys while she handed him her dagger.

A bullet ricocheted off the truck.

"Get in," she ordered Rafe as she opened the door. "Slide over."

Two men were running their way and firing weapons. As Moira was shutting the door, she cried out. "Shit!"

She locked the doors and turned the ignition simultaneously, tears leaking out of her eyes as she bit back the pain and drove fast out of the parking lot.

"You okay?" he asked, glancing behind him.

"I'm fine."

He looked at her left arm and saw a hole in the leather jacket. "You were shot!"

"It's minor. Just hurts like a bitch, but I'm fine."

They weren't out of the woods yet. He saw a car behind them. "The gunmen are in a sedan. They're following."

"I need to lose them. Hold on. Put on your seat belt."

"You're not—"

"Do what I say!"

She had definitely been trained by Rico Cortese, Rafe thought. She sounded just like him. He did as she said and noticed that she winced when she put her left hand on the steering wheel.

He grabbed the door handle as Moira spun the truck in a one-eighty. She then drove straight at their pursuers, turning on the high beams.

"Moira—" Rafe felt helpless as she increased speed.

The game of chicken was quickly over. Moira moved left, which the pursuing car didn't expect, and the driver overcompensated and jerked the car off the road.

Moira braked quickly but steadily. She spun the car around again and continued in her original direction, away from the hotel.

"Rico never taught me that move," Rafe said.

She was shaking. "Rico didn't teach me it either. I just made it up," she said. She glanced in her rearview mirror. No one behind. "I'm good on the fly."

She shot a look at Rafe, then focused on the road ahead. "I heard what those men said outside your room. Fiona wants you alive. What do you have that she needs?"

Rafe slammed his fist on the dashboard. "I don't know!"

"We'd better figure it out sooner rather than later, because she's not going to stop until she succeeds."

TWENTY-TWO

After nearly twelve years as a cop, and the last two as sheriff, very little surprised Skye McPherson.

Today surprised her.

It wasn't just that a teenage girl was left naked and dead on the cliffs in an apparent occult ritual—which may or may not have been murder.

Or that a sweet, mild-mannered librarian had stolen a classic 1964 Mustang and committed suicide by driving off the cliffs and into the rocks at the edge of the Pacific Ocean.

Or that she'd been called to a hostage situation at Rittenhouse Furniture that night that ended in death when David Collins shot the gunman. There were four deaths and two survivors—one of whom was in critical condition. The other, customer Ashley Beecher McCracken, was hysterical and under sedation at the hospital. Skye hoped to get a statement from her in the morning.

It was that Skye had faced all these deaths in one twenty-four-hour period—only ten weeks after the massacre at the mission.

She finally arrived home after midnight. She knew Anthony was there—her sheriff's truck was in the driveway. She'd parked behind it in the marked sedan she'd borrowed from the pool. The shower was on, and she considered joining him . . . but what she really wanted was a shot of whiskey.

As if all this death and dying wasn't enough, the D.A., Martin Truxel, had waylaid her at the hospital after the shooter, Ned Nichols, was declared D.O.A. Truxel made it perfectly clear that he would make Raphael Cooper's disappearance and Abby Weatherby's murder major issues in her upcoming election against his hand-chosen candidate, Assistant Sheriff Thomas Williams.

Whiskey in front of her, she stood at the kitchen counter, palms down, and replayed the conversation over and over.

"You're incompetent, McPherson. I'm watching these investigations closely. And you."

She'd never liked the arrogant, ladder-climbing D.A., but now she was scared. If he dug too deeply, not only was her job at stake, but so were those of everyone else who had helped her cover up what happened on the cliffs during the fire that claimed three lives. Juan Martinez, Rod Fielding, even Deputy David Collins had helped her clean up after the fact, no questions asked, because they trusted her.

David was extremely upset about what happened tonight at Rittenhouse. So was she, but he blamed himself because he'd told Grace Chin to stay in the bathroom, that he was coming in to save her.

And Ned Nichols had shot her while Skye was talking to Grace on the phone. It was a living nightmare. When Skye closed her eyes, she heard Grace's scream, then the gunshots. She would never forget.

"Skye?"

She turned around. Anthony stood there in jeans and no shirt, his skin damp from his shower, his shoulder-length hair brushed slick down the nape of his neck, curling at the ends. The scar from where he'd been stabbed on the cliffs was still dark across his stomach. She'd almost lost him ten weeks ago. She loved him so much her chest ached, and she wanted to break down and hold him forever.

"Skye, honey, what's wrong?"

She wiped at her damp eyes. She wasn't crying, she just wanted to. "It's been an awful day, an even worse night." She looked down at the glass of whiskey she'd poured but now didn't want. She pushed it aside.

Anthony pulled out a chair and sat her down on it, then sat across from her. He kissed her lightly on the lips, so light, so sweet, but she didn't want light *or* sweet. She wanted hot, passionate sex with Anthony right now. She wanted to pull down his jeans, kiss him everywhere, make love to him on the table, the floor, anywhere as long as they were together, touching, naked.

"Talk to me."

She shook her head and pulled him to her, kissed him hard and long, pushing her tongue into his, drawing it into her mouth. He met her lust, kiss for kiss, stroke for stroke.

His lips were hard and warm against hers, his body solid, fresh soap and a hint of something mysterious on his flesh. He made her wild with need, for him, only him.

His hands moved down her back, up her shirt, hot against her cold skin. She wrapped her arms around his neck, fisting his damp hair in her hands, rubbing his neck, his shoulders, unable to keep her hands still.

"Skye—"

"Don't talk. Make love to me."

She pulled off her shirt and felt his bare skin against hers. She was urgent, moaning as her nipples pressed against his chest, as his large hand pushed between them and molded around her breast.

She fumbled with his jeans. He had to stand so she could push them down, along with his briefs, and his semi-hard cock grew under her touch. He knelt in front of her, kissed her, his hands on her breasts. She pushed his head from her lips downward, and he took one small breast into his mouth, his hand cupping and squeezing the other. She gasped as his teeth lightly bit her nipple, then reached down and squeezed him, pulling him closer to her.

"Skye—" he whispered into her chest.

"Shh." He always wanted to make sure she was comfortable, that she was enjoying herself, so concerned about her that he never really let himself *go*. She wanted him to lose control with her, to want her so much that he took everything she offered and more. He was too damn restrained, too damn *noble*.

But she didn't want to talk about it, not now; she just wanted Anthony in her, over her, any way she could get him. He was hers; she wanted to mark him.

Very unlike her. She swallowed uneasily, then Anthony whispered in her ear, "I love you, Skye," as he stood, helping her to her feet.

He slid off her uniform pants and panties together, and she was naked. He picked her up to carry her to the bedroom. Always the gentleman. Always chivalrous.

"Right here, right now," she said, using her body to direct him toward the counter. Uncertain, he sat her on the edge and she wrapped her legs around his waist. He was exactly the right height to make love to her like this.

Before he could protest, she guided him into her, then slid forward to take him completely. She gasped, wrapped her arms around him, and his hands moved to support her. His cock involuntarily jerked inside her. He was trying to control it again, to fight the passion, to make sure she was comfortable, that she orgasmed first, that she had pleasure even if he denied himself.

But she knew his body now, knew how to push him over the edge. She kissed his earlobe, her tongue circling, sucking, moving down his jawline, to his lips where she kissed him hard, drawing his tongue into her mouth, mimicking sex. His cock soon followed the rhythm she set with their mouths and they both groaned, so close to the edge, so close to losing themselves completely in each other.

Anthony couldn't resist Skye when she touched him. She was a siren for him, calling, beckoning, drawing him in. She was his greatest strength and his greatest weakness. As soon as she nipped his tongue he let himself go, pulling out of her, then plunging in, her body open and inviting, her voice a melodious mixture of lust and satisfaction. Her body glistened with sweat as she worked them both up; he kissed her neck, tasted her salty flesh, wanted more. He braced his legs, bending his knees for better control. Her back arched and her head tilted back. He watched her face as her mouth opened on a high gasp of pleasure. Her hands gripped the edge of the counter; her long blond hair fell down her back in damp waves.

He swallowed a grunt, sweat pouring off his skin as he held himself in check, wanting desperately to pump heavily into Skye but not wanting to hurt her, not wanting to deny her pleasure. Then she reached behind him and dug her fingernails into his butt, squeezing as she pushed herself into him. He would have stumbled backward, but she pulled them into the counter. He worried she'd hurt her back, but then her finger touched the tender skin on the underside of his penis and he groaned out loud, pushing himself into her as he came in a powerful, uncontrollable wave of ecstasy. Her body tightened around him and she shook with her own release.

He held her close. "I'm sorry," he whispered.

"Why?" Her breath was short and fast.

"I lost control. I wanted to satisfy you."

"You did. And I like it when you lose control."

"I don't. It's—" He didn't know how to say it. It felt *primal*. Lustful. Wanton and wrong. His discipline required that he remain in complete control of his emotions and his physical needs. There was too much at stake to put aside self-control for personal satisfaction. His love already put Skye in great danger; he was selfish to want to be with her. But he craved this one weakness. He needed Skye.

"You can't control everything, Anthony," she said quietly.

Lights from a car coming up the street cast shadows across the kitchen. Anthony stepped back, picking Skye up and putting her on the floor.

"Someone stopped in front of the house," he said.

She nodded toward his pants on the floor by the table as she grabbed her uniform and underclothes. "Get dressed. I'll be right out."

She walked into the bedroom. Anthony knew something was wrong, but he didn't know what. He started to follow, but the knock on the door stopped him.

He crossed to the front door and looked out the side window. Rafe.

And Moira. They both had blood on them.

Something had gone terribly wrong.

Fiona listened to Ian explain how he—and two other strong, grown men!—had lost Raphael Cooper.

She was beyond furious that Moira—of all people—had found Cooper first.

But it explained a lot.

"Are you certain you shot her?"

"Her arm was bleeding pretty good, and Walter cut her neck."

"He should have slit her throat when he had that knife on her. He's a weak fool. Take care of him."

Ian cleared his throat. "Can you try the blood demon again? We're ready to go out."

"No. Now that won't work."

Fiona paced, the electricity in the room sparking with her anger.

Serena explained to Ian, "It's Moira's blood. If Cooper has any of it on him, it's protecting him. We won't be able to find him."

"What's so special about her blood?" Ian asked. "She's not a witch anymore."

"She'll always be a witch, whether she uses magic or not," Serena said.

Fiona interrupted before Serena said more. Not because it was a secret about Moira's bloodline, but simply because the subject infuriated her. All she'd done to protect Moira as the Mediator was now being used against Fiona.

"That doesn't explain why we lost him after the

cabin," Fiona said. "My Third Eye saw him, we knew he was there, but then he was gone."

Serena cleared her throat. "Maybe it was her physical presence that gave him some sort of protective bubble. Your 'eye' has never been able to find her unless she used magic; maybe if she's near Cooper or anyone else she passes that shield on to them."

"Andra Moira needs to die. She's been an annoyance, and now she's becoming a problem." Fiona turned to Ian. "Take care of the idiot Walter, and make sure everyone understands that Moira is wanted only dead. No excuses, no hesitation."

"Yes, Fiona."

She waved at him to make him go away, and he left. It was her and Serena. The good daughter.

"It's too late to set up the ritual tonight, and we need a new location." She needed Cooper, but it could wait until the Seven were bound in the *arca*.

"I have one." Serena handed her a printout from the local *Santa Louisa Courier* dated only an hour ago.

Local Man Goes Postal; DOA in SWAT action
Four people dead at Rittenhouse Furniture

A tense three-hour hostage situation ended at 10:36 tonight when a SLSD SWAT officer shot Ned Nichols through a skylight at Rittenhouse Furniture Discounters while he held a customer at gunpoint. . . .

"Why are you showing me this?" Fiona asked her.

"Four dead. This guy Nichols lost it . . . violence, rage, lots of blood; it'll draw the demons in."

"We may have ghosts to contend with," Fiona countered.

"*May* have ghosts. And if we do, I can handle them."

Fiona considered the location. It *would* be private, and the spilled blood would be a lure. Though she was loath to admit it, Serena had exceptional control over her powers and could handle any spirits that interfered. Under normal circumstances, Fiona didn't worry about ghosts because lost souls were easily sent to the underworld with a simple incantation. But with all her energy focused on the Seven, she could possibly leave herself vulnerable to a pathetic ghost, especially one who didn't know it was dead—too often the case in sudden, violent deaths.

She smiled and spontaneously hugged her daughter. "Good idea, Serena. Now I think I'll release some of this frustration with Garrett and get my beauty rest. You should do the same—you have bags under your eyes."

Serena closed and locked the library doors behind Fiona and smirked. If she only *knew* that Garrett fooled around with others behind her back, Fiona would be livid. She expected her "men" to be loyal to her, even though she slept around when the mood struck her. But Serena wasn't about to tell on him. She liked the lying minister. Not to screw around with, but as a kindred spirit. They were both good at deception.

She lay down on the chaise lounge and closed her eyes, incanting the spell that allowed her own psychic eye to see. She had never told Fiona that she'd developed the power, so Fiona had no reason to block her.

Serena's mind tumbled and fell, stars swirling, until she felt disconnected from her body, connecting more firmly with the elements. The air, the fires, the winds, the waters—she was everywhere and she was nowhere.

This must be how omnipotence felt.

She watched Fiona and Garrett begin their sexual dance in Fiona's chamber. Fiona was always in charge, always in control, even during sex. Serena grew tired of watching and left them alone, floating through Santa Louisa, watching, watching, watching.

Seeking . . . she looked for Moira, hoping that this time it would work, but it didn't. It never did, but Serena had grown more powerful with the effort.

She searched for Rafe . . . his eyes. His touch. His mouth. She craved him like no other, wanted him back, her seduction complete only in the carnal sense. Yes, he'd made love to her, but he didn't *love* her, not like she did him.

Moira's blood protects him.

Anger bubbled and boiled as Serena realized Rafe was physically close to Moira.

The thought, the mere *idea,* that Rafe and Moira were working together angered her so much that her psychic eye returned to her too quickly. Serena's head ached with a migraine so sudden and fierce that she couldn't get up if she wanted to.

But she had an idea that would lead them to Rafe, if he was still with Moira. And if that were the case, they could take both of them. It would require time and extensive energy on her part, but she realized that she could see all of Santa Louisa *except* where Moira and Rafe were. She'd find them through the process of elimination as soon as she regained her strength.

TWENTY-THREE

Skye watched the coffee drip steadily into the pot while Anthony treated Moira's injuries.

She should have taken Rafe Cooper to the hospital, or into custody. Yet she'd let Anthony talk her out of it. She hadn't protested much—it was two in the morning and she'd been up for twenty-four hours straight. Why was she making coffee? Honestly, no amount of caffeine would keep her awake at this point.

She'd called dispatch and learned about the false fire alarm at the hotel and calls of shots fired, but no witnesses came forward with information that helped. Two deputies were on scene but hadn't found a shooter. And when Rafe told them the story of jumping off the balcony and running for the truck, he'd left something out. She didn't know what, but he wasn't telling the complete truth. He skimmed over the story, and every time she had a question Anthony put his hand on hers, asking a question of his own that had nothing to do with the crime at hand.

So Skye had started the coffee, duty and love coming head-to-head. She should have resigned after the massacre.

She and Anthony had lied about what happened at the fire on the cliffs. No one would believe that Juan Martinez had been possessed and tried to kill her. Not only had she written a false report about how Deputy Reiner died, she'd enlisted Rod Fielding's help in covering up details that would have opened even more questions for which no one would believe the answers. She *should* have quit, but she didn't because she loved Santa Louisa. This was the only home she'd ever known. Her father had been born and raised here, had died in the forest he loved so well. She'd be lost anywhere else. But even more important, she had to protect her people. Not just Anthony, but the innocent citizens who didn't know that demons were alive and thriving in their town, a threat to their lives and their loved ones. That there were people who played around with demons, who wanted to control and use them for specific purposes Skye would never understand.

Anthony came up beside her and rinsed bloody towels in the sink. Pink water swirled down the drain.

"I'm sorry, Skye. I know this puts you in a difficult situation."

"Don't," she said, squeezing her eyes closed. "I understand. But I need some answers soon."

"We both do."

Skye glanced at where Moira and Rafe sat on the couch. A white bandage was wrapped around her upper shoulder—there'd been no bullet, but a large-caliber round had taken a nice chunk out of her arm and she'd lost a bit of blood. The cut on her head was sealed with a butterfly bandage, adding to the bruises she'd sustained earlier in jail.

But it was the thin cut on her neck that had disturbed Skye more than the other injuries. The two-inch wound had already started to heal by the time they walked into Skye's house, but the mark was proof that someone *human* had attacked her.

She brought the pot of coffee over to the table on a

tray with mugs, milk, and sugar. "It's not tea, but it's hot and caffeinated," she said when they stared at it.

Rafe said, "I acquired a taste for coffee after moving to the States." He poured himself a mug and added a hefty dose of milk.

Moira said, "May I have some water?"

Anthony went to get her a water bottle from the refrigerator and Skye sat on the chair across from them. She didn't know how to start.

"This day has been hell," Skye began.

Moira grinned, a raw laugh coming out of her throat as she took the water from Anthony. "You could say that." She drank heavily.

Anthony sat on the armrest of Skye's chair, put one hand on her shoulder and squeezed. She wanted to touch him but didn't move. She said to Rafe, "Tell me why you won't go to the hospital."

"They did something to me there. I don't know what, but I wasn't in a coma. I have memories . . . but I can't focus on them. I had vivid dreams—I'm still having them." He looked at Anthony. "Do you know Father Isa Tucci?"

"His name, not personally. He was killed at the mission."

"I know why he was at the mission." A pained expression crossed his face. "It was because of a snake," he said.

"A snake?" Anthony glanced at Moira. What did they know, what did they share, that Skye didn't understand? She felt such the outsider.

"What's important about a snake?" she asked.

Rafe said, "In hindsight, I think the snake was a lure. But at the time . . . a boy came to Father Tucci with a snake, said he'd hunted it. It was large; Father made a stew. Everyone participated.

"The killers came when everyone was asleep. Father woke up, saved a handful of the youngest children. He survived, but almost killed himself."

It was Moira who asked, "How do you know this?"

He looked at Moira, spoke as if talking just to her. "Remember when I told you I know things I don't remember learning? This is one of them."

Skye said, "If they drugged you in the hospital, we should be able to prove it." She turned to Anthony. "I'll call Rod in the morning and ask him to take Rafe's blood and hair samples and run the tests on the q.t."

Anthony concurred. "We'll find out what happened. I promise."

Skye cleared her throat. "Rafe, we need to talk about what happened at the mission. You're the only survivor."

Moira rushed to his defense. "You sound like you're accusing Rafe."

Rafe interjected, "I will answer any of your questions if I can, but first we need to find the person who has *all* the answers."

"Who?"

"Lisa Davies. She's a witch; she was the daughter of the cook at the mission. If you talked to her, she deceived you or cast a spell so you didn't look too closely. But she was there at the mission when the priests were killed. She, Jeremiah Hatch, and Corinne Davies summoned a demon through a violent sacrifice. I was trapped in my room and heard everything, heard the cries . . ." He hesitated, and Moira took his hand and squeezed. "I don't know how I got out, but I think when the demon was brought forth Lisa loosened her mental grip on my prison in order to control him, and I broke free. When I came into the chapel, I saw them . . . and I saw the demon in his true form. Hideous . . . wretched . . . then suddenly beautiful, trying to lure me. But I broke their concentration, and their circle, and the women ran to the sacristy for protection. I intended to kill Jeremiah to stop the demon, but he was already dead."

Everyone looked at Rafe. He spoke as if he was in a trance, the memory so painful that for a moment no one could speak, feeling his anguish.

Anthony said, "Lisa is dead. She died in the fire on the cliffs two days after the murders."

Rafe shook his head as he rubbed his forehead. "She's not dead. I saw her on the cliffs. She changed her hair, from dark to light, but it was her. She's a witch with strong magic. And I was blinded to it. Because of me, because of my weakness, I didn't see the truth. Lisa's spells and her mother's poison forced my brothers to relive their worst nightmares. Those nightmares really happened. When they died, they wanted to die to escape the unbearable pain of reliving their past."

"Thank you," Anthony said when he and Skye lay in bed awhile later. The grandfather clock dinged the half-hour—3:30 in the morning. "Rafe isn't safe anywhere else, and I know this was difficult for—"

She cut him off. "Don't thank me."

"What's wrong? Talk to me Skye. You're upset—"

She sat up in the dark, the moonlight filtered through her filmy curtains making her look pale and blue, to match her mood. "I just realized that you *knew* where Cooper was and didn't tell me."

"He didn't kill those men. You know that! And you also know that no one will believe it."

"Yes, I get that. But I still need to put his comments on record."

"He can't tell anyone what really happened."

"But he can tell us he saw the Davieses in the mission when everyone died. That he saw the weapons!" She paused. "Do you believe that he saw Lisa Davies the other night? What if she's behind Abby's death? What I don't understand is *why*."

"To release the Seven Deadly Sins."

"Right. Bring forth the demons," she said sarcastically, and Anthony tensed. "What I *mean* is, why the elaborate murders at the mission? Why the ritual with Abby Weatherby and Lily Ellis? Why *now*? What's their purpose?"

"I don't know."

"And Rafe never told us how he ended up at the cliffs. You wouldn't let him. Every time I led the conversation in that direction, you steered it away."

"It's late. We were all tired."

"Tomorrow, you need to let me ask the hard questions. I need to take down a statement."

"Of course."

He rubbed her shoulders, gently pushed her back to the bed. "It's been rough today for you."

"For all of us," she said. She relaxed a little, but her mind was still moving. She asked, "Who did it? Who kept Rafe in a coma? Richard Bertrand was his doctor— I just can't think of him being some sort of Satan worshipper. I've known him most of my life."

Anthony bit back an angry comment. She was tired. "They're not worshipping Satan." He thought hard for a minute. "Maybe the massacre at the mission was the beginning, and this is the end."

"It's not the end until I find out what happened to Abby."

"Your dedication and compassion are two of the many reasons I love you." He kissed her forehead. "Sleep, Skye."

"I'm so tired, but I don't know that I can sleep. People are dying all over town. I had a suicide this afternoon, then a whacked out salesman comes back to work after his dinner break and shoots his co-workers. Why do people do it? Don't we have enough human evil in the world, why do these damn witches have to create more?"

"Shh," Anthony murmured and kissed her long fingers and pulled her to him. He loved her so much. He was worried about her job, her health, and the forces in Santa Louisa. He hated what she'd seen, what she had to do, how she had to keep her feelings closed off so she could do her job. Skye wasn't what he'd call a vulnerable woman, but her deep-seated need to understand the unknowable was her Achilles' heel. She was vulnerable to the evil that roamed the town because she still, even after what she'd seen in November, couldn't wrap her logical mind around the supernatural. But she tried, and he loved her for it.

"Sleep, Skye. I'm here. I love you, and I'll protect you. Just sleep."

He held her until she finally relaxed and slept.

Santa Louisa was a small, quiet coastal town. Could so many deaths, in such a short time, be unconnected? It could be demons, but it wasn't like any possessions he'd heard about. If anyone was possessed there would be residual clues—smells, possible marks on the floor or walls. He suspected Moira would be able to walk the crime scenes and know for certain.

If there was something supernaturally evil responsible for the cases Skye pulled over the last twenty-four hours, Anthony would find out. And if he had to ask Moira O'Donnell for help, he'd do it.

He would do anything to protect Skye.

TWENTY-FOUR

O God! can I not save
One from the pitiless wave?
Is all that we see or seem
But a dream within a dream?
—Edgar Allan Poe

It was the dream that couldn't die.

Gino held a knife. He'd taken a life. Guilt pulsed through his body like a snake slithering through his veins. The nightmare that was real.

The boy had been possessed, moving through the village with singular purpose: to kill. Men, women, children. One after another. No one stopped him. They hesitated in their fear, and he slit their throats. They fought back, and he tortured them in ways Gino had never fathomed, wished he'd never known or seen. When the boy reached the third hut, the screams and cries of the dying awakened those still sleeping.

Gino's friend Ravi, the village elder who had brought him to this forsaken Central American country, tried to stop the boy, yet the boy was no longer of this world but of the next. He held Ravi with one hand—impossible, but Gino had seen it with his own eyes! Held him up and snapped his neck with a squeeze.

Impossible, except that the boy was possessed. His eyes were dead. Evil flowed through his body, not blood.

Ravi collapsed in a heap on the parched earth, his neck at an impossible angle.

Gino ran back to his small hut and took up his crucifix and Bible. He could taste evil, feel it crawling on his skin, hot and seductive and fearsome. He could hardly breathe as the screams and cries of the dead and dying vibrated in his head. His hands shook, but if he did nothing to stop the slaughter, the demon would kill all ninety-seven people in this small, poor village.

He ran out to confront the beast.

"In the name of Jesus Christ, I command you to leave!"

The boy flinched, as if stung by a bee.

Gino, emboldened by the power in his voice, began the rite of exorcism.

"In the name of the Father, and of the . . ."

The boy slit the throat of a woman who knelt in prayer. Her dying eyes accused Gino.

. . . you told me God was loving and merciful . . . you lied to me . . . you brought death to our peace . . .

And Gino knew then that her unspoken words were true. It was his fault; he'd brought evil with him. He must destroy the damn book!

"Gino," the demon mocked, and he saw the true face of evil slithering beneath the boy's skin.

He called upon St. Michael the Archangel.

The demon laughed. "Geeeeennnooooooooooo . . ."

His head hurt and blood dripped from his nose. Still he continued the exorcism. He threw holy water on the boy's body. Steam rose from his skin as the beast cried out in pain, a demonic scream that seemed to come from under the earth as the child fell to his knees.

Gino's strength grew.

Then the demon rose, laughing, and lightning struck a hut, trapping the family inside the blazing room.

Gino spoke the words that had been so effective before. Why didn't they work now? Where was God? Where was St. Michael?

Or was it him? He'd opened the book, but he hadn't read. Had the demon been inside, waiting for his weakness to crack a seal he didn't know was there?

"Leave the boy, Satan!"

He felt his feet rising from the ground.

I am dying.

He hovered two feet off the ground, trapped and helpless as the demon set another hut on fire. And another.

In the demon's excitement over the fires, he dropped the knife.

Gino continued the exorcism ritual even while levitated; the demon faltered, but never stopped. Gino, however, fell to the ground and the knife was within his reach.

He clenched it. It was infused with evil, but he held on. It burned his flesh, but he held on.

The next hut went up in flames. If anyone ran, they were thrown through the air as if by magic.

As if by magic. The book!

Gino rose to his feet, knife dripping innocent blood, and with strength he prayed for, he cut the demon's hand off. Small snakes slithered out of its body, spreading the darkness, the evil, coming for him. He stabbed the demon once, twice, three times . . .

The boy fell to his feet. Smoke filled the air, whirled around him; he felt the demon touch his soul, then scream as he disappeared into the earth, and the ground was scorched.

"F-Father."

The boy's eyes were dying. Dying. Gone. He died. Innocent. At Gino's hand. He dropped the knife and prayed for death, but God wasn't merciful.

Gino searched his hut for the book he'd found last week in an abandoned, crumbling structure that at first he'd believed was a church hundreds of years old. He should have known from the arcane and profane symbols on the remaining walls and floor that the church wasn't dedicated to God. If he'd never gone inside he would never have found the book.

He searched the entire village three times before collapsing in exhaustion.

The book was gone.

His penance, it seemed, was purgatory on earth. Reliving the nightmare, the fear, the suffering, the murder of an innocent boy. The endless searching for a book that seemed to have vanished into thin air.

Gino woke from the violent memories every night these last few weeks. So often, in fact, that he feared the dark and dreaded sleep. He took to walking the halls alone, praying for peace, praying to be free.

For two decades he'd fought the memories, beaten them back, and they were finally gone. For years they were gone. His penance had been paid. He had been healed in the loving presence of God, his faith restored . . . but then the memories had returned, worse than before. Vivid. The taste and scent and feel of blood on his hands, in his nose, twisting him in knots so tight he couldn't eat or sleep or think.

Repent. An eye for an eye, a tooth for a tooth.

Chants from the chapel drew him out of his bed and

he stood, feet bare, his sleep shirt brushing against his old, gnarled knees.

He looked down and saw snakes. Small, baby snakes, slithering. He couldn't scream. He couldn't move. He squeezed his eyes closed.

"Gino, come to us, as it is above, it is below.

"Robert, come to us, as it is above, it is below.

"Lorenzo, come to us, as it is above, it is below."

They were all being summoned to the chapel, every one of them. They were sinners; they needed to repent and be cleansed. Be punished.

You have been forgiven. Stay.

He opened his eyes. The snakes were gone.

"Gino, come to us, as it is above, it is below."

Gino didn't notice the tears streaming down his face as he turned the knob and left his room. He walked down the hall, heard other doors opening, heard the chanting in the chapel.

He needed the pain to stop.

He stepped into the chapel and smelled blood. It was his own.

Rafe's chest burned as if he'd been stabbed with a knife. He reached down to pull the knife out . . .

"Rafe—"

He opened his eyes and saw Father Isa Tucci, a knife in his hand, blood spatter on his face.

"No!" He struck out. Hit flesh.

A grunt—female—registered. He sat up, didn't know where he was.

"Rafe! It's me, Moira. Rafe, please, you're having a nightmare."

Moira. She stood next to him, her hand rubbing her jaw.

Oh, God, I hit her. I hit her.

"I'm sorry. I'm sorry."

"It's okay. I'm tough."

She sat next to him. Took his hands in hers. He looked at her. Her jaw was red, on top of the assorted cuts and bruises from the earlier assault. She wore a black tank top, the bandage Anthony had dressed earlier was clean and startling white. She wasn't bleeding anymore.

He pulled one hand from hers, gently touched the tender spot where he'd lashed out in his sleep.

"What was it?"

He rose from the bed and looked around. Skye's guest room. Moira had insisted on taking the couch, but he'd wanted her to have the bed. She'd refused. She was stubborn. He faced her. That stubborn expression was still on her face when she stood, only inches from him, and asked, "Rafe, was it another memory?"

"It wasn't mine. What did they do to me? *Why* did they do this to me?"

She hugged him close to her. She smelled fresh, of soap and water. Fresh and alive and so beautiful it made him ache.

"I promise you, Rafe, we *will* find out exactly what they did."

He liked the way she felt, the way she smelled. She was solid, whole, real . . . just what he needed. "I—I don't understand anything. But I feel everything, like I was right there. The smells, the pain, the fear."

She repeated, "We will find out what they did and reverse it."

"You were a witch, why don't you know?"

The pain on her face came and went so fast Rafe almost missed it. But it was there, and it lingered in her eyes before she shielded them.

"I didn't mean—"

She cut him off. "Anthony and Skye are still sleeping. I'm going for Lily now, before dawn."

"You can't do it alone."

"You can't come with me. They want you—I told you what I overheard last night."

"But they want to kill you."

"My mother has wanted to kill me for a long time. But they want you for something else, and until we know exactly *what* they did to you in the hospital and what they need you for now, you have to keep a very low profile."

He wanted to explain his comment, that it came from frustration and fear, not because he thought she was one of them. She'd taken off the bandage from her neck; the welt was still red. She'd braided her hair loosely down her back, making her look almost vulnerable.

He'd hurt her. He ached inside and wished he could take the words back.

"I'm sorry," he said simply.

"It's okay."

But she didn't look at him, and then she walked out.

TWENTY-FIVE

As Moira neared the Ellis home, she felt the magic at work even before she saw the Victorian house at the crossroads. The spells were so potent that she feared she'd be discovered before she even crossed the threshold.

She drove past the house without slowing, continued around the block, and parked far down the street behind it. Dawn had just started to bleed over the mountains, and dark shadows shielded her as she walked along the tree-lined street in the early morning fog.

She circled the house, careful to stay off the property, using all her senses in search of a weak spot.

You're a witch, reverse the spell.

She could. She still felt the power inside her, the evil she'd been born with. She could unleash it. She'd find Fiona, if Fiona didn't find her first. If she planned it, she could stop the coven.

And people would die.

The knowledge that Moira *could* do something didn't mean it was right or safe. She and Peter had planned for months before she started using magic to thwart her mother. They'd done *everything* they could to protect her, everything to keep her safe.

And that plan had ended in death.

Enough, Moira. Do your job.

She stared at the dark Ellis house. There was magic at work here, but she discerned that any spells were to protect against evil spirits only. The herbs growing in the garden, the plants under the windows, the talismans above each door—they wouldn't stop a person from walking in, or alert the witch that there was an intruder. Maybe Moira had a shot after all.

She picked the narrow side yard, next to the attached garage, because there was a door that couldn't be seen from the main house. It provided her with a natural barrier from both neighbors and Lily's mother spotting her.

She stepped into the yard, her senses on high alert. A television was on two houses over, a news program, but Moira couldn't hear distinct words. Birds tweeted, high and low, building in sound as dawn grew. She was calm but alert, and had no sensation that the spell cast here was turning on her, signaling the witch.

Emboldened, she approached the door. Locked.

There were no locked doors when you were a witch, but you didn't need to be a witch to use a pick. She pulled her small set from her pocket and three seconds later she was in, mentally thanking Rico for teaching her not only how to kill demons but to break and enter the old-fashioned way.

The garage housed a compact car and shelf upon shelf of dried herbs and canning jars. At first glance it appeared to be the craft shop for a creative sort, but Moira knew what these herbs and plants were used for, and none of it was good. A dried flower arrangement hung above the door. Decorative on the surface, but the herbs were to banish spirits, further protecting those inside.

She hesitated, unsure how to proceed. She didn't know

the layout of the house, and here in the garage she was fully exposed if anyone came in.

She tried the door that led to the house, slowly, carefully. It was unlocked. She listened for movement inside. Nothing.

Moira was about to step in when the hot-water heater behind her turned on. She jumped, swore, then waited. The floor creaked upstairs, reminding her that this was an old house and she needed to be mindful of the sounds her footfalls would make, no matter how carefully she stepped. She itched to rush in and snatch Lily, but Moira resisted the impulse, counting slowly to twenty, forcing herself to be cautious. She crossed the threshold into the small laundry room that separated the garage from the kitchen. The scent of freshly brewing coffee filled the air. She closed her eyes for a moment to focus on movement, however slight. She'd spent months training in what Rico, in his rare moments of humor, called her "spidey sense." Full concentration, releasing fear, slowing heart rate. Listening. Sensing. Being.

Someone in the shower upstairs, the fall of fat drops of fast-running water. Moira almost felt the steam, the air in the house becoming warmer, moister, the longer the shower ran. A shuffling gait—someone larger than petite Lily Ellis. The steady *drip-drip-drip* of water into the coffeepot. The warm air pushing through the floor heating vents, rising.

Heather. The distinct herb faintly tickled her nose. Henbane, a common ingredient for a multitude of spells and incantations, most with nefarious ends. Wormwood, another herb used in witchcraft, primarily as a protection for the home.

She heard a *thunk* from below. *Downstairs?* Was there

a basement? Rats? She shivered. She despised rodents of all kinds. There was nothing redeeming about them.

The movement had sounded too big for a rat. Then, a faint sob, so faint she wouldn't have heard it if she wasn't listening with every cell in her body.

The door to the basement would probably be off the kitchen or under the staircase.

In the kitchen, she opened the only door. Without turning on a light, the smell of bread and cans told her that this was the pantry.

She closed the pantry door without making a sound, then moved through the room to the hall. Above, the shower still ran.

In the short hallway leading to the front of the house, there were two doors. To the right, and to the left, under the staircase. The floors creaked. Though Moira trod with exceptional care, if the water went off, Lily's mother would surely hear the squeaky hardwood floors.

The door under the stairs was locked.

Moira took out her pick. This lock was newer, but she popped it quickly.

As soon as she opened the door, a potent aroma of powder—wormwood, blue cohosh, and something Moira couldn't immediately identify—rushed into her senses. They were herbs used to create a dust to protect against maleficent spirits and opposing witches. To keep a person safe from possession, as well as compliant. Lily wouldn't fight, scream, or try to escape. She'd be calm . . .

A tearful voice came from below. "Mama? Can I come out now?"

And terrified.

Moira crossed herself and whispered her own special

prayer. "St. Michael, you'd better be watching my back this time, and don't let any of our enemies stop me." As an afterthought, she added, "Please."

She walked down the wood steps. A wall was on one side; the other was open, without a railing. The stairs creaked worse than the floor above. The basement was damp and moldy.

"Lily," she whispered in the pitch black. "It's Moira."

"Go! It's too dangerous."

"I'm not leaving without you."

"It's too late. My mother—"

"Tell me later. Move. Now."

Lily shuffled over to her.

"Faster."

Upstairs, the shower shut off.

Moira pushed the teenager ahead of her up the stairs, a faint light coming from the hall as the sun continued to rise and break through the early morning fog.

Lily stumbled, but Moira kept her moving forward. Lily didn't know the meaning of the word *quiet,* but fortunately she was small and her movements reflected that. They rounded the corner and Moira knew that Elizabeth Ellis was standing on the second floor at the top of the stairs, listening. Lily's mother was smelling the mixture of herbs that Moira had unintentionally released when she'd opened the basement door.

Moira pushed Lily into the kitchen.

Someone ran down the stairs.

Moira said to Lily, "Move it, now, out the door."

"Hecate, Beliel, and Achiel . . ." Elizabeth Ellis began when she saw them.

Not about to let her finish the incantation, Moira whirled around and kicked Ellis in the stomach, almost surprising herself that her aim was dead accurate and Ellis was standing exactly where Moira had sensed. Her mental muscle had kicked in. *Thanks, Rico!*

Without hesitating, she kicked again. The white towel wrapped around Lily's mother fell off. Moira almost laughed as she slammed the palm of her right hand in the woman's face, pushing the naked woman to the floor.

Lily screamed.

"Run!" Moira commanded.

"You'll never make it, bitch!" Elizabeth Ellis cried at Moira as she got to her feet. "I call all the spirits, seize—"

"Shut. *Up!*" Moira backhanded her twice. Her left shoulder throbbed and she began to bleed again. The warmth seeped through her bandage. *Dammit,* it hurt.

She knocked over the kitchen table on the way out, to impede the woman's pursuit, then pushed Lily through both doors and outside.

Lily limped toward the street, but Moira shoved her in the other direction, into the backyard. "This way. Over the back fence."

Lily obeyed, though she was hampered by the long, thin nightgown she wore. She shivered, but Moira couldn't concern herself with the girl's comfort.

"Faster!"

Moira cupped her hands for Lily to step in and she boosted the girl over the fence. Her arm ached and the bruises from her mother's attack yesterday made her want to scream, but instead she bit her tongue.

The side door burst open.

Lily was over the fence and Moira grabbed hold of the top and pulled herself up, favoring her right arm. Elizabeth Ellis began an incantation that Moira knew well. Simple and effective.

Dogs all over the neighborhood began to bark. They barked because there was a demon.

"Fuck," she muttered. "Earthquake."

The ground shook as an earth demon rose from the soil in front of her. It was generally harmless because the incantation itself was weak, summoning latent demons out of living, nonhuman organisms. But it would delay Moira—she couldn't let the demon wander and hurt someone.

Lily stumbled and fell. Moira pulled her up and said, "Jared's truck, around the corner! Now!"

Elizabeth Ellis wasn't strong enough to summon a more powerful demon at will—the ritual would take either more time or more witches—but the command of environmental demons was an easier trick to learn. Moira longed to create a short bolt of lightning to zap her. The desire, deep and unbidden, unnerved her and she touched the medallion around her neck, the one that had been Peter's.

She held out her hand and began a short rite of exorcism as the wavering demon came toward her. It was more of a sprite, not a lost soul, and though she intended to send it back into the ground, her powerful words twisted it instead, surprisingly turning the demon inside out before it disappeared.

"What the hell just happened?" Moira said.

Elizabeth Ellis had seen it too and stopped dead in her tracks. Moira, suddenly terrified by what she'd done—because she didn't know exactly *what* she'd done—ran. She caught up with Lily before she reached the truck, and pushed the girl along.

To her credit, Lily no longer cried out, though she wore no shoes. In socks only, she ran over the rough concrete and gravel.

Move move move! Moira willed.

"Jared!" Lily suddenly exclaimed, panting.

"Just his truck. Get in."

She obeyed, obviously disappointed. Moira started the vehicle and sped off. Only then did she glance in the rearview mirror. Elizabeth Ellis was more than a block down, no longer chasing them but still naked.

Moira grinned. "Victory is sweet, but sweeter when your opponent is butt-ass naked in defeat."

TWENTY-SIX

Ari Blair woke up in her bedroom at 6:30 that morning shaking, her sheets wet with perspiration.

You're dead. You're dead. You're dead. The chant repeated until the high school senior felt her head would explode, the dry monotone as disturbing as fingernails on a chalkboard.

She got up, stumbling from bed to bathroom as if she were hungover. She threw up and rested her clammy forehead on her arm.

Her life was over. She was eighteen, and this was the end of the line.

Slowly, she rose from the cold tile floor and stared at her sickly reflection in the mirror. Her skin was grossly pale, matching nearly white hair. She used to think she was so beautiful—tall, blond, and blue-eyed, the girl-next-door type. She had friends and a terrific boyfriend; she was *popular*. A cheerleader, a straight-A student, the student body president, perfect!

"I was accepted into *Berkeley!*" she told her mirror image.

Then Abby had brought her into the coven. It was everything she wanted. A secret society. It matched her New Age sensibilities, her need to elevate to a higher consciousness. She wasn't going to follow her parents in their male-centric religion. She was *smarter* than that.

She would make her own path, live her own life, wholesome and good. She believed in the Wiccan motto: *Do no harm.*

But Abby died! There were evil spirits, *demons,* and they wanted pain. She had felt it very clearly as she stood next to one of them; Ari could have reached over and touched the *thing.* It was there and not there, smoke and solid mass. It was not right.

How could the Goddess be part of something that felt so . . . *bad?*

They'd threatened her. Watched her. Every minute since they'd fled the cliffs.

"If you talk, you're dead."

"Tell no one."

But she couldn't keep silent! She wasn't bad, she didn't want to hurt anyone; she had just wanted to go beyond conventional religion, to understand who she was, why she was here, how nature and humans shared a delicate balance. She needed to know her place, her calling.

They'll kill you.

Now her boyfriend Chris was dead too. His parents were distraught. She went to the hospital as soon as she heard. The doctors thought it was a brain aneurysm.

Ari knew better. It wouldn't have happened except for *her.* What she'd done. She didn't know how but the coven must have killed him. They'd killed Chris because she'd told him what happened. It could be no coincidence that he'd died when Ari planned to expose Fiona's coven.

If they thought killing her boyfriend was going to stop her, they were dead wrong. If anything, their brutal audacity emboldened her.

She dressed without showering, gathered up her supplies, and slipped out of the house before her parents noticed she was up and about. Her mother was still in bed, her father in the shower.

Ari knew she'd never have a moment of peace until she found and trapped the demons she'd helped release, and sent them back to where they belonged.

She *could* fix it. She had the power. It flowed through her . . . she'd controlled the elements, she'd made fire! She'd left her body, had flown over the earth and seen *amazing* things. She could find and trap the demons. She had to.

She couldn't live with herself if she didn't stop this insanity.

And if she failed? She didn't deserve to live.

"Where'd she go?" Anthony asked Rafe.

Rafe hesitated. "Last night we made a plan to rescue Lily Ellis."

"What were you thinking? We were waiting for backup!" Anthony clenched his fist but restrained himself from hitting the table. "I knew Moira was lying to me."

"I agreed with her that it was the right thing to do. We can't wait. She's bringing Lily back here."

"We don't know what they did to you for ten weeks, and you wanted to waltz unprotected right into their territory?"

Anthony's guilt over what Rafe had endured while in the hospital had unnerved him. He had thought he'd protected his friend, but he'd failed in a fundamental way. Rafe's attackers were human, without the vulnerabilities of demons. He'd left Rafe in the hospital, but he'd been far from safe.

And Anthony didn't know what had been done to him, or whether Rafe could even be trusted. Rafe wouldn't consciously aid the magicians, but what if it was unconscious? Hypnosis was extremely dangerous and highly effective if administered properly.

Rafe slowly rose from the table. "Your hatred of Moira has clouded your judgment. Because I agree with her, now you don't trust me?"

"This has nothing to do with my feelings about Moira. For now, we're working together. With the Seven uncontrolled in the world, there is far more at stake. They are gathering strength as we sit here!"

"Exactly! They're gaining strength and we *can't* sit here and do nothing. Moira went for Lily. If the coven can't use her to trap the Seven, that will buy us time."

"That's not it. You know it." Anthony flashed back to the conversation with Skye late last night. *"A guy came in after his dinner break, locked the doors, and killed three of his co-workers, a customer . . ."*

"You think I'm going to the darkside?" Rafe was trying to lighten the conversation, but Anthony barely noticed.

"No, it's something else. Something Skye said last night about a mass murder. Something felt wrong about it, but I don't know why."

Skye entered just then, braiding her long, wet hair as she went. She was already in uniform. "Rod called. He wants both of us at the morgue ASAP."

"Both of us?" Anthony questioned.

"Wants to show us an identical marking on two

corpses that just came in. Thought you might know something about it because it resembles one on Abby Weatherby's body."

"I'll get my shoes."

Anthony left the room and Skye said to Rafe, "I put yours and Moira's clothes in the washing machine, and Anthony put some of his things in the guest room for you. If the stains don't come out, just toss the clothes. I don't think Anthony will care."

"Skye, thank you for everything. I know this is hard on you. You have doubts about me. I would, too, if I were in your position. But I have a favor to ask."

She assessed Rafe. He was similar to Anthony in many ways—how he stood, how he spoke—but he was also very different. Anthony had a strong, dominant personality, a powerful confidence that she was very attracted to. Rafe was quieter, but in some ways seemed even more powerful. He didn't wear his confidence on his sleeve, but it was there, just as strong, but humble. He had the same uncanny way of looking at her that Anthony did: as if he could read her mind.

She knew Anthony couldn't, but perhaps Rafe Cooper had talents Anthony didn't. She was still new to this whole St. Michael's Order and what they did—and didn't do. Maybe mind reading was part and parcel of being a warrior for God.

"You have well-formed instincts," Rafe said to her. "You are extremely intuitive because you understand human behavior. Trust those instincts, no matter what."

She didn't know what to say, so she said nothing, but Rafe's words were disconcerting.

Anthony returned from the bedroom. "I'm ready." He said to Rafe, "Don't leave the house. You're safe as long as you stay put."

Serena fell asleep in the library after unsuccessfully searching for Rafe Cooper. Using her psychic eye was hugely draining. She woke up feeling out of sorts and still exhausted.

"You slept here all night?" Fiona said as she walked in, fresh-faced and glowing. "It's eight in the morning; we have plenty of work to do."

Garrett brought in a tray of fruit and juice. He kissed Fiona lightly, then put the tray down.

"Thank you, darling." Fiona traced a single dark-red-painted fingernail down his cheek and neck and smiled seductively. Serena resisted the urge to roll her eyes. Garrett knew Fiona didn't care about him.

Serena helped herself to the fresh-squeezed orange juice. After two tall glasses she almost felt like herself.

"Can we look for Raphael Cooper now, or do you need more sleep?" Fiona's saccharine tone was annoyingly sarcastic.

"I'm ready." Serena said.

There was a knock at the door of the library. Fiona scowled, waved her hand, and the door opened. "I said no disturbances!"

"Elizabeth Ellis is here."

Elizabeth walked in without waiting for an invitation. She looked atrocious, dressed in jeans and a misbuttoned shirt. She wore no bra, and her boobs sagged noticably. Without makeup, she looked older than her years.

"You left the *arca?*" Fiona snapped.

"Your daughter took her!"

Fiona said nothing for a long time. So long that Garrett and Serena exchanged glances, concerned over her building fury. The energy in the room heated, and a spark here and there told Serena that Fiona was beyond anger.

Elizabeth Ellis didn't seem to notice. "Well? Aren't you going to do something? This is unacceptable!"

Serena's eyes widened and she stepped back, away from Elizabeth, expecting the woman to be struck down for talking to Fiona in such a tone. Serena was used to reading her mother's moods. When there was bad news, you *never* pushed.

Surprisingly, Fiona restrained herself. She turned to Serena. "Bring Prziel back. We'll find Raphael Cooper. I will have him in my possession before sunset."

A chill ran down Serena's spine and she once again began preparations for summoning the blood demon.

"What good is Rafe if we don't even have Lily tonight?"

"Anthony will do anything to save him. He'll give me Moira and the *arca*. We'll have them all. Zaccardi, Cooper, and Andra Moira. None will survive dawn. If the Seven don't want them, I'll gladly kill them all myself."

She crossed the room and stood face-to-face with Elizabeth Ellis, seeming to tower over her though she was only an inch taller.

"The next time you enter my sanctuary uninvited making accusations or demands, you will die."

TWENTY-SEVEN

Anthony had been in the Santa Louisa morgue's autopsy room once before, during the autopsy of three of the victims at the mission. It had been a wholly uncomfortable experience then, as it was now.

Dr. Rod Fielding looked up as soon as Anthony and Skye walked in. "Gloves and gowns, both of you." He gestured toward the storage cabinet.

"Both of us?" Skye asked.

"Yes. You and Anthony."

Skye shot him a surprised look and walked over to the cabinet. She handed Anthony a pair of latex gloves, then a gown. Looking around as she put them on, she walked over to the coroner. "You said two bodies," Skye commented. "There are three bodies here."

"The female over there is new, but she fits."

"What exactly is going on?" Skye asked, impatient.

"Remember the mark we saw on Abby Weatherby? We thought it was a birthmark?" He motioned for them to approach a board in the corner where he had photographs from Abby's autopsy. "See here?"

"Right, I remember."

Anthony stood next to Skye as Fielding crossed the room and removed the sheet from another corpse. "That's Nichols, the shooter from Rittenhouse," Skye said.

"Right. Help me turn him over," Rod said.

After Skye complied, Anthony immediately saw a red-wine stain on Nichols's upper shoulder. It was roughly six inches, but oddly shaped. It didn't exactly match Abby's, but there were similarities. But unlike Abby's there was a darker thread, almost like a tattoo, within the mark that looked familiar:

"It doesn't match," Skye said.

"Not perfectly, but the other two match this guy. I called Abby's parents and asked about birthmarks—I didn't say anything about it, just that we needed information for our files. Her mother said she had no birthmark, other than a small mole on her outer right thigh."

"Did you show her a picture?"

"I think her mother would know if she had a birthmark, especially like this."

Anthony stared at the mark. "This looks too detailed to be a birthmark," he commented.

"Yeah, more like a tattoo," Fielding said, "but it's not. There's no ink in the mark; I already tested a sample." He walked over to another table. "Then I got this eighteen-year-old athlete. Basketball player. Perfectly healthy; I have all his medical files from his doctor, who was shocked when he arrived unconscious at the hospital. He was bleeding from his ears—had lost a tremendous amount of blood before he died. The doctor speculated brain aneurysm, but I've never heard of an aneurysm that resulted in bleeding from both ears. There was no head injury that his coach was aware of;

he didn't play much in the game. He complained about a severe headache shortly before he collapsed. Bleeding from the ear can occur in some infections, but it's usually from a head injury or foreign object. There is nothing external to have caused such an event."

"So what did he die from?" Skye asked.

"I don't know, I haven't started the autopsy. I was prepping him early this morning when I saw the mark. Here, help me." Skye and Fielding turned the body. A red-wine stain, identical to the shooter's, was on the teenager's back, almost in the same place.

"My assistant told me there was yet another body that came in from the hospital early this morning with this mark."

Anthony said a silent prayer for the young man, then turned to the female corpse. She was about forty, and had a mark identical to both those of the shooter and the teenager.

"Could it be a virus?" Skye asked Fielding. "Something contagious? What's going on, Rod?"

"I don't know, but I've never seen anything like it."

"Who's this woman?" Skye glanced at the toe tag. "Barbara Rucker? That name is familiar—she works at the high school."

"Bingo. Secretary to the principal. I don't know the whole story, but she died in a car accident after leaving her husband's office in Santa Maria yesterday evening. Her husband's on his way in." He put up his hand when Skye opened her mouth to protest. "I told him not to, so don't jump down my throat. He's distraught, wants to know what happened to her. I hadn't planned on doing an in-depth autopsy—beyond a standard tox screen for drugs and alcohol—until he called. Based on the accident report, Barbara Rucker was speeding erratically, then ran off the road and into a telephone pole. It was foggy and the roads were slick; CSI is checking the vehicle for possible brake malfunction. Her husband said she wasn't a drinker, didn't do drugs, but hadn't been acting like herself." He glanced at Anthony. "Do you think she was possessed?" he asked quietly.

"Demons don't want the people they possess to die. They lose the body. It doesn't make sense." He frowned and stared at the mark. "This is familiar, but I don't know why."

"Damn," Fielding said. "I thought you'd be able to help. If you don't know what it means—"

Skye interrupted. "This is a criminal investigation. We need to assume that these three people had something in common, so we look into each death carefully, retrace their steps. Maybe they were all at the same place at the same time."

"Like the cliffs," Anthony said.

"Yes." She looked at the young man's body, then asked Fielding, "You said these marks weren't tattoos. Could they have been self-made? Like—" she hesitated, then said, "burned into the skin?"

Fielding considered the question. "It's possible—I'll need to do skin grafts, check the cells underneath for signs of intense heat and dead cells. But if it was recent, I would expect discoloration on the skin surrounding the marks. Still—I'll check. I'll get back to you later today."

"You're doing all the autopsies today?"

"Yes, I just wanted you to see this first."

"Did the toxicology reports come back on Abby?" Skye asked.

"Not yet. I expect them early this afternoon. I'll call you if there's anything suspicious."

"I'm going to wait in the lobby for Mr. Rucker," Skye said.

She stopped next to the young man again. She looked at his toe tag. Chris Kidd. All color drained from her face. "I talked to this boy yesterday. When I was at the school—he came up to me and said his girlfriend might know something about Abby's death. I pressed, and while he didn't flat-out say it, I had the distinct impression that she was on the cliffs that night. I intended to follow up with her yesterday, but then the librarian stole—" She stopped. "Anthony, how can this all be happening? The librarian? Chris Kidd? The secretary . . . they're all from the school."

"But not Nichols," Fielding reminded her.

"Maybe he's not part of the same . . . *thing*."

"He must be," Anthony said. "The marks are almost identical."

"I have everyone working on that case, checking his background, his apartment, his associates. He's not married, but maybe he's friends with someone at the school; maybe he had reason to be there yesterday."

"Or maybe," Anthony said, "he was part of the coven. Maybe he was at the cliffs during the ritual— maybe *all* of these people were."

Skye said, "So were Lily and Rafe."

"I'm going back to the house. I'll look at Rafe myself. After, I'll head back to the mission and research what this mark might mean."

"After I talk to Rucker," said Skye, "I'll check on Lily."

Anthony hesitated, wondering if he should tell her

that Moira had gone after Lily. Instead, he said, "Be careful. Elizabeth Ellis is a witch."

Rod Fielding's head shot up. "Elizabeth?"

"You know her?" Anthony said.

"We go to the same church. She's a nice woman; so is her daughter."

"Don't go back to that church. The new pastor, Pennington, is suspect."

Fielding frowned, and Anthony wondered for a brief moment whether he could be trusted. But why would he call them to the morgue and show them the marks on the corpses? And he'd gone above and beyond after the murders at the mission.

The coroner shook his head. "I don't go often, once in a while. I've only been twice since Pennington took over. I don't really like him much. He has charisma, I'll give him that. Very attractive to the women, and young. Pennington came with outstanding credentials. I don't think Matthew Walker would have turned over his church to just anyone."

"That's something we definitely need to look into," Anthony said.

Skye asked Rod, "Do you know how I can reach Walker?"

"His cell phone number is in my Rolodex. Grab it on your way out. Tell him I said hello. I should have called him at some point. His mother was gravely ill. I just didn't think of it."

On their way out, Skye took Anthony's arm. "Anthony, please be careful. And remember—let me handle the police work. Too many people are watching me too closely. Any hint that the police department is investigating supernatural crimes and everything we've done to

protect Juan Martinez and Rafe Cooper will blow up in
our faces."

Moira wasn't certain *how* she knew something was
dreadfully wrong at Skye and Anthony's house, but before she turned Jared's truck down Skye's street back to
Skye's she sensed a charge, electricity in the air. Maybe it
was the scent of fear.

Lily's feet were bleeding. Moira had forgotten she'd
been injured running from the coven two nights ago
until she saw the blood seeping through her thick socks.
Running three blocks and hopping over a couple of
fences in the process hadn't helped any. Now she curled
into a ball in the passenger seat. The cab was so hot
Moira was sweating, but Lily had complained of being
cold.

Moira approached Skye's house cautiously, looking
for anything amiss. Skye's truck was in the driveway, but
the second car was gone. She drove around behind the
house, since there were no fences to block her view.

A metal chair was overturned on the deck.

It might be nothing; it could have been knocked down
by wind at night. But Moira didn't remember any wind
strong enough to knock the chair over. And Skye
McPherson seemed too . . . meticulous . . . to leave a
piece of furniture in disarray.

She stopped the truck but didn't get out. She couldn't
leave Lily alone, but she also didn't want to bring her
into an unknown situation.

"Lily," she said.

Lily opened her eyes. "Where are we?"

"The sheriff's house. I need to check it out before I
bring you in. How are you doing? Can you walk?"

"I don't know."

"That's okay. Be alert. I'm going to open the windows. I know it's cold out, but if you see anyone, scream bloody murder. Even if it's someone you know. I'll hear you."

Lily nodded, her body shaking.

"I'll bring a blanket as soon as I can."

Moira parked the truck, opened the windows a crack, and left the keys with Lily. "Lock it," she commanded, and got out.

Moira took the three steps up to the deck with one leap, her dagger in one hand, ready to attack. Every nerve was on high alert, every cell listening, smelling, feeling what was outside the house, and inside.

There's no one here.

No movement. No breathing. No life.

Her heart skipped. The idea that Anthony and Rafe were dead, deserting her. Moira couldn't do it alone. She needed backup, anyone to be on her side.

And she wanted it to be someone she trusted. Like Anthony.

Like Rafe.

She felt alone again, cold and helpless and hopeless.

Without hope, you have nothing.

The sliding glass door was ajar. She pushed it open with one finger and stepped inside.

The kitchen was a disaster. Dishes had been thrown around the room and shattered. Large platters and mugs had left gouges in the walls. The table was no longer in the center of the room; it was upside down, in the living room near the front door. The couch had been upended. Pictures had fallen from the wall, the frames and glass broken. Feathers from throw pillows had been scattered everywhere. A crucifix, one that Moira remembered hung over the doorway, had been thrown into the antique hutch, breaking a collection of dishes Skye had stored there.

No one had touched a thing. As certainly as she breathed, Moira knew that a magician had walked in here and had a temper tantrum. Everything she passed by had invisible remnants of dark energy. She had never felt quite like this before. The entire house seemed alive, sizzling, crackling with sorcery.

As she breathed in the pulsating energy surrounding her, Moira's cells tingled. It would be so easy to pull that energy into her, to absorb it, to refuel. She was so tired . . .

She stood in the guest room and stared at the bed Rafe had slept in last night.

She squeezed her eyes shut and pounded her fists on the wall. She had to resist the urge to draw in the magic. Walking in here she had a taste of it, just a taste, and it fed her craving. On her tongue, in her eyes, coating her eardrums. Every sense wanted to absorb the energy, thirsty for it . . .

She must resist. *"Clamaverunt iusti et Dominus exaudivit et ex omnibus tribulationibus eorum liberavit eos!"*

The spells here were powerful, drawing her in. She battled them the only way she knew how. She continued with verse after verse of Latin exorcism rites, until an audible *snap* and a whoosh of air, so subtle, so quiet no one else would have heard it, told Moira the residual magic had dissipated.

The dark craving instantly faded and she could focus on the task at hand.

Where were Rafe and Anthony?

Moira walked carefully over the ruins of the house, checked each room twice, and found no one, living or dead. She was alternately relieved and terrified.

When she returned to the living room she saw the message, pinned to the back of the front door. A message that only Fiona would have left.

An eye for an eye, yours for mine.
The arca and the traitor for your brother.
Two for one, for he has caused trouble.
I am more than fair.
The longer you delay, the more he suffers.

Outside, Lily screamed.

TWENTY-EIGHT

Moira fled the house, heart racing with the fear that not only had Fiona kidnapped Rafe but now she had Lily, too, and Moira had been responsible for both.

Anthony stood on the deck. "What happened?" he demanded, looking over her shoulder.

Maybe it was his tone, or her guilt, or her anger—but more likely her fear—that provoked her to push him. He barely budged.

"You left him alone? You left Rafe and now Fiona's coven has him! How could you?"

Anthony brushed past her and into the house, his own dagger out, not that it would do any good. She raised her hand to Lily, to let her know that Anthony was a friend, and then Moira put her hands on the wood railing and breathed in the fresh, moist, early-morning air. So much like her homeland in Ireland, a much-loved place to which she would likely never return.

Rafe. They were kindred spirits, Moira and he, a little lost and a lot alone. Someone she could finally talk to about all this . . . and because of her, he had been taken by Fiona as a game piece.

Checkmate.

She couldn't allow Fiona to win. She wasn't turning Lily over to her, but she would trade herself for Rafe. Fiona would be hard pressed not to agree. Lily was an innocent, injured. She couldn't even run if she needed to. And she would die if Fiona was successful.

Anthony stepped out of the house, furious. "Where does Fiona want to make the trade?"

Moira whirled around. "What? You can't be seriously thinking of turning Lily over to them."

He scowled at her. "Of course not. But she didn't give any instructions."

"She will. On her terms. And she won't give us much time to prepare." She looked at Anthony as she stuck her dagger back into its sheath. "It looks like it's you and me, Anthony. That's it."

"And Father Philip when he arrives. I spoke with Bishop Aretino last night. Father Philip left before dawn, alone, and is on his way here."

Fear clawed at her throat. "No, no, you have to stop him. Divert him. Call Rico, demand that he intercept him before he gets here. You know that Father is in great danger whenever he leaves the mission!"

Anthony nodded. "Because he is older, not physically able—"

She shook her head. "No! It's because of me!"

He stared at her and she paced on Skye's deck. "Fiona cursed him," she said.

"That won't work. His faith is too strong."

"That doesn't matter."

"Of course it does. Moira, for all our differences, I know you care for Father. I appreciate your trepidation, and I don't want him here any more than you do, but I will do everything in my power to protect him. Faith does matter. It saved me more than once."

He put his hands on her shoulders. She stopped pacing, stunned by his showing of concern for her.

"Even without the curse, if Fiona knows he's here, she will attack him with the same fierceness as she did me in jail, and Rafe here—" She gestured toward the house. "He can't survive something like this."

Anthony's jaw tightened. "I will find him. I won't let anything bad happen to Father."

Moira wanted to believe him, but she also knew that Father Philip believed if he left the sanctuary he would die. "Why is he coming here instead of going to Olivet?"

"I don't know."

Moira was hardly comforted by Anthony's words, "In the meantime, I'll find Rafe."

"How?"

That, she wasn't as certain about. But she had a few ideas. "I would start with Garrett Pennington, the pastor of Good Shepherd or whatever church." She waved her hand dismissively. "If he won't tell us where Fiona is, he'll lead us to her. One thing I'm very good at is following people. He won't know I'm there."

"What if he's a magician?"

She thought about how she'd dissipated the psychic energy in Skye's house. "I don't think he can detect me."

He seemed to take that as an answer, at least for now. "And what about Lily?"

"She can't walk. Her feet are practically raw from running barefoot the other night, and—" She hesitated. "Getting her out this morning wasn't easy."

"How did you do it without magic?"

"My spidey sense. Good old-fashioned intuition, something Rico taught me to listen to." She cracked a half-grin. "Look, Anthony, take Lily to the mission and work on finding out how to trap the Seven; I'll track down Garrett Pennington and, hopefully, Fiona. I'll call you when I learn something, and we can go from there."

He was torn, but nodded. "I have another more immediate issue to research."

"What could possibly be more important than reversing Fiona's spell?"

"Nothing, but I've done all I can on that with what I have. I'm waiting on further information from a few people. But right now there's a string of disconnected deaths that have one thing in common."

"What?"

"The dead bodies each have some sort of identical birthmark, but it's not on any of their medical records. The coroner says it's not a tattoo." He reached into his breast pocket and handed her a color print of a mark on a corpse.

Moira stared, her heart skipping a beat. "Holy Mary, Mother of God." She didn't realize she'd crossed herself until she'd already done it. "This is a demon's mark."

"They were possessed when they died? But—"

She shook her head rapidly back and forth. "No, no, not that. Let me think." She whirled around and stared at the odd-shaped red demon's mark in the photograph. "This only happens when someone goes through a demonic baptism."

"I know a lot about demon worship, but I've never heard of demonic baptisms. It's sacrilegious."

Moira managed a harsh laugh. "Everything they do is sacrilegious! I had one of these." She pulled down her turtleneck to reveal the faint scar where her demon's mark had been. "Father removed it." The procedure had been emotionally and physically exhausting, but it had been successful.

No one but Father Philip and Peter had known about the mark, until now.

"I was marked on my thirteenth birthday," she continued. "When I came of age, I was baptized and marked. A demon—my so-called guardian devil, I suppose—was summoned to mark me. It's rare, I'll admit, because most witches aren't strong enough to control the ritual and the demon possesses the person he's supposed to mark, and it becomes a bloodbath. But Fiona is not a weak witch, and frankly neither was I. I was marked . . . but I didn't know what it was for until later . . ."

Her voice trailed off and she looked over at Lily still sitting in the passenger seat of the truck. Did the girl have a mark on her?

"Moira," Anthony prompted.

"These people had to have been marked by a demon, but I couldn't tell you when. It could have been the other night, during the ritual Rafe interrupted, or today, or ten years ago. I don't know!"

"Skye is investigating their last few days; would that help narrow it down? Abby had a similar, not identical, mark on her. I don't have a picture."

Moira didn't know how so many dead people could have gone through the ritual if they *weren't* on the cliffs. It wasn't fun, and took years of preparation to accomplish. If Lily was marked unknowingly, it had to have been when she was a young child and something she didn't remember.

"Was there anything else weird besides the marks?"

"They all died under odd or unusual circumstances. Three of the four victims worked at or went to Santa Louisa High School."

"That's no coincidence."

Anthony asked the question she'd been thinking but couldn't quite put into words. "Can someone be marked by a demon if they didn't know anything about it? What if they were minding their own business, but somehow were touched—not possessed—by one of the Seven?"

"I didn't think so," she said, "but theoretically it could happen, I suppose." Moira stared at the photo. She shook her head, handed it back to him. "I've seen something like it before, but can't remember where." She took a deep breath. "Don't let Lily out of your sight. I'm going to stop by Santa Louisa High School before I go to Pastor Garrett's church. If I get arrested for breaking and entering, I hope you'll convince your girlfriend to keep me out of jail."

Jared hadn't wanted to come to school, but his father drove him on his way to work this morning and said he'd be calling in to make sure he was in every class.

He wanted to leave for good. Walk out of the school, pack his stuff at his dad's house, get Lily, and *leave*. His father had called him an idiot for giving his truck to a stranger, though Jared didn't consider Moira O'Donnell a stranger. Not after what they'd seen . . . Still, maybe he *had* been stupid to loan Moira his truck. He hadn't talked to her since yesterday morning, and he hadn't spoken to or seen Lily; he felt like he was in the middle of a dream. A nightmare. He couldn't talk to his father, and Mrs. Ellis hung up the phone when he called and asked to talk to Lily.

He considered skipping out second period—by that time, Mrs. Ellis would be at work and he could go see Lily.

He crossed the parking lot when he heard someone call his name.

He turned and saw Ari Blair motioning to him from the driver's seat of a small car, looking like she was waiting for someone. For him? He'd known her most of his life, but they never really moved in the same social circles.

He walked over to her. She looked like crap—no makeup, her hair pulled haphazardly back in a lopsided ponytail, pale as a ghost. "Hey."

"Get in."

He frowned.

"Please, Jared. It's about Lily."

He hesitated. After what he'd seen these last two days . . .

Ari pleaded with him. "I know what happened on the cliffs when Abby died. I was there. I need to fix it. It's the only way, or Lily will die. Please, Jared, I need your help. I can't do this all by myself."

"I'll listen."

"Listen in the car, okay? We'll just drive around. I'll tell you everything; I just really need your help. Or it won't just be Abby or Chris—"

"Chris? *Chris Kidd?* What happened to him?"

"He died last night. He was killed, I'm sure of it, to keep me from doing what I'm going to do. I can't let anyone else die."

Jared walked around to the passenger door and got in. "Tell me everything, Ari, and don't lie. That's the only way I'll help." He only hoped he could tell if she were lying, he thought, as she drove out of the parking lot and onto the main road.

TWENTY-NINE

Before Skye had left the morgue, she'd spoken with Andy Rucker, the distraught husband of the dead Barbara Rucker.

According to Rucker, he and his wife had been happily married for twelve years. Barbara had always been insecure about her weight and upset that she hadn't had a baby, which she desperately wanted. But Andy thought she'd been relatively happy until she turned forty and found out she couldn't conceive.

Barbara had called him yesterday afternoon on his cell phone. He was in a meeting, let it go to voicemail, and when he called her back she was crying and wouldn't tell him why. He almost went home but was delayed by an office emergency.

Just after five in the afternoon, Barbara showed up at Andy's office in Santa Maria. She accused him of having an affair. When his colleague walked into the office without knocking, Barbara stared agog at the very pregnant office worker. Barbara then chased the woman out of the office and pushed her down the stairs.

"Barbara just . . . I don't know, lost it. I thought it was because of the baby. Martha was seven months pregnant, and Barbara can't have kids . . . "

After pushing Martha down the stairs, Barbara Rucker ran out of the building. Fifteen minutes later, her car crashed into a light pole traveling, according to the accident investigation, in excess of seventy-five miles an hour. There were no signs that she'd attempted to brake.

A second suicide by car in as many days? Both women who worked at the high school? It made no sense—unless Skye listened to Anthony. And even *he* didn't know what was going on.

But Andy Rucker was 100 percent certain that his wife was home all night Tuesday—far away from the demon-ridden cliffs. Skye didn't see why he would lie, and though she supposed the secretary could have slipped out of the house for a couple of hours and sneaked back in without her husband waking, that was doubtful.

When she arrived at Santa Louisa high school, the principal had confirmed to Skye everything Andy had told her: Barbara Rucker was sweet, a little insecure, very much in love with her husband, and yesterday she'd been unusually emotional.

After talking to the principal, Skye asked the receptionist to call Ari Blair into the office between periods, but not to alert her that the police wanted to speak with her.

"Ari is absent," she said.

"Did her parents call in?"

"We have two hundred sixteen first-period absences," the receptionist said. "I couldn't tell you if they called yet; we're still processing the attendance slips."

"Is two hundred and sixteen absences unusual? It seems high."

"Extremely unusual. We average thirty-two a day, sometimes double that in flu season. But over *two hun-*

dred?" She shook her head. "Most of them are juniors and seniors."

"Isn't that strange?" Skye asked. "Is it a senior prank or something?" It *was* Friday. Maybe a group had driven south to Disneyland. She dismissed the thought as soon as she thought it. A dozen seniors, sure. But two hundred? Not likely.

Before the receptionist could comment, a student sitting against the wall said, "I saw Ari this morning in the parking lot."

"What was she doing?" Skye asked the girl.

"Nothing. Just sitting in her car."

Skye asked more questions about Ari during the break and learned from three students that Ari was seen sitting in her car in the parking lot until approximately 8:45 a.m., when she talked to Jared Santos and they left together. Skye also learned that Lily Ellis hadn't shown up today, either.

She called Deputy Hank Santos. "Do you know where Jared is?"

"School. I dropped him off this morning."

"He's not here. Several students saw him drive away with another student."

"Dammit! It's that Ellis girl, isn't it?"

"No, actually, it's—" She stopped. "Lily Ellis isn't at school, either."

"I'll be right there." He hung up, and Skye swore under her breath. She didn't need Hank getting up in arms about this, or digging deeper into what had happened at the cliffs. He was already on the cusp of whether he trusted her to be sheriff, and if she lost Hank's support, several other deputies would follow.

While the receptionist pulled Ari Blair's parent contact

information, Skye took a call from Deputy Baca, who'd been interviewing Ned Nichols's neighbors this morning.

"Give me the nuts and bolts," she said.

"Nichols was the manager of the eighteen-unit apartment building. Clean but run-down. The crime scene investigators are still in his apartment, but there's nothing obvious like pictures of his colleagues with targets drawn on them. We caught one tenant leaving for work; he didn't care for Nichols, said he was a stickler for rules like no political signs, only one pet per apartment, things like that."

Skye cut him off. She didn't need to know all this right now, and nothing he said helped her figure out how he had a birthmark that matched those of two other dead people. "Anything else?"

"We're going to track down the other residents. The gal next door works at the high school; since you're there, I thought maybe you could talk to her."

Skye stiffened. "His neighbor works at the high school?"

"Nicole Donovan. English teacher. New, moved to Santa Louisa over the summer."

"I'll talk to her. Thanks."

She hung up, asked the receptionist what room Donovan had, and was informed that Donovan had a free third period starting in fifteen minutes.

Skye stepped out and decided to wait until class was over, make it casual. She had no reason to think that Nicole Donovan was involved in Abby's death, but at the same time this was one of those strange coincidences that got her police instincts humming. Nicole Donovan, English teacher, was the only apparent connection to the high school that Ned Nichols had, other than the fact that he graduated from here nearly twenty years ago.

Donovan, Donovan . . . Skye pulled out her notepad. She had Abby's schedule written down. First period:

English 4, N. Donovan, Rm 119

One more connection. She was heading to room 119 when her phone rang. It was Reverend Matthew Walker returning her call.

"Thank you for returning my call," she said.

"I was surprised that the sheriff of Santa Louisa wanted to talk to me. I heard on the TV news what happened yesterday in Santa Louisa—the murders at Rittenhouse. I'm stunned. I know the Rittenhouse family well."

"I'm calling about Pastor Garrett Pennington, your replacement at Good Shepherd."

There was a brief silence. "Replacement? I didn't know they'd found a replacement."

"Who are 'they'? Your employer?"

"Good Shepherd is affiliated with Lamb of God Ministries. My mother's illness was sudden, and I couldn't stay while they searched for a new pastor. I thought they'd have told me, but . . ." He let his voice trail off.

"Do you have contact information on your ministry? I need to verify some information. So you don't know Garrett Pennington at all?"

"Never heard of him. But Lamb of God is small; they often recruit outside their ranks. Most of our churches have small congregations in rural communities."

He gave her two phone numbers and an address in

San Diego—for Vance and Trina Lamb—and assured Skye that "Lamb" was their true last name.

"When did you leave Santa Louisa?" she asked.

"The first week of August. My mother collapsed and was admitted to the hospital. I drove up, and after talking to the doctors learned she had a brain tumor. They said she could live for a week or possibly a month. It's been seven months, praise the Lord, but she's still not out of the woods."

"You haven't been back since?"

"I returned for a few days to pack up my things, gave my last sermon on August ninth, told the congregation what happened, and asked them to pray for my mother. I contacted Lamb of God and informed them of my leave of absence, and they said they'd start searching for a replacement. Is this a new hire?"

"About five or six months ago, I believe. I don't have those notes in front of me, but he was there at the end of the summer."

"That's odd. I spoke with Vance two weeks ago and he didn't say anything to me."

Odd indeed, Skye thought. She thanked the pastor and hung up, then called the number he'd given her.

A female voice answered.

"I'm Sheriff Skye McPherson in Santa Louisa, California. I'm calling to speak with Vance or Trina Lamb."

"This is Trina Lamb. How may I help you?"

"I'm calling regarding Good Shepherd Church in Santa Louisa."

"Yes?"

"I'm following up on your pastor, Garrett Pennington."

"Good Shepherd has no pastor. Matthew Walker took

a leave of absence, and we haven't filled the position yet."

"Mrs. Lamb, Garrett Pennington has been acting as the pastor of Good Shepherd since the end of August."

"We don't know any Garrett Pennington."

"But Good Shepherd is your church?"

"In a manner of speaking. We don't have the organization of the larger churches with mandates and funding. We supply material like prayer books and stock newsletters, and take care of organizational matters such as tax filings, in return for a percentage of the collection and fund-raising. Matthew really built the church up. When he took a leave of absence, he asked for us to find a replacement for him, but we've been unable to do so. We sent two candidates to the church council, and neither met with their approval."

"Church council?"

"Yes, when Matthew left to care for his mother, three in his congregation volunteered to interview replacements. We sent up two, but they rejected them. They've been holding prayer services, but I fear unless Matthew returns they'll wander away."

"Who is on the council?"

"I don't know all the members, but my contact is Elizabeth Ellis. Do you know her?"

Lily's mother, who Anthony called a witch. "I know of her."

Lamb's voice became indignant. "I'm disturbed that someone would be pretending to be a man of the Lord."

Skye sighed wearily. *You don't know the half of it.*

Moira was relieved that Anthony hadn't asked her *why* she was going to Santa Louisa High. She'd have to lie to him, and she didn't like lying to him. He couldn't read minds, but he was sharp, and even though she was a terrific liar—thanks to years of having to lie to her mother in order to save her own life—she wasn't sure she could come up with a plausible excuse.

She left a voicemail for Jared; she assumed he was in class when he didn't answer. She walked around the silent halls, hoping no one questioned her. The nice thing about Santa Louisa was that it was a smallish town with small-town mentalities. No metal detectors at the doors, no campus cops, no one particularly concerned about someone walking the halls between classes.

But the downside of a small town was that everyone knew everyone, and Moira was a stranger. Worse, she didn't know how far the tentacles of Fiona's coven extended, and people *she* didn't know might know *her*. She was always wary of Fiona's human spies.

She walked around the halls looking for any sign of witchcraft, or the lingering stench of sulphur that demons left in their wake. Slowly by the lockers, breathing deeply at each narrow vent, seeking the subtle aromas of herbs and plants that might tell her someone was practicing witchcraft—or was hexed. Moira didn't know if they would be the next victims of the demon or if they were protected from what they'd brought forth. But each person was a possible lead for her to find Fiona.

She'd passed by several lockers that were suspect, but one stood out as if it glowed with a big neon sign: *witch*.

She glanced around. Heart racing, she took out her pick and popped the lock in less than three seconds, though it felt like three minutes.

It was myrrh that she smelled, fresh and potent. On the inside of the locker was a symbol Moira knew well from her youth—it went with a spell for popularity. As if to reiterate the fact, she found a turquoise charm hanging in the back.

She quickly went through the books. The locker belonged to Ari Blair, student body president. In notebooks were doodles of witchcraft tables, and another notebook was the beginning of her own *grimoire.*

And there was an address book.

The bell rang; Moira pocketed the address book and shut the locker, walking away with purpose, as if she belonged.

No one stopped her, no one commented. She walked right out of the school, toward where she'd parked Jared's truck.

Shit!

A sheriff's car was parked in front of his truck and Hank Santos, Jared's father, was looking in the windows. Moira turned and walked in the opposite direction. She didn't know what was going on, but she wasn't going to waste time finding out—or risk going to prison.

But dammit, she needed a car! Maybe she could just wait a few minutes and he'd be gone.

She found a place on the far side of the main school building where she could stand among the trees and still see Jared's truck without being exposed. She went through Ari's address book, hoping there was information she could use to find Fiona or Garret Pennington.

THIRTY

Serena was taking a huge risk showing up at Santa Louisa high school, but Nicole Donovan was hysterical and hysterical witches did stupid things. Like Elizabeth Ellis's rant this morning to Fiona. Elizabeth was lucky to be alive and breathing. Nicole would be lucky to be alive by the end of the night.

Nicole had third period free, so Serena waited until her students left the classroom before slipping in and locking the door behind her. She'd seen a police car out front. Probably not the sheriff, but Serena didn't want to take too many chances. Skye McPherson was one of the few people who *might* be able to identify her—if she looked close enough.

"Ari drove off with Jared Santos!" Nicole exclaimed in a loud whisper. "That can't be good. We have to find her."

"That's why you called and *demanded* that I come here?"

"Yesterday Ari was on edge, and did you hear that her boyfriend died?"

Serena hadn't heard, but she acted nonchalant. In truth, she was concerned because the death was unusual. She hadn't been able to decipher the entire *Conoscenza* but she knew the Seven behaved differently.

Their coven was protected, but what about those they associated with?

Instead, she told Nicole, "That doesn't concern us."

"Yes it does! I heard that the sheriff brought *Anthony Zaccardi* to the morgue with her. Everyone is talking about Chris Kidd's death. He collapsed, bleeding from both ears. The secretary died in a car crash going seventy miles an hour. The *librarian* committed suicide! No one knows what is happening, but now people are talking about the cliffs, about Abby, about strange things they've seen. We can't keep this a secret! Someone's going to find out and—"

Serena laughed. "You think that the average person in Santa Louisa is going to believe that demons are on the loose? And why do you think they had anything to do with those deaths?"

"They had to."

Serena wasn't going to fuel Nicole's panic, though she agreed. No one had successfully brought forth all seven of the Seven Deadly Sins at one time, and when a coven had summoned one of them, it was under tight control, and returned as soon as they completed the ritual. What Fiona had planned was far grander in scale, to not only summon the Seven, but to keep them trapped in the *arca* instead of sending them back to Hell. The possibilities were endless.

"We have a plan, and we will succeed," Serena said. "Tonight. Either you're with us one hundred percent, without hesitation, without doubt, or you're out."

And Nicole knew damn well what being *out* meant.

"It's on tonight? Where?"

"You'll know in time. But until then—keep your mouth shut."

"What if Cooper shows up again?"

"He'll be there." Serena smiled. "He's no longer a threat."

A knock on the door surprised both of them. "I have to get that," Nicole said. "It's open period, and I don't want any rumors going around. There're too many as it is." Nicole walked to the door and unlocked it.

Sheriff Skye McPherson stood there. "Ms. Donovan? Do you have a minute?"

"Is this about Abby? Poor girl."

"No, it's about your neighbor, Ned Nichols, if you have a minute." Skye glanced at Serena and gave a slight, inquisitive nod. Serena responded in kind. She wasn't going to speak. Some people remembered faces easier, some people remembered voices. And while Serena had changed her appearance back to her usual self, she couldn't change her voice. Even though it had been more than two months, Serena wasn't taking any chances.

Nicole shook her head. "I heard about it on the news. It's so hard to believe that he could do something like that."

Serena didn't need to listen to this, nor did she want Skye McPherson to spend too much time studying her. She waved good-bye to Nicole, nodded to the sheriff, and walked out of the classroom as Skye asked Nicole when she'd last seen her neighbor.

The halls were deserted. Serena was thankful she'd never had to suffer through school.

She left the building by the side door, then started down the path to the sidewalk and toward her car.

The crystal in her pocket vibrated and burned so hot

she yelped out loud, stunned. She'd almost forgotten she'd brought the blood demon with her.

Something was not right.

Serena slowed her stride, moved off the sidewalk and into the trees that lined the road. She willed herself to be camouflaged, murmuring a concealment spell to surround her. The fog had lifted, but the gray sky cast odd light and dark shadows around her, as if the world were black-and-white.

She pulled out the crystal, holding it carefully between her thumb and forefinger. It was glowing, pulsating. She'd never seen this happen before, and for a brief moment she thought that the demon was about to escape. That wouldn't be good; he'd be one pissed-off demon. She needed to send him back before that happened. She could do it alone, and was about to begin the incantation when she saw movement from the corner of her eye.

Someone was partially hidden in the grove of trees to her left. Waiting for a friend? Watching? The crystal in her hand vibrated faster. She ordered the demon to be still, and he did, shaking almost imperceptibly.

A Catholic church loomed across the street, dark and empty. But it wasn't the church that gave her the feeling that something was afoot.

The spell Serena cast around herself didn't make her invisible—that was impossible—but it made it difficult for anyone to see her, a shadow, blending in with the trees, and as long as she didn't move, barely breathed, she was *de facto* invisible.

It was a woman, ten feet from her. A woman with long black hair.

Moira.

Her sister stood in the grove, watching the student

parking lot. A police car was there and as Serena watched, it drove away. Moira continued to watch, but judging by her stance that had been what she was waiting for. She itched to move, always a bundle of energy.

So much like Fiona. A virtual clone, only Moira didn't need spells and magic and supernatural power to achieve that sleek neck and slender nose and those perfectly arched cheekbones. She didn't need to choke spirits of their power to add shine to her hair, or depth to her eyes.

Serena hated her and loved her and wanted to be with her and wanted to kill her.

Moira had been the only thing in the coven's way for so long, until Rafe Cooper. Moira had thwarted them, delayed them, jeopardized their lives. She had to die. Somehow, it was even worse because Moira didn't realize what she was doing, or how dangerous she was to Fiona's plans.

Yet the one time Fiona had the chance to end it, she'd played her stupid mind games and Moira was still alive.

Why did Moira deserve to live, anyway? After the pain Serena had suffered because that *bitch* wanted to be free.

Fiona had always loved her sister more. As the chosen, the sacrifice, the one who would rule the realm between the here and the underworld. The one who could move between the two places as effortlessly as breathing.

Moira had thrown it all away. She'd walked away as if none of it mattered! And she wanted to deny *them* the right to infinite knowledge, to share in the wealth of the worlds.

Fiona hadn't given Moira's chosen position to Serena. She said she couldn't, it wasn't possible, but it was! It was possible! Serena had figured out how she could have everything that Moira had given up, as long as Moira was dead.

You're not free, you'll never be free, and I will kill you.

Moira sensed someone watching her as she stepped toward Jared's truck. She stopped, discreetly slid the address book into her pocket, and listened.

A distant dog was barking; a closer dog responded with a higher-pitched yelp.

Distant voices. Movement. A door slamming shut.

Right here, right now, someone other than she was breathing.

Rico called it "mental muscle," where instincts took over and the reaction to a threat came before conscious, coherent thought.

That mental muscle saved Moira's life.

She hadn't registered the movement when she faked right, then dove to the left, between two redwood trees, as a charge of energy hit the ground where she'd been. She fell into a somersault and jumped up ready, dagger in hand.

A strawberry blonde, taller than Moira. Slender. Willowy. Pale.

So familiar, the laugh a memory from the past. Of green and salt air and clover and lavender fields. Of tea and dark beer and freedom.

Of youth and innocence.

Of hope.

Moira shouldn't have been surprised to see Serena—she'd already gone head-to-head with Fiona—but she was nonetheless startled by her sister's presence.

"Serena." She cleared her throat.

Serena grinned. "You're nervous."

"I'm not nervous. You don't scare me." Not like Fiona.

Serena wrinkled her nose and said mockingly, "You *should* be scared. If *I'd* trapped you in a jail cell, you wouldn't have lived."

Moira's heart nearly broke. She remembered Serena as a little girl, so sweet, so perfect. Moira had practically raised her during the years they lived in Kilrush before Moira knew about Fiona's plans for her, before she realized that the magic she used hurt people.

But she hadn't seen Serena since she'd escaped from her mother and found Father Philip. Serena had just turned thirteen when she helped Moira run away the last time.

Moira hadn't forgiven herself for lying to Serena that day, but she had to—Serena wasn't going to leave the coven. She was too needy, too attached. Moira had given her a chance, two days before she planned on leaving, a small test. Shared a "secret" to see whether Serena would tell Fiona. Serena had failed, revealing the false secret, and Moira accepted that her sister would never leave Fiona.

"It's not too late for you to turn away from the coven. Leave Fiona." Moira was buying time. She doubted Serena was of the mind-set right now to leave. If only Serena would listen and believe the consequences!

Serena shook her head. "You had everything. You could have walked between the worlds—"

"It was a fucking lie and you bought into it."

"I've been there. It's no lie."

"End it now. Tell me where Rafe is and I'll get him. Fiona won't have to know you told me anything. We can stop this. Serena. The demons you released are killing people! You don't have control, but you *can* help stop the insanity."

"*We* didn't release the demons. Rafe did. He interfered. We would have had them under control and he loosed them. Now, we will get them back. You saw the message. We want her."

"I'm not giving you Lily."

"Yes you will."

Moira watched her hands. There was something shimmering, shiny, almost seductive, that Serena was playing with in her palm. Moira felt energy building in the still air, the magic growing as Serena was silently working a spell. Her sister had indeed developed as Fiona wanted—into a strong, powerful magician.

Serena said, "Rafe has caused severe damage to our movement, and Fiona is punishing him. Because *you* stole our *arca*."

Serena was trying to twist Moira's heart and make her feel guilty. Moira forced herself to stay calm and put Rafe—and what Fiona was doing to him—out of her mind. "I don't want to hurt you, Serena. Walk away now—"

Serena laughed, and her hands seemed to shimmer with a faint orange glow.

"*You* hurt *me*? You have no power. You gave up your power. But me?"

She turned her palms toward Moira. A bolt of energy, almost unseen, a sliver of brightness, came forth. Moira put up her dagger as a shield in reflex, but was too late. The energy hit her chest and Moira was thrown back ten feet, right on her ass.

Moira was stunned, but no more so than Serena, who seemed to be uncertain how she'd performed that magic.

Moira knew how Serena had done it. Her sister had somehow tapped into a stream of power from the underworld. An open gate . . . were the gates still open? Few witches could channel such energy directly from their body—they generally used crystals and rituals to generate that kind of charge. Serena had done it at will.

Serena put her hands up again, an odd smile on her face, but this time Moira was prepared. She held out her dagger and repelled the energy into the closest tree. Her addiction bubbled to the surface, the overwhelming desire to use her dormant magic returning. This morning in Skye's house, she had felt it; it was stronger now, as if each small taste made her craving grow.

Serena glared at her. "I will kill you!"

Moira realized that it wasn't a craving to use magic, it was a reflex. She remembered the pain of Fiona's attack in the jail, how she had battled it internally, not with an exchange of magic. She'd survived. Maybe next time she wouldn't, but there was hope for her without turning to supernatural forces.

She held her dagger as if it were her lifeline.

Serena laughed. "I'm not possessed. I'm not a demon. Your religious symbols and amulets don't scare me." She stepped forward. "You have to believe for them to work. You don't."

"I do!" Moira bit her tongue, furious with herself that she'd allowed Serena to goad her into defending herself.

"You don't!" Serena's palms went up and Moira turned the dagger to repel the energy shock, using the power of the relics and her internal hope.

The dagger burned in her hands and she cried out, but

held tight as the sacred blade reflected the energy safely away.

Serena tried again, but whatever energy she had drawn in was extinguished. And worse for the witch, she was drained. Moira could see it in her stance, the way she swayed like a drunk, in her eyes, in her voice.

Moira said, "Walk away, Serena. Leave Fiona."

"She needs me." Her voice was small, almost childlike.

"All the more reason to run away while you can. She'll weaken if you leave. I can stop her. You can't let this go on! You can't continue to play with human lives like we're game pieces. We're flesh-and-blood people, just like you."

Serena attempted to gather more energy, but the attempt pained her, bringing her to her knees, and she struggled for breath.

"I loved you, Moira," Serena whispered, and Moira remembered the little girl she'd raised when Fiona went off on her extended trips. So beautiful, so fair, so quiet, so smart. Sweetly Serena, Moira used to say.

"I love you, Serena."

"Don't talk of love! You don't know anything!" Serena reached into her pocket and Moira raised her dagger.

Serena threw something small, a crystal smaller than a Ping-Pong ball, on the ground, while saying, "In the name of your master Baal, in the name of your master Baltach, I command thee Prziel to steal Andra Moira's soul!"

The small ball of glass shattered on the sidewalk. A thick liquid poured from it, the consistency of pooled blood, moving, growing, into a being, a person, a . . .

Demon.

With a deformed, horned human head and the body of a goat, the demon took shape and continued to grow.

Moira froze. She'd faced possessed people, but never an incarnate demon.

She'd never faced a pure, soulless spirit.

"Mine!" the demon hissed. *"Mmmmiiiiinnnnee!"*

Her fear was absolute and instant, but she couldn't allow fear to win. Her soul was at stake, eternal pain and suffering, and it was time to accept her fate, here, now.

She would not die without fighting back.

The demon was far more fearsome in appearance than in action. He staggered, weak, and didn't seem to see her clearly. Moira could use that to her advantage.

He lunged at her, his body not quite fluid but moving fast and breezily, as if his corporeal form were made of thick gas. He had form, but he over-exerted himself in the failed attack and wavered before her eyes before so-lidifying again.

He was blind, sensing her through smell or instinct. He staggered, screaming in pain. She hadn't touched him, only jumped away, into a controlled fall to bring herself back on her feet and ready to fight.

She pulled out what Rico called a poisoned dart: a three-inch iron barb that had been blessed and saturated in sacred oil and ash from Sunday palms.

"In the name of the Father, the Son, and the Holy Ghost, go back to the pit!"

It took all her willpower and control to stand her ground as the demon attacked again. She held the dart out and as soon as it pricked the demon's corporeal shell, the creature screamed an agonizing bellow that

Moira felt deep in her chest. She fell to her knees, unable to breathe, unable to move. The demon turned to dust, and a gust of hot air swooshed down and consumed the dust like a vacuum. It happened so fast, and Moira was in such pain, she wondered if she were delirious.

When she could finally look up, her sister was gone.

THIRTY-ONE

When Anthony and Lily arrived at the mission, he spotted an unfamiliar car. He pulled up close behind it and proceeded with caution.

Lily had slept during the drive up the mountain, and he let her continue to sleep while he inspected the intruder's vehicle. Just as he noticed the car had a rental sticker in its back window, Father Philip stepped out of the mission's only remaining structure.

"Anthony."

He took long steps to reach the only father he'd ever known, and hugged him tight. "Father. It is good to see you."

"And you, son."

Anthony stepped back. "Why did you come here instead of Olivet? And without a bodyguard. It's dangerous here."

"We have much work to do, but not enough time. Where's Moira?"

"Gathering information on where to find Rafe. The coven has taken him!"

"Anthony—we need to talk. Moira didn't go after Rafe alone, did she?"

"We had to split up. She's at Good Shepherd Church, a front for Pastor Garrett Pennington—one of Fiona's magicians—hoping that there will be information there to help us find where they're holding him."

Father tensed, concern crossing his tired face. Anthony had always known Father was older than most of the elders, but now he appeared even older than his years, and it greatly worried him. "Who is her backup? She shouldn't be alone."

"We had no choice. I need to protect Lily Ellis, the young woman they called the *arca*. The coven wants to trade Rafe for both Lily and Moira."

"They will never exchange him. Rafe's too valuable to them. Come inside. Fill me in while we prepare."

"We? You can't be part of this! You will stay here, where it is safe. With Lily." But Anthony didn't know if Father Philip and Lily were safe anywhere, alone. He'd left Rafe in what he believed was a safe refuge, yet they had found him. No one was truly safe as long as Fiona O'Donnell was alive. He wished Rico could come, but he was battling evil elsewhere. Despair rushed Anthony. How could they possibly battle against a coven as large and powerful as Fiona's with just him, an old priest, and Moira—who wasn't even part of the Order? So far she had been more diligent and useful than he'd expected, but she'd also rushed off this morning without discussing it with him. Moira was a maverick. St. Michael's couldn't function with mavericks; it was their communication and planning and union that gave them the strength and intelligence to fight supernatural battles on earth without succumbing to the dark forces themselves. How could their pitifully small group possibly save Rafe and make sure Lily didn't fall into their adversary's hands?

Despondent over their options, Anthony gently woke Lily and carried her inside. There were two small rooms remaining at the mission, the small entrance and what long ago had been the caretaker's office. He placed her on the cot in the corner, where he sometimes slept when he worked late and the weather was too poor to drive down the mountain.

Father Philip sat next to her and took her hand. "Lily," he said, smiling. "My name is Philip."

"Hi." She swallowed nervously and blinked.

"You've been very brave."

She shook her head. "I'm scared."

"Being brave doesn't mean you're not afraid. I have a few questions for you."

She glanced at Anthony. "You can trust Father Philip," he told her. "I've known him all my life."

Father Philip said, "I don't blame you, Lily, for not trusting me, or Anthony. But—"

She shook her head and sat up on the cot, leaning against the stone wall. "I trust you. Moira told me the truth from the beginning, but I didn't want to believe her. She told me I could trust Anthony, and I do. I'm okay—I just wish I understood what was going on. My mother—she's a witch. I don't understand, but I know what I saw."

"Did you see your mother on the cliffs when Abby died?"

She shook her head. "But she was there! She told me she was; she knew what happened before I told her." She looked from Father to Anthony and asked, "Is Jared okay? I haven't seen or talked to him since yesterday morning, when his dad took me home. My mom took my cell phone, wouldn't let me talk to him, or go on the computer. When I tried to leave, she locked me in the basement and said—" She paused and bit her lip nervously.

"What did she say?" Father Philip prompted.

"That I was here for a purpose and I should be proud. But Abby died, and my aunt came over last night and I heard them talking—"

"Your aunt? Abby's mother?"

She nodded. "Aunt Darcy. She's my mom's cousin, but I always called her aunt. And she wasn't crying or anything about Abby. She was actually mad! At me because I'd run away."

Father nodded. "Abby, I'd like to baptize you. A Christian baptism. I need you to answer the questions I ask truthfully. You are of the age of consent, and if you lie, I can't help you."

"I already was baptized."

Anthony asked, "By Garrett Pennington?"

"Y-yes. How did you know?"

"He's not a minister."

"But—I don't understand."

"He's a witch, just like your mother, just like Fiona O'Donnell and the rest of the men and women you saw on the cliffs. He could not have given you a valid baptism," Anthony explained. "And likely, you were baptized long ago to serve the underworld."

"Lily," Father said, "this is important. It's to protect your soul. I don't know what's going to happen tonight, but a valid baptism removes the stain of original sin from your soul, the sin that Adam and Eve brought into the world."

"It doesn't seem fair that we all are being punished for things we didn't do," Lily said.

"It doesn't seem fair," Father agreed. "But we're human beings, and our faith keeps us strong. Stronger than we think we are. We don't always see the signs of God in action. We think He hates us, that He allows evil to prosper. Good people die. Bad people live. But truly, is God to blame? Are we not culpable because we are blind to His help and the help of others? Anthony, myself, Moira—we all belong to St. Michael's Order."

Anthony's ears pricked. Moira part of the Order? Never had a woman, let alone a witch, been initiated. He would have known. Yet he'd never known Father to tell a lie. He was torn, not knowing which would be the greater error.

"In the Order," Father Philip explained, "we are taught to see signs. To interpret them. If the Seven Deadly Sins remain free, humanity is in great jeopardy. But worse still, if Fiona's coven gains control of them, she can target her enemies. The greatest threat to her power on earth is St. Michael's Order. If we fail, there is no one stopping the reign of evil on earth until Jesus Christ comes again."

"How can we—I—any of us—stop it?"

"By following the signs. And the first thing is to purify you so they can't use you to store the Seven Deadly Sins. Anthony and I will do everything in our power to protect your life; and the first thing is to ensure your body cannot be used by the Seven. Do you understand?"

She nodded.

"Do you want to be baptized into the Catholic Church?"

She nodded. "Y-yes."

Father Philip began the baptism rite. It was bare-bones, but included ancient traditions. He spoke the sacrament quickly, his hands steady on Lily's head. He took a small chalice, removed the lid, and with a gold spoon took a teaspoon of salt and fed it to Lily.

The salt was for wisdom and to help prevent the corruption of sin. It was rarely used anymore in modern baptism, but St. Michael's Order insisted. And in this context, with the pinnacles of sin freed in the Seven, even more appropriate.

"Lily, do you renounce Satan?"

"I do."

"And all his works?"

"I do."

"And all his pomps?"

"I do."

A chill rushed through the room, but if Father felt it, he didn't let on as he anointed Lily with sacred oil.

But Anthony felt it, and heard the voices that had been silent for weeks.

help us help us help us help us

The same voices he'd heard when he first arrived at the mission ten weeks ago, minutes after the murders. He hadn't heard them since those first days, had hoped the souls of the dead priests had found peace, all the while fearing that they were still trapped somewhere between heaven and Hell, imprisoned by someone or something.

help us help us help us help us

Anthony stood perfectly still while Father finished asking Lily questions about her belief in the Holy Trinity.

She answered the last question affirmatively.

Father had poured holy water over her head with each of the last three questions, and when he was done, Anthony felt a slight tremor. Father felt it as well, and said to Anthony, "It's good."

Anthony didn't want to argue with Father Philip, but he'd never experienced any physical reaction to a baptism, which was an *internal* cleansing of sin.

Father finished the baptism by handing Lily a candle and lighting it.

"Lily, go in peace and the Lord be with you. Amen."

Lily was silently crying.

"Child, don't cry," Father said, holding her face in his hands.

"I can't help it. I don't know why I'm crying."

"You are humble. Humility is a virtue. Lie down and rest. We have a long night ahead of us."

She lay on the cot, and Father covered her with a blanket. He turned to Anthony and said, "She will sleep. Let us go to the office and you can tell me everything that has happened. And maybe, together, we can find the answers we need to reverse the evil Fiona O'Donnell has done."

"First, Father, tell me where Rico is. Why can't he be here? Why can't he send someone?"

Father said solemnly, "The Seven Deadly Sins have disbursed. Only one remains in Santa Louisa. Rico and his people have trouble in every—how did he say it?— every *hot spot* in the world. We are on our own, yet they all depend on us to find answers and stop Fiona's coven. If we can't do those things, these battles will be our end. No one in the Order will be left standing."

THIRTY-TWO

When Moira saw the flashing red and blue lights in her rearview mirror, she almost floored the accelerator. She hesitated just a moment too long with her decision, because the police cruiser flashed its brights and flipped the siren on and off twice in a piercing *chirp! chirp!*

Moira looked at the roof of the truck. "You *really* don't like me, do you?"

She kept her hands on the steering wheel and stared in the side mirror as the deputy got out. Hank Santos.

"This is getting better and better." She should have floored it. She'd had a chance.

More likely she would have gone off the road and killed herself. But instead of bliss in death, she'd probably be dragged down to the pit and be summoned by her mother so Fiona could torture her lost soul for the next decade. Fun.

She rolled down the window. She hoped she could talk her way out of this, because not only did she have a knife on her, she also had a gun on her. She couldn't kill a cop, nor could she go back to jail.

Talk about being stuck between a rock and a hard place.

"Deputy Santos, right?" she smiled.

"Step out of the truck, please."

"Sir, Jared loaned me his truck. I wasn't speeding."

She honestly didn't know whether she'd been speeding but thought it sounded good.

"I asked you to step out, Ms. O'Donnell."

"Why did you pull me over?"

"If you don't step out of the vehicle, I will forcibly remove you. Please step out."

Moira slid out of the truck, feeling the same odd sensation she'd had when Santos came to her motel yesterday morning. She concentrated with all her senses, but he wasn't possessed or under a spell. Still . . . something about him was off. She said, "You're mad about yesterday morning. I tried to—"

"Keep your mouth shut, Ms. O'Donnell. You've manipulated my son, but this truck isn't his to do with what he pleases. It's mine. My name is on the registration, and I did not give you permission to drive it."

"Fine. It's yours. I'll walk."

"Your license, please."

She bit her lip and pulled out her wallet. She showed him her driving permit from Sicily.

He glanced at it. "I need your international driving permit."

"I don't have one." She'd been in and out of the United States for the last seven years, and getting an IDP was the last thing on her mind.

"This license is expired as well," he said.

She wasn't surprised. She'd had it for years. Other than her passport, renewing government documents wasn't high on her list of priorities.

"I said I'd walk."

"You've already broken several laws, Ms. O'Donnell. I'm going to ask you to come down to the station while we sort this out."

"Deputy Santos, please, I really can't." She doubted begging would get her out of this mess, but she'd try anything at this point.

His face darkened. "I don't know what game you're playing, but ever since you came to town you have been a thorn in my side."

"What? I haven't done anything to you."

"You are coming between me and my son. He never lied to me before now. He ditched school today. I don't know where he is, but I'll bet you do."

"I don't." What on earth was Jared up to? Moira *was* worried. She should have made it a point to talk to him earlier today, make sure he was keeping a low profile.

"I need to search you."

"No. Do not touch me." She was beginning to panic. She didn't want to hurt Hank Santos, but she couldn't go to jail. "Call Sheriff McPherson."

"Turn around and put your hands on the car."

A car pulled up behind Santos's cruiser. Another cop. Great. Now she was going to be manhandled, searched, and they'd find her weapons, haul her to prison, and . . .

Skye McPherson got out and strode over. Moira sighed in relief.

"Hank," Skye said. "I'll take care of this."

"With all due respect, Sheriff, I don't believe you are impartial in this matter."

"Why did you pull Ms. O'Donnell over?"

"She's driving a stolen vehicle."

"Hank, you know Jared loaned her the truck. He told me yesterday afternoon that he had."

"He didn't have my permission."

"Bring it up with your son. If Ms. O'Donnell wasn't

breaking any laws while driving, you'll need to let her go."

"She's driving without a valid license."

Skye asked Moira, "Is that true?"

"I don't have an IDP."

"I can't let you get back in the truck."

"I'm arresting her," Hank said.

"For driving without a license?"

"I have the right." He rubbed his head as if he were in pain.

"Hank, can I have a word?"

They walked back to Hank's cruiser. Moira breathed easier and tried to pinpoint what it was that disturbed her about Hank—other than his being an asshole.

Whatever Skye said to him, it had to have been good. Five minutes later, Jared's father drove away.

Skye came over and said, "You have to leave the truck. Get your stuff."

Moira grabbed her bag from the backseat. "Thank you."

"I saw him follow you out of the school parking lot. I'd called him when I learned Jared ditched school. But I have a more immediate concern."

"What?"

"I saw something on his neck."

"I saw it yesterday. A birthmark. But—"

"I've known Hank for years. He never had it before. And I have four dead bodies with so-called birthmarks that they didn't used to have. I'm worried about him now, I don't even know if I should have let him go, but what am I supposed to do? Arrest him? Ask him to remove his shirt so I can compare his mark to the dead?"

Skye shook her head, motioning for Moira to get in the passenger's side of her cruiser.

"If it's the same mark that Anthony showed me this morning," Moira said, "I'll tell you what I told Anthony. It's the mark of a demonic baptism, but the fact that these marks are showing up spontaneously makes no sense. They usually come during the ritual baptism itself. Could Hank have been on the cliffs the other night? Is he part of the coven?"

"No," Skye said.

"Can you be sure?"

"I suppose I can't be, but I know that the other victims with this same mark were not at the cliffs—except for Abby. And her mark is substantially different, though it's the same basic shape. All the victims were affiliated with the high school in some way. A secretary. A student. A librarian. And a murderer who lived next door to a teacher. It has to be related to the high school. I just spoke to one of the teachers and even she rubbed me the wrong way—I don't know why. But Nicole Donovan—"

"What about her?"

"Rafe told me this morning to trust my instincts. He was deadly serious. My first impression—my gut instinct—about Nicole Donovan was that she was *too* nice, *too* helpful—without being at all helpful. She didn't say one thing that I could follow up on. And there was a woman in her classroom when I got there who rubbed me wrong, but she left. Donovan said she was a friend."

"Listen to Rafe," Moira said, though she wondered exactly what Rafe meant by his comment, and what he knew that he hadn't shared.

"The student, Chris Kidd, came to me yesterday after

I spoke to the student body. He implied that his girl-friend, Ari Blair, was on the cliffs when Abby died, and was scared about coming forward. Now he's dead, and Ari ditched school. All signs point to her being part of this coven. A witness saw her drive off with Jared."

Moira slammed her fist on the dashboard. Why hadn't she sat on him? She thought she'd made perfectly clear the risks he faced, and since she had his truck she thought he'd stick it out at home.

"I have an APB out on Ari Blair and her car," Skye said. "Basically, I issued an order to detain her as a material witness and contact me immediately."

"Ari Blair," Moira mumbled. Reaching into her back-pack, she pulled out the address book taken from a witch's locker.

"What's that?"

"I was looking for lockers that belonged to witches, okay? This came from one."

"Why would you do that?"

"I was hoping for maybe a calendar or something that could give me an idea of where Fiona is staying."

She opened it and saw on the front page:

Property Of:
Arianne Blair

"This is hers," Moira told Skye.

"Was there anything helpful in there? I can't believe I just asked that. It's an illegal search and seizure."

"I took it, you didn't."

"Fruit of the forbidden tree. I now know you stole it, so I can't use anything in it to arrest anyone."

"Screw that; I just want to stop Fiona from killing

Rafe. She opened the address book to "Garrett Pennington" and tapped the address. "This is where I'm going to start."

"What's that?"

"Good Shepherd Church. Garrett Pennington. He lives in an apartment above the church—she has two addresses here, one for the church and one for Pennington."

"I found a connection between Pennington and Elizabeth Ellis. It's not safe for you to go there alone, and I don't have a warrant."

"Who cares about a warrant?"

"I do. Because if he killed Abby Weatherby, I can put him in jail."

"Rafe could die. I need information, and Pennington is the best bet to get it."

"This is fucked," Skye said, then changed the subject. "Can a witch make someone sick?"

"Sure, it's a standard spell. Not too difficult."

"What about a brain tumor?"

"Harder, but for a skilled magician, not impossible."

"I don't generally like coincidences, but Matthew Walker's mother has a brain tumor, and that was the reason he left Santa Louisa. Then just a few weeks later, Elizabeth Ellis, who is on the church council, hires Garrett Pennington as the pastor. But Walker didn't know anything about it."

"Seems obvious to me when you put it like that," Moira said. "If the coven had something personal of hers—preferably blood, hair, or fingernails, but a personal object can sometimes work—they could curse her. Give her a brain tumor or a heart attack. It doesn't always work, it's not a science, and the farther the distance the harder it is."

"That sounds like voodoo."

"Yeah."

"You're saying voodoo is real."

"Voodoo is witchcraft, nothing more, nothing less. What's so surprising?"

"I have a lot to learn." Skye paused. "Can you help me with something before we go to Good Shepherd?"

"I'll try."

"Ari Blair lives near here; I called her mother earlier and have permission to search her room."

"Good idea—she's young, probably less disciplined than Pennington. We might get what we need there. If not, you'll take me to Good Shepherd?"

"No. I'll drop you off down the street at the Starbucks. You can go wherever you like from there." Skye glanced at her. "I'm still a cop, Moira. I've already broken so many laws that I've sworn to uphold that when I can pretend I'm not breaking one, let me pretend."

It took ten minutes to reach Ari's house. As soon as Moira stepped on the property, she knew a witch lived here.

"Moira? Hey—Moira!"

Moira barely heard Skye's voice when she turned into Ari Blair's bedroom without being told which one was hers.

Magic, powerful magic, permeated every inch of space. The walls, the carpet, the clothing strewn across the desk chair . . . it was as if the room breathed magic.

The energy was strong, but young; powerful, but untrained. Moira sensed an inner goodness in the room, an aura of wanting to please. The aura of kindness. She wanted to weep for the poor girl who lived here, the betrayal she was about to face.

Ari Blair could have been her.

"Do you need to sit?" Skye asked from what seemed to be a great distance but was only feet away.

Moira shook her head and crossed the neat but cluttered room. She touched a book on the desk. A Wiccan spell book. Another was a Wiccan book of blessings, another about the elements in Wicca. All benign in the sense that they promoted the stated belief of witchcraft: *do no harm.* Most practitioners were well-intentioned but misguided people who were searching for truth, balance, and understanding.

They didn't understand the dark underbelly of magic. That noble intentions were simply that: intentions. That *do no harm* was impossible when you messed around with supernatural forces. Ari had been used, her inner goodness and innocence and desire to learn more about herself and the world around her being twisted in order to pull energy from her.

"How did Ari's boyfriend die?" Moira asked quietly.

"Possible brain aneurysm. He complained of a severe headache in the afternoon, then a few hours later collapsed and bled from the ears. He died en route to the hospital."

"I feel fear. Here, in this room. Fear and magic. She's definitely scared about something."

Skye was looking at her strangely.

"What's wrong?" Moira asked.

"You sound like Anthony."

"Anthony is an empath. I'm not."

Moira turned her back to Skye to avoid more questions. Together they searched the room. Moira flipped through the spellbooks one by one.

Skye said, "Jared was here."

"How do you know?" Moira asked.

Skye held up two phones. "This is Jared's cell phone." She flipped it open to show a photo of Jared and Lily on the wallpaper. "I'll bet this is Ari's. They dumped the phones so no one could GPS them."

"Dammit! What on earth was that kid thinking?"

"He's worried about Lily, and he's an eighteen-year-old boy. He thinks he's invincible."

"Idiot," Moira mumbled. "We need to find them."

"I will." Skye looked through Ari's closet while Moira continued going through her books and papers. Moira took the time to study what wasn't as obvious. She noted that Ari was interested in vortexes—intersections of positive and negative energy. Important in balance theory, a yin-and-yang thing.

An idea popped into Moira's head as she reviewed Ari's books. She talked it out to get it straight. "Let's say Ari had no idea what the ritual the other night was about. After, she's terrified and thinks she needs to fix it. Her boyfriend dies. She's panicking, and she comes up with an idea to stop it."

"How?"

"I think she's trying to undo the damage she helped create on the cliffs. Look—" She pointed to books on geography, spiritual vortexes, geometry, and ley lines. "This tells me she believes in intersecting points of power."

"Points of power? What's that?"

"Intersecting points of power. I'd love to explain it all to you, but we don't have time. Ari is playing with fire.

In a nutshell, she's trying to set up a power center. It takes time—she needs to go to specific places the same distance apart, and each the same distance from the chosen power center. When each spot is aligned, it creates a one-way flow of energy, helping in complex rituals, especially for sole practitioners. Most covens have enough people to draw energy from, but individuals use the elements."

"What can that do?"

"The more energy Ari can draw into her, the more powerful her magic. But she can't possibly think she can reverse the ritual. She'll get herself killed. And Jared. Dammit, as soon as she sets up the power center, she's practically broadcasting her whereabouts to Fiona. Fiona's power weakens when Ari draws energy to one spot."

"Okay, assuming this is true, why can't we do the same thing? Buy ourselves some time? Maybe lure Fiona into a trap?"

"Because the energy flow comes from magic, and only begins when the ritual starts. When that happens, you're looking at battle magic, Fiona against Ari. Fiona will win, hands down, but not before more demons are released. Ari is drawing energy toward her—any demons, spirits, ghosts within the boundaries of the ley lines will be drawn to her center. She's a novice. Even a practiced witch like Fiona wouldn't attempt such a ritual without days of planning and preparation to protect her and her coven. Ari probably thinks she can either call on her own demon for vengeance or draw in the demons she released. But either way, she's summoning the damn creatures. And now Jared is with her. It's extremely dangerous. I have to find Ari. Stop her from making the same mistakes I did. I'm ready to go to Good—" She cleared her throat. "Starbucks. Actually, their tea isn't half-bad. Not like a fresh-brewed pot, but for tea in a bag, tolerable."

"You sound just like Anthony," Skye said, not for the first time.

"Well, Italy and Ireland . . . we have a lot in common."

"I'd never have imagined." Skye turned around.

Moira gathered up Ari's material on power points. She'd study Ari's notes and try to figure out where she planned to set up this vortex.

"You can't take—"

Damn, Moira thought she'd been discreet. She slid the material into her bag. "Take what?" She smiled and walked past Skye, relieved when the cop said nothing more.

THIRTY-THREE

Father Philip had listened attentively to Anthony's recap of what he and Moira had learned, asking only a few questions for clarification, and now he sat quietly at the table, his expression contemplative.

Anthony grew impatient but remained silent.

At last the old priest spoke. "You said you have a photograph of the marks on the dead bodies?"

Anthony nodded, retrieved the photo, and slid it across the table to Father. "Moira said it's a demon mark, except these people—other than Abby Weatherby—weren't on the cliffs during the ritual."

The old priest studied the instant picture and frowned. "Moira is right. I don't see how this could happen—but then again, I've seen things during my eighty-three years that I couldn't have imagined. The coven would have set up powerful protections for their members. Perhaps those in the circle were unaffected, but anyone who had contact with the demons *after* the ritual *are* affected."

"But why would a demon possess them, then kill them? It doesn't make sense, not with what we know about demons."

"You're right. We are truly facing the unknown here." He paused, then added quietly, "Perhaps it's the proximity. As the demons move through town they affect people they come in contact with."

"I've read Franz Lieber's notes," Anthony said, pulling out the handwritten journal. "He believed the *Conoscenza* was destroyed."

"We all did." Father sighed and looked Anthony in the eye. "I learned yesterday that there have been secrets in the Order. Raphael was sent here to find the *Conoscenza*."

Anthony shook his head. "None of this should have happened. It didn't have to!" He spun around, angry. He didn't want to be angry at Father Philip, his mentor had learned of the truth only yesterday, but Father *should* have known. "Who hid the truth?"

"The Cardinal."

That stunned Anthony. Cardinal DeLucca was their ally. "He would never have put Rafe in jeopardy."

"I am certain he is horribly distraught at what happened, but we can only do our best with the information we have at the time. Faith, instincts, intelligence."

"Where did the cardinal get his information?"

"Hervé Salazar."

Anthony knew Hervé well. The young priest meant well, but he had been so damaged by past experiences battling the occult that he saw things that weren't there. Anthony had been called to no fewer than sixteen places around the globe where Hervé was certain demons lived within buildings. He feared the apocalypse was imminent, that demons were everywhere. Nothing had been proven, and Anthony's specialty was architecture. If there was a demon embedded in a building or artifact, Anthony could identify and exorcise it.

"The cardinal didn't believe him," he said.

"The cardinal needed to verify what Hervé told him, and Raphael was in California at the time. He has a natural gift of communication, speaks multiple languages, and we had need for a caretaker here."

"What happened to the last caretaker before Rafe was called up?"

"He resigned. He wasn't of the Order, and the cardinal felt he had problems handling the special needs of the priests in his care."

"Could he have been lured away by the housekeeper and her daughter, the witches? They could have cast a spell over him, poisoned him, done almost anything so they could continue unencumbered. They were poisoning the priests; they didn't want interference."

"You may be right. I don't know."

Anthony sat down. He couldn't help but feel that the Order had failed not only Rafe, but all the priests who were murdered that night. If they'd been more alert, more suspicious, they might have stopped the slaughter. He asked quietly, "Where do we go from here? It's you and me."

"And Moira and Rafe, and even your Skye McPherson. And Lily. She is stronger than you believe."

"Rafe is—" He couldn't say it. He looked down. "I failed him," he whispered. "Again."

Father Philip reached over and touched his forearm until Anthony looked at him. "No self-pity, son, no regrets. We don't know the future; we do the best we can. Intentions matter. Your intent was not to allow Raphael to be taken. He is still alive, and we will do everything to get him back. We may die. But what is it that the Americans say? We won't go down without a fight."

Anthony smiled. "I'm glad you're here, though I am worried about your safety. There are many witches who want you dead."

"My safety is unimportant right now. We have a fundamental problem with the Seven. They grow stronger by feeding on the sins inside human beings. The sins that came from Adam and Eve. The stronger they become, the harder they are to trap."

"I understand this, from what Franz Lieber has written, but what can we do?"

"I don't know how to send them back, but I believe I know how to trap them." Father Philip pulled a small journal from his breast pocket. It was stained, and very old.

Anthony recognized the tattered book as *The Journal of the Unknown Martyr.* The stains were blood, the book hundreds of years old, written in Aramaic, the language of Jesus Himself, but virtually unused in the thirteenth century when the Unknown Martyr penned it. The fact that the book had survived nearly one thousand years was testament to its importance. That Father Philip had taken it from St. Michael's vault was against everything they believed.

Father Philip carefully, reverently, opened it to a page near the end. He translated as he read:

"Your humble servant begs you, O Lord, to end our suffering. I have seen the Seven Sins, with my own eyes, in their True Being, and I fear great for mankind. They come for me, I beg You for deliverance. When the last was interned, they broke the traps we set. Now we pray and hide, hide from their collective Wrath, and pray to You, O Lord, for Mercy. Virtue conquers Sin. Give me a sign, O Lord, we who battle the demons in Your Name, Your most Humble Servant, I."

He put the book down. "That is the last entry."

The pain in the words was not lost on Anthony. "Yet the Seven were sent back, so there must be a way."

"Not without loss." He stared at the book stained with blood.

"What does it mean, Father? I see that together they are stronger, yet Lieber said that when released they disband."

Father nodded. "Yes. Because they are drawn to their nature. Lust to lust, sloth to sloth. They can be trapped, but the journal ends and we don't know how the Unknown Martyr and his fellow soldiers did it. We only know that they succeeded, and then they died."

Anthony was solemn. "We have no choice."

"You can find another way. It will take time to find all Seven. But first we trap the Sin that is in Santa Louisa. It is imperative we know which of them we are dealing with."

"Why?"

"Virtue traps Sin."

Anthony frowned, then realized what Father was saying. "We can trap them with a vessel that negates them."

"Yes. I believe that is what this means. I've read the entire journal. The language is archaic, but based on the facts I believe the Martyrs trapped them one by one in different pure vessels. It is with the last that they encountered death."

"For every action there is an equal and opposite reaction," Anthony mumbled. "For lust, chastity would keep it inert. For pride, humility."

"Yes. What sin is out there now? What are we fighting?"

Anthony paced again, this time in contemplation.

"The bodies I saw in the morgue. The ones with the demon's mark. A woman who couldn't have children pushed a pregnant woman down a flight of stairs. A man who had been passed over for a promotion killed the woman who was promoted in his place. But what of the basketball player who died of an aneurysm? He had the same mark, yet he hurt no one."

"Perhaps he was battling the Sin internally."

Anthony stopped pacing. "So we either kill or die?"

"When touched by one of the Seven Deadly Sins, our own conscience becomes twisted. We act on our impulses, we take what we want, do what we want; we have no barrier, no standard of right and wrong. If someone covets his neighbor's ox, he takes the ox."

"Covets—envy." Anthony knew it as soon as he said it. "Envy is in town. How do we trap it?"

"Envy is the first sin, the original sin. The serpent lured Eve to taste the forbidden fruit, to eat from the Tree of the Knowledge of Good and Evil. He was envious of God's newest creation, human beings. Humans who had free will. Humans who were favored. He couldn't have what they had, so he took Paradise away from them."

Anthony frowned. "What object can contain Envy?"

"A tabernacle," Father responded solemnly.

"But how do we trap Envy inside it? We can't summon it without drawing on the evil we are trying to stop." Then the solution came to Anthony. "So we have to find where Envy is most likely to be lured, and set the trap there."

Fiona watched the demon walk around Raphael Cooper on its six clawed hooves, its psychic leash but a fine line. Cooper mumbled a prayer, invoking God, and the demon hissed and yelped.

She gave the demon room and it attacked Cooper.

Fiona called back her pet and Cooper cried out in pain for the first time that day. Finally! The man was human after all.

"I am weary of your silence, Raphael," Fiona said. "Who taught you the ritual? Who else knows the *Conoscenza*? Raphael, speak to me!"

"Your black magic. Does not work." He bit back a scream as the demon clawed him. "On. Me."

Serena walked into the room. She stared at Raphael. She tried to keep her face impassive, but Fiona knew the truth.

"Would you like to play with your lover?" Fiona asked her. "Go ahead. He can't get away this time."

Serena turned her back on Raphael and said, "It's nearly time."

"You're not going to offer a sacrifice for his life? I'm surprised, daughter; I thought your love was eternal," she mocked.

Serena said, "He chose the wrong side."

She walked over to him. Fiona watched her daughter with interest shielded under a veil of boredom. She had worried a bit that Serena's lust for Raphael Cooper would blind her to what needed to be done.

Rafe drew in an unsteady breath and watched as the young woman approached him. Calling herself Lisa, she'd played him, used him, seduced him, in order to torture and kill the priests for her evil sacrifice.

Now, Lisa—or Serena, or whatever her name was—took a long look at him. Her eyes, green and catlike, filled with pain and rage, but her voice was well-modulated when she told Rafe, "Every death after the moment on the cliffs when you broke our circle is on your conscience. If you had left us alone, all those people would still be alive."

She touched his head and chanted something familiar. He recognized the sounds, the language, but not what it meant. It was the language he'd spoken the other night, but even at the time he hadn't known what it was he was saying.

Suddenly he was on his knees. Images of violence, bloody and vile, played in his head.

She'd drawn out the memories of that night when the mission priests died. The memories he desperately wanted to forget, and now they played over and over and he could do nothing to stop it.

"Stop!" he begged, holding his head as he curled into the fetal position.

Fiona turned to her daughter, proud. "Impressive, Serena."

"It's time," she said and walked out.

Fiona told her pet to guard the prisoner, then she followed her daughter. She *was* impressed, and not a little bit surprised.

Fiona would need to keep a watchful eye on Serena.

THIRTY-FOUR

Late Friday afternoon and no one was in or around the vicinity of Good Shepherd Church. Lucky for her, Moira thought, as she picked the lock to the back door of the church. At the last moment she considered that there might be an alarm—half-worried, she looked around for a panel, motion sensors, or anything to indicate there was an auditory or silent alarm system. Nothing.

The church was one large room. There was definitely magic in here. Not a lot, and she suspected that none had occurred since Sunday, but it felt strong enough that Moira knew spells had been cast here. Something retained magical energy. She looked quickly around, taking in the simple room instantly.

It appeared that this building used to be a business of some sort. Multiple outlets along the floorboard, for plugs and phones, indicated there were probably twenty desks or cubicles. Real estate was Moira's guess. Now the room was filled with padded folding chairs; the carpet was new and lush, and the altar was a simple polished wood table with a gold cross hung on the wall above it. Moira didn't want to stay here too long—though the sky was darkening as the sun rapidly set, the front of the "church" was all glass. But she took a moment and looked under the table with her flashlight.

Just as she thought: a sigil. The sigil—a demonlike creature in a hexagram—was unique and likely the patron "demon" of Pennington's order. Whether it was Fiona's or a special mark just for Pennington, she didn't know. She looked around and saw protections over every doorway—herbs disguised as decorative flowers, or framed posters with sayings like "With God, nothing is impossible." She'd bet there were occult symbols on the flip side of the paintings. Maybe that was the magic she felt, the simple protective spells cast to keep demons and spirits at bay.

There were four smaller rooms off the main room, all on the northern side of the building. The front room—with all the window exposure—was a classroom and day-care center. The next looked to be a meeting room. The rear two were offices. Moira searched both of them, not certain what she was looking for but hoping she'd recognize a clue if she saw it.

Since Pennington was one of the twelve at the ritual, he had to be in Fiona's inner circle. He'd know where she was living. It wasn't a hotel, not here in Santa Louisa, where the choices were sparse with no five-star hotels in sight. And Fiona had been here awhile—months. She may have arrived after the murders at the mission, but Moira would bet her money that Fiona had been here for much, much longer. Fiona wouldn't have trusted even her most trusted circle with every detail of her plans. She would want to be nearby. To watch, supervise, and criticize.

Pennington had arrived in August. The priests died in November. Was he part of it? Directly, or on the periphery? She hadn't pressed Rafe on the details of the murders, but maybe she should have. She had her theories based on what she *did* know, what Anthony and Rafe said, and what had been written about the murders in the papers. But she didn't have details, and if she was missing something . . .

She searched both offices. The computers were passcode protected, and while Moira could pick any lock and hot-wire almost any car, she knew next to nothing about technology or code breaking. The file cabinets were locked, and those she easily picked. She found little inside—though a printed copy of the membership directory might come in handy. She snatched it, glancing through what looked like over three hundred names. She prayed they weren't *all* witches. Chances were only a few of them were practitioners. People like Elizabeth Ellis.

The desk in Pennington's office drew her in particular. There was magic here, strong and powerful, and for one fear-filled moment she thought she was being watched. It took all her willpower not to cast a shield around herself, knowing that the shield might protect her for that moment, but the magic it generated would alert Fiona to her location.

She shook off the feeling, searched the office, and found a hex bag meant to curse any who entered without permission. She dumped out the bag and said a prayer, then left.

Pennington lived upstairs. Another door, another lock, and she was inside.

He didn't actually live here—she knew that as soon as she stepped into the stale rooms. These, too, had once been offices and converted into an apartment. It was clean, smelling antiseptic, and furnished with cheap but trendy furniture. The door opened into the living room—two couches and a couple of chairs. The kitchen was in the middle and windowless, the bedroom in the rear. Again, windows faced the street. She kept the lights off; it was not completely dark yet and a few cars had driven by. The church and apartment were on a side street that dead-ended into a park. There were only a handful of businesses here, and most were closed at five. A small café on the corner, which she could barely see from the bedroom window, appeared to be the only place still open, and it wasn't doing a brisk business.

Still, she wasn't going to take chances. She walked through the kitchen, looked in the refrigerator: sparse. Cans of soda, water bottles, and expired orange juice. The freezer had more food, probably used if he had to stay for a reason.

One of the two bedrooms had been converted into an office. Unlike Pennington's official office downstairs, this space looked well-used. She searched the desk first. There was no computer, but there was a cord to connect a laptop to a nearby printer. Nothing of interest in the desk, except the bottom drawer, which was locked.

From that drawer something magical pulsated with dark energy. She hesitated, then picked its lock. Sliding open the drawer, a wave of heat washed over her, brushing by her on a stench of evil. She shook involuntarily and barely resisted slamming the drawer shut.

Inside was an old wooden box as thick as a ream of paper, but half the size. Carved on the outside was a sigil similar—possibly identical—to the one under the altar in the main room. The wood was dark and aged, the corners worn and black. Two dark orange eyes looked in opposite directions yet seemed to look right at her— through her—like twin flames. She stifled a scream, as if the demon on the box were alive.

The box was locked and required a number code. Seven wheels—old and worn so dark she could barely make out the numbers—would need to be set exactly right to open it. She considered taking it, but as her hand neared the thing, every instinct inside her told her not to touch it. She wished Anthony were there. He'd know exactly what this was and how to handle it.

Instead, she took a picture of it with her cell phone and emailed it to Anthony with the message:

This scares me to death; I don't want to touch it. Dark magic—the blackest—is coming off it in waves. But if you want me to grab it, I will.

She clicked *Send,* pocketed her phone, and turned her attention to the file cabinets. She was looking through the paper documents for property—where did Pennington *really* live? She'd bet her last dollar that he stayed with Fiona. Fiona liked her inner circle close.

Good Shepherd owned a lot of property, not only in Santa Louisa but all over the country. She wanted to grab everything but couldn't carry it all, so focused on places in or around Santa Louisa.

Fiona would live somewhere private. Preferably near the ocean, but that wasn't a requirement for her mother. Size—it had to be big. Opulent. Fiona liked to live well, and she was good at manipulating people into giving her things. Anything she wanted, including money. Moira wondered how wealthy Good Shepherd was—with three hundred church members, it was neither large nor small.

It took her several minutes, but she found three properties in Santa Louisa that seemed to fit Fiona's criteria, at least on paper. Moira pulled up Google Earth on her iPhone and looked at the property images. The first was a Victorian house in downtown Santa Louisa. Large, on half an acre, but on a busy corner. The second was promising—in the mountains, in fact off the same road that led to Santa Louisa Mission. Fiona would appreciate that irony.

But when Moira pulled up the last property, she instantly knew this was the one. Just south of the county line, no one lived a mile in any direction. The highway was close, but no other residences were. Fiona could see the ocean, and the place had three separate buildings aside from the main house, which had six bedrooms and eight bathrooms. This was it.

If Fiona was there, so was Rafe. There had to be some way she could pinpoint where he was being held without sending out her own magical feelers.

"Use all your senses, but focus on feeling. You are empathic when you allow yourself to be," Rico had told her more than once. *"Drop the shields and* feel *the emotions. Search for the emotions."*

Rafe would be scared. Hurting. She could do it. She didn't want to—she'd spent years building up her shields so she didn't feel the emotions of others—but to save Rafe she would.

Just in case she was wrong, she grabbed the files for all three properties before leaving the room.

Back downstairs, she realized at once something was very wrong.

Magic, active magic, vibrated off the walls. Moira could practically *see* the energy building in the room. Where was it coming from? It wasn't directed at her, and it was coming from all around. Coming *into* the building.

She was at the center of an energy vortex. Someone was drawing in the energy. This didn't happen spontaneously.

But no one was here.

She listened, then discerned the voice chanting. Downstairs? There was a *basement*?

Moira searched for another door, but there wasn't one inside the building. She pictured the alley next to the church. And there *had* been another door to the right of the church's rear entrance. She should have checked it out, but she hadn't planned on being here this long.

She ran outside. The door was closed but not locked. She said a prayer, along the lines of *I hope you're in a helpful mood, Big Guy, because this feels very bad right now.*

Moira pulled open the door. Incense swirled around her as she silently stepped inside. Candlelight flickered down below.

From the top of the stairs, she recognized that this was a permanent ritual spot. Many spells had been cast here, most so black that fear nearly made Moira run. How could she, one person, fight such dark magic?

She hesitated, listened to the voices. Felt the magic around her. Most of the spells were old. Lingering, but harmless. She focused on the spell being cast now. The energy being drawn into this room, the energy she saw upstairs. The vortex.

Ari Blair.

Was Jared still with her? Among the shadows and candle flames Moira couldn't clearly see what was happening down below. Then she heard a male voice chanting along with Ari. *Jared*. She didn't know whether to be relieved or pissed off or worried. Probably all three.

Ari was calling on a variety of names to aid her, using a mixture of Latin and English, common among amateur Wiccans. Moira listened to the words, and only a moment later realized what Ari was doing.

It was a reversal spell. Relatively simple and easy if a witch wanted to reverse a curse or illness, but trying to recall the Seven Deadly Sins? Ari was not only going to get herself killed, she was risking the release of more demons.

Moira rushed down the stairs. Ari and Jared knelt in a pentagram surrounded by a double circle, candles all around them.

"Stop!" she shouted.

Ari looked up from the chalice she was incanting over. Fear, then irritation, crossed the girl's face. Jared saw Moira and sighed in relief.

Ari scowled. "You need to leave." She tried to sound tough, but Moira heard the hesitation in her tone.

"You need to stop right now. Turn over the chalice and tell me exactly where those three altars are so I can destroy them."

"No!" She glared at Moira. "They killed Chris!"

"One of the Seven Deadly Sins killed Chris, and one or more of them are going to kill or possess you if you don't stop playing around with black magic."

"I'm a white witch."

Moira shook her head. "That's what I used to think. Until a demon used me to kill my boyfriend."

Ari sucked in a sob. "I didn't kill Chris!"

"You might as well have. It was a demon from the cliffs who touched him."

"But Chris wasn't there."

"You were, though you were safe in the protective circle. Everyone else in the world is in jeopardy."

Ari was listening, and Moira was relieved. The magic was stagnant now, without the continuing ritual to build it up.

But Ari was unconvinced. "That's why what I'm doing here is so important! I'm sending the demons back so they can't hurt anyone else. I didn't know what was going to happen. I never wanted anyone to get hurt."

Moira continued to walk forward. She stood on the outside of the circle. "I believe you. You don't want to harm anyone."

"*Do no harm.* That's what we believe."

"That's what *you* believe. It's noble. You didn't want to hurt anyone. I don't think you planned on releasing demons."

Ari nodded. "I want to do good. I created the energy vortex. I researched it, plotted it out, and it's working! Don't you feel it?" She put her arms up. The crystals on her wrists drew in the energy, practically drugging the teenage witch.

Moira was losing the argument. "I feel it. And you need to stop it right now."

"No," she snapped petulantly.

Moira said to Jared. "Follow me."

"Please don't go, Moira," Jared pleaded. "They have Lily! They're going to hurt her just like they did Abby."

Moira said, "Jared, Lily is with Anthony. Safe. No one can get to her." *I hope.* "Ari is playing with fire, and she doesn't want to listen to the truth."

"Lily's okay?" Jared asked, rising from the floor and walking over to Moira.

"Jared, no!" cried Ari. "Don't go. None of you understand the power that I have!"

Moira lost her temper. "You don't think so? I understand it better than *anyone,* even better than Fiona. I know what the power does to people. To people I love and care about. I also know what it does to you. You feel invincible. You believe you can do anything. You've probably left your body, floated among the clouds, watched people. That was my favorite part of being a magician. Flying. And I still miss it."

"Then help me if you can!"

"I'm trying."

"You're trying to stop me, not help me!"

"That's the only way I can help you. I have to stop this now." For the last several minutes Moira had been feeling the energy turn from neutral to black. Something was coming. She had to convince Ari to break the circle and destroy the chalice. If Moira walked into the circle, the energy would be drawn to her, because of her blood. "The energy is changing. Don't you feel it, Ari?"

But Ari was already drunk with the power, and said, "I'm getting stronger."

"You're losing control!"

Ari put her arms up and chanted the end of the ritual.

"Under the stairs!" Moira commanded Jared. She didn't have to tell him twice.

A tornado of dark gray smoke rotated along the perimeter of the circle in which Ari stood. Ari held her hands up and commanded the spirit to go back where it came from.

The whirlpool of evil rotated faster. Every candle went

out except those within the circle. Moira's hair blew all around her; she could barely stand upright against the pressure. She had her flashlight in hand, but it was all she could do to hold on to it.

The entity didn't obey Ari's commands, just as Moira feared. She had no idea whether the demon was one of the Seven or a completely different devil. But with all the energy being directed into the center of Ari's circle, the demon either didn't know Moira and Jared were there or didn't care.

Moira's arsenal of weapons wouldn't work until the demon took a physical form. She knew the exorcism prayer by heart, but the demon wasn't trapped. As soon as she began it, it would turn on her. She wouldn't be able to help Ari, or Jared, or save Rafe, if she were dead.

Ari held up a crystal.

"Smash it!" Moira screamed at her. "Break the crystal and you'll break the spell!"

Whether Ari couldn't hear her over the demonic winds or whether she ignored her, Moira couldn't say, but Ari said, "I command thee, as it is above, it is below. I command thee to come—"

"No!" Moira shouted helplessly. "Don't!"

It was too late. Ari had invited the demon into her circle. The girl screamed silently as the demon invaded her body. The resulting silence as all the air seemed to be sucked out of the room terrified Moira.

The possessed Ari stared at Moira, her eyes a red-tinged opaque.

"I know *you*," it said.

Fiona cast the circle, but nothing was working the way it was supposed to. Her anger mounted as her coven grew wary. They were doubting her, she felt it in her pores, and that doubt, that mistrust, infuriated her nearly as much as the weak circle at the Rittenhouse furniture showroom.

She turned to Serena. "This isn't working! We should have returned to the cliffs."

Serena was upset, as she should be since her error had cost them valuable time.

"We leave. Regroup tomorrow night at the cliffs—"

"Wait," Serena said.

Fiona despised being interrupted or contradicted, but she stopped just short of backhanding her daughter. Serena was in a half-trance, pulling information from the psychic energy in the region.

"It's Ari," said Serena. "Her magic. I told you she was stronger than you wanted to believe!" Serena put her hands up, trying to discern what Ari was up to. "She's drawing energy to her location. She created a . . ." She closed her eyes, her fingers on her temples as if in pain, but Fiona pushed.

"What?" she demanded.

Garrett stepped over to her. "Fiona, let her be."

She glared at Garrett. He was too soft on Serena. He stepped back from them, and Fiona turned back to her daughter. "Serena, what did Ari do?"

"A triangle. She is drawing in all energy within a perfect two-dimensional prism."

"How can that little witch do it?"

Serena didn't answer. Instead, she said, "All the energy is being directed toward Good Shepherd Church."

"The fool!" Fiona paced. "She doesn't know what she's doing. Only the strongest of magicians should attempt even the most minor spells. All our work! She's going to destroy it! Garrett, you and Nicole. Go."

"I could do it faster," Serena said.

"I need you here. We'll work together to break the triangle."

Serena stared at her, mouth open. "You've never said that before."

"What?"

"That you needed me. That we are stronger together."

Fiona frowned. "Of course I have." Had she?

Serena shook her head. "Maybe you thought it, but I can't read your mind."

"That must be it." Fiona touched her good daughter on the cheek. "I am hard on you, Serena, but that is necessary to make you strong. Let's continue."

Serena smiled. "Yes, Mother."

Though Anthony wanted to leave Father Philip and Lily at the mission, where he felt it was safest, he worried that leaving them alone anywhere was just as dangerous as bringing them with him.

The tabernacle he needed was in a secure storage room of St. Francis de Sales in downtown Santa Louisa. Two years ago, the parish priest died of a heart attack. Since then there had been five priests assigned, all leaving for a variety of reasons, which now seemed odd. The priest with the longest duration was Father Isaac, who had come out of retirement to tend to the dwindling flock. Anthony had never before considered that witchcraft had been involved in keeping the sole Catholic church inert and inactive, but now it seemed the only logical reason—other than general human apathy.

It was after seven p.m. when Anthony arrived. The

church was dark; the parish house next door had a single light in the living room. Father Isaac would retire for the night by eight. Anthony brought Father Philip and Lily with him to the door, not wanting to leave them alone in the car.

Father Isaac took several long minutes to reach the door. When he opened it, Anthony felt the waves of pain coming from the old man, who looked even older now than he had when Anthony arrived in town two months ago. "Are you well?" he asked.

"I'm old," Isaac replied. "My suffering is less than many."

"Father, this is Philip Zaccardi of St. Michael's in Sicily."

Isaac's eyes widened as if he were meeting a saint. "Reverend," he said with a deep nod. "It is truly an honor."

Isaac had been a supporter of St. Michael's efforts, but like most priests not affiliated with the Order, he remained quiet about it.

"Thank you," Philip said humbly. "We are in need of a tabernacle."

"The original from the mission," Anthony clarified.

Isaac nodded. "Of course. It is in the vault."

"We also need a eucharistic ceremony. Can you do it, or may I have permission?" Philip asked.

"Let's share in the consecration."

"We don't have much time," Philip said. "I baptized Lily earlier today. This will be her first Eucharist."

Isaac smiled solemnly. "I know the prayers in my heart; let us proceed expeditiously. Anthony, you know how to get into the vault. I will begin preparation."

Anthony pulled his phone from his pocket and

frowned at the message from Moira. He pulled up the image she'd sent. As soon as it loaded, his heart froze.

"Father," he said to Philip. "Moira found this."

Father Philip crossed himself as he looked at the picture. "The Mark of Cain."

Anthony stared. "So help us God." He wasn't surprised—Fiona's coven had the power behind it to suggest they were in deep—but seeing the sigil was chilling. Covens who invoked Cain were vicious, ruthless, and unstoppable until death.

Lily looked at the photo and stifled a scream. Her hands flew to her neck as she swayed in terror. "No. No!"

Anthony caught the girl as she fainted.

THIRTY-FIVE

There were two ways—at least, two ways Moira knew about—to exorcise a demon while keeping the victim alive.

Moira didn't have time for a traditional exorcism. Not only was Rafe still in grave danger, Ari's ritual would have already attracted the attention of Fiona and her merry band of witches.

But stabbing Ari, though effective and fast acting, didn't appeal to Moira, either.

Damn, damn, damn!

Moira started the exorcism rite, keeping her dagger firmly in hand.

"Deus, in nómine tuo salvum me fac, et virtúte tua—"

The demon laughed, Ari's voice deep and unnatural. *"Andra Moira."*

She ignored his intimidations and continuted her invocation.

The demon twitched, but continued to taunt her. "You know me. We're old friends."

She would *not* listen to his lies.

The candles all relit simultaneously, and it was all she could do not to jump. Jared came out from under the stairs. "Is Ari going to be okay?"

"Get back!"

The demon was strong, and while he couldn't break

the spirit trap and attack her, he could summon dormant demons in the room. Some were residual spirits from past rituals; others were trapped in ritual objects on the black magic altar. The ground shook and several evil spirits wrenched themselves from the captivity.

"I can—" Jared began.

"Stand behind me!" Moira commanded Jared, then continued shouting the exorcism prayer while facing off three demons of uncertain shape moving toward her.

They were not unlike the earth demon that Elizabeth Ellis had summoned when she'd rescued Lily. Moira tried the same prayer she'd used before, and one of the demons evaporated. The other two still came at her. Out of the corner of her eye, she saw a large, solid demon wrenching itself from the old, moldy brick walls. The building shook around her and Moira flashed on the image of killing the demon the same way Dorothy took out the Wicked Witch of the West, dropping this building on him. Except that she'd be under the house, too. She would have laughed but she had both her hands full—one with holy water, the other with her blessed dagger.

She flicked holy water onto the weak demons in front of her and both of them dissipated.

That seemed too easy.

Noise at the top of the stairs distracted her. A stranger was running toward them and Moira at first feared he was another witch. He stopped and stared at the destruction of the basement and the charging demon.

"Watch out!" the man cried.

Moira whirled around as a hoofed demon, looking

much like a deformed mythological centaur, charged her.

This was no earth demon. It was a corporeal demon, no question about it. Straight from the pits of Hell and smelling as vile as a decomposing corpse on a summer day.

Moira backed up, reaching into one of her pockets and pulling out a vial of sacred chrism. She broke it across her blade, coating the iron with oil that was poison to demons. A sliver of glass from the vial cut her finger, but she pushed back the sharp pain, which was far less important than imminent death at the hands— hooves?—of an ancient demon.

The demon spoke a language she didn't know, and she didn't ask for a translation. It rushed her and she deliberately fell to the ground, to urge the demon to run over her. It reeked of rotting flesh and black magic, and she could scarcely breathe. She stabbed her arm out and into the underbelly of the demon, slicing its guts open with her oily dagger.

One hoof stomped her in the thigh and she screamed, but her voice couldn't be heard over the agonized high-pitched cry of the tortured creature as it hit the wall. She jumped up, shaking out the pain, thankful her leg wasn't broken, which would have been icing on the cake of this shitty day.

The demon centaur was bubbling ooze as it liquefied in front of her, steam rising from the remains. The ooze stunk worse than the demon itself.

Was it dead? *Dead?* As in no longer in existence in this world *or* the underworld? Impossible. Its form was dead; there was no way to annihilate a demon.

"Holy shit, what the *fuck* was that?" Jared asked.

The demon inside the trap was surprisingly silent.

"What did you do to . . . it?" the stranger asked.

She looked at her dagger almost as if she'd forgotten it was there. The demon's blood—if it could be called blood—was black. It dripped from the oily knife until the knife was clean.

"Are you okay?" the stranger asked.

She turned to him, careful to keep a fair distance. He was in his forties, tall and attractive, with short, sandy hair and a solid, square jaw to match his solid, square shoulders. He wore a white button-down shirt and jeans.

"Who are you?" she demanded.

"I should be asking you the same thing," he said. "I'm Matthew Walker. This is my church. Or—it used to be." He looked pained. "We need to get out of here."

"You're the pastor who left last summer?"

"Sheriff McPherson called me earlier today and told me someone was defrauding my congregation. I got here as fast as I could."

The demon in Ari began to laugh.

"Let me help," he said.

"You're an exorcist?" she asked skeptically.

"No, but I've assisted in exorcisms."

The demon continued to laugh, and Moira felt the energy building again.

"Matthew Walker," the demon hissed.

Matthew jumped and began a prayer.

Moira continued her exorcism and Matthew said a parallel prayer in Greek. While she recognized the sound of the language, she didn't understand most of it. But the dual exorcisms seemed to be working, faster than she expected. The demon stopped laughing almost instantly, and Ari's body began to convulse. Within minutes, the demon screamed and left Ari's body in a tornado of smoke. Ari collapsed.

The energy in the room had stabilized but not disappeared. "We have to destroy the altars Ari set up," Moira said.

"I know where they are," Jared said. "I'll do it."

"Be careful."

"You mean you're not coming with me?"

"I trust you. Just—later, we need to talk about you and this." She gestured toward Ari.

"I'm sorry, Moira. I wanted to help."

"I know you did," she said, understanding Jared more than he knew. "Once the first altar is down, it breaks the vortex, so get to the easiest location first."

"Got it." He started up the stairs.

Matthew walked over and felt Ari's pulse. "She's okay, but we should call a doctor."

"Can you stay? I need—"

"Well, hello," a voice bellowed from the top of the stairs. "I'm—surprised to see you both here."

Garrett Pennington walked down the stairs, pushing Jared in front of him.

Matthew stepped in front of Moira in a protective gesture. It gave her the opportunity to quickly assess the situation. Pennington didn't have a weapon in hand. That gave her the edge. Though a woman, she played dirty when warranted. And three against one? Was Pennington a fool? He had witchcraft on his side, but the numbers benefited the good guys this time.

"Who are you?" Matthew demanded.

Pennington raised his eyebrows and touched his chest mockingly. "*You* don't know *me*?"

"Are you the bastard who did this"—Matthew waved his hand toward the altar—"to my church?"

"Church? If you want to call it that."

Matthew stepped toward him, and Moira put her hand on his arm. "Watch it. He's a witch. Or, I suppose, technically a *wizard*."

"I prefer magician," Pennington said.

"I prefer you get the hell out of my way," Moira said.

"You'd be insane if you thought I'd let you walk out of here. Fiona will be thrilled to see you again." He continued down the stairs, pushing Jared hard to the ground.

Moira said to Pennington, "Listen to me. We have a problem here. Ari created an energy vortex and it's still here."

"She's unconscious," Pennington said. "It'll dissipate soon."

"No, something else is drawing it in here and it's probably something in your office or behind your altar, asshole, or she created a loop of some sort, because I *feel* it. If we don't stop it, a hole is going to be punched into the underworld, and I don't think Fiona wants to spend her time battling wayward demons celebrating new-found freedom when she's trying so desperately to re-capture the Seven."

For a moment, Pennington waffled. "How do you know that will happen?"

"What good are you if you *don't* know? Seriously, how do they train you guys? I'm not even using magic and I can feel the charge! Dammit, I'm not fucking with you! Call Fiona if you don't believe me!"

"Let's go, then."

"We can't leave her here," Moira said, pointing to Ari.

"Why not? She created the problem in the first place. She should have to suffer the consequences."

"I'm not leaving her."

"Yes you are."

Pennington made a move toward Moira, and he wasn't using magic. Just brawn.

A street fight. Just what she was waiting for. Moira almost jumped for joy. She'd take this kind of physical battle any day over magic.

The fake preacher didn't bluff well. He feigned right—it was so obvious that Moira anticipated his real move, countered effectively, and flipped him. He lay there on the floor twenty seconds after he'd made his first step.

Moira said to Jared, "Can you carry Ari?"

He nodded, ran over to the petite teen, and picked her up.

Pennington tried to stand, and Moira kicked him in the ribs. He began to cast a spell, but Moira hit him on the head with the butt of her dagger to shut him up. He tried to get to his feet, stumbled, and collapsed.

"Up the stairs!" she commanded Walker and Jared.

They ran up and outside, and suddenly Moira was face-to-face with a woman she'd never seen before. A witch, based on the protection spell Moira sensed surrounding her. But the witch knew her limitations, because she also held a gun in her hand.

"I don't have time for this," Moira said.

She was on the verge of attack when Jared said, "Ms. Donovan? What are you doing?"

Donovan? Moira searched her memory and then realized she was the high school teacher.

"You're the reason they all died," Moira said.

"I don't know what you're talking about," Donovan sneered.

"You were on the cliffs." Out of the corner of her eye, she sensed more than saw Matthew Walker edging away from her and toward Donovan.

The woman rolled her eyes. "Apparently that's not much of a secret anymore."

She was the connection. Donovan and Ari Blair, but Donovan was the neighbor to the guy who killed his co-workers last night. Moira was finally beginning to make sense of how the demons were operating. All those on the cliffs must have become catalysts for the demons. What about Lily? Rafe? Jared said, "You're dating my dad! Was that all a lie?"

"We all do what we have to," Donovan said.

"That's why Hank Santos is marked," Moira muttered.

"What?" Jared said, turning to her. "My dad? What happened to my dad?"

Shit, Moira, that was smart. "Jared, we're trying to find a solution, but we really have to get out of here. Now."

Donovan said, "I've got other plans, and you're all coming with me. No one is going to stop it this time."

Matthew was only feet from Donovan, who was focused almost solely on Moira. No surprise; Fiona had probably offered a sweet reward for Moira's heart in a box. To distract her away from Matthew, Moira said, "You know, Nicole—right? Nicole Donovan? It's over. We know who you are, and no one at St. Michael's is going to let you get away with imprisoning the Seven Deadly Sins—if every last one of us has to die to ensure it."

"Good to know," Donovan sneered.

Suddenly, with feline grace, Matthew leapt onto the woman and they tumbled to the ground. He grabbed her wrist and slammed it on the cement walkway. She screamed and cursed, and Moira ran over and grabbed the gun, aiming it at Donovan.

"Shut up or you get a bullet in the brain, and I don't think you're a good enough magician to stop it."

Donovan screamed in frustration, and Matthew got up with the witch, holding her wrists.

Moira told Jared, "Take Ari with you. Get to one of her altars as fast as you can and break it apart. Destroy all three and then head to Skye's house and stay there. If Ari gives you shit even after what she's been through, tie her up, I don't care. Just don't let her do anything stupid."

"My dad—"

"I'll find a way to save him. I promise. He's acting weird, but he hasn't done anything wrong." *Yet.* "Go."

Jared carried Ari to her car and Moira breathed slightly easier. "Thanks for your help," she told Matthew, who stood contemptuously next to a weepy Nicole Donovan. "If you want to call the police, tell them Pennington is a con artist, whatever you want. But you might not want to mention what happened here. No one would believe it."

"You can say that again."

Donovan started crying in frustration. "You can't do this!"

Moira ignored her. "I have to go. They hurt a friend—" She stopped. Matthew had helped her, but he didn't need to know details.

"Are you sure you're okay?" he asked.

"Fine." She pulled out the papers to the property where she felt Rafe was most likely to be. She hoped and prayed that the ritual Donovan spoke of was nowhere near this place. She looked around for Jared's truck. "Shit."

"What?"

"I don't have a car."

"I'll take you wherever you want to go."

"No—"

"Please. I would feel better. After tonight—I've never seen a . . . *a demon* . . . like that."

"Neither have I." Not the black ooze, anyway. "But this is going to be dangerous. These people don't play nice, and they'll condemn you just for helping me."

"Just a ride. And maybe a little backup? You might think I'm a male chauvinist, especially since you can obviously take care of yourself." He grinned, revealing boyish dimples that clashed charmingly with his square jaw. "But I don't like the idea of you going off by yourself and fighting anyone, human or . . . not." He lost his smile.

Moira didn't want to accept his help, but she didn't know how long it would take for Anthony to arrive if she called him for a ride. And Pennington wasn't dead—he could come up those steps any minute. And the longer Moira waited, the more danger was not only to Rafe, but everyone in town.

"All right, thank you." She glanced at Donovan. "Can you tie her up downstairs with Pennington?"

"Gladly."

Matthew went down the stairs and Moira picked up his keys, which had fallen to the ground when he'd tackled Nicole Donovan. Moira sprinted across the church parking lot to Matthew's car.

Matthew Walker's timing was too good. He might be exactly who he said he was—after all, he had taken down the teacher. But Nicole Donovan hadn't seemed concerned about Walker. And the demon knew his name. She *wanted* to trust him, but she'd rather be safe than dead.

Besides, if he wasn't involved with Fiona, she didn't want to risk his life. She didn't know what she'd face when she found Rafe.

Walker's car had a GPS. Great, he could call in a grand theft auto and the cops would be on her ass in minutes.

She'd have to take her chances.

She typed the address of her first-choice property into the GPS and it gave her a map. Ten point four miles away, near the ocean. She memorized the route, then ripped the device from the dash and tossed it out the window as she drove off.

She called Anthony. "I have a lead on Rafe. I'm following up on it."

"Where are you?"

"I'm leaving Good Shepherd now." Moira filled him in on the highlights. "This place has been used as a center of black magic for some time, at least since Pennington arrived," she said. "I sent Jared off to destroy Ari's altars and break the energy vortex."

"Can he be trusted?"

"Tonight? Hell yeah, he got a good scare. Oh, speaking of Pennington, he's unconscious in the so-called church basement. Can you call your girlfriend and get her to arrest him? He tried to kill me. I'm happy to press charges. And Ms. Donovan, the teacher from the school, is there too. She pulled a gun on me. Fiona's web has spread far and wide. And she implied they're working another ritual to recall the Seven. I'll find Rafe, you find where they're setting up." She put on a brave front, but she knew tonight was it. She would walk straight into the lion's den, and she was no Daniel.

Anthony said, "The photo you sent. Of the box? You didn't touch it, did you?"

"No. I told you that. It's bad news."

"It's worse than that. I'll retrieve it myself when I get there. It's evil incarnate."

"What is it?"

"The Mark of Cain."

"Cain, as in Cain who slew Abel?"

"Yes. I'll fill you in later. But don't go after Rafe alone. Father Philip is very concerned."

"I'm fine," she said, then glanced in her rearview mirror. She was already out of sight of Good Shepherd. "I had some help at Pennington's place. Matthew Walker, the original minister of Good Shepherd. Skye talked to him earlier, and I guess they put two and two together and came up with Garrett Pennington is a lying sack of occult shit. The good pastor Matthew held his own against the two witches. But I left him there. He probably won't be happy because I kinda borrowed his car without asking."

"Moira—"

"It's Rafe's life on the line. When you get over there, could you explain it to him?"

THIRTY-SIX

By the time Skye arrived back at the sheriff's station, it was after 8 p.m. She was exhausted, hungry, and worried. They'd already had two homicides, three attempted rapes, one assault and battery, and an astounding *twenty-four* felony thefts. That didn't count the nearly one hundred misdemeanor thefts—including a woman who went to a boutique, tried on a wedding dress, and walked out wearing it. Without paying.

Before she could sit down at her desk, Rod Fielding came in. "I have something for you," he said.

She collapsed in her chair. "Take a number."

He sat on the corner of her desk and said in a low voice, "It's related to our conversation this morning."

"Another marked body?" she guessed.

"Not exactly. Same M.O."

"M.O.? We're not dealing with a serial killer here." Though as she said it, Skye couldn't help but think that the Seven Deadly Sins *were* supernatural serial killers. They were racking up victims faster than any human killer.

"I don't have the body myself, it's out of my jurisdiction—up north in San Luis Obispo. But I called the coroners and pathologists I know in the surrounding areas, asked them discreetly about the mark. No one has seen one yet, but Karen up in SLO had a case that came in today that was unusual and she was chatty about it. A woman who lost her house in foreclosure a few months ago burned it down this morning—and the family living inside it barely escaped. They'd just moved in over the weekend. The grandmother, who was living with them, died."

"They caught the arsonist?"

"She's in the county jail."

"And this fits the M.O. how?"

"I called one of the deputies up there, to see what he knew about the case, and get this—the arsonist rents an apartment in Ned Nichols's complex."

The Rittenhouse shooter. "Odd coincidence."

"Coincidence? You think so?"

"No. Keep the connection to yourself. And if you hear of anything similar—or any corpses with similar marks—let me know."

"Will do."

"Thanks, Rod. And—be careful, okay?"

He stood and said somberly, "I've checked my back ten times today in the bathroom mirror."

She would have laughed, but Rod was serious.

"You be careful too, Skye. Just because you got a demonologist on your side doesn't mean you're invulnerable."

That was certainly true. She'd had a couple of close calls back in November when she'd been investigating the murders at the mission.

As Rod was leaving, he said, "I just wanted you to know I've taken care of Abby's body. She was cremated this afternoon."

"Thank you." She watched him leave, then called a

friend who worked nights at the SLO county jail. She asked if the arsonist had any distinguishing marks. Ten minutes later the woman returned to the phone and said, "How'd you know? She has a big-ass birthmark on her upper shoulder. Odd shaped, part of it looks almost like a crescent moon."

"Thanks for your help," she said and hung up. What would Anthony think about this?

Before she could call him, her cell phone rang. It was Anthony.

"Funny, I was just thinking about you," she said.

"There's been trouble at Good Shepherd."

She straightened. "What kind of trouble?"

"The kind I seem to be lucky enough to find," he said with a rare hint of sarcasm.

"I'll meet you there."

"No—not yet. Let me go over and assess the situation first. I don't know what we'll find there."

She unfortunately knew what he meant. "I'm in the office less than ten minutes away," she said. "Do you know what happened?"

"Moira tracked Ari and Jared to Good Shepherd, where the girl set up a dangerous ritual. Ari ended up possessed, Moira took care of it—she had some help in the form of Matthew Walker, the former pastor. He said you called him today about Pennington?"

"Yes. He seemed upset about it. Are the two kids okay?"

"Apparently. But as they were leaving they encountered two of Fiona's coven: Pennington and a teacher from the school, Donovan. Said Donovan is involved with Jared's father. Which matches what you said about Santos earlier and the mark you saw."

She remembered Rafe's words again. *Trust your instincts.* "There've been a huge number of calls tonight," Skye said. "I've been trying to find Rafe, but—"

"I heard. We've been listening to the police scanner."

Right. Anthony was driving her truck. "What does it all mean? That half the town is possessed?"

"They are not possessed. Their inhibitions—their conscience—has been removed. They are acting on envy. Taking what they want. Consequences be damned. I have a tabernacle to trap the demon Envy. We're ready for it."

"I hope so."

"Moira thinks she knows where Rafe is. She went to check it out. But I'm concerned about the coven right now. Moira said they're staging another ritual. I fear that the results will be the same as what Ari Blair tried to do."

"So they'll be defeated. What's wrong with that?"

"Skye, the more souls they take, the stronger they become. They can become invincible—at least to mortals. When that happens, only the last great battle can stop them. And that comes only once—at the End Times."

"I was being sarcastic, but you succeeded in scaring the hell out of me."

"I'm sorry. I love you."

"Love you too. Be careful." She reluctantly hung up.

Her desk was full, but she couldn't focus on the stacks of paperwork. More would be coming in over the course of the night. She glanced through files, then saw a note on top of a rubber-banded stack from Deputy Jorgenson. He'd felt awful about letting someone drug him the other morning—though Skye had assured him it wasn't his fault. He must have jumped on the research she'd asked him to do since she'd put him on desk duty for forty-eight hours pending blood tests.

> *Sheriff—*
>
> *Here are the background checks you'd asked for this morning. Still waiting on military records on Nichols. There's nothing on Fiona O'Donnell, and I contacted ICE for immigration status, but haven't heard back. A few things seemed odd to me and I flagged the files. The Doc cleared me for duty this afternoon, so I'll be back graveyard shift Sunday.*
>
> *—Dep. Jorgenson*

She'd almost forgot about the slough of background checks she'd asked Jorgenson to do. She hadn't expected them until Monday. She'd run them on each of the dead, plus Pennington, Walker, Fiona O'Donnell, Rafe's doctor Richard Bertram, and Andy Rucker, the husband of the woman who he claimed pushed a pregnant woman down the stairs. The victim was in the hospital under full bed rest after her doctors stopped premature labor.

He had all the reports here, with a note on each file indicating what was missing. He'd flagged Matthew Walker's report.

She frowned. She'd put his name in this morning, but after talking to him she didn't have any red flags and wouldn't have looked at it tonight—considering everything that was going on—had Jorgenson not flagged it.

She flipped it open and skimmed the summary. Frowning, she flipped pages. This couldn't be right . . . she picked up the phone and called Jorgenson. "Hey, are you certain you have the right Matthew Walker?"

"Yep, I triple-checked when you mentioned the sick mother. It's the same Matthew Walker who was the pastor of Good Shepherd. You'd think the church or whatever would have done their own background check, 'cause I sure wouldn't want to be hearing about God from some pervert ex-con."

"Thanks," she mumbled. "I appreciate how fast you got this to me."

"Anything. And I want you to know," he cleared his throat, "you got my support this June."

"I appreciate that, too." She hung up and stared at the file, shaking her head.

Matthew Walker was a well-versed liar. He had gone to Bethany Bible College with Vance Lamb, just as Mrs. Lamb said. He then moved to Sacramento, where he was the associate minister for a large church. He'd been accused of rape, but the charges didn't stick when the victim recanted her statement. Jorgenson made a note that he was checking with neighboring states, but included a verbal conversation with a detective in Portland, Oregon, that he'd recorded and transcribed:

Walker is slick. He started this storefront church downtown, had a huge congregation after two years. Said he was Christian, but it was generic as anything. All feel-good crap. Got real chummy with Edith Lyttle, an eccentric woman with millions in the bank. Edith changed her will, left all the money to his church, and then two months later died. I had the coroner autopsy the body twice, but he swore it was a heart attack. No drugs, no violence, nothing. But damn, I'm a 22-year veteran and my gut told me that

Walker killed her. Left Portland when his mother got sick. Funny coincidence, that happened right after I exposed the jerk for those rape accusations you mentioned. Said I had slandered him, destroyed his ministry. He's good. Yeah, left Portland with Edith Lyttle's three million dollars.

That was four years ago. Jorgenson found nothing on him—other than that he had a California state driver's license issued in San Francisco—until he opened Good Shepherd two years ago.

But the kicker? Jorgenson had found Georgia Walker's obituary—dated nine years ago . . .

. . . . widow of Judge Neil Walker, survived by a sister, Corinne Davies of Portland, Oregon and a son, Reverend Matthew Walker, of Austin, Texas.

Walker had no dying mother—his mother was already dead. Then why did he leave Santa Louisa? Why the elaborate lies?

The man had lied to Skye, and she smelled blood. She'd bet her badge that he knew Garrett Pennington, his replacement at Good Shepherd. Whether the Lambs were involved, she didn't know, but she would before the weekend was over.

She called Jorgenson. "If you come in this weekend, you get overtime. I want a complete background check on Matthew Walker. I want every church he worked at, every article he's quoted in, a birth certificate, his mother's death certificate, where he was born, who his next-door neighbor was growing up. Call every cop who suspected him of a crime. He is trouble with a capital T."

"I'm on it, Sheriff."

"Thanks."

She hung up, then looked at Walker's mother's obituary again.

Sister to Corinne Davies.

Corinne Davies, the cook who poisoned the priests at the mission. No mention of Lisa Davies, her daughter, who'd also worked at the mission.

Skye called Anthony to tell him, but he didn't answer his phone.

Shit, shit, shit.

She ran to the desk sergeant. "I need four patrols, two to go to Good Shepherd and two to go to the cliffs where Abby Weatherby died."

"We have no one. Everyone is out on a call. Day shift is working overtime."

"You have *no one*?"

He shook his head. "I'll prioritize it for you: send the first out to Good Shepherd?"

She hesitated, then nodded. "I'm headed to Good Shepherd now." She walked out, then walked back in. "Hey, do we have a patrol at Rittenhouse?"

He looked at the sheet. "Yeah, Tom Young is working that beat. He's checking the site every hour. Worried about kids vandalizing the place or something?"

She nodded. "Exactly." *Or something.*

Skye ran back to her car and prayed that nothing had gone wrong with Anthony. Or Moira.

THIRTY-SEVEN

What's worth the price is always worth the fight
Every second counts 'cause there's no second try
—NICKELBACK, "If Today Was Your Last Day"

Anthony stood in the basement of Good Shepherd. There was no one here, unconscious or otherwise, though the place was a complete mess.

Father Philip crossed himself when he stepped down into the basement. He looked around, fear in his eyes, then started back up the stairs. "This room is a nest of slithering snakes, full of darkness. There are many demons here, waiting for release. We must leave immediately."

"I didn't know this was down here," Lily said. "It's spooky. I'm scared."

Father took her hand and squeezed. "So am I, dear."

Anthony didn't like the place either, though he didn't sense the same evil that Father did. It was what he saw that disturbed him—the altar, the destruction, the unusually dark blood in the corner. He shook his head. "What they must have been doing—I haven't seen magic this evil in a long time."

"Let's find the box and leave, Anthony. Moira needs our help."

When Lily came to at Father Isaac's church, she had been borderline hysterical. She couldn't explain why she'd been so deeply terrified of the photo of the sigil carved into the box. She said nervously, "Do we have to take the box?"

"Yes," Father said. "We must destroy it."

They left the basement and Anthony tried the door to Pennington's apartment. Unlocked. "Be careful," he said. He listened for movement, breathing, any sign that someone was waiting for them upstairs. He proceeded cautiously, quickly searching the apartment with Father and Lily in tow. It was empty.

"Moira said it was in his desk drawer. I don't want to be here any longer than necessary," he said.

The three entered the small office with Father Philip standing in the doorway, looking down the hall. Anthony searched every drawer. "It's not here. Moira swore she didn't take it." Pennington must have nabbed it before he left.

Moira had said that she'd left Matthew Walker, the real pastor of Good Shepherd, with Pennington. Either Walker was injured, or he wasn't who he said he was.

"We need to leave," Anthony said. He led the way down the hall, looking again in every opening.

As he reached the door, it slammed open, hitting him. He almost attacked the man who came in, gun drawn. It was Deputy Tom Young. Anthony breathed easier.

"Tom. Anthony Zaccardi, we were—"

"There was an alarm here." Tom moved into the room, still holding the gun, aimed at Father Philip.

"The door was unlocked—" Anthony hesitated. Alarm? That wasn't right. Moira had been in the building for more than an hour and hadn't triggered an alarm.

Tom didn't holster his gun. He called down the stairs, "Got them!"

Anthony's blood chilled. Tom was a cop who worked for Skye, but he obviously had another agenda. Tom was the deputy who'd taken Moira to jail—he might have been the one who'd drugged the others and contacted Fiona.

Anthony reached for his dagger. A well-aimed knife could kill. But Tom's gun could go off, and Father and Lily were both in the line of fire.

Tom swung his weapon toward Anthony. "Hold it, Zaccardi. Hands up."

Slowly, Anthony complied.

Tom Young searched him, removed his dagger, then began to pull out all Anthony's defenses—the vial of holy water, the vial of salt.

He karate-chopped Young's arm and reached for the gun. Young swore, but he kept his hand around the gun. Anthony moved right, but Young pistol-whipped him, bringing Anthony to his knees. He tasted blood in his mouth and spit it on the floor, his eyes unfocused. Lily screamed.

A man walked into the room. "Lily. So good to see you again."

"Pastor Matthew—"

"Come with me."

"No, please—what are you doing?"

"I suppose you wouldn't believe me if I said God's work?" Walker said with a half-smile that didn't reach his eyes.

"Bastard," Anthony said as he got to his feet, staggering a bit as he shook his head to clear it.

Matthew Walker was a tall, good-looking man of average build. Though Tom had both the gun and the brawn, Walker was clearly in charge, and right now he looked bemused.

Tom Young grabbed Lily, his gun pointed at Father Philip. "You're pathetic, Zaccardi. And Fiona said you were smart." He laughed. "As soon as we figured out that Moira had passed Lily on to you, she was easy to track. Every sheriff's vehicle has GPS that's monitored at dispatch. I tracked you here, easy-peasy."

Walker glanced at Tom, irritated. "Your incompetence is nothing to brag about. If you'd done what you were told, we'd also have Andra Moira, but I had to let her go because you didn't have the *arca*."

"You wanted me to be discreet, I was *damn* fucking discreet."

Walker ignored him and said, "Zaccardi, I wish I could say it's been a pleasure—your reputation was well deserved, though a bit exaggerated, don't you think? But honestly, you've been a pain in the ass since you came to Santa Louisa. Finally, I'll get my town back."

"Did you take the box after Moira left?" Anthony asked.

"That's pretty obvious, isn't it? But I didn't *take* anything. It's mine."

Father Philip spoke up for the first time since the men entered the apartment. "Walker, it would serve you well to remember that Cain turned on his own. I would strongly advise you to destroy the box."

Anthony didn't know why Father was trying to reason with the magician.

Walker stared at Father Philip, his face hard. "Let's go, *Father*."

A voice came up the stairs. "Sixty seconds!"

Anthony hated being helpless as he watched Young push Lily at Walker, then grab Father Philip. He couldn't see a way to stop Walker from taking them. He clenched his fists.

Walker smiled warmly at Lily and touched the side of her face with the back of his hand. "I've missed you, Lily. Your ignorance was so pleasurable for me."

"You know what to do, Anthony," Father said as he passed by.

"He can't do anything if he's dead." Young aimed the gun at Anthony. The split second before Young pulled the trigger, Anthony dove to the side behind the couch, feeling the heat of the bullet against his bruised cheek.

"*Ciao*," Young said and started down the stairs with Father Philip.

"Forty seconds!" the voice downstairs said.

"Move it, old man!" Young ordered. "Walker? You coming or staying?"

Anthony heard them jog down the stairs.

Forty seconds 'til what? The anxiety in Young's voice . . . Anthony had to get out of here.

He couldn't follow them down the stairs. Young would be waiting—with the gun—for him to emerge from the building. He ran to the front of the building, mentally counting down how much time he had left.

The bedroom had two large double-paned windows. Anthony grabbed the heavy metal bedside lamp and used the base to hit the window with all his strength. It cracked. He hit it again. Again.

Twenty-eight. Twenty-seven.

He smelled smoke in the rooms below, and the reflection of flames on the building across the street told him the fire was building rapidly.

The window splintered in a mass of fine cracks. Shielding his head, Anthony threw the lamp at the window. It finally shattered.

Fourteen. Thirteen.

He kicked out the shards along the bottom frame as he judged the distance he'd need to jump to not only get clear of the glass but the explosion he knew was about to happen.

He couldn't do it. He looked left—nothing. To the right there was a narrow balcony with metal railings. He judged the distance at about eight feet.

Six. Five.

He stood on the frame and balanced. As he leapt on *three,* the explosion came, the force of the air pushing him beyond the balcony. He reached out and tried to grab the railing, the heat and debris from the explosion hitting him.

The railing slipped from his fingers and he was falling . . .

Moira drove up to the mansion she'd found in Good Shepherd's property records. Its lush grounds glowed with soft lighting. The house was majestic and sprawling, with high windows and numerous porches and porticos. There were even two turrets, which would satisfy Fiona's pretensions of nobility.

Aside from the physical trappings, as soon as Moira stepped onto the property she felt the undercurrent of magic. Many spells were at work here, and Moira had to tread carefully. Chances were that Fiona had alarms on the place, but Moira couldn't worry about that right now. She'd rather take her chances with the police than with Fiona any day.

Fear bubbled up, fear she'd suppressed at Good Shepherd. When she could act and focus on a plan, the fear stayed buried. But her adrenaline rush had disappeared during the drive out to the coast, and now all she could think about was how high the odds were stacked against them.

When you played by the rules, the odds were never in your favor.

Moira stayed in the shadows while she walked the perimeter, getting a sense of how the house was laid out and whether anyone was inside. No one was moving downstairs. There was no music, no television, no noise whatsoever, except the filter working in the pool and the waves crashing against cliffs three hundred yards behind the house.

It was now or never. If Rafe wasn't here, she had two other places to check.

The dozen French doors were impossible to pick, and *if* people were inside she didn't want them alerted by breaking glass. The kitchen door at the side of the house had a spell cast over it and it took Moira nearly three minutes to get the lock open.

The rich scent of Irish stew lingered in the kitchen, and for a moment, she stopped and breathed deeply, her eyes stinging. There *had* been some good times in her childhood. Before she knew what was planned for her. Like when her grandmother cooked stew that smelled exactly like this kitchen.

The good memories were too few and far between.

Moira methodically, silently, walked through the first floor, checking each room quickly. She didn't sense anything other than magic.

Frustrated, she reached the back of the house and as she put her hand on a pair of double doors, a jolt of energy hit her. For a second she thought someone was inside the room attacking her with witchcraft, but as she pushed open the doors into what was obviously a library, she realized no one was inside.

This was where Fiona and her people created the bulk of their spells. Compared to the magic outside, the energy in here was a hundred times stronger.

She stopped in the middle of the towering room, her dagger in one hand and her last bottle of holy water in the other. Her senses were practically screaming caution, she was on edge and agitated, but she saw nothing out of the ordinary.

More than at any time in her life since she'd renounced it, in the last forty-eight hours she'd been immersed in dark magic energy. More magic in a short period than at *any* time in her life. It was no wonder she was weirded out: Moira was walking around the house of her mother, who'd sworn to torture and kill her.

She released a pent-up breath and focused. Opening her senses to the emotions imprinted here, trying to feel Rafe's presence. *Relax. Breathe.* As soon as she calmed, she realized that it wasn't just the magic that was stronger in here. There was a demon nearby.

She cautiously approached a set of double doors in an alcove to the side of the vast space. An unfamiliar sigil was posted *on* one of the doors, instead of above it. She turned the handle and pushed the door open.

Moira stared at Rafe, clad in jeans and nothing else, unconscious in the center of a spirit trap. Claw marks across his chest were barely dry. Her heart nearly stopped at the thought that it was too late, that Rafe was dead, but then she saw the slight rise in his chest.

She started toward him, but her instincts saved her at the last moment.

Demon!

It came for her, and she realized belatedly what the symbol outside this door was. It trapped the demon inside with Rafe, to guard him. If he left, the demon would devour him. Like a Cerberus, with teeth and fangs and an insatiable appetite for human souls.

She splashed holy water on it, its scream piercing her ears, as she jumped into the spirit trap with Rafe. The pea-brained Cerberus, for it looked like one of Satan's guard dogs with one head instead of three, growled and barked at her but couldn't breech the trap. It saved her . . . and trapped her.

Well, fuck.

She felt Rafe's pulse. Strong and steady. The Cerberus yelped, and she turned to the animal and shouted, "Yahweh!"

The animal bucked and foamed at the mouth, enraged, and physically grew in size.

"Oh, that's showing him," she mumbled to herself. "Piss off the demon dog and see him grow." She knelt by Rafe, brushing his hair off his face. "Rafe, I'm so sorry. I'll get you out of this. I promise."

Right. You promise. How are you going to defeat Fiona's demonic pit bull?

The poisoned dart had worked with the fierce demon Serena sicced on her this morning, giving Moira confidence. She took out another dart, willed herself to stop shaking. She didn't know what was worse, facing the demon now or facing Fiona when she returned.

She didn't have time to compare. She stepped to the edge of the trap and, with an ancient prayer and a "pretty please," she extended her hand outside the circle.

The demon attacked, ran right into the poisoned dart and screamed, but didn't disintegrate like the other demon. Before Moira had time to react, the demon bit her forearm and she fell to her knees. Acidlike pain ravaged her body. She heard nothing but her own agonized scream, which sounded as if it were pulled out of her lungs by force. Quickly, she jerked her arm back into the spirit trap and held it close to her chest.

Rafe sat up and reached for her, pulling her toward him. He groaned in pain, but held her tight. Tears streamed down her face, but she said, "Glad you're alive."

"Are you okay?"

"I will be," she said through clenched teeth.

"Let me see."

"No."

"You're being a baby."

"Damn straight. It hurts." She took a deep breath and let Rafe pry her arm from her chest.

Two deep holes from the demon's canines and a hundred pin pricks between them pierced her skin. The blood that poured from the wounds burned and bubbled with the acid of the demonic bite. Her entire body was on fire and she cried out when Rafe touched near the bite, as if yelling would rid her body of the pain.

Rafe frowned and inspected the wound. She turned away, willing the pain to subside, and she realized that the dog was no longer growling at her, no longer pacing. She looked around, where did it go?

Then she spotted it, lying in the corner, its mouth a bloody mess. Its eyes were wide and unfocused. Its legs, with impossibly long claws at the end of each of its six paws, were stiff and unmoving.

She stared, unbelieving. This couldn't have happened. She shook her head. Of course it had. A belated reaction to the poisoned dart. She breathed easier, though she was still nervous. The Cerberus was too dumb to play opossum . . . she hoped.

"It's dead," Rafe said in disbelief.

"Appears so."

"How?"

"Poison dart."

"That's how it works? I thought demons couldn't be killed."

"Not, um, usually." Two dead in one night. That had to be a record. "But we can't be sure. Let me check."

She jumped up, but he pulled her back down. "No. You're not going to risk your life."

"I already did," she replied, "and we can't stay. Fiona could be back any minute. We need to get out of here."

He raised his eyebrows but didn't say anything. He held out his hand and helped her up. She gently touched the claw marks on his chest.

She had a sudden urge to kiss him, to soothe the pain he was in, but instead she turned away, heat rising to her face.

"Moira."

She looked back at Rafe. The dim light coming in from the library made his dark eyes fathomless as they locked on to her face. He reached up and touched her cheek, firmly turning her to face him. Her lips parted to speak, but no sound came out because she couldn't think of any words. His dark hair was damp with sweat and fell forward, partly obscuring his eyes. Her uninjured hand shot up, as if it had a mind of its own, to brush the loose strands out of his face, but he grabbed hold of her wrist and pulled her to him.

He kissed her. One hand held her face, the other her wrist, and he kissed her. Too passionate for a good luck kiss; too long for a friendly good-bye. Too . . . *good*. All pain slipped away, just for that moment. The weight of Moira's responsibilities eased, just a fraction. As if one kiss, one oh-so-hot kiss, could take away some of her misery, claim a share of her obligations.

His unshaven jaw rubbed against her skin erotically. She could scarcely breathe, sinking into Rafe's passion, her need for him growing not unexpectedly. From the moment she'd found him in the abandoned cabin, she'd felt connected to Rafe Cooper in ways she couldn't begin to explain. And maybe she didn't want to understand.

Rafe stepped back, just a half step, severing the kiss with a primal groan that made Moira quiver. He didn't apologize, nor did she want him to, but the shock on his face must have mirrored her own surprise.

Any other time, any other place, and she'd have continued moving toward where that kiss was heading. The craving in Rafe's eyes, the firm set of his jaw, indicated that he would be more than willing to join her in the exploration.

But Moira couldn't forget who she was and what she had to do. Nor could she forget Rafe was spoken for— he was a warrior for St. Michael's Order. Neither of them could afford to be distracted by attraction or affection. It was dangerous for them, and those they were responsible for. Rafe knew it as well as she, but still pinned her with a gaze that said: *This is only the beginning.*

She swallowed the words she wanted to say and handed Rafe a plastic three-ounce container with the last of her holy water. He took it, and she retrieved her dagger.

"Ready?" she asked, her voice low and raw.

He nodded, and together they stepped outside the circle, their eyes locked on the unmoving demon in the corner.

Why was the demon still here? It should have slithered back to Hell by now. Its essence at least should have made a flashy show of falling back into the pit. Could it really be dead?

Moira would have liked the time to explore the house, to see if there were any clues as to what Fiona's plans were, but they didn't have time. She had to figure out where the witches were re-creating the ritual. She took Rafe's hand and they ran out of the house as fast as they could.

Less than five minutes later, they were at Matthew Walker's car. Moira took a bottle of water and poured half of it on her arm. It stung and she swore.

Rafe found a towel in her bag. "Here," he said. "Let me."

He gently wiped away the blood. She squeezed her eyes closed, holding back tears of pain. She felt a kiss on her arm and her heart skipped a beat.

Her eyes opened and Rafe smiled at her. "You okay?"

She nodded, and examined the wound so she could avoid looking at Rafe, not wanting to think too much about what was happening between them. This . . . nothing. Nothing was happening. It was the adrenaline of the moment, the panic, the rush of escaping. Same as with the kiss.

You're lying to yourself. She ignored her inner conflict about what the kiss *might* have meant and studied her arm even more intently. The small pricks weren't bleeding anymore, though they still hurt like hell, but the two canine bites had gone deep. "I have a first-aid kit in my bag," she said. "You could use a bandage or two as well."

"I'm fine," he said and retrieved the kit. He opened it and smiled. "Bandages, tape, antiseptic, a crucifix, and holy water."

"Never know what you might need," she said.

As he taped gauze over the two deep wounds, Rafe said, "Fiona went to kill you."

"She didn't find me."

"You weren't at Rittenhouse?"

"Rittenhouse? The furniture store?"

"She said you'd end up there. That's where they went to complete the ritual. Where they are now."

"That was where the guy killed his co-workers, perfect for them. Shit!" She started the car. "I don't know where it is, and I kinda threw the GPS out the window."

Rafe smiled, "Go back to the highway and head north. It's just before the county line."

She did as Rafe said and tried to call Anthony. The call went right to voicemail.

"Anthony, it's Moira. They're at Rittenhouse Furniture. I have Rafe; I'm on my way there."

She tried Skye, and after four rings got *her* voicemail and left her a similar message.

Why wasn't anyone answering their phone?

Rafe took her hand. "What's wrong?"

"I sent Anthony to Good Shepherd. He's not answering his phone." Rafe didn't say anything for a moment. "Rafe? What?" she prompted.

"Anthony is well trained. We have to trust him."

Now it was Moira's turn to remain silent.

"Spill it," Rafe said, squeezing her hand.

"Good Shepherd is on the way. It's a short detour."

"You care," he said.

"Excuse me?"

"You couldn't reach Skye, but you're not worried about her. Anthony is just as capable—maybe more so—of taking care of himself, but you're on the verge of panic."

"I'm not." She *was* worried, though. "I'm just going to drive by the place, make sure everything is kosher."

She turned off the narrow highway and headed into town. It was late, the roads were empty, but as they neared the downtown area, sirens howled. Alarms rang in businesses. People walked the streets. There were fights, smashed storefronts, and chaos.

"What's going on?" Moira asked, horrified at the apparent anarchy.

"Envy." Rafe dropped her hand. "Give me your gun."

She took it from her holster and slid it across the seat to him. He checked the ammunition, then held it ready.

"It's a riot," she said.

She slowed down and moved over to the right for an ambulance to pass. When she did, two teenage boys jumped on the hood of her car and told her to stop.

"Floor it," Rafe said.

She did and the sick thud of a body falling off and onto the side of the road made her stomach flip. She glanced in the rearview mirror, relieved to see both boys getting up.

"Now I know why Skye didn't answer," Moira said. "She has her hands fu—"

An explosion rocked the car.

It came from the direction of Good Shepherd.

THIRTY-EIGHT

Pride, envy, avarice
these are the sparks that have set on fire the hearts of all men.
—DANTE ALIGHIERI

Skye heard the explosion before she saw the flames in the direction of Good Shepherd.

She floored it and radioed the fire department.

"Dammit, Anthony, if you're dead . . . ." She would not think of it. She would *not* think of it.

She pictured herself standing over Anthony's charred body in Rod Fielding's morgue, while Rod went through his autopsy checklist.

Tears stung her eyes. Anthony was her life. She couldn't lose him.

Her sheriff's truck passed her. She glanced over, not sure if Anthony was in the car, but the man behind the wheel was definitely not Anthony. Big, beefy shoulders and a hat. He looked like a uniform, but he went so fast Skye couldn't identify him.

She wanted to continue to Good Shepherd, to see if Anthony was there. To see if he was hurt. If he needed her.

But someone had stolen the truck Anthony had been driving. If Anthony was injured, the fire department would be there in minutes. If he was dead, she would know it far too soon.

Torn, but making her choice, she made a U-turn and followed the truck from a distance. There were at least three people in the vehicle.

She called dispatch with her cell phone, in case the thief was monitoring police radio transmissions. "It's McPherson. I need to get a GPS reading on my assigned vehicle."

"Lose it again?"

"Excuse me?"

"An hour ago I had a request for a GPS on your truck, that someone had stolen it."

"Who made that request?"

"Deputy Young."

Skye felt both betrayal and rage. Young—she'd worked with him for eight years, ever since he was fresh out of the police academy. He was born and raised in Santa Louisa. He was one of *them*? A spy—a *witch*—in her own department? Were there more?

"Sergeant," she said, "I don't know what's going on with Young, but my truck wasn't stolen until five minutes ago." She wasn't supposed to let anyone else use her official vehicle; as sheriff she was supposed to set an example. She'd have a lot to answer for when this was over.

If she survived.

"Yes, ma'am," the sergeant said. "Here it is. I'm tracking it. Will send the coordinates to your car—what are you driving?"

"Unmarked vehicle number six-niner-zero."

"One sec . . . okay. You should have it on your computer."

She tapped a key and there was her truck five blocks ahead, still going north on Main Street.

"Thanks. I may need backup." Who could she trust? She didn't know anymore.

"Everyone is tied up, but I can pull a team."

"Jorgenson. Call him in."

"You sure?"

"Yes." He had given her the key information on Matthew Walker; he had to be on her side. She hoped she hadn't read him wrong.

Trust your instincts.

"Jorgenson and David Collins. Have them track my unmarked car and meet up with me ASAP. Radio silence on this. Cell phones only. Over."

"I'm sorry, I'm sorry, I didn't know," Ari blubbered. Jared wanted to slap her to make her shut up, but he didn't.

He'd destroyed the first altar, the easiest one he could get to, and they'd just arrived at the second. When Ari woke up, she remembered everything and seemed to have turned into a wailing lunatic.

"Either help me or shut up," he said. "Or both."

"I—" She stopped. "I'm sorry, Jared."

She was calmer now, so Jared responded, "It's okay. It's my fault too. I helped you."

"I didn't really give you a choice."

"Of course I had a choice."

She shook her head. "I cast a spell of compliance. I wanted you to agree with everything I wanted to do. You argued, fought it, but I got everything I wanted. Do you think you would have agreed to be part of my circle if you weren't under a spell?"

He didn't know.

"I'm worried," he said. "I've been trying to reach

Moira and Anthony. No one's around. I feel like I should be doing something!"

"We are." She overturned the altar and scattered the herbs, dirt, and stone far and wide.

Bright lights came up the road, followed by police lights and the whirl of a siren.

"Shit," Jared said.

When the cop got out of the car Jared recognized him. "Dad!"

Hank Santos approached. He looked angry, but he rubbed his head as if in pain. "What are you doing out here this late? This town is insane tonight. I've been on call after call; I've been worried sick about you."

Jared almost argued with him, but the worry and stress in his dad's voice melted away his anger. It had been a hard two years after his mom died, and Jared had been upset when his dad started dating again a few months ago. He was being selfish and critical, and now was a good time to grow up.

He said, "Dad, I need your help. Please. You're the only one I can turn to. I need *you*."

Hank stared at him. Tears came to his eyes; he took off his glasses, pinched the bridge of his nose, then put the glasses back on. "You still need me?"

"I'll always need my dad. We're family, and that will never change."

The relief and love on Hank's face eased Jared's mind. Family mattered, Hank used to say. And now Jared realized why it was so important. Forgiveness meant pushing aside all the crap, the hard feelings and mistakes. They loved you, unconditionally, if you let them.

"Tell me what's going on, son."

Jared sighed with relief. "It's going to be hard to believe, but I swear it's the God's honest truth."

"After the things I've seen tonight, I'd believe just about anything."

Good Shepherd was a wall of flames so hot and bright that Rafe and Moira didn't dare get close.

"Where's Anthony? Where's Father?" Moira said as she jumped out of the car.

Rafe followed. "Hold on, Moira," he said.

"No, no! What if they're inside? I told them to come here! I told them—"

Rafe spun her around and gave her a shake. "Moira. Listen to me."

Her brows came together and he felt her biceps flex. She didn't like being manhandled or ordered around, but he needed her one hundred percent focused. "Let go," she said quietly.

He loosened his grip but didn't let go. "No panicking."

"I don't panic," she said, but glanced down. "I'm sorry."

"Can you feel any magic?"

"No! I can't feel anything—"

"You need to relax. Be calm."

"I can't, dammit! What if they're dead? Because of me?"

"Moira, listen. The only way you can help them is to focus, and you can't use *all* your senses if you're panicking." Rafe took her hands in his and squeezed tight. "I'm right here. Relax. Is there any magic at work? Can you sense if anyone is inside? Injured?"

The heat from the blaze uncomfortably warmed the

air around them. His back was hot, sweat was beading on his brow. He watched Moira work to get her emotions under control.

"I can't," she said, though she was breathing easier.

Rafe stared into Moira's eyes. "Yes, you can. Breathe. Now let it out."

He saw the moment she found her balance. Her entire body relaxed as if the panic had *whooshed* out. Her grip relaxed in his hands, but he didn't let her go. "What do you sense?"

"Old spells. Old demons. They're burning. There's a new gateway here. Dammit! They opened another gateway. Too many and we'll lose control—"

Rafe interrupted, calm but firm. "That's for another day. Right now, is anyone *working* a spell?"

She shook her head. "No. No active spells. Nothing—" She stopped, her mouth dropped open, and she stared over his shoulder.

"What is it?" He glanced behind him, saw nothing but the evil building engulfed in bright orange flames. The fire was spreading, but the fire department hadn't arrived yet. He saw nothing unusual and turned back to Moira.

She didn't say anything, her gaze unfocused, her body shaking uncontrollably. Sweat poured from her skin, from something other than the blaze. What was happening to her? Fear clawed at Rafe. He needed Moira. He couldn't do this alone.

"Moira? Please, please, snap out of it. Tell me what's happening, dammit!"

He pulled her to him, hating that she was suffering. Something—had Fiona sent a nightmare to her as she'd done to him? Was Moira reliving pain of her past? Did she have to watch over and over people she cared about die? Painful, horrible deaths? He would take it from her if he could.

He repeated a prayer for deliverance, over and over as he held her close. She stiffened in his arms and he tilted her chin up, but she pushed him back and started running, staggering, down the street.

He caught up quickly and grabbed her hand. "Watch out, the debris."

"Anthony!" she shouted. "He's here. The building is about to collapse and if we don't get to him first, he'll die."

He didn't ask how she knew—she'd had a vision. It was the only explanation.

"Where?"

"He's in the back of a truck. He fell into the back of a pickup, but when this building goes it's going to suck everything down with it."

"Get the car. Now. I'll find Anthony."

She nodded, and ran down the street to where they'd parked.

Staying on the opposite side of the road, Rafe ran past the burning building. He searched for trucks. None in the church parking lot. He looked in front of the building next to Good Shepherd. There!

He ran across the street, the heat searing his skin, making the claw marks on his chest burn. He jumped into the bed of the pickup, his hands burning on the hot metal, and there was Anthony, on his back, trying to get up, blood running down his face and into his eyes.

"Anthony!" Rafe opened the back of the pickup. "Come on, it's coming down right now."

"Walker," Anthony said, his voice dry and low.

"Later, buddy, we got to go."

Headlights came at him and he jumped out, helping Anthony, who staggered under his own weight.

Moira leaned over from the driver's seat and opened the passenger door.

"Get in *now!*" she said as the earth started shaking all around them. Anthony fell to the street and Rafe half dragged him to the car. He got in first and used his weight to pull Anthony in after him. The door wasn't even closed when Moira floored it.

"Hold on!" she yelled, going from zero to sixty in six seconds. The door swung closed, and Anthony struggled to sit upright as the two large men were crammed in the front next to Moira.

Rafe turned his head and watched as Good Shepherd blazed bright red and disappeared into the earth. The pickup truck Anthony had fallen into was sucked in with it, along with the buildings on either side.

By the time Moira reached the top of the hill on the edge of town, all that was left of Good Shepherd was scorched earth.

Candlelight flickered inside Rittenhouse Furniture. The inventory shielded the activity, but each piece was outlined by the light, casting odd, dancing shadows out the large showroom windows and into the fog. The street lights along the edge of the small parking lot shined in interlocking circles, revealing several empty vehicles. Warehouses and light industrial businesses on this road were all closed at night. No one else was around for miles, and with the thickening fog and damp air, Moira felt as though they were the only people in the world as she approached, fifteen minutes after Good Shepherd disappeared in a blaze of hellfire.

She drove without headlights to the back of the building and parked behind the Dumpsters. It didn't conceal them completely, but at least they weren't obvious at a glance. She hadn't even stepped out of the car, but the dark magic rolled off the building as the fog rolled in from the ocean: slow, ethereal, unstoppable.

She breathed deeply, concentrating all her senses on the building and surrounding area. She felt small, cleansing spells and bigger, more dangerous protection spells. She didn't sense anyone outside watching the back door. There was a river of fear flowing through the building. She didn't know whether it was residual emotions from the violence of the night before or fear being generated right now.

"That's Skye's truck," Anthony said.

She opened her eyes and looked where he gestured. On the far side of the back lot, the sheriff's truck was parked in the shadows.

"Is she here?" Moira said. "Is she crazy?"

Anthony said, "Walker and Deputy Young must have taken it after they tried to kill me at Good Shepherd. Thank God. It's here."

"Why?" asked Moira, taken aback that Walker was one of them. Why had he helped her earlier?

"The tabernacle. It's inside the truck. We need it to trap the demon."

"Trap? You don't know how to send it back?"

"Not yet, but we can contain it," Anthony said.

"You're certain?" Rafe asked.

"Yes."

Moira concentrated. "There are many spells in play; I'm having a hard time discerning them," she said. "Let me try again, see what they're doing right now."

The harder she concentrated, the greater her headache until she visibly winced. Rafe grabbed her shoulders. "Stop. You're going to hurt yourself."

"I have to figure this out!"

"Sometimes you have to have faith."

"I'm going for the tabernacle," Anthony said. "Stay here."

"You need backup," Moira said.

"I'll go," Rafe said.

"No," Anthony and Moira said together. Then Anthony added, "I don't need backup. The truck is only a hundred yards away."

"It's not up for debate," Rafe said. "I'm going."

Reluctantly, Anthony agreed. Moira didn't like this at all, but she didn't have an alternate plan.

"Be careful. And, um, take this." She handed him her dagger.

He took it, then squeezed her hand. "Thank you."

She watched the two men sprint across the back of the parking lot until they hit the trees. She breathed easier when they had some camouflage.

And she waited. And waited.

The car door opened.

"It's about—"

She stopped.

Matthew Walker stood there looking bemused.

"Somehow, I knew you'd end up here."

She spat in his face.

His face hardened until she thought he was capable of

pummeling her to death, then he relaxed. "Tom," he said to the cop standing behind him, "make sure she doesn't have any friends hanging out around here."

To Moira, he said, "Come inside. Your mother's waiting for you."

THIRTY-NINE

They had Lily.

Matthew Walker pushed Moira into the center of the showroom floor. The furniture had been pushed aside to make room for the large, elaborate ritual circle to recapture the Seven. In the center, Lily was tied to a raised altar.

Anger pulsed through Moira and she fought against her restraints, intentionally slamming the back of her head into Walker's jaw. He grunted, but tightened his hold and pulled her close. "You're making it worse. Look. We have another surprise for you."

Fiona, dramatic as ever in a silvery velvet gown that flowed around her body like a waterfall, sashayed into the room, holding Father Philip's hand. "Look who I found?" she said and laughed.

Father had a cut on his head and was unusually pale. He saw Moira, and sadness darkened his eyes.

"Father—" She blinked back tears of fear. She couldn't give them fear. There was already too much fear in the room, and demons thrived on the emotion.

"Yes!" Fiona exclaimed. "You remember him."

"Are you okay?" she asked him.

"Do what you have to," he said cryptically.

"That's enough chitchat," Fiona said. "He's just a lit-

tle upset because poor Anthony died in a tragic fire."
She pretended to wipe a tear from her eye. "So sad."

Though Moira ached at the pain in Father's expression, she didn't let on that Anthony survived the explosion. If they suspected, they'd go out and hunt him
down, and he'd never get to the tabernacle in time.

Rafe had been outnumbered worse on the cliffs two
nights ago, yet he had stopped them. It was possible.

Garrett Pennington stood to one side with two other
men. He looked like he wanted to kill her, his handsome
face bruised and bloodied from fighting her. It looked
like she'd broken his nose as well. She hoped it healed
crooked.

Several women stood around in filmy white gowns, including Nicole Donovan, the teacher, and Elizabeth
Ellis, Lily's mother. Others she didn't know, men and
women of all ages, from a teenager to a middle-age wizard. Eleven . . . twelve . . . no, fourteen she counted.
Covens didn't always operate with thirteen members,
though many preferred to keep the group to less.

Moira felt all eyes on her, but someone was staring at
her, trying to work a clandestine spell over her. Something Moira didn't recognize but felt deep down to her
soul. She strengthened her will and turned her head.

Serena stared across at her, her face emotionless.
When Moira caught her eye, she smiled.

"Everyone's here," Fiona said, holding her and Father
Philip's joined hands up. "Let's begin." She smiled at
Moira, then at Matthew Walker. "Darling," she said,
"I've missed you."

Walker moved Moira into the center of the circle. Incense burned in seven chalices, set on the altar with Lily.
The herbs weren't protective incense that was burning

outside the circle. These herbs attracted demons. These people are officially insane, Moira thought. They *may* attract one or more of the Seven Deadly Sins, but they were also going to draw in every wayward demon roaming the area. How could they control it? How could they possibly think this was going to work?

"You're all nuts."

Walker squeezed her arm. "I saw what you did. I will learn how you did it. That's the only reason I didn't kill you earlier."

"Did what?" She had no idea what Walker was talking about.

He didn't answer, but pushed her down.

Next to the altar were two steel balls attached to a chain and foot manacle. For a moment Moira thought they were made of iron, and that would offer some protection against spirits.

"They're lead, dear, not iron," Fiona said as she walked Father Philip into the circle. "I'm not stupid. Had you remembered that, you wouldn't have tried to find me."

"I didn't try," Moira said. "I succeeded. Funny, you were looking for me for seven years and never could figure out where I was, even with your dark magic and psychic eye. Maybe you've lost it, *Cailleach*."

Fiona roughly pushed Father Philip down, and he stumbled and fell to his knees, his glasses falling off his face. Moira reached for him, her heart quickening for the old man. Walker pulled her back before she could touch him.

Fiona stepped on the old man's spectacles, grinding the lenses into the cement floor with her spike heel. "He won't need these where he's going."

Walker attached Father Philip to one lead ball, and Moira to the other. Then he pulled Fiona into his arms and kissed her deeply. "I've missed you far more than you've missed me, sweetheart," he told her.

Serena stepped into the circle with them. Matthew turned to her and gave her a squeeze. "Hey, I've missed you too, kiddo. Staying away all these months was the hardest thing I've had to do."

"Glad you're back, Dad." Serena smiled, then turned to Moira, gloating.

Dad? Moira's disbelief must have registered on her face, because Serena said, "Why do you find that so hard to believe? Just because you didn't know I knew my father? I'm good at secrets too."

Walker laughed. "Sorry, Moira. Serena's my daughter, but you aren't. Can't say I'm choked up about it." His laughter ended abruptly, and he said to her in a low voice, "You've caused my women trouble and heartache for years, and now it's time for you—and your friends— to pay for it."

Moira assessed the situation. Matthew Walker had almost—but not quite—taken control from Fiona. Fiona hadn't seemed to notice, and Moira would be shocked if she condoned it. Her mother was subservient to no one, man, woman, or demon. Yet she'd sighed in ecstasy when Walker took her in his arms and kissed her, playing the role of a love-struck woman. She loved no one but herself. No one.

Yet . . . there was something different about Walker. And suddenly Moira feared him more than anyone else in the room.

"Fiona, dear, are you ready?" He waved his hands

dramatically, then bowed, essentially giving her the floor. The three of them backed out of the circle.

Fiona beamed and began the incantation.

"I have called the Seven to Earth, I have called the Seven from Hell, through a Gateway I consecrated in the blood of the righteous. It is right and just that the Seven are to be contained in the *arca* that has been consecrated for them to live and walk on earth as they did in ages past."

"As it is above, as it is below," the women outside the circle shouted.

Serena lifted a chalice and spoke in an ancient language. The magical energy in the room instantly doubled. Moira felt it as a hot, electric wash over her skin.

"Father?" Moira asked. "What's she saying?"

Walker said, "Quiet!" He lifted his hand, drew in energy, and threw it at her. It hit her like a bullet in her shoulder and she screamed. The magic painfully surged through her and she willed it to dissipate, mumbling in Hebrew.

Serena continued. The chanting responses of the coven increased in volume. Moira inspected her chain and the lock. It was old; if she had her lock picks she could get out of it in two seconds. A bobby pin would work, but she didn't *have* a bobby pin or anything *like* a bobby pin. She had nothing—Walker had taken her jacket, every one of her weapons, even her medallion and crucifix.

The furniture shook, and she wondered why they weren't concerned about the heavy pieces flying across the vast showroom and killing them.

She watched the faces of the coven members, saw that they were concentrating, focusing on keeping the ritual under control. Even Matthew Walker was no longer paying attention to her, but using powerful magic to keep the demonic elements at bay.

She slid her body closer to Father Philip. She heard him talking, but not to her. He spoke in Latin, and it took her a verse before she realized it was Psalm 54, a prayer of confidence while facing great peril and imminent death.

"Turn back the evil upon my foes; in your faithfulness destroy them."

Lily was unmoving, in shock, staring at the ceiling. "Lily, help is coming," she quietly told the girl. She prayed it was true. That Anthony and Rafe were able to get to the tabernacle and find a way inside and . . . *shit.* It was a lot of hopes and dreams and ifs. But other than them, who else was there? Skye was a cop, not an exorcist or demon hunter. Bullets would do nothing to a demon, but would certainly kill the victim.

"Father, what is Serena saying?"

He whispered, "Pure evil from the *Conoscenza.*"

"What language?"

"The language of demons." He looked at her. "Only you can destroy the *Conoscenza.*" Tears sprang to his eyes.

It dawned on her slowly why only she could destroy it. "Because I'm a witch," she said in shock, her eyes burning. "Is that how you see me?"

"No, child, I only see you through eyes of love."

An armoire fell over, and Moira jumped. She had to get out of these restraints. She could do nothing trapped like an animal.

She saw the broken glass from Father's lenses. And the twisted wire frames.

She glanced around. The witches were all chanting and concentrating while Serena continued her summoning ritual. She scooted over inch by inch until she could reach the frames, then discreetly palmed them.

Father Philip saw what she was doing and helped shield her hands from the surrounding coven. As they huddled together, the air in the room heated and swirled around the demon trap.

Moira snapped off the side from the frame, still watching the coven. She carefully worked the shaft into the manacle lock. Dammit, it wasn't as easy as she thought it would be.

Father continued his praying, and Lily moaned. "Moira," she sobbed. "I feel something. Something is coming for me. Help me, please. Please. God, please!"

Her cuff opened. The movement was subtle, and rather than immediately jumping up, she started working on Father Philip's restraints. "How do I destroy the *Conoscenza*?" she whispered. "Is it here?"

"Yes, but I haven't seen it."

"How?"

"Blood and fire."

She shivered. "That sounds like something *they* would do."

"You're not sacrificing anyone, dear. But . . ."

Moira understand. "My blood. But why? Why mine and not Fiona's?"

"Because magic can't destroy it. I don't have all the answers. But—it's dangerous." Father Philip's shackle snapped open. He said, "The cardinal has answers."

"Who? The cardinal? Which cardinal?"

Before he could respond, a black cloud rushed into the

room through the vent above the circle and filled the double circle, swirling around and around the altar.

Moira had seen the strange and supernatural in her life, but never had she seen anything like this. Never had she felt raw evil as it brushed past her, hot, vile, reeking of decay. But it wasn't the malevolent personality that terrified her. It was the intelligence within the creature that made her realize there was no way they could defeat it—not one of the Seven and certainly not all of them.

There was no way to survive. She wanted to curl up into a ball and pray to God to make death quick.

It was not just her soul on the line. Inaction was not an option.

Moira jumped up, shaking off the shackles she'd unlocked only moments ago. She kicked over every candle and threw each of the seven chalices outside of the circle. But it didn't matter. It was too late.

The Demon Envy had arrived.

FORTY

I am about to take my last voyage, a great leap in the dark.
—THOMAS HOBBES, 1679

Envy took form.

Moira stared, standing in front of Lily and Father Philip, protecting them with nothing because she had nothing to protect them with.

Envy was alternately hideous and beautiful. A man with long, golden hair turned into a hoofed creature standing on hind legs, horned and deformed. The changes were fluid, but the creature was corporeal. It had mass and body like the demon that had wrenched itself from the walls of Good Shepherd. But there was something different about this one. The eyes had intelligence. The demons she'd encountered before were driven by one thing: destruction. They acted purely on instinct.

Envy acted on forethought and intelligence.

It smiled at her.

Father recited a psalm; Moira knew it but couldn't remember which one. Envy didn't react to the invocation of God.

"Your words have no effect," it hissed.

Envy's voice was low, rumbling, loud. It echoed throughout the warehouse. That was when Moira first noticed the chanting had stopped. The coven watched those trapped in the circle with Envy. Moira didn't dare take her eyes off the demon, but she felt fear all around her and it wasn't coming from just those in the circle.

The damn coven *should* be scared. They would be next.

"I am the One," Envy said.

"God is the One," Moira spat out.

Envy growled.

Good going, piss off a demon while you're trapped with it.

"I am the one who gave you knowledge. I am the one who felled mankind. I am the one you should bow to." Envy smiled as it changed form, its legs turning into a snake, a rattle at the end, its body a hairy chest, its head turning back to the golden-haired Fabio, now with fangs that dripped poison. It slithered on the floor, seven feet tall, growing and shrinking as it circled around the trap.

"You think you can keep me here?" it asked.

"Don't blame me," Moira said, circling the altar to keep herself between Lily and the demon. "It was them—the witches and wizards who want to trap you."

"And *you?*"

It slithered toward her so fast she couldn't help but scream, her shriek short as her breath was stolen from her. Envy's breath reeked of dead flesh, sulphur, and maggots. Its narrow, forked tongue shot out, impossibly long, and touched her cheek, burning her skin.

Moira flinched from the demon's touch. With courage she didn't know she had, she said, "You have delusions of grandeur to think you were the serpent who spoke to

Eve. You're but one of seven; the serpent didn't have to share his power."

She had no idea why she'd intentionally antagonized Envy; she had no idea if he was the demon who'd lured Eve or was just making it up because that's what demons do best: lie. But all she could think about was buying time, otherwise Rafe and Anthony would have no chance to get the tabernacle in place.

The demon hissed in rage and pushed her aside with such force she flew across the room and hit a hutch. Glass broke around her, cutting her arms, and she fell to the ground.

Get up! She couldn't move. She tried to rise, but glass dug into her hand, cutting it open. She bit her tongue to not cry out as she rolled away from the glass and lay on her back looking at the ceiling. She couldn't save them—what was she thinking? She was one human against a demon who could kill her without straining itself. It could have killed her then, thrown her farther, higher, harder . . . like Peter.

Lily screamed. Moira forced herself to her feet, shook off her dizziness, and stepped forward.

Envy was sniffing Lily, its tongue touching her flesh. It reached her mouth, shot the forked end in, and leapt backward, its form turning back into the hoofed creature. "You are contaminated!" it screamed. Envy spat onto the floor; steam rose where its black saliva fell.

Moira ran over to Lily. The girl was shaking. Blood oozed from where Envy's tongue had cut her skin. "Hold on," she said, though she had no clue how they were going to get out of this.

The coven members started chanting again. Serena

held an oversized book with thick pages and began to read.

The *Conoscenza*. Moira could destroy it now.

Blood and fire.

How could she destroy it with Father Philip and Lily here? Moira was prepared to die to destroy the book, but she wasn't going to take innocent lives with her.

As Serena read, the demon writhed, losing form. It was furious; anger was rolling off the creature, palpable, as it grew in rage and jealousy.

"You think you're better," Envy growled. "I took your lives before, I can take them now!"

Envy grew as it lost shape. It moved faster and faster in the circle. Furniture in the building began to shake.

Serena read faster. Envy hovered over Lily, drawn to her in spite of her "contamination." Moira looked around for a weapon, anything to fight with, though without form how could she kill Envy? Envy wrapped its form around Lily and she screamed.

Father Philip began an exorcism prayer, reached out, his hands touching the demon. Envy hissed in agony and rapidly fled from Lily. It screamed at him, taking the form of a beast. "You can't stop *ME!*"

It exhaled and Father Philip was brought to his knees, his hands at his throat, his face turning red. The demon rushed him, drawing out Father's breath.

"NO! Let him go!" Moira screamed. She put herself between the demon and Father, but it didn't stop. She glanced behind her. Father was convulsing as he fell to the floor. No, not him. Not Father.

"Damn you all!" she screamed. *"Avertet mala inimicis meis in veritate tua disperde illos! Voluntarie sacrificabo tibi confitebor nomini tuo Domine quoniam bonum!"*

Envy turned his attention to her.

"Release him!" she commanded.

"You have no power over me. You gave up your power," it hissed. Father lay still. Too still.

Why him? Why not me? Why the only good thing in my life, you take from me?

Envy laughed, turning into dark smoke, washing over her. She was frozen, encased by Envy as it sought a way into her body.

Then it pulled back, again took solid form. Showing off. Proving it was powerful. Proving it was in charge. Moira was inches away from its face as it stared at her. Envy opened its mouth and Moira saw the fangs, the maggots, as it came toward her.

A commanding voice resonated through the room, overpowering the demon, the chanting, the rumbling.

"In the name of the Father, and of the Son, and of the Holy Ghost," Rafe shouted, "you are banished back to the lowest level of Hell."

Then he spoke in the same language that Serena had used.

Moira turned from Envy to Rafe, stunned.

Rafe knew the ancient language of demons! The language of the *Conoscenza*, the book of evil, the spells that focused on the destruction of all that was good in the world.

How did he know it?

Her heart broke when she realized that Rafe was using battle magic to counteract Serena's spell, repeating the opposite of everything Serena said—Moira understood that not in the words, which she didn't understand, but in the conflicting energy in the room. As the energy increased in strength, each kind battling the other, it was growing, expanding, practically visible to Moira, light and dark, hot and cold. Her senses were overloading and she could scarcely think.

The pain in her head was so intense she fell to her knees, her hands on her ears, on the back of head, willing the agony to end.

With the tabernacle in a sack on his back, Anthony couldn't reach the roof. There was no place to climb up. He didn't have the keys to Skye's truck to drive it to the building to use as a ladder.

"Dammit!"

He ran around the corner and right into Tom Young.

"You're supposed to be dead." Tom looked upset and scared. He pulled his gun. "You don't get two chances."

Bright lights shone on the side of the building. When Tom glanced at them, Anthony kicked the gun from his hand. A shot went wild.

Hank Santos jumped from the car. For a minute, Anthony feared he was on an Envy-induced rampage. If Hank stopped him, there was no way to trap Envy and Lily would be possessed. Father Philip, Rafe, Moira— they'd all die. He stood his ground.

Jared got out from the passenger side. "Where's Lily?"

Anthony looked from Hank to Jared. "Are you both okay?"

"Yes," Jared said. "My father is fine."

Anthony didn't know whether he could believe the kid, but he didn't really have much choice now.

"I need to get on the roof."

Jared looked at his father. "Dad?"

"I have an idea." Hank jumped back into his truck and drove it to the edge of the building.

Anthony climbed up to the hood, then the roof, and with the sack on his back, he pulled himself up using the gutter.

He ran along the flat roof to the ventilation access panel and prayed he wasn't too late.

Envy screamed and slithered to the edge of the circle. "Let me out!" it screamed to Serena. "I want *that one!*"

Its tail stabbed toward Rafe. Rafe froze in his place, like a deer in the headlights. He couldn't speak. He couldn't think. He only saw Envy. It stared at him, silently calling him.

You have power. Power I want.

Rafe fought the demon's will. He couldn't give in.

You are mine. You were always mine.

Rafe turned his head from the demon, tried to block the slick voice in his mind. He reminded himself that demons could get into his head, but they couldn't read his thoughts or know his soul until he gave it to them or they stole it. He fought, but was weak. And getting even weaker.

He saw Lily on the altar, tried to focus on saving her. He had done it before; what was fighting him now?

Moira was on her knees, her hands over her head, in pain. He stepped toward her, and she looked up at him. "Stop," she cried. "Stop."

He didn't take another step. Her mouth opened and her eyes closed as she withstood another wave of pain.

Who was doing this to her? He looked around the room, saw Matthew Walker—he knew him. Not the name, but the face. Rafe's head ached as he tried to place how he knew the man.

Fiona walked over to the edge of the circle and used her foot to rub out a small section of the trap.

Moira screamed. "No! Fiona, don't!"

"He deserves to die." Fiona stared at Moira. "You'll be responsible for killing him. You brought him here; he's your responsibility."

Rafe began a traditional exorcism, buying more time for Anthony to get the tabernacle in place. The demon laughed, turned back into black smoke, and wrapped itself around the inside of the demon trap, blocking Rafe's line of vision.

Suddenly, a searing pain hit Rafe in the back. He thought he'd been hit by a bullet but realized as he fell to his knees that it was electricity, a magical bolt coming from Matthew Walker.

Rafe kept the rite going, stumbling over the words as the spell Walker used sucked the air from his lungs. The more he inhaled, the less air he brought in. And the demon grew in size. Rafe cried out and saw Moira leap from the circle and tackle Walker with savage ferocity. Walker went down and Rafe regained his legs.

Serena was practically screaming her spell, and Rafe seemed to be countering it. The words came to him—he didn't know from where, he didn't want to think about where, he just wanted to survive. To save Lily. To save Moira.

Fiona was successful in breaching the spirit trap and she ran back to safety, a protective circle that she shared with her daughter Serena. But Envy didn't want them, not yet. Envy wanted Rafe, and it slithered forward smiling, a hideous grin of death. It breathed his name.

"*Raaaphaeeelll.*"

Rafe reached behind his back and retrieved the dagger.

He held it in front of him, expecting to be terrified, but instead experiencing complete calm. His eyesight sharpened, the pain from earlier attacks fading. He breathed fully, in and out, and stared Envy in the face.

"Come here, you bastard."

Envy growled, lunging with a speed Rafe didn't expect.

As the demon rushed him, Rafe charged. All thought left his mind; all he could think of was stopping the demon. Stopping Envy from spreading its wickedness throughout the earth.

He leapt, and slit the demon's throat with the blessed dagger. The demon ripped off its own head and threw it across the room. The head turned into a thousand flies that buzzed all over, swarming.

What had he done? Why had he slit the throat? He didn't know what he was doing. He froze, uncertain, his head throbbing.

The demon came for him, its head growing back, its eyes red and focused on him. Rafe stared. This was the end.

Moira screamed. Walker had her pinned, but his magic failed as he grew enraged. The bastard had his hands around her throat. He would choke her to death, a good old-fashioned *human* murder.

"I'll kill you, Moira," he said through clenched teeth. "And I will enjoy it."

Moira had no doubt that Walker wanted her dead, and no doubt that he would enjoy squeezing the life out of her.

But Moira was not ready to die.

Simultaneously, she kneed him in the balls and shot her arms up between his, aiming right for his eyes. He turned his head at the last minute, avoiding permanent damage, but he loosened his grip and Moira slammed his biceps to push his hands away from her neck. She caught her breath, head butted him—*Shit! That hurts*—and flipped him.

Her backup dagger that Walker had seized earlier was in his pocket, and she pulled it out, unsheathed it, and ran to Rafe's side.

Envy towered over Rafe, turning to gas, ready to fuse with the man.

"Don't even think about it," she said, and continued the exorcism where she'd left off.

Envy turned to her, retaking shape, and backhanded her with its clawlike hand. She fell to the ground and spit out blood.

Rafe rose from where he'd fallen and chopped off the demon's arm. Baby snakes slithered out of the beast, winding their way rapidly around the room.

The women in the coven began to scream as snakes crossed their feet, red and black, vile creatures. Moira feared if any escaped they'd create even more problems than they already had.

Like they could have bigger issues than this!

Rafe cut off the other limb, but the demon slammed him with its tail. He flew across the room and hit the wall.

Moira couldn't allow Rafe to die, not like Peter, not like the man she had once loved. "Damn you," she said. "*Veniat mors super illos: et descendant in infernum viventes!*"

She took her dagger and with all her strength brought it down on the rattle of the demon's tail.

Envy screeched, so loud, so violently, that Moira fell

to the ground and put her hands to her ears. The witches covered their ears; some collapsed, as Envy tried to regain its strength.

Serena held up the book and intoned a command. All the flies that swarmed, all the snakes that slithered, were drawn to the book.

Serena called upon the living darkness, invoked names of demons that made Moira's blood freeze, and all the vile creatures in the room turned and headed straight toward Lily.

Moira fought the pain and crawled toward the girl on the altar. "Stop," she tried to plead with her sister, but Serena either didn't hear or didn't care.

"Rafe, help!" she cried as she stumbled.

Lily screamed as the snakes slithered up the altar, wrapping themselves around her feet, her ankles, faster and faster, flies buzzing around her head.

Rafe got up from the ground. He ran to Moira and grabbed her.

"Trust me," he said.

She nodded, terrified, not knowing what he was going to do.

He raised the dagger over her.

"No," she tried to say, but nothing came out.

He cut her hand and held it over the torso of the demon that lay on the ground trying to regrow its limbs.

Then he pressed her hand into one of the holes in the demon's body.

She screamed as pain surged through her body. Rafe seemed shocked by what he'd done and pulled her arm out, holding her.

"I'm sorry, I'm sorry," he said.

She couldn't see, the pain blinding white. She blinked, and it began to subside.

All parts of Envy's body pulled together into a dark gas and turned into a whirlpool, moving faster and faster.

Moira watched as the demon fought being drawn up into the ventilation system. It fought a losing battle as it was drawn up to the ceiling, right into the tabernacle that Anthony had used to cap the vent.

There was sudden complete silence. Moira breathed again.

Fiona turned her magic on Moira as she said, "I will never underestimate you again."

Moira tried to stand, but Fiona had both hands on her head, just the tips of her fingers. She couldn't move. She could scarcely breathe.

"If you die now," Fiona said, "it will be too soon. You will suffer. I will ensure that you suffer. If you love again, I will take him. If you trust again, I will ensure you will be betrayed. You have no one. You have nothing. You will find me and beg me to kill you. You do not know what pain is, Andra Moira."

Moira stared into Fiona's blue eyes, as if she were looking into her own. Bottomless, deep, but Fiona's were filled with the passion of hatred.

The front doors burst open.

"Police! Freeze!" Sheriff Skye McPherson and three cops rushed in, guns drawn.

Fiona glared at Moira. "Remember this?" she said. "Enjoy the sweet memories!"

Moira felt the spell invade her as Fiona's eyes fluttered.

"Freeze!" she heard, but saw nothing but the library at St. Michael's seven years ago.

She was there with Peter. In slow motion she watched as he was thrown across the room. She saw every frame individually, as Peter's body fought, twisted, moved. The fear on his face. The fear and the pain and the look of the betrayed.

She cried, but the malevolent vision would not stop. Again and again, Peter slammed against the wall, his eyes accusing her, death stealing him from her.

Death would be better. Death would be better than this. *Dear God, make it stop, make it stop.*

Peter's body hit the wall again, this time slowly. Blood spattered inch by inch by inch. She could almost reach out and touch it.

"Moira!"

"Stop, stop! Make it stop, make it stop!"

Holding her tight, Rafe spoke quietly. Soothing. His words filled her mind, though she barely heard what he said. The memory grew fuzzy and faded. She began to cry and he held her, rocking her. She clutched him as if she were drowning.

Chaos was all around her. Magic flew through the air, as the coven members tried to avoid arrest. Shouts and orders as Skye cuffed Elizabeth Ellis. "Secure the scene! Back door!"

"Rafe—" She caught her breath. She had so many questions. What he'd done, what he'd said. But now, she was so tired and his embrace gave her blissful peace.

"Your hand," he said, holding it to his lips. The bleeding had stopped. She stared at the wound.

"You're in shock," he said.

"Lily?"

Rafe looked over her head. "Anthony and Jared are

with her." Then his body tensed. He rose and put her on her feet. He took her hand and she saw what he saw.

Father.

They ran to the middle of the damned spirit trap. Father Philip lay on the floor.

Moira knew he was dead, but she said, "He's going to be okay, right? He's going to be okay." She knelt next to him, remembering what the demon had done to him. How he'd fallen, saving Lily.

Father Philip's eyes were partly open. His neck was bruised, his mouth open. Anthony checked for a pulse and breath, tears dropping on Father Philip's body.

"He's okay," Moira said. "He's okay. He's okay."

"He's gone."

"No. No!" She held him. "Father, please. Please don't leave me."

Rafe put his arm around her. Anthony took Father Philip's hand and gave him Last Rites, his voice breaking.

"Amen."

FORTY-ONE

Fiona packed her things quickly, rage fueling her energy.

"I hate them!"

Matthew squeezed her shoulders. "It's not over. We'll confront them again. It's inevitable."

"They trapped my demon! It's mine!"

Matthew tilted her chin up. "Sweetheart, we don't have time to rant about Andra Moira or Raphael Cooper. All in due time. The police must know where we are. I sent Serena and Pennington to get the boat."

"You should have let that idiot die in the fire."

"I considered it. But he's useful."

Fiona reluctantly concurred. "We need a good plan to retrieve the tabernacle. I think they'll store it at the mission, or at the church downtown."

"You're right, dear, but I have another plan."

"Does it involve gutting Raphael and choking Moira with his intestines?"

"You are imaginative, dear, but I prefer subtlety. Rafe will soon remember how he knows me. He stared for a long time, but couldn't place me."

"Then you should never have left Santa Louisa. How I missed you!"

He kissed her. "I missed you too, darling."

"How many women did you sleep with while you were gone?"

"Only you, my love." He kissed her again. "Serena should be on the beach soon. We need to go."

"You didn't tell me your brilliant plan."

He paused for a moment. "We allow them to do the hard work."

"Meaning exactly what?"

"Why should we expend our energy tracking and trapping the Seven? Anthony, Rafe, and Moira will do it for us. And when they're done? We'll take them back. All seven of the deadly sins will be ours."

Fiona considered the idea. "I can see how that might work." She smiled. "And we can spend the extra time finding a new *arca*."

"Yes, that is truly our one stumbling block. They don't realize they can't keep the Seven together, except in an *arca*. But we have the luxury of time. And I know just the place we can go."

Fiona took a last look around the library where she'd spent so much of the last two years. This had been a good place for her, for her family, for her coven. And Andra Moira had destroyed it. Her daughter and Raphael Cooper. Though Matthew was trying to ease her anger, she didn't want to let it go. How could they have such strength without magic? The heavens didn't grant power; only demanded blind faith and obedience. Neither Cooper nor her traitorous daughter were obedient to anyone.

"Darling, we must leave." Matthew had gathered their most important materials, the rare herbs, the priceless *grimoires,* and the last of Cooper's blood, the latter in a small cooler. Everything else could be bought or taken wherever they went.

Fiona turned to her lover. It had been Matthew from the beginning, for now and forever. None of the men she played sex games with meant anything to her, including Garrett; they were merely a distraction when Matthew was away. She trusted him—until tonight.

"You could have killed Moira tonight. At Good Shepherd."

"Yes," he said. "But we need her alive."

"No! What she has done to me, to our cause! I suffered when she ran away."

"Darling, I know, and I promise you, we will find her again and make her suffer tenfold. But we need her alive—she has a power I don't understand."

"Is that how she killed my demon?" Fiona looked into the room off the library where the demon had lain. She and Matthew had sent the slain body back to the underworld, but she was surprisingly upset over the incident.

"It's about her, not her tools, not St. Michael's Order. I just haven't figured out exactly how she's doing it. Perhaps it is magic, but she's masked it somehow."

"I haven't felt any magic coming from her. She would have used it tonight."

"There was so much energy in that warehouse, I had a difficult time discerning where the power was coming from."

"Even you, my darling Matthew, are not infallible."

He frowned. Like her, he didn't appreciate being reminded of his imperfections. She kissed him to ease the sting of the criticism.

"Cooper cut her, poured her blood into Envy," she

said. "It weakened the demon, allowed Zaccardi to trap it."

"Her blood is your blood."

"And her father's."

Matthew said quietly, "It is time."

Matthew didn't have to explain what he meant. He was the only one who knew who Moira's father really was. It had been a dangerous game from the moment Matthew approached Fiona when she was sixteen, and he ten years older, but they had been successful in everything—except keeping Moira in line. Exposing Moira's biological father was risky, but the stakes had been raised after the release of the Seven Deadly Sins. The added danger meant bold action.

"He will be hard for us to get to."

"But not impossible."

The final pieces were moving into place, but it would take all her concentration, all her magic, to ensure victory for her and her people. "With us," Fiona smiled slyly, "nothing is impossible."

He held her eyes with a promise of the ecstasy that awaited them. "I love you, Fiona. Now, we must leave before the police arrive. We have a long journey."

Moira sat in the back of an ambulance while a paramedic picked small pieces of glass out of her hands and arms. "This is a nasty scar," the guy said, pointing to where Fiona's pet demon had bit her only a few hours ago. The injury looked months old. "What happened?"

She just shook her head. Anthony and Rafe spoke in hushed voices just outside the doors. Anthony still held the tabernacle. They were discussing where to put the box until they figured out how to send Envy back to Hell.

They'd caught only three of the witches, including Elizabeth Ellis. That gave Moira a small satisfaction. She really didn't like that woman.

Fiona, Serena, and Matthew Walker had escaped. Skye had sent patrols to the house where Rafe had been held captive, and the other two properties Moira had identified, but there was no sign of them.

Without Father Philip, nothing was the same. She felt desperately alone. Her eyes burned; she thought she had no more tears, but they came, hot, fast, unstoppable.

Without Father Philip, she had no one who loved her. No one who cared what happened to her. No one to love. He was her anchor, the reason she could get up every morning and continue the battle. For him.

He was gone.

Never had Moira felt so lost since the day she ran away the first time, before she'd met Father Philip. When all she knew how to do was run.

She'd made her stand and failed. Father Philip was dead.

Rafe climbed into the ambulance and sat next to her. "Is she going to be okay?" he asked the paramedic.

"Yes," Moira responded, blinking back the tears, unable to look at Rafe.

The paramedic said, "I want her to go to the hospital, but she's being stubborn."

"I'll take care of her." He looked her in the eye and she saw he meant it.

Maybe she wasn't completely alone.

Rafe turned to the paramedic. "Our friend Anthony has a nasty cut—can you take a look at it?"

"I'm not done here."

"Five minutes."

The paramedic sighed, then left Moira and Rafe alone.

He frowned at her hands. "It was pure madness in there," he said quietly.

"I don't know what happened. I don't know why Fiona let the demon out of the circle. It could have attacked her or any of them. But it went right for you." She considered that. "Fiona knew it would go for you. It wanted you, Rafe, specifically. Why?"

"I wish I knew. Was it something I said?" he half-joked. "Or did? I don't know. Anthony said that Fiona is a powerful magician."

"With Walker by her side, she's even stronger."

Rafe made her look at him. "What did she do to you?"

She didn't want to talk about it. But she owed Rafe an explanation. "She turned a memory of mine, a nightmare, into vivid Technicolor slow motion. I couldn't get out of it. I tried, but I couldn't."

Rafe touched her cheek. "Come here." He put her head on his chest. The paramedics had given him scrubs to wear, reminding Moira of when she found Rafe two days ago.

"I have to do this again. And again." She closed her eyes. "I'm not strong enough."

"You're stronger than anyone I know. But you are not alone. *We* can do this."

She hoped so. The world was a dangerous place without the Seven Deadly Sins making it deadlier.

"We'd better get started. They're not going to wait around for us to get our act together."

"Sleep first," Rafe said.

Rafe looked at Moira's arm and the bite marks. There had been so much blood, and the acid dripping into Moira's cuts, her cry of pain. He would never forget what happened in that room. The bite . . . Moira's pain . . . the demon's dying scream. And now . . . he looked at the cut he'd made on her hand.

"How did you know?" Moira whispered.

He shook his head. "I remembered how when the Cerberus bit you, it died. I hoped . . . maybe your blood . . ." He stopped, not knowing what he was going to say because he couldn't get his mind around it. "I just knew."

"Like you knew the magic words."

"Magic words?"

"How you slowed him down. The exorcism or whatever it was you did. It was the language Serena was speaking. Is that what you did on the cliffs the other night?"

He didn't know. "Moira, I'm sorry, I wish I had answers—I don't."

"We'll figure it out."

"How did I earn your trust?" It mattered to him, greatly.

"I don't know, but—we're in this together. All of us."

Anthony appeared, joining them inside the ambulance. "I agree," he said. "Together." He looked at Moira's arm as well. "Are you sure it was a demon that bit you? I've never heard of anything like a demon dying from biting a human. I'll research it." He didn't sound hopeful.

Rafe smiled woefully as Moira dozed off. "Let's keep it quiet. There are a lot of people who don't like Moira."

Anthony nodded. "I'll be discreet. Skye's wrapping up the explanations."

"Which are?"

"I'm not sure yet, I think she's winging it. She knows how far she can go." He put his hand on Rafe's shoulder. "As soon as she's done, we'll go back to my place. You—and Moira—need sleep." He left.

Rafe looked at the sleeping beauty beside him. Her expression was uneasy and she moaned. He pulled her closer to him and kissed the top of her head.

"I'll do anything to protect you, my love," he whispered. "Anything."

Read on for an excerpt from
CARNAL SIN
by Allison Brennan

Published by Ballantine Books

Moira woke up with blood on her hands.

Her heart raced as she sat upright in the strange bed, staring at the dark red blood *drip, drip, dripping* onto the white sheets, disappearing as each thick drop spread. She swallowed the scream that fought to escape.

She blinked and the blood was gone. The panicked rage faded. She almost—almost, but not quite—forgot the feeling of her hand clenching the heavy, balanced dagger. Almost forgot the sickening sound of the blade slicing through tendons, hitting bone, cutting out an invisible soul, and throwing it to demons that tore it to shreds, feeding.

But she'd never forget the fear. It never left. She lived with it day in and day out, sometimes buried so deep *almost* could believe it was gone. When she lied to herself.

She couldn't lie to herself now. The nightmare faded, but her vision blurred in the dim light coming from the edges of the closed blinds. The nightmare faded, and the vision hit.

Was it a vision? While she was awake? It felt like a vision, but she'd never been fully awake for one before and her gut reaction was to stop it. But she couldn't, even if she'd tried. In a rush, her mind was filled with thoughts not her own, sights she'd never witnessed, feelings she'd never had. Not like this. Not this evil.

* * *

She flew across the continent and back. Tired. Bored. Frustrated. There were many places she could stay, but none of them appealed to her. The desires of the body were weak, and she was anything but weak. She didn't want just any body. Only the perfect body. One who wouldn't fight. One who wanted her. One who welcomed her. A physical body to lose herself in and control. Freely. Openly.

The Seven Deadly Sins had been released, and with them other demons, and they had freedom. Their time had come again. The Seven would protect them. The Seven would feed them.

She grew stronger with each passing day.

She landed where her Protector was.

"I found you a vessel," Lust said. "She's yours."

Yesssss.

Moira saw the woman sleeping, not knowing her fate.

"No!" she screamed.

The demon turned and stared at her. It saw her. Saw her vision. Shared her vision.

It wasn't possible.

Was it?

"Moira!"

She jumped out of bed, shaky, knife in hand without even thinking about reaching under her pillow for it.

It was Rafe. She swallowed, blinked, tried to regain her focus. It wasn't real. It wasn't real.

She knew damn well she was lying to herself.

"I'm sorry," he said quietly. "You were looking right at me, but you didn't see me."

She shook her head to clear her mind and sat back heavily on the edge of her bed. She had to get out of this place. She'd been in Santa Louisa for nearly a month, but for the last two weeks she'd been doing *nothing*. Anthony Zaccardi, Santa Louisa's own resident demonologist, had his books and research, trying to track down the remaining Seven Deadly Sins. Rafe had his physical therapy and training. And what did she have? Exercise until her body ached. Nightmares that reminded her of her deadly flaws. Visions almost daily for the past two weeks that left her drained and on edge. And *still* no trace of Fiona O'Donnell or Matthew Walker. She was going stir-crazy. In the last seven years she'd never stayed in any one place this long, except Olivet when she was training to be a demon hunter with Rico.

"I'm okay," she said, but not fast enough. He didn't believe her, but he didn't need words to question. He never did. His dark, bottomless blue eyes questioned her, compelling the truth from her lips.

"I had another vision," she admitted.

That she could say it out loud showed she'd accepted the fact that she was a freak. She'd always known it, but now? Well, it sounded even crazier. And it was. But Rafe didn't think so, which was both comforting and scary as hell. They were so much alike . . . yet so different. He never left her alone anymore, and she was scared to death. Of what was happening between them. Of what would happen if she let down her shields. There was no future for her, she couldn't lose her focus. Not again.

"I think . . ." how could she explain? "One of them—one of the demons—found a host."

"Anthony doesn't believe they're seeking possession."

"Anthony doesn't know everything," she snapped.

Rafe walked over to the dresser and leaned against it, crossing his arms over his chest. Already, two weeks after he miraculously woke from his coma—if that's what it was that had kept him unconscious for ten weeks—he'd regained his color and much of his strength. They were staying at Anthony and Skye's place—hardly big enough for the four of them—with Rafe sleeping on the couch. She needed to get out of this place. Not just because she itched to find where her mother had disappeared to, but because the close proximately to Rafe was distracting. Not to mention Anthony's need to control both of them day and night, and Skye's constant questions. Moira liked the cop, but there were some things better left outside of the law. If Sheriff Skye McPherson knew even half the laws Moira had broken . . .

Rafe *still* didn't say anything. Damn, how annoying was that? He just pinned her with his sharp eyes, his unshaven square jaw locked, waiting for her to tell him the truth.

"I know it's not possible," she began—*hoping* it wasn't possible, "I just—it felt—like the demon saw me. Or—" she hesitated, then said what she truly feared. "Or I was looking through the demon's eyes. Then it turned and looked inside itself. At me. Knew me and that I was there. And it wasn't one of *them*, not one of the Seven. But—I think—" She bit her lip.

"What?"

"Do you think that the Seven are somehow collecting demons who are already here? Like bodyguards. Or distractions."

Rafe didn't say anything. Why was he always so damn

quiet? Why couldn't he get angry like Anthony or frustrated like Skye? Instead, he was *calm*.

"I won't let anyone hurt you, demon or human."

He barely whispered, but she heard every word as if it was etched onto her bones, and every hair on her skin rose. He appeared serene, but he was a tightly controlled bundle of energy. His words had movement to them. Weight. She wanted to believe him. He meant what he said, but he wasn't strong enough to protect her or anyone. Neither was she. None of them were. She felt so much despair, and feared it was residual contact with the Seven. That their power was still present even though they had long left Santa Louisa.

All but the demon Envy, who was trapped in the tabernacle in the secure vault at St. Francis de Sales in downtown Santa Louisa—a vault that Moira commented was the supernatural equivalent to Fort Knox. Anthony hadn't been amused. He never was.

But Rafe had smiled at her joke behind Anthony's back, and winked at her, another reason why she was drawn to him. He liked her sarcasm, and he made her smile.

"I'm scared," she now admitted. "I've been doing nothing for nearly two weeks. Nothing but waiting for something we can't even identify. How can we stop the remaining Seven Deadly Sins if we don't know where they are? Do we have to wait until someone drops dead? Do we have to wait until we hear on the news that Greed is working its evil magic on Wall Street or people die because they're too lazy to eat? And dammit, where is Fiona? Where did she go? I can't *feel* her magic anymore. They're just gone and I'm waiting for them to come after me! And what if—"

She stopped. She was turning into a complainer. God, she hated herself right now. When had she become a sniveling brat? She had to put the fear aside or it would bite her in the ass. Yeah, she was worried—so was everyone else involved. She needed to stop feeling sorry for herself, accept her fate, and move forward. Maybe if she repeated the mantra enough it would come true.

"What?" he asked.

She gave voice to her hidden fear. Maybe if speaking it out loud she could stop it from seeming so real. "What if the Seven have infected me?"

He stared at her and shook his head. "They haven't."

"How do you know?"

"*You* would know."

"But I *don't* know."

He smiled. "This is a silly conversation, Moira."

She shook her head, biting back a smile.

"I saw that," he said and sat next to her. He took her hand and kissed it. "Come on, smile."

She raised an eyebrow. "Think you're up for a little wrestling match at the gym?"

"Why do you always do that?"

"Do what? Workout?"

"Every time I get close to you, you take me to the gym. Or for a run. Anything to avoid talking about what you feel when I touch you. What I feel when I think of you. Why I can't get you out of my mind. I know you look at me when you think I'm sleeping. I know you're worried. What are you worried about?"

"This isn't the time—"

"It's never the time for you."

She jumped up and walked to the window, her heart racing. She couldn't explain to Rafe what she was feeling, what she was thinking, when she couldn't figure it out herself! But there was far more at stake than this *connection* she and Rafe had. She *was* worried about him. They still didn't know what the coven had done to him at the hospital, and Dr. Bertrand had destroyed all of Rafe's files. Destroyed or stolen. Rafe had secrets, secrets he was keeping from her and Anthony.

She had to be able to trust him, but didn't know if she could. It hurt. Deep inside it hurt, but if she couldn't learn to trust him—if he couldn't tell her the truth he harbored deep inside—no matter how she felt about him, she couldn't get too close. It would cloud her judgment, and right now she needed a straight head.

Rafe's voice hardened. "Tell me what you saw."

"It was more what *she* saw."

"She? Demons aren't male or female."

"It *felt* feminine. She was flying. It felt like astral projection, but I know I was right here, all of me, mind and body and soul. But I was also with her, flying, looking for a vessel. A willing participant in whatever insanity she has planned. But—" she frowned. "She found someone. I saw her."

"You saw the demon?"

"The person she was looking at. Brunette. Petite. Very pretty. I can see her as clearly as I can see you."

"Do you know where she is?"

Moira concentrated but her head ached and she just didn't know. She paced the small room, unable to sit still. "I hate this! If God wanted to help us in this battle, he'd give us clearer instructions."

"We just need to figure them out," Rafe said.

"I'd rather have a rule book, thank you very much."

Anthony stopped in the doorway. With bags under his bloodshot eyes, he looked like he hadn't slept the night before. "Rico's plane just landed. He's on his way for the meeting. Twenty minutes." He glanced at Rafe. "I need to talk to you."

She raised an eyebrow at Anthony. "Secrets already?"

He didn't answer her, didn't even look at her.

She pushed by him. "Whatever. I'm going for a run."

"Twenty minutes," he repeated as she walked by.

Rafe had grown beyond annoyed at how Anthony treated Moira. When he heard the front door slam shut, he said, "Hasn't she proven herself to you? She nearly *died* at the warehouse to save everyone inside. If it wasn't for her, *you* would have died at Good Shepherd."

He didn't mention that she'd also saved Rafe's own life, not once but twice. Anthony was still skeptical about how—or if—Moira had killed the Cerberbus-type demon. Even Rafe wasn't certain about what happened in Fiona's library, or how Moira had been bitten by the demon and survived with only a small scar, yet he'd witnessed the entire thing. He knew what he'd seen. He knew what Moira had suffered. And he'd *seen* the demon, been attacked by it and still had the scars.

Anthony was struggling with a response, and Rafe pushed. "You stood by me. You believed in my innocence, that I had nothing to do with the murders at the mission. Why can't you give Moira the benefit of the doubt?"

"That's different."

"Why?"

"Rafe—I don't want to go into it."

"It's because Moira was a witch? Because she made mistakes?"

"She's *still* a witch! You know it, I know it. I don't

want to hear how she's not using magic, she has witch blood and there's nothing that can change that. What do you want from me, Rafe? I'm trying to accept her because of her value to our mission, but you weren't there when Peter died. You didn't see what happened. You didn't bury his broken body. She was responsible, and it still hurts. Peter was my brother."

"You think I don't understand the pain? I was just as responsible for the murders at the mission, yet you aren't blaming me."

"You weren't—"

"I was. In the same way Moira was."

"It was completely different. You weren't using magic, you didn't open the door for a demon to breach the sanctuary."

"I was blind. I was ignorant. I didn't see the clues."

"They were powerful witches. We don't know what spells they cast. And even though you didn't know about the spells, you were suspect enough to send them away."

"But I didn't know Jeremiah Hatch was one of them," Rafe said quietly.

"Rafe—it's not the same thing and you know it."

"No I don't."

Anthony rubbed his eyes. "I can't argue this now. Father Issa is bringing the Bishop to the meeting."

Rafe frowned.

"I know what you're thinking."

"No, you don't."

"I met Bishop Carlin when I first arrived in Santa Louisa. You're thinking that because he was friendly with Corrine Davies he is one of them, but he could have been under a spell or simply overworked and didn't see the signs. He's not part of St. Michael's Order, he doesn't know what to look for. It's important that we keep him close. Friend or enemy, he's our connection to the hierarchy here in the United States. We need his tacit agreement. Any opposition from Carlin creates problems for us."

Rafe understood that intuitively, but he'd been the one to confront Carlin last fall when he fired Corinne Davies. Carlin had been livid—and that was an understatement. If Carlin was under a spell, that made him weak; if he had been involved on a more personal level with Davies, that made him part of Fiona O'Donnell's coven, and that made him culpable in mass murder, not to mention crimes against his vows and God.

"Moira would be able to tell," Rafe said.

Anthony hesitated.

"Dammit, Anthony! You didn't hesitate to use her before, when her life was on the line, you think she's going to deceive us?" Anthony still didn't say anything. "I can tell if she's lying," Rafe added. It ached that Anthony was putting him in an adversarial position with Moira, even if she didn't know. He didn't want to have to scrutinize her. He didn't want to think of her as a potential enemy.

Anthony said, "Don't tell her."

Rafe understood his meaning. "You're still testing her. When will it stop?"

"Knowing what we want may cloud her judgment."

Rafe disagreed, but said. "Whatever you want. I'm going for a walk."

"Rico—"

"Is coming. I know." Saint Rico. With Father Philip gone, he was essentially their leader here in America. None of the others in the Order would leave the sanctuary in Italy to lead them. And there were so many battles in so many parts of the world, they could count on no one but one another.

It didn't give them a lot of hope to find, trap, and send back to hell the Seven Deadly Sins.